Michelle Smart's love affair with books started when she was a baby and would cuddle them in her cot. A voracious reader of all genres, she found her love of romance established when she stumbled across her first Mills & Boon book at the age of twelve. She's been reading them—and writing them—ever since. Michelle lives in Northamptonshire, England, with her husband and two young Smarties.

USA TODAY bestselling and RITA® Award–nominated author **Caitlin Crews** loves writing romance. She teaches her favourite romance novels in creative writing classes at places like UCLA Extension's prestigious Writers' Programme, where she finally gets to utilise the MA and PhD in English Literature she received from the University of York in England. She currently lives in the Pacific Northwest, with her very own hero and too many pets. Visit her at caitlincrews.com.

THE FORBIDDEN INNOCENT'S BODYGUARD

MICHELLE SMART

HER DEAL WITH THE GREEK DEVIL

CAITLIN CREWS

MILLS & BOON

First Published in Great Britain 2021
by Mills & Boon, an imprint of HarperCollins*Publishers*
1 London Bridge Street, London, SE1 9GF

The Forbidden Innocent's Bodyguard © 2021 Michelle Smart

Her Deal with the Greek Devil © 2021 Caitlin Crews

ISBN: 978-0-263-28243-6

MIX
Paper from
responsible sources
FSC® C007454

This book is produced from independently certified FSC™ paper
to ensure responsible forest management.
For more information visit www.harpercollins.co.uk/green.

Printed and bound in Spain
by CPI, Barcelona

THE FORBIDDEN INNOCENT'S BODYGUARD

MICHELLE SMART

To Millie, happy reading. x

CHAPTER ONE

Elsa Lopez couldn't stop pacing. She'd spent the past week hiding in her Viennese apartment obeying her mother's request to stay inside until the man tasked with escorting her home to Valencia arrived, and her nerves were shredded.

Her usually unobtrusive security detail had quadrupled with no warning a week ago. She now had a bodyguard stationed outside her front door, another guarding the front entrance to the apartment building and another guarding the back entrance. In a top-floor apartment on the other side of the courtyard were more guards watching every person who came within its vicinity. Her trip home to Valencia for her sister's engagement party had been bought forward. Her mother wanted her home and within the safety of the Lopez estate as soon as possible. That could only mean there had been a specific threat against Elsa.

Still pacing, she read her mother's latest cryptic email again. Their communications were supposed to be secure but both women worked on the assumption that every call was listened to and every written communication read. After what had happened to their family, paranoia was to be expected. Jumping at shadows had become a part of Elsa's life.

Be ready to leave on the day of Samson's birth. Your escort has made all the arrangements. Trust him. Trust no one else.

Samson had been Elsa and her sister Marisa's first pet. Their parents had bought the dog for them when they'd been in infant school. They'd faithfully celebrated his birthday on the ninth of July for every one of his twelve years of life.

Today was the ninth of July.

There was a rap on her front door. She checked the security camera before opening it, just in case. Since her father's murder a year ago, 'Just in case' had become something of a mantra.

'Your escort has arrived,' the unsmiling guard told her.

'Is he one of your men?'

He shook his head.

'Who is he?'

Her question went unanswered. The guard indicated the oversized handbag sitting by the door. 'Is this all you're taking?'

She picked it up and secured it over her shoulder. 'Yes.' She always travelled light when she returned to Valencia. She'd lived in Vienna for five years, but her childhood bedroom was still hers, the wardrobes still stuffed with all her clothes and accessories. All she'd packed were her cosmetics, purse and passport.

Elsa's apartment was set above a pizzeria and book shop in a beautiful building with white walls and green window frames. She followed the guard down the narrow stairs to the ground floor and stepped out into the cobbled courtyard. Mid-morning and the coffee shop on the other side was spilling over with people. Summer in Vienna was hitting its stride, the students and hipsters who usually made up the bodies wandering through this laid-back district increasing rather than decreasing in numbers.

A tall, well-built figure with a full, thick black beard standing propped against a lamppost caught her attention. Arms with biceps the size of her thighs were folded across a powerfully built chest. There was something familiar about him, something that made her heart give a sudden jolt. Shielding her eyes against the glare of the rising sun, she stopped walking and stared.

It couldn't be…?

She dropped her hand from her brow and stared some more. The figure moved towards her. Incongruously dressed for the weather and bohemian vibe of the district in a pair of dark grey trousers, a dark blue shirt unbuttoned at the neck and a charcoal waistcoat, the unruly curly black hair had been slicked back, dark shades along with the new beard covering much of the face she'd tried her hardest to forget.

Santi.

Her mother had sent Santi.

He was standing in front of her before she could unfreeze her shocked brain, straight white teeth flashing in a wide smile, bear-like hands lightly gripping her shoulders. He leaned down and placed his cheek against hers as if this was a planned meeting between two close friends and whispered, 'Smile and look pleased to see me.'

But her shock was too great. The cologne she'd caught in ghostly fragments over the years had already engulfed her senses. The skin on her cheek tingled from the soft brush of his beard. Elsa reared back. Her frozen mouth managed to form one word. It came out like an accusation.

'You.'

He tightened the hold on her shoulders and increased the wattage of his smile. 'Me. Now, as delightful as this reunion is, we need to get moving.'

His gravelly voice dived straight into her stunned senses.

The courtyard began to swim around her. Of all the people in the world she'd have wanted to escort her home, Santiago 'Santi' Rodriguez would have been at the very bottom of the list.

It had been five years since Elsa had left his bed crushed, shamed and chastened but those years melted away and, cheeks now burning under the weight of his stare, the old humiliation slapped her afresh.

In desperation, she turned to the bodyguard who'd accompanied her but he'd melted away too.

Santi hid his impatience and kept the smile on his face as he released Elsa's slender shoulders to take her hand. She tried to jerk away but he didn't relinquish his hold. 'We don't have time for this, *chiquita*. We need to move. Now smile and come with me.'

Tugging at her hand, he set off, forcing her to move alongside him.

'Of all the places you could have set up home, you had to choose a pedestrianised area?' he joked in an effort to ease the tension as they weaved through the crowds and onto Mariahilfer Strasse. 'I thought I might have to kill someone for a parking space.'

She didn't respond. Her pretty face was clenched from smooth brow to heart-shaped chin.

Using his excellent internal sense of direction—Santi had never been lost in his life, had only to look at a map once to memorise it—they crossed the wide road bursting with shoppers and slipped down a side street. Although Elsa trotted beside him in mute obedience, he didn't release her hand. His intuition, which was as excellent as his sense of direction, told him strongly that should he let her go, she would bolt.

After the way she'd ignored him at her father's funeral, he hadn't expected her to greet him with whoops of joy but did she have to act so repulsed when he was putting his life on the line for her? The woman who'd once been his little shadow now recoiled from him. The first word she'd spoken to him in five years had been hissed at him as if he were dirt on her shoe.

The last time they'd spoken was the night he'd found her in his bed. Considering how drunk she'd been, he'd be surprised if she remembered any of it, actions *or* words.

He'd done his damned best to forget it too.

They reached the Naschmarkt, a mile-long market already bursting at the seams with locals and tourists. If anyone was following them, this was where Santi intended to shake them off. Keeping a firm hold of Elsa's hand, he cut through food stalls and restaurants, backtracked a few times, cut through a coffee bar and then led her outside and down another side street where the car he'd acquired was parked.

Elsa took one look at the tiny, battered white car and raised a brow. 'You're saving me from what I assume are kidnappers in *that*?' The car had to be the same age as her and could in no way be called a classic.

He grinned and unlocked the passenger door manually. 'If you aren't expecting it then the kidnappers aren't either.'

This confirmation of her suspicions hit her like a needle of ice being injected directly into her veins and she grabbed hold of the opened door to stop her weakening legs dropping her to the ground.

Santi must have read something on her face for his smile fell. 'You didn't know?'

She tried to get moisture into her arid mouth. 'I knew there was a threat to me but not the details,' she croaked. 'Mamá said my escort…you, I suppose…would explain.'

'I'll explain everything once we're on the road,' he promised.

In the car, she dropped her head between her knees and breathed deeply. At least she hadn't fainted. That was one good thing.

Santi leaned in through the driver's door. 'I need your phone.'

'Why?' she asked dimly.

'They're probably tracking it.'

Mutely, head still dipped, she pulled it out of her bag and handed it to him. He dropped it to the ground. It crunched beneath his giant foot.

'I have a replacement for you in the boot.'

'Okay,' she whispered.

'Are *you* okay?'

She raised her head and took another deep breath. 'I'm fine.'

'Then buckle up, *chiquita*, and let's get this heap of junk to the airport.'

Only when he'd turned the engine on did she cast him a sideways glance. The sick, faint feeling that had enveloped her disappeared and she was suddenly struck by an urge to laugh. All six feet four of pure muscle that was Santiago Rodriguez was folded into the driver's seat. His head skimmed the roof, his knees touching the steering wheel so intimately he could use them to drive.

He flashed the grin that had once made her insides melt and put the heap of junk into gear. With a screech of tyres, they were off.

Elsa stared out of the window while they drove out of the city she'd made her home. Her heart had lodged in her throat. When would she next see her apartment? Sit at her desk in the calm open-plan office? Enjoy a quiet cappuccino with a good book at her favourite coffee shop? Would she ever feel safe again? Would she ever *be* safe again?

When they were safely crawling on the Ost Autobahn,

she cleared her throat. 'You said you were going to tell me everything.'

Santi waited until the articulated lorry overtaking them had safely passed before answering. 'How much do you know about the efforts to bring the cartel who killed your father to justice?'

The dizzy, nauseous feeling started up again, white noise buzzing in her ears at the mention of the cartel.

Elsa's family owned a shipping company that transported freight across the world. Fifteen months ago, a representative of the cartel in question approached her parents offering a ridiculous amount of money to use their cargo ships to smuggle drugs. Her parents said no. The cartel increased their monetary offer. Her parents still said no. The next day they found their dog, Buddy, drowned in the swimming pool. Things escalated from there. Her parents refused to be intimidated and called the police. They also increased their personal security.

Three months after the cartel's initial approach, Elsa's father Marco had kissed her mother goodbye and set off for a round of golf. While he'd played eighteen holes with his regular golfing friends, someone had tampered with the brakes of his car. Whether they'd intended for him to die or just wanted to scare him was irrelevant. Marco Lopez had driven into the back of a delivery truck at a set of traffic lights five hundred yards from the golf course and died instantly.

'I know the new security guy Mamá hired, that Felipe Lorenzi, has a team working to bring them down,' Elsa croaked.

'Things have moved quickly in the last month. International authorities are involved. They've been putting the final pieces into place to make a co-ordinated swoop on the cartel and arrest them. One of Felipe's men received a tip-off that the cartel have got wind of it and are planning pre-emptive action.'

She could hardly unfreeze her throat enough to whisper, 'Me?'

'Yes. They want to frighten your mother into dropping her evidence. Right now it's the only solid non-circumstantial evidence the authorities have against them.'

A day after her husband's death, Rosaria Lopez had received a phone call from the cartel's representative. The caller had commiserated about Marco's death then casually asked about the health of her heavily pregnant daughter Marisa. The threat had been implicit. Rosaria had agreed to a meeting with the representative, which she'd attended wearing a pair of teardrop earrings with a recording device implanted in them. Elsa still struggled to comprehend how her formidable but grieving mother had found the courage to walk into the lion's den, but walk into it she had and, during the conversation in which the cartel had laid out their fresh demands, came a concrete admission of guilt for Marco's death. And more threats.

The cartel were satisfied they had the Lopezes in their pocket. They completely underestimated the Lopez women's steel. Rosaria made numerous copies of the recording, fired her security team and, on Santi's advice, hired Felipe Lorenzi in their place. Felipe's team beefed up their protection and formed an impenetrable fortress around them. Communications from the cartel suddenly ceased. None of the Lopez women dared believe that would be the last they heard from them, and set about bringing the cartel down before they could go for their family again.

Elsa tried to process this specific threat to her but there were so many emotions ravaging her that it was hard to get her thoughts in order. 'Why am I in your care and not Felipe's?'

'Your mother asked me,' he answered with a shrug. Santi couldn't be completely certain but he thought they'd escaped the city without being followed.

He thought back to the conversation of five days ago. He'd been sat in the garden with Rosaria and her elder daughter Marisa. Santi had been regularly updated about the situation, had thrown his own time and resources at assisting the Lopezes' fight for justice, and he'd listened to the revelation about the new specific threat to Elsa without a flicker of emotion.

Rosario had fixed the green-brown eyes her younger daughter had inherited on him. 'Bring her home to me, Santi,' she'd said.

Although he'd had a good idea she was going to ask him to do this and had learned skills over the past year in anticipation of something like this happening, he'd still sucked in a breath. 'Wouldn't it be better for Felipe and his men to bring her back? They're the experts.'

'They will give you every assistance but I trust *you*.' Tears had glistened in her eyes and her voice had caught before she could continue.

Marisa had been the one to finish for her. 'To them, Elsa's just another job.'

He'd understood. God help him, he'd understood.

Santi had been as near as dammit a part of the Lopez family since they'd employed his mother as their housekeeper when he'd been a boy of ten and Elsa had been incubating in Rosaria's womb. Everything he had and everything he was was because of this family. There was nothing he wouldn't do for them.

Elsa rested her head against the window and closed her eyes. Her parents had always believed the sun shone out of Santi's backside. She'd once believed that too.

A memory flashed in her mind. Her first house party

without adult supervision. She'd been, what, fifteen? Sixteen? Her parents had, of course, believed there would be responsible adults there. It had never occurred to them that their baby girl would lie. She'd had a cigarette. It had made her cough so hard and had tasted so disgusting that she'd never touched another. One of her friends had smoked dope but Elsa's throat had been too sore from the coughing fit to try it for herself. She'd drunk beer, though. She hadn't liked the taste but there had been no other alcohol available, not that she'd found anyway.

As was often the case with unsupervised teenage house parties, alcohol and illicit drugs meant things got pretty raucous. When a game of Beer Pong resulted in a flat-screen television being smashed, Elsa had still been sober enough to know it was time to leave, and had sent a message to her dad asking to be collected.

A little woozy but still the right side of drunk, she'd waited out front with her friends Lola and Carmen. A handful of older boys joined them, boys the three virginal girls had whisperingly agreed were *sexy*. When offered a bottle of beer each, the giggling girls had accepted, too naïve to realise the boys expected payment.

That payment had been of the tongues down throats and hands up tops and down skirts variety. Elsa had never expected her first kiss to be of the drunken, unwanted kind, but that's what it had been. The boy in question hadn't even *asked*. It had been disgusting, all slobbery, like what she'd imagine kissing Rocco, her dad's English mastiff, would be like. She'd pushed him away. He'd grabbed hold of her again and pinned her hands behind her back to stop her resisting.

There hadn't been time for her to feel scared because that had been the moment a shadow had fallen over them and then suddenly the boy had released her and levitated... But he hadn't been levitating, she'd realised a blink later.

He was hovering inches off the ground because Santi had hoiked him into the air by his neck.

He'd grinned at Elsa and, still holding the boy aloft with one hand, had dug into his pocket with the other and thrown his keys to her. 'Wait in the car for me, *chiquita*. And your friends.'

From the safety of the car, the three girls had stared with their faces pressed to the window as Santi entered the house. Moments later teenagers of differing stages of inebriation had flooded out.

When he'd finally joined the girls in the car, he'd told them to buckle up, turned the radio on and, singing along to the song playing, driven away.

'What did you do to that boy?' Elsa had asked after Santi dropped her friends at their homes. There had been no need to question why he'd collected her rather than her father. He'd always been happy to run errands for him and act as occasional chauffeur to the Lopez girls.

'Nothing you need worry about,' he'd answered.

'Did you hurt him?'

'How would you feel if I had?'

She'd thought about it. 'Good. But bad too.'

He'd laughed. 'I didn't hurt him or his scum friends, but I promise you this much—those boys are never going to manhandle you or any other female again.' His voice had then become serious. 'I want you to promise me that when you are out with your friends, you all look out for each other. I get that you're at an age where you want to experiment but you need to keep safe too and for women, safety comes in numbers. You understand?'

That was the night Elsa had fallen madly in love with Santiago Rodriguez. Overnight, the chiselled face with the broad nose, wide mouth and black eyes surrounded by lines that seemed permanently crinkled with amusement turned into the most handsome face she'd ever seen.

The next day she'd received an enormous bunch of flowers from the manhandling boy with a note that simply read, 'Sorry.' She'd received presents from Santi that day too—a rape alarm, a can of pepper spray and self-defence classes.

And now, as much as she wanted to seethe that her mother had entrusted her safety in the face of such danger to Santi, Elsa understood why she'd done so.

Santi would never let anything happen to her. He might have gained a fortune in his own right over the past decade that put her family's wealth to shame but he would put his own life on the line for any of the Lopezes. His loyalty was unwavering and eternal.

For all that being with him made her want to curl into a ball and cover her face, and for all that she hated him for his cold cruelty that night five years ago, the fear that had gnawed in her belly all week had settled. The old feeling of safety she'd always had when she'd been with him had smothered the fear.

Elsa was pulled from her trip down memory lane when Santi entered the car park of an airport hotel. He found a space near the entrance. She went to open her door but he put a hand on her arm.

'Wait.'

She waited.

When satisfied no suspicious cars had joined them, he said, 'Follow my lead and save any questions until we're alone.'

Striding into the hotel, he headed straight to the reception. To her surprise, he produced two passports which he handed over with a credit card. A room key was given in return and then Elsa found herself being led to an elevator. Thinking he intended for them to stay hidden in a room until the last possible moment, she was further surprised when he pressed the button to the basement.

'Where are we going?'

The doors pinged open before he could answer, revealing a loading area for deliveries and rows of industrial bins, trolleys and other random items. The most random of all was a gleaming Aston Martin with tinted windows nestled between a row of overflowing green bins and a pile of discarded crates.

Santi waved an arm with a flourish. 'Your chariot awaits.'

'I know the other car was a hunk of junk but isn't this a bit excessive for a short drive to the airport terminal? Can't we take the shuttle?'

He raised his brow.

'What?'

'Didn't your *mamá* tell you? We're not flying to Valencia.'

'Then how are we getting home?'

White teeth slowly exposed themselves under his widening grin. 'We're taking the scenic route. You and I, *chiquita*, are going on a road trip.'

CHAPTER TWO

'A ROAD TRIP?' Elsa said dumbly. 'We're driving all the way to Valencia? But that will take…*days*.'

He pulled a musing face. 'There's some sailing involved too. But saying "road trip" has a much better ring to it than "road and sailing trip", don't you think? And speaking of which…' he opened the passenger door '…we need to get going. We only have a little breathing space. I want the airport to be dust before they realise they've lost you.'

She slid into the luxurious interior, put her bag between her feet and fastened her seat belt while Santi climbed into the driver's side. When he closed the door, the motion sent a waft of his cologne into her airwaves, a scent that was earthy and musky and made her breath catch in her throat and her abdomen clench.

'Can't we fly from a different airport?' she asked in desperation. 'Hire a small plane or, better still, take one of *your* planes. You know everything about the aviation industry. You can get us there undetected. We can be home by dinner.'

He sighed and pressed the start button. The engine purred gently to life. 'Your family, Felipe and I agreed it would be better to take you home via the scenic route.'

'But driving and sailing?'

He put the car into Reverse and swung out of the parking space. 'The plan to bring down the cartel starts now, and we want you safe and far from the action while it happens. If the gods are smiling on us and Felipe and his men and the authorities do their jobs properly, the cartel will be history by the time we arrive in Valencia.' He nosed the car out of the hotel's delivery area, looked from right to left and pulled smoothly onto the road. 'It was all supposed to happen in a few weeks but the threat to you has bought it forward.'

'What about my family? Where have they been taken?'

'The villa's been turned into a fortress.'

Angry, terrified heat filled her head and she slammed her fists on her thighs. 'Why haven't they been *moved*?'

'Because that would have tipped the cartel off,' he answered calmly.

'And turning the villa into a fortress didn't do that?'

'The estate has been heavily guarded since your father's death. You know this. The extra security was brought in very discreetly.'

She threw him the filthiest glare she could muster before turning her face to the window and clamping her lips together.

Elsa didn't care how heavily guarded the estate was. She didn't care that the villa had a panic room with provisions that could keep her family protected and fed against a month-long siege. They should have been taken to a safe house in a different country. Somewhere like New Zealand.

'Your mother told you to trust me, *chiquita*,' he said, his gravelly voice suddenly soft. 'So trust me when I say your family are safe. Nothing will happen to them. I swear.'

Her throat was too choked to answer, eyes brimming with tears that were certain to unleash if she looked at him.

'Have I ever broken a promise to you before?' he asked gently.

Keeping her gaze out of the window, she gave a small shake of her head.

Promise not to tell my mamá.

Promise not to tell my papá.

Promise you'll get me there on time?

Promise you'll be there?

You promise?

Variations of promises she'd made him swear throughout her most formative teenage years. He'd kept every one of them. Got her out of more scrapes than she could remember.

And then he'd broken her heart.

Santi spent the next hour or so concentrating on the road before and behind them, watching for a tail. He didn't think anyone was following but wouldn't take anything for granted. Traffic was heavy but once they'd driven through Margarethen am Moos, it lightened and the tension in his shoulders loosened a little too.

While his remaining tension was all internal, Elsa was as taut as a wind-up clock. She needed to relax before rigor mortis set in. He had complete confidence in Felipe Lorenzi and his men. The Lopez family couldn't be safer if they were in Fort Knox.

He turned the radio on, found a station that played the kind of tunes he liked, and cranked the sound up. Santi had a special loathing for randomised non-curated playlists. In a world where technology and streaming ruled, he still preferred the human touch.

'How can you sing?' the rigid woman beside him asked accusingly.

'How can you not?' he retorted.

'Because…'

'Because you want to let your demons control you?'

When Santi felt the old familiar tension and anger stir

in his guts, a good blast of music usually helped diffuse it. It was a trick he'd learned many years ago, reinforced and perfected when he'd ached with every fibre of his being to pulverise the teenage boy who'd tried to force himself on Elsa. The tautness in his guts right now felt very different from that long-ago tension.

'It's not your family in danger,' she said.

'Isn't it?'

His words hung in the enveloping silence.

A few miles later and he saw the tell-tale colours of a fast food restaurant.

'Hungry?'

'No.'

'Well, I am.'

The restaurant had a drive-through. He pulled into it and opened his window to give his order.

Minutes later and he reached for the bulging paper bag and drinks tray, passed them to Elsa who had no choice but to take them, then drove into a bay.

Taking the paper bag off her lap and putting it on his own, he then un-wedged the coffees from the tray and put them in the car's cup holders. He pulled out squares of sugar for Elsa from the bag, then removed a burger box and fries and handed them to her too.

'I said I wasn't hungry,' she said stiffly.

Unwrapping his double burger, he shrugged and took an enormous bite. 'I'll eat it if you don't want it.'

Despite her private vow to ignore him for the duration of their journey, Elsa couldn't help but notice how he devoured his food with the same appreciation he'd always shown, and found herself flooded afresh by memories. How many times had Santi collected her from parties and, in an attempt to sober her up before she had to face her parents, bought her fast food and black coffee doused with plenty of sugar?

Looking back, she could see she'd deliberately drunk too much on those nights out with her friends just so he would look after her.

When she finally looked at the food on her lap, a huge pang rippled through her heart to see it was the chicken burger she'd always favoured.

He'd remembered.

She didn't doubt he also remembered the night she'd waited in his bed for him, and as she thought that, the little appetite she'd regained by smelling the food vanished, and she handed the box to him. 'Have it.'

'With pleasure.'

Their fingers touched as he took the box and a shock of heat danced through her. Suddenly breathless and unsettled, Elsa leaned as far from him as she could and pressed her cheek against the cold window.

When he'd finished every scrap of both his meal and hers, he drove to a bin, opened his window, and dropped their rubbish into it.

And then they were off again.

'How come you ended up studying in Vienna?' Santi asked. The Autobahn stretched before them. He estimated they had another four hours of driving before they reached their first destination, and Elsa's cold silence was fast becoming intolerable. The Elsa-scented air had stopped the radio working as a distraction. Her perfume was much lighter and more subtle than the heavy, cloying fragrance she used to douse herself in. This one had a gorgeous, delicate fruity tone and his nostrils twitched to drag it deep into his lungs.

'It seemed like a nice city,' she muttered.

He worked at loosening his jaw. Everything felt tight, as if all the bones in his body had locked together. 'You were going to study in Valencia.'

'I changed my mind.'

'Why?'

Elsa closed her eyes. She didn't want conversation. Santi's voice...

She clenched her jaw tightly. Barely half a day together and already his voice, deep, gravelly, *sexy*, was doing things to her.

It was because she'd been taken so unawares, she told herself. No time to prepare for being with him. This heated, sickly tension was just a muscle memory. An echo.

She wasn't that obsessive, reckless girl any more. She walked rather than ran. She listened carefully rather than talk nineteen to the dozen. She was in control of herself. Feelings didn't dictate her actions. She considered things carefully. Impulse had no part in her life.

'I asked why you changed your mind,' Santi pressed.

From the corner of his eye he saw her raise a shoulder. 'University is supposed to broaden your horizons. Marisa kept telling me I was a fool for wanting to live at home rather than experience everything university had to offer. I decided she was right.'

'So why stay after you graduated? You were going to join the business.'

He remembered the hours she'd spent talking about the day she took her place in the family business, her excitement for the travelling and adventure that would come with it, all her ideas for it. Instead of doing the thing she'd spent her whole life looking forward to, she'd taken an office job with a Viennese recruitment company. He couldn't begin to imagine what kind of excitement recruitment gave to someone with Elsa's zest for life.

Another glimpse of shoulder rising. 'Vienna suited me.'

'How did you find the language?'

'It took a while for me to pick it up but I'm fluent now.'

'Did your Austrian boyfriend help you?' He dropped this question casually. For some unfathomable reason his heart seemed to stop while he waited the few beats for her answer.

'Which one?'

He laughed at her chutzpah. 'How many have you had?'

'Enough.'

'Your parents told me you were serious about someone called Stefan.' He reflexively tightened his grip on the wheel. 'They kept waiting for you to bring him home so they could meet him.'

'It didn't work out.'

'Why not?'

Another shoulder rise. 'We wanted different things.'

'What did you want?'

'A man who didn't keep bombarding me with questions like someone from the Inquisition,' she said pointedly.

He laughed again. 'We haven't spoken in five years. Is it a crime to want to know how you've been?'

'From what you've said, you already know everything.'

'I only know what your *mamá* has told me. She's very proud of you. Your *papá* was too. And I know *you*, *chiquita*, and what an accomplished liar you are.'

'I am *not*.' It was the most animation he'd heard since he'd forced the conversation on her.

'Don't get defensive. People lie. Teenagers especially. It's human nature. You happen to be very good at fooling your family.'

'I'm not a teenager any more. And you lied to them too.'

'Not in words. I omitted a few things but if they had ever asked me directly, I would have told the truth. I'm glad they didn't ask. It is better for parents not to know everything their children get up to, I think.'

'I didn't do anything more or less than others my age did.'

'And that's why I never had to tell them. You experimented like all teenagers do but compared to how I behaved as a teenager, you were an angel.'

He felt her curiosity pique in the subtle way she straightened. It was a little tell he remembered from the days when they'd been as close as cousins.

'What did you get up to?'

'Stuff you wouldn't believe.' Stuff he would never have dreamed of sharing when she'd been an impressionable teenager. And stuff it shamed him to his core to remember.

'Try me.'

'Okay...' The woman beside him was no longer an impressionable teenager, he reminded himself. 'You remember the day you went cliff jumping and hurt your back?'

Elsa reluctantly allowed the memory to surface. It had been a forty-foot drop into the sea and she'd landed badly. The exhilaration as she'd flown through the air had been worth the pain. Rather than get a lift back with a friend, she'd called Santi. He'd kept his mouth shut when she'd blithely told her parents she'd hurt it after falling down some stairs. 'Yes...'

'I did the same thing at the same age but I was drunk out of my mind. I nearly drowned. I was wild, always drinking, always on the lookout for trouble, fighting anyone who looked at me the wrong way, rarely attending school and when I did it was to cause trouble. I never knew when to draw the line.'

Elsa knew boys like Santi had described. They were the kind of boys he'd always warned her about.

'I don't remember you being like that.' She couldn't remember Santi as a teenager at all. In her mind, he'd always been a man. Eleven years older than her twenty-three years, he'd been a part of her life for all her life, the long-dead housekeeper's son who'd continued to live on their estate in the cottage he'd shared with his mother, but in Elsa's younger years he'd been a shadow in the background.

By her tenth birthday he'd become her father's right-hand man, the man who occasionally picked her up from her private school or ballet lessons and occasionally joined the family for Sunday dinner; an elusive big brother with no time for pesky little girls who only wanted to talk about ballet and horses. He'd only taken solid form in her mind when she'd gone to that first unchaperoned house party and he'd turned into her unofficial chauffeur and protector.

'You were too young to have known, and in those days I was kept away from you and Marisa.' Those were the days Santi looked back on with shame and self-loathing and his knuckles tightened over the steering wheel again as the vision of his PE teacher's pulverised face flashed in his eyes. 'If not for your father, my life would have taken a very different path. He was a good man. The best. The best mentor a boy could have and, *damn*, I *miss* him.'

'I miss him too,' Elsa whispered. Her heart throbbed with the sharp pain that had rarely dulled since his death. 'I know you do.'

She closed her eyes and breathed in deeply through her nose, only to find Santi's earthy, musky scent filling her lungs.

A tear spilled down her cheek. She brushed it away and swallowed back more tears. The confines of the car were closing in on her. She didn't want to talk any more. Didn't want to think. All she wanted was to be home with her family and for this nightmare to be over.

But Santi's scent was growing in intensity, feeding the nightmare, and now she imagined she could feel the heat from his body too. 'Can we open the roof?'

'Not a good idea.'

'Why not?'

'Your hair is very distinctive.' The curse of being a redhead in a country where less than two percent of the population were naturally that colour. 'Best we don't take unnecessary risks.'

'Do you mind if I open the window then?'

'Go ahead.'

As the fresh air pooled in, she put her face to it and welcomed it into her lungs, welcomed it pushing out Santi's scent. The way her body reacted to it frightened her. It reminded her too sharply of the hunger she'd felt for him all those years ago.

That had been a hunger categorically not reciprocated.

The sun was descending when Santi parked the car. He removed his shades and checked the messages on his secure phone, then rolled his neck to loosen it and stretched his back.

Elsa had fallen asleep an hour ago. When calling her name failed to rouse her, he placed a finger on her shoulder and gently prodded it.

Her eyes flew open and locked onto his.

It had been a long time since Santi had gazed into those eyes, a curious combination of green and brown, as clear as crystal but with unfathomable depth, and as he stared, his sinews tightened.

He'd spent the day running on adrenaline, assuming the knots in his guts were caused by the situation. He'd filled the tension between them with music and conversation, never allowing himself a moment to acknowledge the beautiful woman Elsa had blossomed into. She'd always been a pretty thing but now... Oval-faced with rounded cheekbones, a cute little nose, lips shaped like Cupid's bow and long silky locks the colour of autumn leaves... Elsa was stunning. The most ravishing woman he'd seen in all his thirty-four years.

A pulse beat loudly in his head. He could only have been trapped in her gaze a matter of moments but in those moments time became elastic, stretching until he forced himself back to the present.

He cleared his throat. 'We're here.'

She blinked a number of times before turning her face and covering her mouth to hide a wide yawn.

Elsa took in her surroundings, glad to have something to focus on that wasn't Santi, glad to have a moment to settle her heart without his all too knowing gaze on her face.

He'd parked in front of an enormous log cabin situated at the base of a steep forest. Craning her neck, she caught a glimmer of water a short distance behind them. 'Where are we?'

'Carinthia,' he answered.

She knew of the popular Austrian spot with mountains and lakes, situated within the Eastern Alps but had never visited. 'You're sure we've not been followed?'

'I detected no tail. I've had a message from Felipe—the cartel know you've disappeared. They're looking for you but nothing in their communications suggests they're close.' His teeth flashed. 'They think you took the train.'

'Good.' She gave another yawn and looked again at the picturesque lodge. 'I'm guessing the cartel won't expect us to stay in a holiday resort?'

'Who knows what they think? But this isn't a holiday resort. I own it.'

That shocked her. Santi had bought a property in *Austria*? 'Since when?'

He shrugged. 'I bought it as an investment last year under a business name. The lake's on the doorstep and in the winter it's within easy reach of the ski resorts, so should be popular with summer vacationers and winter sports enthusiasts. I've had a team renovating it. Luckily for us, the renovations were completed a couple of weeks ago.' He opened his door. 'Come on. Let's get inside.'

Elsa got out. Absolute silence filled her ears, not even a rustle of breeze disturbing the stillness.

The beauty of the setting made her heart sigh. It was as if nature had carved a secret horseshoe into the verdant terrain for the lake to fill, the lodge hidden beneath the forest from prying eyes. She pictured it in winter: the lake frozen, the roof of the lodge and the tall trees and mountains thick with snow. Magical.

She turned and found Santi removing cases from the boot of the car.

Her heart swelled and caught in her throat.

Why had he chosen this spot? Why here, in Austria?

Five years before she'd left Valencia, he'd set up his own business. By the time she'd left, it had grown into a billion-euro venture. She'd barely noticed his growing wealth because nothing had changed between them. He was still just Santi.

In the five years she'd lived in Vienna, his wealth had grown to such an extent she could barely comprehend the figures. It seemed like every conversation with her mother involved a brief telling of his latest acquisition. Rosaria's pride rang in her voice. The years Elsa had been away, his business had turned into an empire. Santi had the Midas touch, and when she followed him up the steps and into the lodge, she found the interior worthy of King Midas himself.

Walking beneath high, oak-beamed ceilings and over gleaming oak floor covered with numerous exquisite rugs, she soaked everything in. The last of the day's light poured in through the plentiful high windows and bounced over highly expensive furniture that was both luxurious and inviting.

'Is this really a holiday let?' she asked, already awe-struck despite having seen only a fraction of the lodge. If this was hers, she'd want to keep it all for herself and her family.

He ran his fingers through his black slicked-back hair and nodded.

'I'm guessing it's for an elite clientele,' she murmured, her attention now captured by a carved oak table placed in a nook that had a map of the world inlaid in marble on its round top.

'It's for those who can afford it. There's eight bedrooms upstairs. Take your pick, they're all made up. Dinner's been delivered and is keeping warm in the kitchen, so follow your nose when you're hungry. Explore. Use whatever facilities you wish, just bear in mind there's no staff here at the moment.'

As he spoke, Santi edged away from her in the direction of the stairs. She told herself she didn't care that he obviously couldn't wait for some distance from her. *She* couldn't wait for some respite from *him*.

'We'll be leaving early in the morning so relax and get some sleep,' he continued. 'I'll leave your case upstairs for you.'

'*My* case?' In all the day's drama, she'd forgotten she didn't have any spare clothes with her.

'Your sister packed it for you. The phone I told you about is in it. You can call your family but no one else. There's also a wig in there.'

Her heart sank. Marisa's taste in clothes differed greatly from Elsa's. Her big sister liked to tease her about how conservatively she now dressed, as if there was something wrong with stylish jeans and pretty tops, and knee-length skirts and dresses.

'What's the wig for?'

'I told you, your hair's distinctive. You'll need to hide it under the wig or a hat when we're in public.'

Then he picked the cases up and, without another word, disappeared with them.

CHAPTER THREE

By God's grace and spacious accommodation, Santi managed to avoid Elsa for the rest of the evening.

It proved impossible to avoid her presence, though.
Barely a day in her company and he felt more wired and
on edge than he'd felt since...

Since those torturous days after he'd found her in his
bed.

To keep his mind occupied and far from Elsa, and to
pass the hours before he slept, he checked in on his business and satisfied himself that there weren't any serious
issues that needed his attention.

It had been many years since he'd taken time away from
the business he'd formed a decade ago. Santi had had the
idea of starting a complementary business to the Lopezes'
shipping one, a fleet of airliners that were exclusively for
the transportation of goods. He'd picked up a lot of knowledge through his work as Marco's right-hand man and had
saved virtually all the money he'd earned from him. He'd
been ready to strike out on his own.

Marco, as was his generous nature, had been more than
happy to guide him. He'd willingly shared his contacts and
office space, and invested a chunk of his own money in
Santi's venture. They'd worked as closely together as they'd
done since Marco had bailed him out that final time. Five

years later, all the investment had been repaid and Santi's business had started to make a killing.

The same week Elsa had left home for Vienna, Santi had moved out of the housekeeper's cottage, which they'd insisted he could live in for ever if he wanted, and into a villa he'd had built a kilometre away. He'd moved his arthritic grandmother from her cramped fourth-floor apartment in Seville into a spacious ground-floor one in an exclusive retirement complex. He'd bought himself a fleet of cars. He'd commissioned a two-hundred-foot super-yacht. He'd bought himself an apartment in New York, a penthouse in Milan and a three-storey house in London, the last of which he was still to spend a night in. This Austrian lodge was just one of many business investments he'd poured his money into.

His success would have been dizzying if he'd had time to think about it but he was always busy working, expanding and micromanaging the business, investing in new ventures...

Far from enjoying the fruits of his labour, he'd become a workaholic. Long, lazy lunches followed by relaxing siestas became a thing of the past. Long, lazy evening meals with good company followed by dancing in smoky clubs until the early hours had been similarly eschewed. For five years Santi had done nothing but work.

One day, when the time was right, he would board his yacht—since delivery, he'd used it once, for entertaining purposes—and sail the Caribbean. He hoped to have found a wife by then. Maybe have a few children. The days of feeling imaginary shackles on his wrists and ankles at the thought of marriage had long gone, but how could a man like him find a wife? Overnight, he'd gone from playing the field with relish to rarely dating. The few lovers he'd had in the past five years had been fleeting affairs that had satisfied nothing more than his basic needs.

That this morph into workaholism had coincided with Elsa's move to Vienna was pure coincidence. That he'd bought this lodge in the country she'd chosen to base her life was coincidence too.

Infuriated that he was *still* thinking of her and certain his brain was too wired for sleep, he decided to take a swim and work some of the tension out of his body.

Grabbing his swim-shorts, he padded quietly past the room Elsa had picked for herself, and headed down to the ground floor spa.

The room Elsa had selected was so elegant and beautiful that, if she hadn't been so desperate to get home to her family, she'd have loved to spend more than a night in it.

A pang rent her chest to imagine spending time here over winter with her family, enjoying the white Christmas she and Marisa had dreamed of as children. The picture came fully formed. Her. Marisa. Baby Nikos. Their mother. Their father. Santi…

No mental image of her family came complete without Santi.

But it was picturing her dead father that turned the pang into a deep, tearing wrench and, aching to hear a familiar loved voice, she snatched up the phone Santi had given her and called Marisa.

Just hearing her sister's voice was enough to soothe her. When Marisa put the phone on loudspeaker so Elsa could talk to their mother and hear baby Nikos babbling away, her chest loosened enough for her to breathe properly. Once she was satisfied that the three people she loved most in the world were safe, she lay back on the sleigh bed and closed her eyes. Santi's face swam before her.

Frustrated at her brain's inability to switch off, even more frustrated it seemed to be locked on everything Santi, she threw the covers back and rummaged through her case for one of the swimsuits she'd spotted earlier.

Thankfully, the clothes Marisa had packed *were* Elsa's own...mostly. Marisa had also packed a couple of her own dresses. They exposed way too much flesh, especially around the cleavage and thighs. Under no circumstances would she wear them, especially not around Santi, not when the disgust that had oozed from him all those years ago still plagued her. Overnight, she'd gone from being a body-confident young woman to someone who could hardly bring herself to look at her naked reflection.

She changed into the swimsuit then slipped on the towelling robe hanging in the bathroom and secured it tightly before creeping out of the room and tiptoeing down the stairs.

During her solitary tour of the lodge earlier, she'd found a vast spa facility on the lower ground floor, but she'd only given it a cursory glance, too on edge about bumping into *him*, before finding her dinner in the rustic kitchen and taking it to her room, where she'd intended to hide until morning.

She hadn't had the chance to fully appreciate the spa's breathtaking glory earlier. She appreciated it now. Completely different in tone and feel from the rest of the lodge, its marble flooring and ornate pillars made her think of Roman baths from millennia ago. So taken was she by the life-sized marble statues lining the walls of the swimming area that it took her a beat to notice the human figure climbing out of the water at the far end of the vast pool.

Santi.

Her abdomen clenched then released in ripples.

Oblivious to her presence, he leaned over to snatch a towel from a lounging chair and rubbed it over his face.

Her heartbeats echoed in her ears. Even if he'd noticed her there, at that moment she wouldn't have been able to react. Her feet were rooted to the floor. The magnificent torso, all hard muscle with a smattering of dark hair across the pecs that had fascinated her from the age of fifteen, was *right there*, only the gold chain with an attached cross he'd worn for as long as she could remember and a pair of swim-shorts on his skin.

Dimly, she remembered Marisa's eighteen birthday. Their parents had thrown a pool party at the villa to celebrate. The sun had shone brightly. Everyone had been there, a melding of generations all having fun, diving in and out of the pool, eating barbecued meats, drinking cocktails and singing along to cheesy party tunes. Elsa and her friends Carmen and Lola, all of sixteen but trying desperately to act like adults, had stretched out on sunbeds and ogled Santi from behind their huge sunglasses.

Santi had been the one to notice when she'd helped herself to her third margarita. Wearing only a pair of swim-shorts, his glorious body damp from the pool as it was now, he'd plucked it from her hand, shaken his head with an indulgent smile, then grooved his way back to the pool, drinking her cocktail.

If she hadn't been so breathless at the accidental brush of his finger against hers when he'd pilfered her drink, she would have been furious.

She was breathless now too.

He turned slightly and froze.

Despite the distance of the pool between them, their eyes clashed. Held.

Eyes not leaving Elsa's face, Santi slowly lifted the towel to his head and rubbed it over his hair.

Whatever good his vigorous swim had done had been shattered in an instant. Caught unawares, no time to shield his thoughts or responses, awareness rippled through him like a riptide.

Her trim, slender body was hidden behind an enormous robe but his heated blood flowed as if she were wearing provocative lingerie.

The image he'd spent five years doing his damnedest to suppress flashed through him. Elsa. Naked on his bed…

He slammed the memory shut.

As if she were privy to his mental turmoil, Elsa suddenly reared back. Her gaze held his for barely another beat before she turned around.

Santi expelled a slow breath and closed his eyes. When he opened them, she'd gone.

Were it not for the arousal filling him so painfully, he would believe he'd imagined her.

Elsa gripped the bannister tightly as she descended the stairs early the next morning.

She refused to think about why facing Santi should make her stomach feel as if it was in a milk churn and her heart thump loudly.

Why did she have to dream about him? Wasn't it enough that he'd pushed himself to the forefront of her mind so that every time she closed her eyes his face was there before her without invading her dreams too?

It had to be that brief late-night moment by the pool. A brief moment that had passed like an eternity.

It's just an echo, she told herself stubbornly. All of it. An echo from the days when she'd been obsessed with him.

That echo reverberated through her now as she followed the scent of bacon to the kitchen, becoming violent when she found him spreading butter over thick slices of bread.

He looked up as she entered and flashed the familiar, easy-going smile that made the lines around his eyes crin-

kle. 'Good morning, *chiquita*. I'm making bacon sandwiches if you want one? Not quite a full English breakfast
but we need to hit the road soon.'

The thought of food made her stomach roil. Santi's good
humour and nonchalance while she'd spent hours torturing herself over her growing unrequited awareness landed
like barbed wire on her skin. There was not a single sign
that *he'd* spent the evening torturing himself, she thought
bitterly. And why would he? What had she ever meant to
him other than as his mentor's daughter? Whatever she
thought she'd detected in his eyes in unguarded moments
were echoes too of the time when her feverish imagination had been desperate to believe her feelings were reciprocated.

'I'm not hungry,' she said curtly, not looking at him as
she walked to the coffee pot.

A sugar pot swished over the counter and came to a stop
beside the mug he'd left out for her.

'Help yourself to extra sugar,' Santi said, his efforts at
good humour gone. 'It might sweeten you up.'

Far from a good night's sleep brightening Elsa's mood,
she seemed as hostile as she'd been yesterday. Under the
circumstances, he didn't expect her to be carefree and light,
but she was making little effort to hide her antagonism and
it was becoming more and more obvious that it was directed
at him and not the situation.

Could she be holding a grudge from that night? He'd
hurt her when he'd rejected her, he knew that. He'd had to.

She would never know how much he'd hurt himself too.

He took the two sandwiches he'd made for himself and
the one he'd made for Elsa to the kitchen table and took
his first bite. Definitely not as good as a full English, a
feast he'd discovered years ago after partying all night at

a British stag party and then joining them for breakfast, but enough to stave off the hunger pangs.

By the time he'd eaten the first, his anger had quelled a little. He kept his gaze fixed on the lake view from the window. He would not look at her again until he was certain he had his emotions under control. It didn't help that she was dressed in a pretty knee-length red floral wrap dress that hugged her slender body sensually.

How the hell did she evoke such wildly disparate emotions in him? She should elicit nothing but platonic familiarity. He should *not* be sitting there fighting the stirring in his loins, fighting his own mind from mentally undressing her. He didn't care that Elsa was a fully-grown woman now. She was forbidden fruit. She would always be forbidden fruit.

But he hated this tension. Hated to feel his muscles bunch together as if priming for a fight. The fight, he knew, was against himself.

When she broke the silence by quietly asking, 'Where's the road taking us today?' he made sure to keep his voice and features neutral with his reply.

'Portofino.'

'Isn't that in Italy?'

He nodded. 'If we leave within the hour, we should be there by sundown.'

'How many kilometres is it?'

'About seven hundred.'

'We're going to do the trip in one go?'

'The sooner we're at sea, the better.'

As Elsa was in complete agreement about that, she headed to the door. 'I'll get my stuff together.'

It was a relief to leave the kitchen. The scent of bacon was too reminiscent of the days when Santi would take her out for breakfast. Say what you like about English food, their traditional breakfast was amazing. The first time she'd had one had been after he'd picked her up from a sleepover at Lola's house. That had been an extra-special delight because she hadn't been expecting him. Her mum was supposed to collect her, but she'd double-booked herself with her hairdresser and asked Santi if he could get her instead.

Thinking back on it, she was certain he'd taken her to that café because he'd had a hangover. It had never occurred to Elsa that he might have had other plans for that Saturday morning, plans that had included sleeping.

Was this what the rest of their trip would be like? she wondered miserably as she climbed the stairs. Wave after wave of forgotten memories punching her?

Back in her room, she went to the bathroom and pinned her hair to the crown of her head and carefully put the chin-length brown wig on. If she wore it for the car journey, she'd be able to put the car's roof down and not have Santi's cologne invade her airwaves. She could take it off once they were at sea on his luxury yacht. With its five decks, ample cabins and large crew, she would have the space to hide away from him until they reached Valencia.

A loud knock on her door set her pulses racing and then Santi's handsome, rugged face appeared. A slight frown appeared on his brow as he took in the wig but he made no comment about it and made no effort to enter her room. 'Are you ready?'

She nodded and slung her bag over her shoulder.

An hour after leaving the lodge, they crossed the border into Italy. Santi was confident they had no tail.

Soon, surrounded by Alpine mountains, they entered the Canal Valley town of Tarvisio. He drove them straight to a hotel with an unobserved car park where he pulled up beside a Maserati GranTurismo. The fob for it was nestled behind the driver's wheel.

Elsa said not a single word while they made the switch. She hadn't said a voluntary word since they'd left.

'Can you work the radio for me?' he asked when they were back on the autostrada.

In silence, she complied. In no time they were listening to an American singer wailing an upbeat tune about her rotten bunch of previous lovers. It did nothing to ease the tension he could feel in his every sinew. Every inhalation dragged Elsa's light fruity scent into his lungs. God help him but the urge to lean into her and inhale deeply was growing by the second.

He gritted his teeth. Music wasn't working. He needed a distraction.

'Tell me about Stefan,' he commanded.

'Why?'

'Just making conversation.' Although why he wanted details of her old lover as a distraction was something he didn't know. Santi pictured Stefan in his mind, one of those strait-laced men who'd excelled in school academically and on the sports field, and had as much personality as a bucket of paint.

'Can't we make conversation about something else?'

'It ended on a bad note, did it?' he guessed, pitching his tone at cheerful. When she refused to answer, he added, 'You know, we're going to be together for a long time. You can't keep ignoring me.'

'I can.'

He laughed. 'You'll never keep it up. You were always such a chatterbox.'

'I'm not that girl any more.'

That much he did know. Elsa had changed. The springy girlishness she'd oozed had been replaced with something far more self-contained.

'Then tell me who you are now. What does the grown-up Elsa Lopez like to do?'

'She likes to go for walks and spinning classes, read books and watch boxsets.'

'But does she still party like it's going out of fashion? Is she still the Queen Bee amongst a large circle of friends?'

'I was never Queen Bee.'

'You were,' he contradicted. 'Your friends flocked around you. You couldn't go anywhere in the villa or the grounds without tripping over a teenage girl.'

'That's because they all fancied you.'

'What?'

'Don't pretend you didn't know.'

'How would I have known that? I was old enough to be their…'

'Big brother,' she supplied drily. 'And they all fancied the pants off you.'

'Teenage girls are not my thing,' he dismissed. He'd noticed them—he'd have had to be blind not to, otherwise he really would have tripped over them—but never as females to be pursued. He liked his women to be women, not giggling banshees.

'You made that abundantly clear,' Elsa muttered.

She only realised she'd said the words aloud when he replied, 'If you're talking about the night I found you in my bed then—'

The old mortification rushed through her. 'I don't want to talk about that,' she interrupted.

'We *need* to talk about it.'

'I was drunk. I barely remember it.' Remembering how drunk she'd been was mortifying too. She'd helped herself to her mother's rum for courage then, when her nerve had almost deserted her, helped herself to a little more.

If only she'd drunk enough to forget everything about

that night. Instead, it was stained in her memories. The night her heart had broken and her dreams had died.

'Really?' he asked sceptically.

'You can't think I actually *fancied* you? You were far too old for me.'

'Then you should thank me for not taking advantage of you,' he retorted. 'Some men might get their kicks from sleeping with drunken virgins but I'm not one of them.'

Elsa wanted to cover her face from the flames of humiliation his words provoked.

What a fool she'd been to think Santi had been waiting for her to come of age. She'd spent her eighteenth birthday on tenterhooks, waiting for the moment he declared his love for her as she'd spent three years fantasising, only to go to bed after her party disappointed. But then, the very next morning, in the villa's kitchen, she'd seen something in his eyes that had made her heart leap, a look that had consumed her for hours until she'd become convinced that Santi was waiting for *her* to declare herself.

The idea had bloomed as the day had gone on. Panic had already been building over his imminent move from his cottage on the Lopez estate to a newly built ten-bedroom villa a kilometre away.

She'd cycled past the construction site of his villa many times, plotting ways to sabotage the build and keep him with her for longer, until it had occurred to her that sabotage was unnecessary—he must be waiting for her to turn eighteen before asking her to move in with him!

Well, if he wanted her to move in with him, he needed to hurry up about it. Her pathetic little brain had decided that it must be shyness or old-fashioned chivalry preventing him admitting his feelings. She'd *had* to act. The best part of a bottle of rum had greatly aided this mind-set. Declaring her love had been the only logical course of action.

If she could go back in time and stop herself entering his cottage that night, she would.

The morning after, she'd wanted to crawl into a hole and die.

Remembering the anguish…oh, it was all coming back to her in unvarnished colour. The cruel things he'd said. The look on his face as he'd said them…

'Thank you for not taking advantage of me,' she said as coldly as she could manage with her heart being wrenched into pieces and the old worthlessness and shame sitting heavily in her stomach.

'I'm sorry if I hurt you that night. I never—'

'You didn't hurt me. It was a drunken mistake and I don't want to waste another breath talking about it. In fact, I don't want to talk about anything so if you don't mind, let's skip playing getting-to-know-each-other-again. I don't *want* to know you. All I want is to get home to my family.'

Santi had to force his knuckles to loosen on the steering wheel. He had to force his jaw to loosen too. Elsa's tone told him quite clearly that she hated him. 'If I didn't hurt you, why all the hostility?'

'I *said* I don't want to talk about it.' To accentuate her point, she turned the radio up so high the sound pierced straight through him.

'Cut it out,' Santi snarled, turning it down. 'Are you trying to make me crash?'

'Just stop *talking*!' she suddenly screamed, her voice as ear-splitting as the radio had been.

'What the hell is wrong with you?' he demanded.

'*You* are what's wrong with me.'

His fingers tightened on the wheel again. 'Very mature.'

She mumbled something under her breath that he couldn't make out and folded her arms tightly across her chest. He didn't have to see her face to imagine the defiant expression on it, which only added to his anger at her attitude and behaviour.

'Spend the rest of our journey sulking all you like,' he said, 'but if you pull another stunt like you just did with the volume, I'll chuck you in the boot. Understand?'

'I'd like to see you try.'

'Would you really?'

'Oh, do one,' she muttered mutinously, shifting to lean against the door.

Clamping his teeth together, he pushed the roof control button and in what felt like seconds, the roof disappeared and warm, fresh air blew around his face. It did nothing to blow his anger away.

And then he caught a glimpse of Elsa's dark wig blowing in the breeze and his heart ached to remember the reason she was wearing it.

Once, they had been friends. Good friends. Elsa had been his little buddy. He couldn't have been more protective of her if she'd been of his blood.

And then one day he'd looked at her and everything had changed.

CHAPTER FOUR

THE CHANGE HAD come the morning after Elsa's eighteenth birthday. Santi had gone into the villa to collect some paperwork he'd needed her father's signature on. She'd been at the breakfast bar, clutching her head, dressed in a thin pink robe.

'Hangover?' he'd asked without an ounce of sympathy. Her parents had thrown a pool party for her, just as they'd done for her sister. Unlike at Marisa's party, Santi hadn't needed to police Elsa's alcohol consumption since she had technically become an adult.

She'd groaned and got to her feet. 'Can you take me for an English breakfast?'

'Sorry, *chiquita*, but I've got a full day ahead of me. Tomorrow?'

'I'll try not to have a hangover for it.'

He'd grinned.

Her green-tinged face had managed a small smile in return before she'd staggered to the kitchen door. Morning light had pooled in through the vast windows and suddenly illuminated her.

His throat had run dry.

The light illuminating her slender frame had made the robe transparent. Elsa had clearly been naked beneath it.

And then she'd turned around, walked back to the

breakfast bar for her phone, mumbling something under her breath, oblivious to the fact that Santi had been able to see *everything*.

Less than twenty-four hours earlier he'd watched Elsa dance around the pool in nothing but a skimpy bikini and felt not the slightest stir of arousal. His mind and body had never gone there.

Their eyes had met. There had been a breathless feeling in his chest, as if his lungs had been slowly collapsing. He'd been unable to tear his gaze from her.

It had felt like he was seeing her for the first time, seeing her as a woman...

Desire had pooled deep within him, hot and thick, as disturbing for the depth of its intensity as for the object of his sudden craving.

His departure had been abrupt and he'd driven away from the villa in turmoil, unable to rid himself of the image of Elsa's naked silhouette. He'd arrived at the mammoth new warehousing complex he'd had built next to his airfield and ironed out the issues his manager had identified, all the while wishing he could scrub his eyes clean. Then Marco had turned up to sign the documents and the guilt had hit him like a truck.

If Marco or Rosaria knew Santi desired their youngest daughter...

They would have been horrified. And he wouldn't have blamed them. The cruellest thing, though, was that it wouldn't be the age gap that would bother them, Marco being ten years older than Rosaria. He, Santi, was just not good enough. He might have built himself a thriving business and a small fortune but the new trappings of his life didn't change his humble beginnings. It didn't change who he was inside. It didn't change the fact he'd once put a teacher in hospital with his fists and that if Marco hadn't stepped in, Santi would have gone to prison for it.

Marco's quietly delivered decade-old words had echoed loudly in his ears that day. 'I can't do this again, Santiago. One more incident like this and I'm sorry but I'll have to ask you to leave. It would break my heart but I need to think of the girls.'

It had been the final warning after Santi had put the Lopezes through three years of hell. He would never forget the sorrow and disappointment that had been reflected in Marco's eyes. That, more than anything, had been the impetus for Santi to make the behavioural changes so desperately needed.

What kind of man would he be to repay everything Marco had given him, which *was* everything, by falling for his daughter? The Lopezes were good people who wanted their daughters to make good marriages with good, clean-living men.

That night, Santi had returned late to his cottage and found Elsa in his bed.

It was five years ago, he reminded himself grimly, refusing to think about that night. The past. History.

He turned the radio up to a not quite ear-splitting level and drowned the past out with music.

Three hours later Santi drove into an exclusive gated road and stopped in the underground car park of a sprawling medieval home that had once belonged to nobility but now belonged to an acquaintance he'd got to know at a private members' club. The acquaintance in question had used Felipe Lorenzi's services himself and was completely trustworthy.

'Why have we stopped?' Elsa asked. They were the first words either had spoken since their earlier bitter exchange.

'Food,' he replied shortly. 'There's a decent coffee shop close by. If you're not hungry, you can watch me eat.'

Elsa practically jumped out. The lowering of the car roof had done nothing to stop her lungs filling with Santi-scented air.

After hours spent in the car, it felt good to stretch her legs.

As they walked the narrow streets lined with centuries-old buildings, Elsa had the sense of walking into the past. She wished she could explore properly. In the five years she'd lived in Vienna, she'd explored every inch of it on foot. She liked to walk. It was a good way to clear her mind and bring herself to a state of calm. At least, it had been before her father's death. Since then there had been too many shadows for any kind of peace.

Five minutes after they'd left the car, she followed Santi into a small but crowded café.

'We can't spend too long in here so I'm going to have a panini,' he said, having to lean in close to make himself heard over the bustle of chatter coming from all directions. 'What do you want?'

She looked at the chalkboard menu at the back of the serving counter. 'A mozzarella and prosciutto panini, please.'

'Coffee?'

She nodded and cast her gaze around for a table. A pair of elderly gentlemen were rising from a corner one, and she indicated to Santi that she would try and get it for them. When no one else tried to claim it, she quickly parked her bottom on the closest chair. She leaned back and let the warm, friendly atmosphere infuse her.

'You've lost your frown lines,' Santi observed when he joined her. He took the seat she'd placed her bag on to stop anyone else using it, and placed a couple of bottles of water on the table.

'It's nice to have a moment of normality,' she admitted wistfully, but the brief inner peace she'd found was over even as she spoke, the café so crowded that Santi was forced to shuffle his chair right next to hers to accommodate his massive frame.

Their coffees and paninis were brought to them.

Painfully aware of Santi's closeness, Elsa kept her elbows as tight to her sides as she could. Their thighs were a hair's breadth from brushing together and no matter how hard she tried to ignore him, her skin seemed to be inhaling the heat from his muscular body the way a plant breathed in sunlight.

God, but her heart was jumping all over the place. Her stomach had tightened too but she forced the food down her throat. She must keep her strength up. And, though she tried her hardest to keep her eyes averted, she was still so *aware* of him. He'd devoured his panini before she'd eaten a quarter of hers.

His appetite was something that had once fascinated her. His appetite was *huge*, and not only for food. Life for Santi had been something to be lived to the full. The only aspect of it she'd tried hard not to think about was his appetite for women. She couldn't remember a single meal they'd shared that hadn't been interrupted by some woman or other calling or messaging him. Whenever she'd slyly asked if she needed to buy a wedding hat, he'd put his wrists together as if they were cuffed and give the most exaggerated shudder.

She'd dreaded the day he confided that there was a woman he was becoming serious about. He was supposed to be waiting for her!

Had he found a woman to settle down with? For all she

knew, he might have spent the past five years living with someone. But he hadn't married or had children, that much she knew with confidence. If Santi ever married, her mother would be guest of honour. If he had children, her mother would be godmother.

Elsa had once believed, with the naïve self-absorption teenagers pulled off so well, that when Santi married her mother would be mother of the bride, and that when he had children her mother would be their grandmother.

Why was she thinking like this? What good did it do to remember how deeply her obsession of him had infected her?

And why did she feel like crying?

Shoving her chair back, she grabbed her bag and got hurriedly to her feet.

'Where are you going?' he asked.

Already walking, she called over her shoulder, 'To the ladies'.'

Alone in the bathroom, there was a moment of shock when she saw the dark-haired woman staring back in the mirror. She wished she could rip the wig off her head and stamp on it.

How was it that she was on the run from the cartel who'd killed her father and instead of looking over her shoulder like a frightened rabbit and fretting about her family, all her thoughts and feelings were consumed with Santi?

The walk back to the car went quickly and with the silence that had characterised their existence together since their hateful exchange earlier. They had hours and hours of travelling left, hours to be endured next to Santi with nothing to distract her. He opened the driver's door and was about to climb in when Elsa was struck by an impulse.

'Why don't I drive for a while?'

He raised a brow.

She bristled at the look. 'I know how to drive. I passed first time.'

He held his hands up for peace. 'I was surprised at the offer, that's all.'

'We've still got four hundred kilometres to cover if we're going to make it to Portofino by evening. I can share the load.'

He raised his other brow. 'Have you driven a car as powerful as this before?'

She narrowed her eyes. 'I hope you're not implying that I'm incapable of driving it?'

'I wouldn't dream of it. I'm thinking only that we want to get to Portofino before the sun comes back up again.'

Lips pursed, she held her hand out for the fob.

With obvious reluctance, he dropped it into her waiting palm. She closed her fingers around it, passed her bag to him, then got behind the wheel.

Santi put the bottled water in the glove box, sent up a silent prayer and fastened his seat belt. He remembered Marco telling him with complete bemusement four years ago that Elsa had passed her driving test in Vienna, even though she had no intention of getting a car. He was about to give her some basic instructions when she turned the engine on, put the car into Reverse, did a U-turn with the smoothness of a seasoned pro, and drove out of the vast garage.

Then she stopped, turned her face to his, smiled sweetly, and said, 'Do you want to give me directions or shall we use the satnav?'

'I'll give directions.'

'Great.' Then she cackled. 'Hold tight.'

Elsa carefully nudged the car into the traffic and joined the throng leaving the city. By the time they'd crawled their way back onto the autostrada, Santi was breathing easier... right until the moment she put her foot down.

'Whoa!' he shouted. 'What's the hurry?'

In answer, she threw her head back and laughed with complete exhilaration, throwing him back in time to the days when Elsa had embraced life and thrilled at adventure. She'd been born with a thrill-seeking gene, he'd long ago come to realise. Nothing scared her. He guessed that's why she'd waited in his bed for him, just another thrill to be explored.

Understandably, that Elsa had been missing these last few days, but she was with him now. Down the fast lane she zoomed, overtaking car after car, the hair of her wig blowing behind her and the biggest smile on her face. Even with his stomach dropping with the same effect as if he were on a rollercoaster, Santi couldn't help but wish it was Elsa's beautiful natural hair blowing around her.

'Since when have you been a racer?' he asked when his stomach had settled enough for him to speak.

'My employer took us to the Nürburgring six months ago for a team-building day. I *loved* it. I haven't driven since,' she added regretfully.

He shook his head in amazement. 'You're a natural.'

'That's what the guy running the event said.' Elsa laughed again as she remembered the only good day since her father's death. 'Lots of my colleagues play racing games on their consoles. Their faces when I got the fastest lap of the day was the *best*. Beaten by a girl!'

'Very wounding to the male ego.'

'And very satisfying to the female one.'

'Why haven't you driven since?'

'I don't need to. My work's a ten-minute walk from my apartment.' But the temptation to buy herself a little sports car after that team-building day had been almost irresistible. The *rush* she'd felt…

It was a rush and a temptation she'd quickly put to one side as she'd settled back into her calm, safe life.

Seeing the traffic ahead of them was gridlocked, she slowed down.

'Other than sulking when they're beaten by a girl, what are your colleagues like?' Santi asked, after she'd brought the car to a stop. Driving had done Elsa good, he decided. She had colour on her cheeks and was answering his questions without any sense of hostility. He considered it progress.

'They're okay. It's a good company to work for.' Even though they weren't going anywhere—lights twinkling in the distance signified the stalled traffic was due to an accident—she kept both hands on the wheel. The nails that used to be manicured and painted weekly were now bare and kept to a functional length rather than resembling talons.

'You enjoy it?'

Her mouth made a funny little swirling motion while she considered her answer. It was a motion so familiar and yet from such a distant time that his heart tugged to see it.

'It's a good job,' she eventually said. 'Generous pay. Lots of perks. Lots of potential to progress up the ranks.'

'You socialise much with your colleagues?'

Her mouth pulled in. 'Not really. Can I have a bottle of water, please?'

Recognising she'd deliberately changed the subject but figuring he had plenty of time to discover her real reasons, he opened the glove box and pulled out one of the bottles.

'What the hell is that?' she suddenly squeaked.

'What?' He closed the glove box and held the water out to her, which she ignored.

'In the glove box. Please tell me it isn't a gun.'

'You want me to lie?'

'Oh, God, it *is* a gun?' She unclipped her seat belt and

leaned over him to wrench the glove box open, then immediately reared back as if she'd been scalded. '*Why?* What the hell possessed you to bring a gun? My God, Santi, are you trying to get us arrested? What if we get pulled over by the police…? Look ahead of us! There's emergency lights flashing everywhere!'

'It's perfectly legal,' he assured her.

'It is *not* legal to carry a gun!'

'I have a special permit, so chill, okay?'

She ripped her sunglasses off and eyeballed him wildly. '*Chill?* That's a *gun*!'

'It's for your protection.'

'I don't want a gun protecting me!'

'So if the cartel find us, you expect me to use *what* to protect you? A water pistol?'

'I don't know!' She slammed her hands against the steering wheel and accidentally hit the horn, making them both jump.

She put her hands back to wheel and curled her fingers around it, straightening her back, taking deep breaths in through her nose, clearly trying to regain her composure.

'Do you know how to use that thing?' she asked in a tight voice.

'Yes.'

'And would you use it?'

'Without hesitation.' Seeing the way her throat moved, he sighed. 'It's nothing but a precaution. I don't expect to use it but if the unexpected happens, I'll be ready.'

'We get into trouble and you'll shoot our way out of it?'

'We don't expect it to come to that. All the signs so far indicate that the cartel has no idea where you are and our plan is working. Felipe Lorenzi has excellent inside intelligence. His team will know when the cartel know and warn us immediately.'

'What if they can't warn us?'

'I can communicate with Felipe's team in a number of ways. The moment I send the signal, a team will be sent to us.'

'What if they can't get to us in time?'

Hating to see the fear that had gripped her, Santi dropped the bottle of water and prised her hand off the steering wheel. He held it tightly, not speaking until she turned her face to him.

'If you want me to tell you exactly how we've co-ordinated everything to protect you then I will, but it will take until we arrive in Portofino to go through it in detail. Just know this—for as long as I draw breath, nothing will happen to you.'

Something flickered in the green-brown depths of her eyes.

'When your *papá* was killed... I cannot tell you the guilt I felt that I wasn't there to save him.'

Tears formed from nowhere and glistened in her eyes. 'There was nothing you could have done,' she whispered hoarsely.

'My head knows that but my heart...' He placed her hand to his chest and tightened his grip. 'I didn't know about the cartel. I'd been working in the US, expanding my business, when it all happened. Your parents didn't tell me because they didn't want to worry me. They should have told me. I would have dropped everything in a heartbeat to get back to them.'

She swallowed and croaked, 'That's why they didn't tell you.'

'I know, and it doesn't make me feel any better. If I'd known...' He breathed deeply and brushed a finger down her cheek, felt her quiver at his touch. His face inched closer to hers as he stared intently into the green-brown pools. 'I can't change the past. God knows, I wish I could but I can't. But when I stood by your father's grave at his funeral, I swore that I would do everything in my power to keep the rest of you safe.' And, he remembered with a deep pang, that he'd been looking at Elsa when he'd made that silent vow. 'I was the one who hired Felipe to protect you all, and over the last year he and his men have trained me.'

Confusion flashed in her eyes.

'They trained me in the techniques needed to be an effective bodyguard.'

The hand enveloped in his against his chest squeezed. 'You knew the cartel would come for us again?'

He found his gaze drawn to her Cupid's bow mouth. Their faces were so close he could feel the vibrations of her skin and inhale the sweetness of her breath.

His voice dropped to a whisper. 'I knew only that if anyone came for any of you again that I would be prepared, and I swear to you now, as God is my witness, that I will *never* let anything happen to you.'

He heard her hitched intake of breath. Saw the anguish in her eyes…and something else. Something darker. It drew him in. Hypnotised him. Made his veins and skin buzz…

Moisture filled his mouth. His lips tingled. His loins tightened. He could feel the vibrations of *his* skin pulling him to her.

He closed his eyes, senses filling with her delicate fragrance and the underlying warm scent of her skin. The tightening in his loins became a throb as their lips whispered together…

A long blare of a horn behind them had them simultaneously release their clasped hands and rear away from each other.

CHAPTER FIVE

ELSA BLINKED FRANTICALLY and put her trembling hands back on the steering wheel, holding it so tightly she felt it could easily snap. Her heart thumped so hard she feared it would burst out of her chest.

Nothing had happened, she told herself desperately, trying even more desperately to get air into her lungs. They hadn't been a breath away from kissing. It was just a moment between two people who'd lost someone they'd both loved. Nothing more. A moment of pure emotion.

But not until she'd inched the car forward to fill the small gap that had opened in front of them could she whisper, 'They didn't tell me either.'

'What?'

She would not allow her imagination to believe Santi's voice had a dazed quality to it.

'My parents.' She sucked in another breath and fought for vocal strength. For *any* kind of strength. 'About the cartel. They didn't want to worry me or make me feel guilt into returning home.' Only Marisa, who'd been working for the family business by then, had been told, and she'd been sworn to secrecy. Her devastated mother had explained everything when Elsa had arrived back home after her father's death.

Hot tears suddenly threatening to fall, Elsa blinked frantically, groped in her lap for her sunglasses and clumsily shoved them on.

How badly she wished her parents had confided in Santi. He would have seen in an instant that the protection they'd placed around themselves had been inadequate.

For all the guilt she and Santi shared for not being there, it was nothing on her mother's guilt. Deep down, her mother blamed herself for abiding by her husband's wishes to keep the threat of the cartel from their youngest daughter and the man they'd considered a son.

'If they had told you…would you have told me?' he asked after a long pause. She knew it was her own fertile imagination making his voice sound huskier than normal. Once, she had imagined all sorts of things from the tone of his voice. None of it had been right.

'Yes.'

'Even if they'd asked you not to?'

'Yes.' She had not a doubt in her mind. If she'd had the slightest hint of the danger they had been in, she would have swallowed her pride and called Santi.

The traffic started moving again. Elsa put the car into gear and crawled along with it. 'It was only because you took charge of our security that I felt able to go back to Vienna. I could trust the new security team only because you trusted them.'

On her visits home before her father's death, being in Santi's orbit had always been difficult. Avoiding his gaze, avoiding his company had always left her emotionally drained, and she'd felt it even more deeply in those weeks after her father's murder. But Santi's stepping in to take control of her family's security had given her a peace of mind she'd barely understood. She'd barely understood anything back then, too racked with grief to do more than go through the motions of life.

Why had she listened to her mother and pregnant sister when, ten days after the funeral, they'd insisted she return to Vienna?

Valencia or Vienna, it made little difference. Her life was destroyed wherever she lived. But she hadn't known that then. Her bereavement leave from work had been up and she'd returned to her self-made life not realising the safety of the world she'd blindly, selfishly, trusted to always orbit in her favour had shattered to pieces. *She'd* shattered. She'd become suspicious of everyone. She'd only left her apartment in daylight hours and even then had still seen shadows everywhere.

She'd spent the past year trying her hardest to put the shattered pieces back together. Only in the last month had she felt that she'd finally turned the corner.

They were crawling closer to the cause of the traffic. The number of emergency services vehicles gave an idea of the seriousness of the accident.

'Don't look,' he urged.

The compulsion to reach over and touch him shocked her with its strength, and she tightened her hold on the steering wheel. 'Don't worry,' she said softly. 'I won't. Don't you look either.'

A lump had formed in Santi's throat. It had been steadily growing throughout their conversation and now felt big enough to choke him.

The call Rosaria had made to him a year ago had come vividly back to him.

He'd known in an instant that something terrible had happened.

When he'd first heard her sobs, in those few moments before she'd found the words to speak, Santi's heart had stopped beating, every part of him frozen to ice with terror that she would say Elsa's name.

There was a coldness on his lap now too, the bottle of water he'd removed from the glove box for Elsa to drink. Glad of something to distract him from the painful memories, he unscrewed the lid. 'You still want water?'

'Yes, please.' She held her hand out for it.

He pressed the bottle into her palm and, as her fingers closed around it, they brushed against his. Hands that had only just stopped tingling from holding hers became electrified. He clenched his jaw tightly to expel the image of the look in her eyes when they'd come within a feather of kissing.

He must not drop his guard like that again, must not do *anything* to encourage this accelerating awareness.

He placed his clenched fists onto his lap and breathed deeply.

They passed the scene of the accident in silence. Both looked straight ahead, neither wanting to look at an accident that would force their minds to conjure the scene when Marco had been killed.

Then the autostrada cleared and Elsa visibly relaxed and sped up.

As the kilometres passed by, Santi began to relax too. He watched her drive, enjoyed the way her pretty hands manipulated the steering wheel...

But that only brought the craving in his blood back to a heated simmer and let loose fantasies of those same hands manipulating parts of *him*. Dragging his attention away from them, he tried to focus on the scenery surrounding them.

A song he liked came on the radio. He started singing along at the same moment Elsa did. There was a brief moment where she turned her head to look at him, their gazes holding through their dark shades for a short beat before she looked back at the road.

He dropped his own gaze and suddenly noticed the skirt of her dress had ridden to mid-thigh. Once he'd noticed it was *all* he noticed, and he became aware of the muscles in that succulent golden thigh tensing whenever she changed gear. It was enough to make his own muscles tense...

He cursed himself. *Stop looking.*

But he could no more stop his eyes from darting glances at her than he could stop his nostrils inhaling her heady scent.

Two hours after Elsa had taken the wheel he could stand it no longer.

'Let's stop at the next services and get coffee,' he said in a sharper tone than intended.

'Okay.'

When they stopped, he would drive the final leg of their journey to Portofino. With the road to concentrate on rather than Elsa, he could put a firm halt to this sick desire that was starting to consume him.

He had to.

When Elsa opened her eyes, night had fallen. Santi, who'd parked at the back of what looked like a busy hotel, was stretching his back and neck. She looked at her watch. In all, they'd been on the road for twelve hours. He must be exhausted.

'Are we there?' she asked, smothering a yawn.

'Yes. We'll sleep on the yacht and set off first thing in the morning.'

It took only minutes to walk to the marina, which was alive with twinkling lights from the yachts and other boats, people strolling, chattering voices and bursts of music. Pulling her suitcase along, she walked in step with Santi as he took the well-lit right-hand path, and peered at the two super-yachts moored in the distance. It was too far and too dark for her to tell which belonged to him. As they walked, people, many dining and drinking on their sundecks, waved and hailed them.

Santi stopped beside a row of mid-sized gleaming yachts that, while obviously luxurious, were only a fraction of the size of his new yacht.

He pulled a set of keys out of his pocket. 'This is the one.'

'This isn't yours,' she said, confused.

His brow creased. 'We aren't using mine.'

'But you said…' Her voice tailed off as she remembered he hadn't actually said they would be sailing on his yacht, only that they would be sailing. She'd assumed.

He must have caught her thinking for he grimaced. 'We need to be inconspicuous, *chiquita*. *The Conchita* can hardly be described as that.'

'No,' she agreed with a sigh and an internal despairing curse. *The Conchita*, named for his mother, was two hundred feet of ostentation, including the obligatory helipad and submarine, and had taken three years to complete. There had been much fanfare in the European yachting community about it. If the cartel knew about Santi's links to her family, which she assumed they did, and if they were smart, which they were, then they would have spotters reporting on *The Conchita*'s movements.

This yacht was, she estimated, no more than seventy feet.

A gangplank had been lowered onto the mooring path. Santi picked up the cases and carried them on board.

Despite the urge to march herself down to the distant super-yachts and beg a lift to Valencia, Elsa made her legs follow Santi.

She stepped into the interior of the main deck. The quality of the materials used to create the living and dining area, U-shaped galley and helm near the bows were undoubtedly expensive; cherry wood panelling and soft leather furnishings made the whole yacht scream luxury. Everything blended together with seamless panache and under any other circumstances she would have been thrilled with it.

'Where did you get this?'

'Felipe organised the charter. I don't know who owns it.'

She hardly dared to ask. 'How many cabins does it have?'

'Two. Both en suite. They adjoin but have private entrances too.' He pointed to steps heading down beside the helm. 'Those stairs lead to the master suite. The stairs behind you go to the second one. They're identical, so take your pick.'

'Where does the crew sleep?'

He didn't look at her while he answered. 'There isn't a crew.'

Her heart stuttered then roared back to life.

The only thing that had kept her going through the long, torturous drive with Santi had been the thought of a huge yacht she could get lost on and the presence of a crew who would act as buffers between them.

Clasping at straws, she said, 'So who'll…?'

'I will.' He grinned. She knew him well enough to know it was forced. 'I've sailed and navigated similar yachts before. Some owners employ a small crew but these are designed for owners to sail themselves. Remember, *chiquita*, we need to blend in. On this yacht, no one will look twice at us. We'll be just another pair of wealthy lovers enjoying a summer break sailing the Mediterranean together.'

Her stomach flipped violently at the casual way he bandied the word 'lovers,' but somehow she managed to force brightness into her voice. 'That's a shame. I was looking forward to spending a day or two on *The Conchita*...' As she spoke, it came to her that the much smaller proportions must mean comparatively smaller horsepower. She braced herself before asking, 'How long will it take us to get to Valencia?'

'Four or five days.'

The time she'd thought she had left being stuck with Santi had more than doubled in an instant.

She could feign brightness no more. 'I'm going to explore.'

'Go ahead. I need to check in with Felipe then we can order food. Most of the restaurants on the harbour deliver. There should be menus around somewhere.'

'Feel free to order for me. You know what I like.'

She scuttled down the steps at near the bows of the yacht without looking back, hating that he did know what she liked, probably better than anyone else. Santi was the one person in the world she'd always been completely herself with. She'd never needed to put on a front with him, never told any of the white lies she'd liberally told her parents and sister, never had to act confident when she was feeling insecure like with her friends, never felt she had to prove herself in any way to him.

Yanking the wig off, Elsa forced her thoughts away from Santi and the past to take stock of the cabin. It was far more spacious than she'd expected and tastefully decorated. To the left of the king-size bed was a small dining area, to the right a door she suspected opened to create a private balcony. She'd have to wait until they were at sea to find out. There was also a compact dressing table and plenty of storage. The en suite was beautiful, complete with a large walk-in shower with colourful mosaic tiles. Next to the bathroom door stood another door with a sliding lock. She turned the handle and it opened to reveal the second cabin, laid out as a mirror to the first. She closed the adjoining door quickly and locked it.

She couldn't deny that the yacht would be considered huge by any normal person. For an ordinary couple in love, this would be heaven.

Whatever Elsa's confused feelings for Santi were, romantic love no longer had any part of them but the last thing she wanted was to be stuck in these intimate confines for days and days with him. Not when every nerve in her body vibrated just to think his name.

Santi had just finished his call when Elsa reappeared. She'd removed the wig, her dark auburn hair flowing around her shoulders.

He noticed she kept a healthy distance between them as she eyed the phone in his hand. 'Is everything okay?'

'They're putting the final pieces in place. If everything goes to plan, the cartel's takedown should happen within the next forty-eight hours.' While he accepted the need to ensure every aspect of the takedown was planned to the nth degree, the sooner it happened the better. As soon as it was over the pre-planned contingencies to speedily return Elsa to her family would be enacted.

It couldn't happen soon enough for his liking. When the plans had been drawn up, he'd hardly given a thought to the prospect of spending days on end confined on a small yacht with her. Being confined in a car with Elsa had been a thousand times more difficult than he'd anticipated but at least he'd had the road as a distraction. Here, with the most advanced navigational technology available, distractions would be hard to come by.

'My family?' she asked.

'Safe. Did you choose a cabin?'

'Can I have the front one?'

'Sure.'

He picked up her suitcase and carried it down the steps. Only when he'd placed it on the bed did he realise she'd followed him. The spacious cabin reduced in size in an instant. The only thing that didn't appear shrunken was the bed. It was impossible to look at it with Elsa so close to him and not remember that night...

He'd closed his bedroom door and smelt the alcohol in the air before he'd seen her reflection in the full-length mirror. She'd been lying in his bed.

Trying his damnedest to slam the memories shut, he backed out of the cabin. 'I'll leave you to unpack. Dinner should be with us in half an hour. Do you want to eat inside or out?'

He'd turned slowly to face her. Her returning stare had been bold but the movement of her throat had shown her boldness to be a front. Silently, she'd pinched the covers and pulled them off. Beneath them, she'd been naked.

He punched the image away and willed the heat in his loins to cool. It had been a long day. His brain was exhausted, his mental defences weakened.

'Is it safe to eat outside?' she murmured, gaze resting on the floor.

'As long as you put your wig back on.'

Her auburn hair had fanned across his pillow...

She pulled a face.

He cleared his dry throat. 'Does it hurt?'

'No. It's just a little uncomfortable.'

'I'm sorry.'

'Don't be.' She grimaced and shook her head and then those mesmerising green-brown eyes locked onto his. 'Don't apologise for trying to keep me alive.'

His guts clenched but he kept his voice steady. 'So, inside or out?'

'Out.'

'I'll see you on the sundeck.' He closed the cabin door, tilted his head back and expelled the huge breath of air he'd been holding.

CHAPTER SIX

AFTER HIDING IN her cabin for precisely thirty minutes, ostensibly unpacking and changing for dinner into an emerald-green high-neck maxi-dress, Elsa ventured up to the sundeck.

She found it easily enough, climbing the steps she'd passed at the back of the yacht to find a sizeable dining and seating area, a hot tub that could fit a handful of people in it, and Santi, whose back was to her. He turned at the sound of her footsteps and she saw he'd been examining a second cockpit. He could steer the yacht inside or out. In front of that was a section she guessed was for sunbathing.

It cheered her to know there was more room for privacy—Santi avoidance—than she'd first thought. Judging by the way he'd left her cabin as quickly as he'd entered it, she imagined it cheered him too.

The awkwardness that had emanated from him in those few moments he'd been in her cabin had gone. He grinned to acknowledge her and pointed over her shoulder, where a man carrying a large tray approached their yacht. 'Good timing. That's our dinner. Get comfortable. I'll bring it up.'

The dining area had corner seating around a table that could comfortably accommodate eight people. She sat with her back to the harbour path and noted an outdoor grill and food preparation area. Certain no one could see her, she closed her eyes and welcomed the cooling fresh sea breeze on her face.

Her heart sped up when she heard Santi's nearing footsteps and she swallowed hard.

She'd rid herself of her attraction to him before, she reminded herself grimly. She could do it again. And if she couldn't... She would control it. Hopefully kill it. But she'd never let him see it. Never put either of them in the situation where he had to reject her again.

Santi didn't want her. He never had. He would protect her with his life but physically she repulsed him. That near-kiss had been...nothing. Whatever she thought she kept glimpsing in his eyes was a lie her brain had conjured to torment her.

'Dinner is served.' He placed the tray, which had two covered plates and cutlery on it, on the table before opening a cupboard beside the grill. The cupboard was in fact a fully stocked drinks fridge. He selected a bottle of white wine then opened another cupboard and pulled out two wine glasses.

'Just water for me, thanks,' Elsa said.

A thick black brow rose before he shrugged and exchanged one of the glasses for a tall one. From the fridge he removed a bottle of still water and then placed it all on the table. Once settled, he lifted the silver lids to reveal plates artfully arranged with linguine, clams and delicately roasted cherry tomatoes. One mouthful proved this simple dish had a bagful of flavour.

'Sure you don't want any wine?' Santi asked as he poured himself a large glass.

'I don't drink.'

He remembered all the times he'd picked her up from parties the worse for wear and how she'd often commented about looking forward to turning eighteen so her alcohol consumption couldn't be policed any more. He also remembered her parents' bemusement that their party-loving daughter had obtained a first-class degree and been given a special award from the university. The most they'd hoped for was that she would scrape a pass. 'Since when?'

She shrugged and set her gaze on the horizon. 'What are we going to do about food when we're at sea?'

'We're fully stocked with provisions. Since when don't you drink?'

She placed another forkful of linguine into her mouth.

'You're not going to answer?'

She pointed to her full mouth with one hand and twirled linguine onto her fork with the other. 'Why do you want to know?' she countered once she'd swallowed her food.

'It's a simple question requiring a simple answer. I don't understand why you're making it into an issue.' And he didn't understand why the answer felt so damn important.

'I'm not. I haven't touched alcohol in a long time.'

He watched her put another forkful into her mouth, observed the tightness of her jaw as she chewed, noted the way she looked at everything but him.

'How long? What made you give up?' What would she do if he leaned over the table and ran his tongue over her tight jawline…?

What in hell was he *thinking*?

'This is sounding like the Inquisition again.'

'If this was the Inquisition your red hair would have you burned as a heretic,' he teased, even as his mind once again conjured that flame of hair over his pillow. 'Is a little light conversation too much to ask?'

Light conversation to get them through this meal before he escaped to the privacy of his cabin where he would do his damnedest not to think that only a door separated her from him.

'Not at all. I just don't get why I have to be the one answering everything.'

'Then let's take it in turns. Truthful, non-evasive answers of more than one syllable only. You start. Ask me anything.'

'Okay…' Her mouth made the swirling motion as she thought. 'Why the beard?'

He rubbed his fingers over it. 'When your *mamá* asked me to escort you home, I thought I should disguise myself a little.'

'You grew that in a few days?'

'Five days.'

'Impressive.'

He rubbed it again. 'Must be all the testosterone. Do you like it?'

Why the *hell* had he asked her that?

She shrugged. Did he imagine the tinge of colour on her cheeks? 'If you like beards.'

'Do you like beards?'

He was going to cut his tongue out, he thought grimly. The tongue now tingling as he imagined running it down the arch of her neck…

He straightened his spine and willed the heat in his loins to abate. Mind over matter.

'I've never thought about it.' Not until Santi had grown one and Elsa had found her fingers itching to stroke it and her skin tingling to remember that one brief brush of it against her cheek when he'd met her in Vienna. 'Is your hair slicked back for disguise purposes too?'

'Yes.' He had a large drink of his wine and flashed his teeth. 'My turn.'

She braced herself for a personal question she wouldn't want to answer.

'Can you see yourself moving back to Valencia?'

Relief made her relax and smile. 'One day.'

'Elaborate.'

'I love Vienna but don't see myself living there for ever. I still think of Valencia as home.'

He twirled a large heap of linguine expertly around his fork before it disappeared into his mouth.

Suddenly aware that she was raptly watching him eat, Elsa wrenched her gaze back to her own food.

Frightened that her fingers had as much substance as the linguine and that her heart rate had accelerated again, she hurriedly said, 'My turn. What was the worst thing you did as a teenager?'

His features tightened. His eyes narrowed and visibly darkened.

Having thought he'd laugh and say something along the lines of petty vandalism, she was taken aback at the visceral reaction and put her fork back on her plate. 'What did you do?' she repeated quietly.

A pulse beat loudly in Santi's head. He rubbed the back of his neck and met her stare. 'Have you ever done something that makes your stomach twist and shame hit you like a hot wave whenever you think of it?'

Something flickered over her face. A wince of pain. Colour stained her cheeks. She gave a short, sharp nod.

He grimaced. 'I put my PE teacher in hospital.'

Her eyes widened then blinked. Blinked again. *'Why?'*

He took a large swig of his wine before reaching for the bottle to top his glass up. 'Because I lost control.'

Elsa stared at him. *'You* lost control?' The Santi she knew was always in control. Always. The only times he'd lost his cool around her had been that fateful night and when he'd threatened to shove her in the boot of the car. Both times, she admitted painfully, she'd deserved his temper.

He pushed his plate to one side. 'My mother's death… Look, I'm not going to make excuses but her death ripped me in two. I couldn't handle it. The pain. That's when I started acting out. If not for your father I would have been expelled for any number of reasons. Fighting. Stealing. Truanting, and Mr Perez hated me for that. He was a sadistic bully at the best of times, but the thing he really despised me for was setting fire to his personal fiefdom: the school gym.'

'You *didn't*?' she breathed, partly in awe. Elsa had hardly been considered a good girl at school but her bad behaviour had been more mischievous than actually bad.

His eyes glinted. 'I set a firework off in it. Don't worry— it was empty. No one got hurt. Your father paid for the repairs and gave a hefty donation to the school in exchange for me getting away with a short suspension.'

'Is that what caused the fight?' she asked, agog. She hadn't known *any* of this.

He grimaced. 'A fight means two or more people hitting each other. This was no fight.'

'So what happened?'

'My last day of school. I left thinking I would never return but I'd forgotten to clear my locker out. It had a pair of trainers your parents bought me for my birthday in it, so I went back. I got my trainers but when I went back outside, Mr Perez was walking to his car. The place was deserted. As soon as he saw me he squared up to me. Shouted abuse. Taunted me. Told me I didn't deserve your family. That I was a nasty piece of shit. All the things he'd spent three years wanting to say.'

His features tensed immeasurably. 'Something in me snapped. I dragged him behind his car and beat the hell out of him. Knocked him out cold. Broke his jaw and nose and fractured an eye socket.'

Elsa had always known her giant protector was more than capable of looking after himself but, even though he'd already said he'd put the teacher in hospital, the details still made her wince with horror. 'Oh, Santi, *no*,' she whispered. What a thing for him to have to live with.

He pinched the bridge of his nose and jerked a grim nod.

'Were you arrested?'

'Not that time.'

Her brows drew together in confusion.

'I'd been arrested twice before that. Your father bailed me out both times. This time I panicked. I called an ambulance and ran home. Confessed everything to your father—he knew the issues I'd had with Mr Perez. I wanted to hand myself in but he asked me to wait a day.'

'Ah…' She sighed, understanding. 'He paid him off?'

He gave a grim nod. 'A million euros for his silence.'

Her jaw dropped. Even for her father, that was a staggering act of generosity. Or desperation. The latter, she decided. Her father had loved Santi like a son.

'Your father pointed out to Perez that I had no money of my own. I could go to prison and he would receive nothing or he could take the money that would set him up for life. He chose greed over justice.' The ghost of a smile played on his lips. 'He quit teaching and moved to Thailand. He even sent me a postcard.'

Her chest loosened. 'He wasn't too traumatised then?'

'If he was, he hid it well. He always was a hard nut but I shouldn't have let him provoke me. I was eighteen. An adult. Your father had done everything to get me back on the straight and narrow, and while he paid Mr Perez off and hushed everything up, he made it clear it was my last chance. That, and the guilt I felt, was the wake-up call I needed to turn my life around.'

'Did he read you the riot act?' she asked, feeling a pang of melancholy.

'Yes. He did it in that quiet way he had. You remember?'

'He didn't have to raise his voice, did he?' she whispered.

'He never raised his voice.'

'That was always the worst. I used to wish he would shout at me like Mamá did.' Elsa often looked back and wondered why she'd ever felt it necessary to lie to someone so enduringly kind and non-judgemental.

Those bastards who'd killed her father had extinguished a candle of light in this dark world. She wished she could be there to witness their downfall. She prayed it involved excruciating pain.

'Does it make you think differently about me?' he asked, eyes locking back on hers.

She shook her head. 'Maybe it would have done before Papá died but not now. You lost your mother so young… Sometimes there is no rhyme or reason to how we react to grief.'

Growing up, Elsa had assumed everyone had the same happy life she'd enjoyed. She remembered feeling intensely sorry for Santi when his mother died because he didn't have a *mamá* any more, but at only four she'd been far too young to understand the finality of death and the grief that could tear a bereaved person's soul in two. She'd only truly understood that a year ago. She couldn't imagine how it would be to lose a parent you loved when you were only fifteen and full of combustible hormones.

Frightened by how badly she wanted to wrap her arms around him, and feeling a strong need to lighten the heavy mood, she said, 'I hope Papá made the teacher sign something that stopped him coming back for more money. If he hears how much you're worth now, he'll kick himself for selling out too cheap.'

She was rewarded with a rumble of laughter that dived straight into her bloodstream and heated her unbearably. 'It was water-tight.'

'Good…' She wanted to add something but hesitated.

Santi noticed. 'What?'

She sighed.

'When have you ever not been able to say what's on your mind to me?' he asked gently.

Her smile contained such sadness that for a moment he thought his heart had splintered. The tips of her fingers extended to touch his, just a light brush of skin against skin but enough to make his blood tingle.

'I was just thinking of how proud Papá was of you. And now I know why. You really did turn your life around.'

His brain told his hand to move. His hand disobeyed.

'All thanks to him,' he said heavily.

Her throat moved. Something glimmered in her eyes. 'I think you might have had a little involvement too,' she rebuked softly, threading her fingers between his…or was it him threading his fingers through hers?

Darts of desire unleashed and fired through him, and he finally got control of his hand and pulled it away, but it was too late. The spread was relentless. He clenched his teeth together and fisted his hands but still awareness flickered in every part of him, and suddenly he knew that when it came to Elsa, mind over matter was impossible. His desire for her had infected him. Every minute spent together had seen it burrow deeper under his skin, and when she looked at him the way she was looking now, as if she was trapped in his stare and helpless to pull out of it, the infection burned through his barriers.

He would not let it burn any closer.

With huge effort, he un-fisted his hands and placed them heavily on the table, then leaned forward so she could not mistake a single word he said. 'After the incident with Mr Perez, your father kept me close. Gave me a role in his business. He put his faith in me and taught me everything I needed to be a man. Do you understand that? I cannot state this enough—everything I am and everything I have is down to him, and I would *never* betray him.'

Her eyes widened slightly. Her chest rose.

Listen to me! he wanted to shout. *Understand. Keep your distance. For both our sakes.*

It felt as if for ever passed before her eyes flickered and her lips formed into a taut smile. She got to her feet, her movements far jerkier than her usual elegance, but her voice was clear and light when she spoke. 'I know what my father meant to you and what you meant to him but you can't give him all the credit for what you've achieved. That was down entirely to your own hard work.

'Now, I hope you don't mind, but I'm going to bed. I'm exhausted. Thank you for dinner. Sleep well.'

Santi watched her silhouette disappear down the stairs with a heart so tightly clenched that any relief was nullified.

Twenty minutes later and Santi hadn't moved. He didn't dare. The longing to follow Elsa into her cabin was just too strong.

He put his face in his hands and kneaded his fingers into his skin.

This was impossible. His desire for her. It could never be.

Their conversation had taken an unanticipated route. Her horror had been apparent but so too had her empathy. He didn't know why the latter should shock him, not when she had Marco's and Rosaria's blood in her.

That was the first time he'd spoken of the incident with the teacher since it had happened. From that day on, he'd had two goals in life—to repay Marco's faith and make him and Rosaria proud.

Any pride he'd earned would be stripped away if they could read his thoughts and see the depth of his torturous desire for their daughter. It was the main thing that had stopped him acting on it that night five years ago, and nausea swelled inside him as the doors he'd slammed on the memories swung on their hinges and that night replayed itself to him in full, vivid Technicolor for the first time.

He'd arrived home to his cottage late and badly out of sorts. He'd carried the image of Elsa's naked silhouette with him all that day. He didn't imagine how he could feel worse about himself.

And then he'd found her in his bed.

He could still remember the exact way his heart had thumped. The way his stomach had dropped. The way his throat had run dry. The fire that had burned his blood.

Without a word, she'd pinched the bedsheets and slowly pulled them off her.

The body he'd spent the day trying to banish from his memory had revealed itself in its full glory. The fire in his blood had become a furnace, heating his skin as his violently beating heart had pumped it relentlessly through him.

Dear sweet Lord. She had been perfect.

Creamy golden skin, plump high breasts topped with dark rose nipples, a slender waist, a pubis with a light triangle of hair a shade darker than that on her head, perfectly rounded thighs, lithe golden legs...

'Are you not going to join me?' she'd asked.

Later, he was to think gratefully that if those seductive words hadn't been delivered with a slur, he would have succumbed to her wanton invitation. Dear God, he was only human.

He'd grabbed the back of his neck and breathed in

deeply, trying to get control of himself. He'd felt like *he* was drunk and had stumbled into the sweetest nightmare possible.

'Santi?' She'd propped herself up a little. Her breasts had moved tantalisingly.

He'd screwed his eyes shut. 'You shouldn't be here. You need to leave.'

'You don't mean that.' She'd hiccupped. And then she'd laid her head back and spread her arms wide. Welcoming him. Inviting him. 'Make love to me, Santi.'

Something inside him had snapped and he had suddenly been filled with utter self-loathing and, at that moment, hatred for Elsa too for putting him in that position.

'You're drunk,' he'd said, still trying to keep a lid on the temper now rising with as much passion as his longing.

'I know.' She'd hiccupped again.

'Go home, Elsa. I'll leave you to put your clothes on.' Determined not to look at her, he'd walked to the door but her reflexes had worked much better than he'd have thought considering her state of inebriation. Giggling, she'd thrown herself across the bed and grabbed hold of his arm before he could escape.

'Don't be like this, Santi.' Her words had become so slurred they'd been barely recognisable. 'I *love* you. I've been waiting for you *for ever*. And you love me. We're going to get married and...'

He'd shaken her off his arm as if she were a terrier biting into his skin. 'What the *hell* are you playing at?' he'd snarled. 'Do you have any idea what a dangerous game this is? You break into my home and wait in my bed for me like a common slut? You were raised better than this. You should be ashamed of yourself.'

Her eyes had widened and she'd shuffled unsteadily back, shaking her head as if he'd suddenly sprouted a second head. Her voice became very small. 'Don't you want me?'

'*No*!' he'd roared, as much to himself as to her. 'You're my mentor's daughter!' He'd needed to get away, out of the cottage and off the Lopez estate before he did something he regretted. Like haul her into his arms and take every ounce of pleasure she had been offering.

But only animals took advantage of drunken women and he was not an animal. And only disloyal bastards betrayed those who'd saved them and given them everything by bedding their virgin daughter, and he would sooner cut his hands off than betray Marco.

Damn Elsa. Damn her for putting him in this position. Damn her for betraying their friendship. And damn her for turning his blood to liquid and his loins to fire in the blink of an eye.

Her chin had wobbled, eyes filling with tears. 'Is that all you see me as?'

'Yes, it is.' The knowledge he'd spent the day doing his utmost not to imagine himself making love to her had only fuelled his fury.

Her clothes had been in a pile by the side of the bed. On the top of it had been a lacy red bra.

His self-loathing had ratcheted to self-combust level. He'd picked the pile up and thrown it at her. 'Cover yourself up. Next time you want to lose your virginity, do it with someone who actually wants it and preferably your own age.'

And then he'd walked out of the room, slamming the door behind him, not knowing those would be the last words he spoke to her for five years.

CHAPTER SEVEN

MOVEMENT OVERHEAD WOKE Elsa from the light sleep she'd finally fallen into. She shuffled to the edge of the bed and peered through the blinds. All she could see was the deep blue of the surrounding sea and the azure of the bright cloudless sky. Santi had set sail.

Just to think his name was to set her heart racing. To remember how their fingers had laced together, the feelings that had erupted through her…

She put a hand to her chest and breathed deeply, told herself to get a grip and then propelled herself to the en suite.

The touch of their fingers… What had she been *thinking*? It had happened without any conscious thought on her part. She could only assume that their conversation, what he'd confessed, the way he'd opened up to her… The impulse to touch him had been beyond her control.

And then he'd yanked his hand away as if her touch had scalded him. Had he been able to read her mind? Had he known the effect that small touch had had on her? Was that the reason he'd felt it necessary to put her back in her place with the reminder that she was his mentor's daughter and nothing more?

She stepped under the shower and vowed not to dissect the evening again. She'd spent enough time doing that during her mostly sleepless night spent fidgeting and pacing and doing her very best not to look at the door separating their cabins.

After she'd dressed, she made her bed and just…hovered. She might have hovered for hours if her stomach hadn't rumbled.

She kneaded her forehead. She couldn't hide away like a frightened squirrel and starve just because *she* was the one having a problem with her self-control. Santi was there for one reason only and that was her safety. He'd disrupted his life to protect her. It wasn't his fault she responded to him so physically. It never had been.

Squaring her shoulders, telling herself that she could do this, could act like everything was fine, she left the cabin.

She found him on the main deck. He was sat at the helm, studying the screens surrounding it. All he wore was a pair of tan shorts, a sight that immediately made her belly turn to mush and her resolve to act normally was almost scuppered from her first look as her greedy eyes absorbed his hard muscularity.

He lifted his head to greet her. 'Good morning, *chiquita*. Did you sleep well?'

She dragged her eyes from his chest to his face but there was no relief to be found there, not when her heart sighed with joy to meet the glittering black eyes.

She forced her lips into a smile and was thankful she could speak coherently. 'It took a while but I got there.' A while being a good eight hours of wakefulness compared to probably three hours of actual sleep. 'How long have you been up?'

'Hours. I wanted to set sail before the marina woke up.'

'Have you eaten?' she asked politely.

'Hours ago. If you look through the cupboards you'll find breakfast stuff. Don't worry about running low, there's extra supplies below deck.'

She wandered to the galley. Although small, it had ample storage, the cupboards filled with provisions. The tall fridge was crammed with fresh goods and from it she pulled out a pot of yogurt then took a banana from the fruit bowl.

'Do you want anything?' How hard it was to keep her voice even. How much harder to keep her eyes to herself. She couldn't stop them darting to him or help the throb of heat low in her abdomen to see the smoothness of his bronzed back and the way the muscles bunched as he went about his business at the helm.

'I could murder a coffee if you don't mind making it?'

'Of course not,' she answered airily, relieved that when she set her mind to it, she could act so…*normal*. That was the key to getting through the next few days, she decided. To mask all the heated feelings consuming her and act normal.

While Elsa busied herself in the kitchen, Santi concentrated on the job in hand. It had been a while since he'd last been at the helm of a yacht and he wanted to have total confidence that he'd done everything correctly in setting their course before he turned the autopilot on. He'd been immersed in it and now found himself having to concentrate hard to get his head back in the zone and tune out Elsa's presence as she swished around in her pretty knee-length caftan.

It had been many years since he'd had such a bad night's sleep and he knew it was reliving the locked memories that had caused it. For five years he'd tried his damnedest to block that night from his brain. He'd refused to allow his mind to travel there. Elsa's move to Vienna had freed him. In truth, he'd been relieved. No more crippling guilt for desiring his mentor and saviour's daughter.

But the image of Elsa in his bed had sneaked up on him

in those times when he was tired. He would bat it away but the image would linger.

Forgetting that night had been hard. Forgetting Elsa had been impossible. Now that the memories had been unlocked, the desire he'd been battling had accelerated in its intensity.

Shame on him but he'd found his ear pressed to the adjoining door to her cabin, his heart thudding as he'd listened to her movements before he'd come to his senses and hastily moved away.

He'd lain on his bed with the air-conditioning set to arctic and tried to think of anything but Elsa.

It had proved impossible. Everything about Elsa was proving impossible.

'Do you need my help with anything?' she asked, interrupting his moody thoughts. She held his coffee out.

He removed the cup carefully, making sure their fingers didn't touch. 'No. I'm good, thanks.'

She smiled and stepped back. 'I'm going to my cabin. Shout if you need me.'

'Will do,' he lied. If he had his way, she could stay in her cabin until this whole nightmare was over.

After spending the day sunbathing on her private balcony—she had been right, the door in her cabin did open to create one—Elsa had run out of bottled water. With great reluctance, she ventured out to the main deck for only the second time since breakfast. The first time, when she'd come out for some lunch, she'd quickly chopped herself a hunk of French bread, grabbed a handful of grapes and scarpered back to her cabin without seeing him. She wasn't so fortunate this time. He was sitting at the dining table, chatting on his phone. His olive skin seemed to have turned three shades darker since breakfast.

Avoiding direct contact with his eyes, she hurried past him. Her hands trembled as she raided the fridge, blood pounding in her head, but she forced her spine to stay straight and tried with all her might to tune out the sound of his voice.

She was just about to walk back to her cabin when his call finished.

'That was Felipe,' he informed her.

Apprehension building, she swallowed before looking at him, still avoiding direct eye contact.

'It appears the cartel has fallen for the decoy.'

She didn't have the faintest idea what he was talking about.

'When we set sail this morning, a crew of ex-special forces set sail on *The Conchita* from Genoa. There are three suspicious yachts keeping distant pace with it.'

'The cartel think we're on your yacht?'

'When you and I left Vienna, a redheaded lady of approximately your age and size and a dark-haired man of approximately my age and size were spotted fleeing the city by a different route. They arrived in Genoa last night and boarded *The Conchita*. They set sail this morning at around the same time we left Portofino, taking a different route to ours.'

She was too desperate to escape to give more than a fleeting acknowledgement to the cleverness of the plan. 'That's brilliant,' she said, inching closer to the steps back to her cabin. 'Where are we sailing to?'

'First stop Corsica. There's an excellent bay we can anchor in tonight—it's safer to avoid the marina. I don't want to take any chances.'

Why did the mention of night set butterflies loose in her belly?

'We should arrive within the hour,' he continued. 'I'll rustle up something for dinner when we're safely anchored.'

'Okay. Thank you. See you in a few hours.' But in her haste to escape, she caught her arm on the seat of the helm and dropped the bottles she was carrying.

Cheeks flaming, she crouched down to pick them up. One of the bottles had rolled and landed at Santi's giant foot. Everything then happened very quickly. She extended an arm to it but at the exact moment her fingers wrapped around it he leaned down for it too and his fingers wrapped around hers.

Their eyes clashed before she could stop it happening.

A breathless moment passed.

A pulse shot out of the blackness of his eyes. A depth that made her feel stripped to the bone and filled with such longing that, suddenly, she couldn't breathe. Heat flowed through her veins as if an electric current had been set off inside her, melting her like ice cream.

The connection was severed abruptly when Santi jerked his head and let go of her hand. 'I need to be on the sundeck,' he said tightly, before straightening and heading outside.

He didn't look back.

How desperately could a man crave a woman? And how deep could the craving run before madness set in?

Those were the questions plaguing Santi as he tried to force his brain to engage with the navigation systems. It felt like he'd had some form of kinetic energy injected into his veins.

Never in his life had he wanted a woman the way he wanted Elsa.

Damn it, he wasn't made of stone. He was a flesh and

blood man and she was the woman his flesh and blood sang for. One look was enough for his body to come to life.

As hard as he fought it, something was happening between them. It had started when their gazes had caught in the Viennese courtyard, a nebulous chemical reaction swirling around them, pulling them closer together, a powerful force of nature it was growing almost impossible to push back against.

Why did it have to be *her*?

And why was his heart already thrumming with anticipation for what the rest of their time at sea would bring when he knew it would not bring anything?

He wouldn't, *couldn't*, allow it.

Elsa locked her door and tried her hardest to catch her breath. For a few, heady moments she'd stared into Santi's eyes and thought she'd seen...

What?

Desire? Real emotions?

Fool.

The beats of her heart wouldn't settle.

She had to fight this. She'd deluded herself once about Santi. She'd allowed herself to believe her feelings for him were reciprocated because that's what she'd *wanted* to believe. She'd read things that simply weren't there. The one time when she'd really felt something from him, that electric connection the morning after her eighteenth birthday party, had proved itself to be the biggest delusion of all.

Never again would she put herself in the position of waking cold and ashamed with the memories of Santi's cruel rejection ringing in her ears before she'd even opened her eyes. She would not read things that weren't there. She would not allow herself to be torn apart by her own imagination again.

She was not that girl any more.

The sun was setting magnificently, an orange haze on the horizon, the first stars winking their presence in the darkening skies. Santi, staring at the distant Corsican landscape, bottle of beer in hand, didn't think there had existed a more perfect, romantic setting.

Romantic?

Where in the bowels of hell had that thought come from? Until that exact minute Santi had never had a romantic thought in his life. Romance was for women, and for the unscrupulous men who wanted to bed them by taking the easy route. The only flowers Santi had ever bought were yellow roses for his mother's grave. He'd been in exactly one jewellery shop and that had been to purchase the watch on his wrist.

Faint footsteps echoed below. He turned his head and held his breath. A moment later, Elsa joined him on the sundeck.

The sensation of his lungs slowly collapsing filled him and he reflexively tightened his hold on the rail.

Like him, Elsa had showered and dressed for dinner, a habit as natural for her as breathing but one he'd adopted through all the meals he'd shared with the Lopezes.

All his good manners came from observing and copying the Lopezes', from not bolting his food, to opening doors for ladies, to speaking respectfully to his elders. His mother had been a diamond in the rough, born in a bad neighbourhood and raised with kids for whom school had been a dirty word. While she'd taken pride in sending Santi to school every day in immaculately clean and pressed clothes, it would never have crossed her mind that her son eating with his mouth open would be considered rude.

For all the trappings of his wealth, Santi was still that poor, rough, ill-mannered boy.

Elsa's good breeding was an innate part of her. Everything, from the way she ate to the way she sat, was graceful. Even when she'd drunk a little more than was good for her she'd been inebriated with style.

He'd only seen her properly drunk that night in his bedroom.

Tonight, she wore a high-necked sleeveless rust-coloured dress with tiny buttons running from the neck that fell to her ankles and tied at the waist. To complement it, she'd donned a pair of gold-heeled sandals that gave her a couple of inches of extra height, applied a little make-up and added a pair of gold hooped earrings.

She could only look more beautiful if her natural red hair was flowing around her shoulders rather than the much shorter dark brown wig she was forced to wear. There were too many other vessels anchored in the bay for them to risk her not wearing it.

He had another drink to settle his careering pulses before saying evenly, 'You look nice.'

'Thank you.' Elsa felt her cheeks flame and looked down at her feet before her eyes were drawn back to him. 'Your hair's gone curly,' she murmured unthinkingly, and clenched her hands into fists to stop them reaching out to touch it. She'd always wanted to touch it.

His lips curved. 'You prefer it curly?'

She nodded. 'It's more…you.' The black shirt he wore with charcoal trousers was more him too. He'd buttoned it to just below his throat. The gold chain around his neck glinted.

His chest rose as he inhaled deeply. That look in his eyes...

She couldn't tear her gaze from the black depths, swirling and ringing with...

Not with what she was looking for, she scolded herself quickly and firmly, pulling herself out of the spell she'd been in danger of falling into. That was *not* a look of desire in his eyes.

She found a smile and said, 'Something smells good.'

He blinked. If she didn't know better she would think he'd been pulled under a spell too. 'That will be the red snapper on the barbecue.'

'How old is it?' she asked doubtfully. She only liked fish if she could taste the sea in it and they hadn't been near a fishmonger in four days.

'About three hours.' His face broke into a wide grin that made the lines around his eyes crease and her heart sing. 'Caught by my own fair hands. Please, take a seat. Our appetisers are served.'

She pinched the skirt of her dress and sat, admiring the spread he'd laid out for them: slices of salami and prosciutto, tomato and basil bruschetta, olives and breadsticks.

And then she sighed.

What a perfect setting for a romantic meal.

Dusky though the skies were, Corsica's beauty still dazzled. The marina in the distance was packed with yachts of all sizes, overlooked by a citadel and surrounded by mountains.

Yes. The most perfect romantic setting.

But not for them. Never for them.

She filled her glass with iced water from the jug and helped herself to the appetisers, all the while chanting the mantra 'Act normal, act normal,' as she'd prepared herself before leaving the cabin.

'Have you spoken to your family today?' he asked after they'd eaten a few bites.

Relieved at having something neutral to talk about, she told him, 'I had a chat with Marisa earlier. She's determined that whatever happens, the engagement party will go ahead... Have you met her fiancé?'

He gave a dismissive snort. 'He's a wimp.'

Elsa couldn't help her bark of laughter.

He held his hands up defensively. 'I don't understand what she sees in him.'

'He knows the shipping industry inside out so can help her run the business—you know Mamá wants to retire,' she explained. 'He's too rich to be a gold-digger, and Nikos needs a father.'

He pulled a face. 'I agree he needs a father but when you compare his real father to that wet biscuit...'

'His real father's dead.' Nikos Manolas had died in a tragic yachting accident eighteen months ago. His body had never been found.

It suddenly occurred to her that the tragedy should have made her wary of stepping on a similar vessel. It should have made her mother and sister wary too. Elsa knew as well as she knew her own name that they'd swallowed their concerns for the same reason she'd not had any. Because of Santi.

To Elsa and her family, his name was synonymous with safety.

If only she could say the same for her heart.

'I know.' Santi's voice brought her back to the present. 'I knew him well.'

'Were you friends?'

'As much as anyone could be friends with him.' His eyes narrowed. 'You know Marisa's fiancé has a lover?'

'Marisa knows it too. She doesn't care. She doesn't love

him. She just wants protection and security for the business and a father for her baby.'

His eye were scrutinising. 'You think she's making a mistake?'

'It's not for me to judge. I'm not in her shoes.'

His expression changed in an instant, a rumble of laughter escaping his throat. 'You can't have changed that much! You used to have an opinion on everything.'

Remembering how he'd always humoured her ill-informed opinions, she poked her tongue out at him before she even realised she was doing it, but the giggles about to escape her lips faded before they could form.

Sharing food, sharing laughter, sharing memories...

These were things that filled her with so much emotion it hurt to look at him.

'Go on,' he urged. 'Your real opinion on your sister's engagement.'

'I'll tell you my opinion if you promise to keep it to yourself.'

Promise not to...

Promise to...

'I promise.'

Leaning forward so she could hug her constricting belly and trying desperately hard not to let him see how this rework of so many long-ago conversations was affecting her, she said, 'Okay, if you really want my opinion...'

'I do,' he assured her.

She took a deep breath. 'I think she's making the biggest mistake of her life. How either of them think they can create a marriage when there's no feeling between them is beyond me, and how Marisa can expect him to grow feelings for baby Nikos when it's obvious Raul only has feelings for himself is beyond me too. But there's no talking to her. Nikos's death almost destroyed her. Marrying Raul is the safe option. She doesn't love him so there's no chance of him hurting her, and while I think she's wrong, I understand completely why she's doing it. When your heart's been broken you do everything you can to protect it from ever happening again.'

Elsa knew immediately that she'd said the wrong thing. It was there in the sudden stillness of Santi's huge frame and the penetration of his stare.

After long, tense moments, he quietly said, 'Who hurt you?'

CHAPTER EIGHT

ANGUISH ROSE FROM deep inside her. How badly Elsa regretted her past openness with Santi. All her hopes and fears, her dreams, all the trials of her life; the fallings-out with friends, the screaming arguments with her mother, the fights with her sister…she'd shared everything. As a result, he could read her like a book.

She fought to keep her poise, reminding herself that he *used* to be able to read her like a book. 'I was talking hypothetically.'

His eyes narrowed and he drained the last of his beer before getting to his feet and taking the three steps to the inbuilt barbecue. He lifted the lid, releasing a wonderful lemony aroma. 'Are you sure? Because if someone's hurt you, I want to know about it.' He used tongs to remove the foil-wrapped fish and place them on a plate. 'Was it Stefan?' he added casually.

She shook her head, tearing her gaze from him and fixing it on the yacht closest to them. 'Looks like they're having a party,' she said, somehow managing to speak through a throat choked with emotion. Music was playing and there had to be a couple of dozen people on the deck.

'Why don't you want to talk about him? What did he do to you?'

'Nothing.'

'Look me in the eye and tell me he did nothing to you.'

Laughter from the partying yacht carried in the air. A pang of envy ripped through her. Elsa had forgotten how much she'd loved to party. She'd loved dressing up and dancing and gossiping and trying concoctions created from whatever she and her friends had been able to pilfer from their parents' alcohol cabinets.

'Elsa.' There was a warning tone in Santi's voice that pierced the beats thudding painfully in her head.

Her gaze flew to him. He stood beside the grill facing her with his arms folded across his powerful chest, black eyes glittering with something that made her belly dive and swoop in one seamless motion.

'Stefan's married,' she blurted out.

The shock on his face would have been comical if her heart hadn't been shredding. 'You had an affair with a married man?'

'There was no affair. He's my boss.'

So many emotions flickered over his face that it was impossible to pick out only one. He blew out a long breath and rubbed the back of his neck. 'Explain.'

She shrugged helplessly. 'I lied.'

And lies always caught up with you. It was a lesson every child learned.

'Why?'

'To stop them worrying. Mamá latched on to Stefan's name when I told her about work. I let her believe we were a couple only because I knew how much she wanted me to meet someone.'

'And the other men you said you'd dated? Were they lies too?'

'Not all of them.' She'd accepted the occasional date over the years. Desperation to rid her head of Santi had driven her to accepting them but they'd been fool's errands.

'Were you serious about any of them?'

'No.' Her admission came out as a whisper.

'Were your tales of partying lies too?'

'Yes.'

'Have you drunk alcohol at all since moving to Vienna?'

Her features tightened, lips clamping together, but she shook her head in answer.

'What did you spend your student years doing, then?'

'Studying.'

Studying? Elsa? The girl who'd had screaming matches with her mother over her refusal to do homework, the girl with such a zest for life and adventure, had spent her student years *studying*?

'*Why, chiquita*? Why all the lies?'

'To stop them worrying.'

His laughter had a sarcastic tinge to it. 'You let your family think you were drinking and partying too much to stop them worrying? How the hell does that work?'

'Because they would have thought there was something wrong.'

'But there *was* something wrong.' Santi knew it in his guts. He'd known it since he'd detected that first lie at the beginning of their road trip. 'What happened to you, Elsa? Someone hurt you.'

'Santi, will you please drop it? Let the past stay in the past.' The plea was in her voice as well as her words but he ignored it, too close to unravelling the mysteries that were driving him insane to be deterred any longer.

'Not until you tell me why you went from a fun-loving young woman to a recluse.'

Her shoulders hunched as she bunched her hands together on her lap. 'I didn't turn into a recluse. I changed, that's all. People do change, you of all people should know that.'

'I've learned to control the worst of my instincts but I haven't changed. I'm still the same person underneath.' Still the same poor, rough, ill-mannered boy but in bespoke tailored clothes.

'And I've learned to control my instincts too.' Her eyes flashed. She spoke with an air of triumph, as if she'd found an excuse to latch on to. 'I stopped abusing alcohol…'

'You abused it no more than your average teenager.' Other than that final night.

'I moved to Vienna for a fresh start. I always intended to take university seriously.'

'I don't believe you,' he said flatly.

'I don't care if you believe me.'

He picked up the bowl with the accompaniment he'd made for their fish and slammed it on the table. 'I think you're lying through your pretty little teeth.'

She flinched. 'Don't say that.'

'Then stop lying,' he snarled, leaning down so his face was directly before her. 'Do you forget I have known you since you were a bump in your mother's stomach? I've watched you tell your parents a hundred lies. I hear it in your voice. I know all your little tells. Look at your fingers—they're rubbing together like they always do when you're spouting your bull.'

Something flickered on her face. She looked down at her hands then back to him. Colour saturated her cheeks then, in one quick, fluid motion, she shoved her chair back, placed her hands flat on the table and leaned forward so it was her face directly before his. 'My bull? *My* bull?'

Her angry breaths feathered against his lips. Her green-brown stare knifed through his chest.

'Why do you need me to spell it out for you?' she said scathingly. 'Have you been so deprived of a woman telling you how wonderful you are these past few days that you'd make me dredge up everything I've spent the past five years trying to forget just to boost your fat ego?'

Santi found himself frozen. The thuds from his heart rose up to join the white noise filling the space between his ears, drowning out everything, even the noise of revelry from the nearby yacht.

'You're an intelligent man, Santi, so stop insulting us both by pretending you don't know who hurt me when all you have to do…' Her voice caught. Her eyes closed, features softening. Her body swayed. And then her eyes flew open and she backed away to the steps with a whispered, 'All you have to do is look in a mirror.'

Elsa fell onto her bed clutching her chest and trying frantically to get air into her lungs.

Days and days of putting on a face and fighting feelings that ballooned by the hour… It was too much. She was exhausted. Tired of pretending. Tired of fighting her turbulent feelings.

But there was no time for her to find any kind of composure for the door opened.

An unbidden wail flew from her mouth and she covered her face before Santi's shape could take form.

'Leave me alone,' she said in a voice that sounded excruciatingly like a whimper.

There was no verbal response and neither did she hear his footsteps walk away or the door close.

'Please, just leave me alone,' she begged. 'I'm sorry for lashing out but I can't do this any more. I can't pretend that spending all this time with you isn't tearing me apart.'

There was a pause. *'Chiquita…'*

'Don't say anything,' she pleaded. 'Please, just let things—'

But her words were cut off when her hands were pulled

away and Santi's face was right there, hovering only inches from hers, the black eyes boring into her.

Crouched before her, he was breathing heavily, the strong nostrils flaring, the sensual lips pulled into a tight line.

Suddenly she couldn't breathe. She could hear nothing but her pulse drumming like a tattoo inside her ears. The world went off kilter and began to spin.

Sensation wafted over her neck as a large hand burrowed into her wig and carefully pulled it off.

Trembling, she closed her eyes, felt his fingers skim over her hair and remove the clip keeping it in place then drag through the tresses. Her trembles grew more violent when he cupped his palm to the back of her head and she felt herself being gently pulled forward. The skin on her face tingled as it sensed him inching closer and closer until the firm lips she'd spent so many years dreaming about pressed against hers.

She couldn't move. Her senses were on overload. The scent of Santi's skin, the warmth of his mouth, the heat of his breath, his touch…

An arm slipped around her waist. The tips of her breasts brushed then flattened against his hard chest. Her pelvis throbbed. His lips moved against hers. Heat suffused her. Her heart thumped so hard the beats echoed all the way to her toes.

He doesn't mean it.

His mouth moved again, lips parting. Her own lips parted with the motion. Her tastebuds sparked to life as a brand-new taste filled her. Santi. His tongue slid into her mouth…

He doesn't mean it.

Her shaking hand found his neck and crept up to the curly hair she'd spent so many years dreaming of touching.

The texture was softer than she'd imagined. She splayed her fingers deeper into it, kneading into his skull as he deepened the kiss and tightened his hold around her. Tiny embers of sensation fired through her from low in her abdomen, growing and pulsing as the desire Santi ignited in her bloomed into a furnace.

He doesn't mean it!

The voice echoing with increasing panic in her head finally penetrated and sanity crashed through her.

Wrenching her face from his, she pushed hard against his chest. *'Don't!'*

Elsa's abrupt rejection almost knocked Santi onto his back.

Heaving himself to his feet, he rubbed the nape of his neck and tried to focus through the pain of his arousal. His skin was scorched from Elsa's touch. Flames licked him. Every part of him.

What was he even doing in her cabin?

Why had he followed her?

His legs had paced behind her before his brain could stop him. His only justification had been to ask her what the hell she'd meant about him having to look in the mirror.

But he knew what she'd meant. God help him. A part of him had known all along.

That night…

It *had* haunted her. As much as it had haunted him. The only man who'd hurt her had been him.

'I'm sorry,' he said hoarsely, backing himself against the adjoining door. His lungs had stopped working properly, the violent thrashing of his heart paralysing the rest of him. 'I shouldn't have done that.'

'Why did you?' she whispered, raising her ashen face to his.

Because he couldn't not. Because one minute he'd been staring into her beautiful eyes and the next he'd lost himself.

'Was it a punishment?' She must have read the cluelessness on his face for her face contorted. 'I know you don't feel like *that* for me, Santi.' Her head dropped and she clutched tightly at her hair. 'Get out and leave me alone.'

He took a deep breath. He was struggling to think coherently.

'What you said…' He swallowed another constriction in his throat. '… About looking in a mirror. I—'

'I said *get out*!' she interrupted with a scream, jumping to her feet, and before he had the chance to realise what she was doing she'd rushed at him, her fists beating at his chest with a desperation that made his heart ache. 'Don't you think you've done enough damage? Leave me *alone*!'

Grabbing at her flailing hands, he pinned them to her sides. Elsa would never hurt him or anyone intentionally but at that moment she was like a woman possessed.

'How can you be so cruel?' she cried. 'To kiss me like you mean it when we both know I disgust you—'

'What…?' Disgust? Was she crazy? 'How can you say that?' he demanded. 'You're *beautiful*.'

She yanked her arms from his hold with a strength he wouldn't have believed from someone so slender and shoved at his chest again. 'You liar! And you know what? I'm a liar too. I *do* remember that night. I remember everything about it and God alone knows I've spent the past five years trying to move on with my life and forget my shame and the cruel things you said, but I *can't*. Your words and your disgust are stained in my memories, and for you to kiss me like that and call me beautiful… How can you do that to me? Why do you hate me so much…?'

He grasped her shoulders and pulled her to him. 'Are

you insane? I don't *hate* you. I could never hate you, and you don't disgust me...'

A groan ripped from his throat as a wave of crippling self-loathing battered him.

'Don't you understand?' he implored with a roar. 'The disgust wasn't aimed at you. It was for *me*.'

Her eyes widened. A hitching sound came from her moving throat.

'When I found you there... Can't you understand what that was like for me? The position you put me in? This beautiful young woman inviting me... How could I have lived with myself if I'd taken advantage of what you were offering? You were *drunk*. And, Elsa, I owe your parents everything. They trusted me to look out for you and I would have sooner ripped my throat out than abuse that trust.'

A tear spilled down her cheek. He brushed it away with his thumb and pressed his forehead to hers, staring deep into her eyes. 'I'm sorry I hurt you, *chiquita*. I should have handled it much more sensitively, but I was too angry with you and furious with myself to think straight. I have never known temptation like that before...' Fingers spearing her silky hair, he brushed his lips lightly over hers. 'Not until you came back into my life. These past days have been torture. I know it's wrong but I ache for you. You're in my head all the time. All I want is to touch you.'

The tips of their noses rubbed, eyes locked together. Her hand tentatively inched up his arm and over his shoulder to the nape of his neck, her fingers brushing against the soft strands of his hair.

'Why is it wrong?' Her voice was throaty and barely audible. Her sweet breaths whispered against his lips, diving straight into his already overloaded senses.

He groaned again and fisted her hair, doing his mightiest

to hold on, to remember all the reasons why he shouldn't do this.

What *were* they? He fought to remember, fought to re-sist...

The beats of Elsa's heart were so violent the echo slammed like a pulse in her head.

Had she fallen into a dream?

Was this really Santi leaning into her and staring at her as if she were someone to be worshipped? She could feel the tremors coming from his powerful body. Every part of her trembled too.

And then his lips crashed against hers. In the beat of a moment Elsa found herself crushed against him, his mouth devouring hers, tongues clashing as if trying to eat each other whole.

She had to be dreaming. This couldn't be real.

The scorching of her skin where his fingers and palms were sweeping over her back and sides, his touch pene-trating the material of her dress, felt real. The brush of his beard against her cheek as his mouth devoured hers felt real too. The burning heat in her pelvis...

The feelings ricocheting through her, the *intensity* of them...

The groaning of her name as he severed the kiss but not the connection made her heart sing. She felt a delicious scratching along her throat as his cheek buried into it be-fore her stomach dipped and she found herself being lifted into his arms and carried to the bed.

Santi laid her down gently. Her golden cheeks were flushed, her lips plumped from his kisses. Her chest was making rapid rise and fall movements. He rested the back of his fingers at the top of the slope of her left breast. The ragged beats of her heart drummed against them, perfectly matching those of his own.

All his nerves had gone crazy. He felt intoxicated. The world had become a blur, his only focus the woman staring at him with such heady wonder.

Slowly, he dragged his fingers down and over the swell of her breast, his thumb encircling the jut of her roused nipple through the fabric of her dress.

He felt her tremble. Heard the faint hitch in her throat. Her breaths had shortened to quick, erratic exhalations.

He could hardly breathe at all.

Taking great care not to put all his weight on her, Santi propped himself on his elbows to stare again into her mesmerising eyes. And then he kissed her, a long, deep hungry kiss that had her moaning into him and sliding a hand around his neck to pull him closer.

He dragged his mouth from hers and kissed and inhaled his way across her cheek and to her neck, ravenous to taste and touch every inch of her. Lower he inched until he reached the top line of her dress. The buttons were tiny and his strangely clumsy fingers had trouble undoing the first two, becoming only slightly more dextrous by the third.

When he reached the fourth button, Elsa felt a sudden tendril of trepidation and covered his hand tightly to stop him going any further. All the illumination in the cabin came from the moonlight flooding in through the large window.

'Close the blinds,' she whispered urgently. The intensity of her feelings were so strong she didn't want to lose them through fear.

His face hovered back over hers for a moment, black eyes boring into hers questioningly.

She palmed his cheek and rubbed the soft bristles of his beard, then lifted her head to kiss him. 'Please. Close them.'

A draught of coldness replaced the warmth of his body as he left her just long enough to release the blind at the side of the bed before the warmth returned with the enveloping darkness and Santi picked up where he'd left off, kissing her, exploring her body with his hands…

Elsa sank back into the pleasure he was eliciting in her.

'You're beautiful,' he whispered when he kissed the base of her throat. He opened the next two buttons of her dress and slipped a hand into the exposed part to cup one of her breasts, sending such a jolt of sensation through the sensitive flesh that she gasped.

More buttons were undone. He reached her abdomen. His fingers pushed beneath the lace of her panties and brushed over her sex, making her gasp again, this time with shock at the unexpectedness as well as the pleasure.

There was something in Elsa's gasp that set alarm bells ringing. Santi shuffled back up to gaze down at her, wishing she hadn't asked him to close the blinds so he could look at her clearly.

He stroked the soft skin of her cheek. 'Have you done this before?' he asked quietly before the question had even formed solidly in his mind.

She stilled in his arms. She hesitated then slowly shook her head.

His heart fell. A distant ringing played in his ears. A weight compressed his chest.

But there was another emotion at play too, one he could hardly bring himself to admit. Exhilaration.

Since that late summer morning when her naked silhouette had shone through the light streaming in the villa's kitchen window, Elsa had been a constant itch in Santi's psyche. He'd gone for months at a time—years—without seeing her but not a single day had gone by when he hadn't thought of her. He'd listen to her family's stories about her new life in Vienna and feel lightened to hear she was happy and thriving, but the lightness had masked the knotted heaviness in his guts that had been there since he'd woken the morning after kicking her out of his bed. The knots had always tightened at tales of Elsa's varied love life.

Those had been the times he'd sought release with other women, he now admitted to himself. Fleeting satisfaction to drive out the selfish ache in his heart at the thought of Elsa being with another man.

She hadn't been with anyone. He didn't dare dissect what he felt about that.

He brushed his fingers through her hair. 'We don't have to do this. We don't have to do anything.'

She touched his head and her fingers sank into the curls. 'Santi…' She sighed. Her voice was barely audible. 'It feels like I've waited my whole life for this.'

He squeezed his eyes shut and breathed deeply. At that moment in time, it felt like he'd waited his whole life for this too.

And then he took another step into the fire and kissed her again.

He'd never known kisses alone could fuel fire. The feel of Elsa's lips against his. Her sweet yet headily addictive taste. The scent of her skin. All of it took mere kissing to a whole new dimension of sensuality and at that moment he wouldn't have cared if she'd said she wanted to do nothing more than kiss. It would be enough.

Slowly, tenderly, he undressed her. There was no frustration in having to take things slowly despite arousal bleeding through his pores. For the first time perhaps in for ever he *wanted* to take his time, not just for Elsa but for himself. He wanted to savour each and every moment.

When Elsa was naked and under the covers, she watched Santi strip with a heart that felt like a hot air balloon threatening to burst out of her chest.

Once he was naked, he lay back on her. She wished

she could put into words and share with him how incredible it felt to be living this moment…but then he kissed her with such tender passion that she *knew* those feelings were shared.

And then he kissed her some more. His lips left a burning trail over her body that felt like it was penetrating her skin, drugging her, turning her from a sentient person into a mass of nerve-endings and sensation. When he took her nipples into his mouth and cupped her throbbing core, she could no more stop her cries of ecstasy than a baby could stop its cries of hunger.

He trailed his way back to her mouth and kissed her with a passion that left her boneless then parted her thighs to accommodate his solid bulk. The even heftier weight of his arousal pressed against the lips of her opening.

His voice was thicker and huskier than she'd ever heard it when he said, 'We need protection.'

She dragged her fingers into his hair and whispered, 'I'm on the Pill.'

'You trust me?'

'Always.'

She'd thought her heart couldn't beat any harder than it already had but it smashed into her lungs and up to her throat, making her tremble with the strength of its reverberations.

This was it.

Santi rubbed his nose to hers and tried to breathe through the thuds of his heart. It felt like it was *his* first time.

But it was hers, and the magnitude of what they were about to do was not something he took lightly.

'When I found you on my bed all those years ago…' He brushed a light kiss to her mouth. 'Elsa, I have never in my life seen anything so beautiful.' He feathered slow kisses over her cheeks, over her eyelids, and pushed just the tip of his arousal inside her. 'You were—*are*—perfect.' He kissed her mouth again and drove a little further. 'Rejecting you was the hardest thing I have ever done.' There was only the slightest resistance before her tight, velvet warmth opened for him. He drove even further inside her and groaned at the undiluted pleasure of her muscles gripping him. He'd never known sensation like it.

Elsa had been so caught in Santi's magical words tasting like nectar to her senses and the explosions of heat pulsing through her that it wasn't until he stilled and moaned in her ear that she fully comprehended that he was inside her. Massively inside her, stretching her, filling her...

Dear sweet heaven...

The feelings that erupted in her were so deep and powerful that she cried out and hooked an arm around his neck.

He stiffened in her arms. 'Are you okay, *chiquita*? Do you want me to stop?'

Stop? He'd have to kill her first.

Her pelvis tilted with no input from her brain to deepen the penetration and then she was holding onto him with all her might, clinging to him, pressing and rocking, her head thrashing, no thoughts in her head, her body moving on pure instinct, desperate for the relief it knew only Santi could provide.

His hand clasped her bottom as he ground into her, increasing the friction, and then, without any warning, she shattered into a million pieces, torn apart by the waves of the most intense pleasure lashing and rupturing through her, barely aware that she was calling his name out over and over and over.

CHAPTER NINE

ELSA LAY WITH her head on Santi's chest, feeling the rhythmic beats of his heart against her ear. The soft hair on his chest tickled her cheek. There was a delicious lethargy in her limbs and a strange tingling sensation in her pelvis.

She didn't want to fall asleep. Didn't want to lose the wonder. Didn't want to wake and find the most magical night of her life had been a dream.

She'd lain there so long her arm was starting to seize up. Carefully, she disentangled herself and propped herself on an elbow. She could see the outline of his handsome face through the darkness and placed a gentle kiss to his mouth.

His head moved and he mumbled something. His hand groped for hers. She laced her fingers through his and pressed it against her heart. Could he hear its beats in his sleep?

Was he dreaming? Was *she* dreaming?

Only when her arm started to hurt again did she lie down and, wrapped snugly in his sleeping arms, finally close her eyes.

When Elsa next opened her eyes, it was to find the side of the bed Santi had slept on empty and dusky early light filtering through the blinds. She rolled onto her back and closed her eyes again.

What had he thought when he'd crept out of her bed? Had he already been regretting what they'd shared?

Was she?

She showered and dressed in record time, pausing only once to stand in front of the mirror with the towel around her. Santi had said she was beautiful. Were they just words given to appease an over-emotional woman? What did he really see when he looked at her?

Smoothing her oversized scoop-necked silver T-shirt over her black shorts, all ideas of playing it cool around him were lost when she found herself hesitating at the steps. She didn't have a clue how she was supposed to act. Was there a special etiquette for facing the man you'd made love to the morning after?

She didn't have a clue how he was going to act either, knew only that she needed to prepare herself for any outcome.

She forced her legs to climb the stairs and compelled the muscles on her face into a semblance of nonchalance.

Santi was busy fiddling with the coffee pot, wearing a pair of loose-fitting beige shorts and an unbuttoned short-sleeved black shirt.

Just to look at him was to knock all the wind from her.

Their eyes met. The silence between them was so complete that if a feather floated in the air, she'd be able to hear the barbs rustling through it. It took what felt like for ever for his mouth and eyes to crease into a smile.

'Good morning, *chiquita*,' he said softly.

She couldn't make her vocal cords work. All she could do was smile through the flaming of her cheeks and press herself against the dining table to support her weakening legs.

'Coffee?' he asked in the same soft tone.

She cleared her throat and managed to croak, 'Please.'

He removed a mug from a cupboard and placed it beside the one already set in front of him. 'I spoke to Felipe earlier,' he said in a more conversational tone. 'It will happen tomorrow.'

Elsa's head was so full of the man she'd spent the night with that it took her a moment to understand what he'd said. 'For sure?'

'First thing in the morning.' He poured coffee into the mugs. 'As soon as we have confirmation it's over, we can get the extraction plan in place and get you home.'

'Okay.' She didn't need to question him about it. Santi would never put her in harm's reach, and that was good enough for her.

It was emotional harm she had to be wary of. Especially now. Especially when she didn't have a clue what he was thinking or feeling and barely understood her own thoughts and emotions.

He carried the coffees to her, lips curved as held hers out.

A frisson sparked as their fingers brushed.

Nothing was said for the longest time. They faced each other by the table, gazes locked. The longer they stood there, the faster the beats of Elsa's heart became and the more ragged her breaths. She ached to touch him. Put her arms around his neck and kiss him. She ached for him to touch her too. More than all that, she wanted him to do or say something to ease the fear building inside her that they'd made a colossal mistake.

Just as she feared she would self-combust with all the emotions tearing through her, he put his mug on the table then plucked hers from her hand and placed it beside his own. Then he put his hands on her waist and pulled her to him. The relief was so great that for one frightening moment she feared she would cry from the magnitude of it.

He traced a finger over her cheek sending shivers of sensation racing through her. 'Any regrets?' he asked seriously.

How to answer that with his black eyes so intent on her? How to answer with such a jumble of emotions frothing in her?

She'd given her heart to Santi once and his rejection had shattered it and shaken the foundations of her happy, carefree life. Her father's death and the circumstances around it had ruptured the loosened foundations beyond repair. It had destroyed her faith and trust in *everything*.

To feel such joy in Santi's arms was dangerous, felt too much like the old, reckless way she'd thrown herself into experiences for the sheer exhilaration of it, blithely assuming she would fall on her feet or if she stumbled then never mind because Santi would be there to catch her and deliver her safely home.

That safety was gone. The lynchpin of her family was gone. Elsa had had no choice but to find safety on her own terms and under her own control. She'd made a life for herself. By no means could it be called exhilarating but it was safe…or had been until the cartel had reared its head again. She'd worked too hard to claw herself out of the black pit of terror and despair to risk ripping herself apart emotionally again.

She could trust Santi to catch her if she fell but she couldn't trust him with her heart again. Couldn't trust he'd give it back to her whole.

But to regret their night together?

She sighed and looped her arms around his neck, shaking her head in answer. Elsa couldn't regret something that had given her more pleasure in one night than she'd felt in the past five years combined. And she wasn't a naïve teenager any more, associating sex with love and love with for ever.

Santi had watched the conflicting emotions flitter over Elsa's beautiful face with his breath held.

When he'd woken, limbs entwined with Elsa's, her silky deep red hair splayed over his chest, everything they'd shared in the night had flashed before him and he'd been consumed with a wave of guilt and self-recrimination. And then he'd stared at her sleeping face and an even stronger wave of desire had blown the self-loathing away…and tenderness. Such tenderness.

He felt it now. The desire and the tenderness. The latter was an emotion he'd never felt before in his life, and he'd slipped out of her bed sickened with himself.

He couldn't wrap his head around her being a virgin. Was that the reason she'd been shy about him seeing her naked? Or did it run deeper? The girl who'd been happy to parade herself in a tiny bikini had grown into a woman who dressed conservatively and hadn't even stripped to a modest swimsuit during their time on the yacht. It sat heavily that the reason might have its roots in that long-ago night.

It made his heart clench to think that night had haunted her as much as it had haunted him. He'd spent five years believing she was getting on with her life and living it to the full. He'd been happy for her. He'd *wanted* Elsa to be happy. A happy Elsa could light a room with a smile.

But, with sunlight starting to filter through the windows, these were thoughts to be contemplated another time. His primary focus had to be on setting sail before the bay came to life. He would not drop his guard until he knew for certain that the danger to Elsa was over and that meant avoiding people in daylight.

'I need to raise the anchor and set our course,' he murmured, and, though he knew he shouldn't, was unable to resist placing a lingering chaste kiss to her lips and inhaling a brief taste of her sweetness.

Her head tilted back, exposing her beautiful throat. 'Can I help?'

'It's too light out there. Stay inside. Relax. I shouldn't be long.'

He stepped back, stroked her cheek one more time and walked out into the bright early morning light.

He breathed the fresh sea air deep into his lungs and tried to banish Marco's sad, reproachful face from his mind.

Censuring himself was pointless, he thought grimly. There would be plenty of time for self-recrimination once he'd delivered Elsa safely to her family. Until that time...

He'd just have to contain it as much as he could.

But something told him containing it was no longer possible. The genie was out of the bottle and couldn't be put back.

The moment Elsa was alone she sank onto the nearest seat and closed her eyes. Her pelvis tingled. Her veins buzzed. Her pulse whooshed in her ears. In her mind was the look in Santi's eyes when he'd traced his finger over her cheek. There had been emotion. Desire. The same look as she'd seen all those other times.

She hadn't imagined it.

A bubble of laughter rose up her throat, as uncontrollable as all the other feelings ravaging her, but then cut itself off as her brief rise of spirits crashed back down to earth.

A part of her, the old reckless Elsa, felt like she could leap over mountains in single bounds. The other, newer, sensible Elsa screamed caution. Caution, caution, caution. Lock her heart tightly. Throw away the key. Don't let him anywhere near it.

But the buzz in her veins told her very clearly that if

Santi tried to make love to her again, she would respond with the opposite of caution. Just to imagine it was to set the butterflies loose all over again.

Santi stared from the panini that had been placed on the ledge next to him at the helm of the yacht's sundeck to the woman who'd delivered it. 'Is that for me?'

Teenage Elsa had hated cooking and vowed never to learn. Something else that had changed about her.

Her beautiful hair flowed around her, no wig needed as there was no other vessel in their immediate vicinity. 'I thought you must be hungry. You only had a small breakfast.'

A small breakfast of fruit shared once they were on the open seas, interrupted by the constant pinging of the radar. This was the first moment of peace they'd had since they'd set sail three hours ago.

Touched, he put his hand on her hips and squeezed without thinking. 'Thank you.'

She smiled shyly and lightly, tentatively, ran her fingers through his hair. Then she stepped back. 'Aren't you going to try it?'

He picked up one of the wedges from the plate and took a huge bite...and immediately wished he hadn't.

Her face screwed up. 'Don't you like it?'

Fighting back his body's efforts to repel it, he forced his throat to swallow the bite. 'Not at all. Out of curiosity, what's in it?'

'Serrano ham and salad stuff. Tomatoes, peppers, those pickled things you like...'

That's what the taste was! 'Gherkins?'

She nodded. 'I thought that as they go well with burgers, they'd be nice in a panini.'

Not a whole jar of them! he wanted to say, but kept it

to himself. She'd gone to the effort of making him some-thing and he wasn't going to hurt her feelings by telling her it was inedible.

With Elsa's watchful eyes on him, he took another bite and chewed as little as he could before swallowing.

Her whole face lit up in a beaming smile. 'I'll pour the coffee and join you.'

The moment she disappeared from view, he gave a silent apology to the fish and chucked what was left of the panini into the sea, then grabbed the bottle of water by his foot and downed it to wash the taste out of his mouth.

Confident the yacht's co-ordinates were set properly, he set the autopilot and was about to rise to his feet when Elsa bounded up the steps scowling...

Well, her mouth was scowling. Her eyes were dancing with a mischievous light he hadn't seen in five years.

Putting her hands on her hips, she shook her mock-scowling face. 'You're such a liar! You said you liked the panini. I made one for myself and it's the most disgusting thing I've ever tasted!'

His lips twitched. 'I never said I liked it.'

'You said... Oh.' She stuck her bottom lip out and folded her arms in mock anger, but then lines creased her beau-tiful face and she burst into a peal of laughter so infec-tious that Santi found himself laughing too, and all the awkwardness that had lingered between them since early morning vanished.

Taking hold of her hips, he pulled her to him. The size difference between them was such that with him seated and her standing, they were the same height. 'How does a woman reach the age of twenty-three without knowing how to make a sandwich?'

'I *do* know.' She sniggered, looping her arms around his

neck. 'I just made the mistake of trying to impress you with something fancier than serrano ham and tomato.'

'I'm touched…' He kissed her lightly, even though he knew he shouldn't. 'Please don't do it again.'

'I won't.' She gazed into his eyes, smiling, then her eyes clocked his empty plate and narrowed. 'Don't tell me you finished yours?'

'I fed it to the fish.'

'Poor fish. I'll make us something else.'

'No! *I'll* make lunch.' He spoke with such force that Elsa burst into another peal of laughter.

God, she was beautiful when she laughed. Her head tilted back, elongating the elegant arch of her neck, and he was suddenly engulfed in the heady fantasy of sinking his teeth into the golden skin…

Arousal shot through him so sharply his fingers tightened their grip on her hips.

She caught his eye and her laughter abruptly stopped.

For a long, long moment they did nothing but gaze into each other's eyes until suddenly their arms wound around each other and their mouths fused together in a kiss of such hunger that Santi was immediately consumed by it.

His hands slipping up her caftan to touch the silk of her heated skin; his last coherent thought before the pleasure took control was that he was already going to hell. Making love to her again couldn't add to his sentence.

Elsa sat at the sundeck's dining table with her face tilted to the sun. Every cell in her body tingled with the after-effects of their sudden lovemaking.

She was beyond regrets. Regrets were pointless.

Couldn't she satisfy both parts of herself? she wondered. Couldn't she embrace this seductive desire that made her feel more alive than she'd felt in so, so long without losing the essence of herself and still protect her heart? Keep it locked tightly away? They had so little time left. The only thing stopping her going mad with fear for what tomorrow could bring was Santi. Tomorrow, her world could turn on its wheel again. It could be ripped apart at the seams.

If all she had was today then she wanted to live it.

Santi appeared from below deck with a tray. He winked at her, then unloaded two plates filled with the most beautifully presented tuna salad, a bowl of black olives, slices of warmed crusty bread, olive oil and a jug of iced water onto the table.

'This looks amazing,' she said.

'It's nothing. It took me ten minutes to prepare.'

'Don't be so modest. If I made something like this it'd end up looking like something Rocco would eat.'

His deep rumble of laughter made her belly go all squidgy. The little whorls of exposed hair on his chest—he'd put a white short-sleeved shirt on—made the rest of her go all squidgy too. Remembering how that hair felt against her cheek made her pelvis contract, and she hurriedly pressed her thighs together.

She'd been a virgin only a day ago and now all she could think of was sex?

She had her first bite of the salad. Her tastebuds pinged. Aromatic and lemony, the avocados giving it creaminess, the chickpeas giving it bite, it was delicious, and she told him so, adding, 'How come you're such a good cook?'

'My mother taught me. She believed everyone, man or woman, should be able to feed themselves, no matter how poor they were.'

'Were you poor?' All Elsa knew of Santi's early life was that he'd spent his first ten years in Seville.

'Very. My mother was only seventeen when she had me. She had no qualifications so had to work her backside off doing menial work to put food on the table. All our clothes came from the church's charity box. The car she drove was falling to pieces and she could never have afforded to replace it.' His smile had a faraway look. 'She never complained. She just got on.'

As hard as she tried, she couldn't picture Santi as a child. 'It was just the two of you, wasn't it?' That was something she'd always known, although she didn't remember how.

'Yes. My father died before I was born. A motorbike accident.'

'How horrible,' she said softly. 'Did you have much to do with his family?'

He swallowed his food and shook his head. 'Not since I was a baby. My mother had a big falling out with them. Her family were too busy trying to scrape a living themselves to help her much so it was mostly just the two of us until we moved to Valencia.'

'Was that for the job with my parents?'

'Yes.' He broke off a hunk of bread and used it to mop some of the dressing clinging to his plate. 'She wanted a fresh start for me. The area we lived in was rough. The school I went to was rough—lots of little thugs in the making, and I was one of them. She wanted a better life for me. When she saw the advert for a housekeeper in Valencia, she applied thinking she had nothing to lose.'

'How did you feel about the move?'

He shrugged. 'I had my *mamá*, so I didn't care where we lived. We were tight.' He crossed his fingers for emphasis.

Elsa drank some water thinking this explained so much. No wonder Santi had gone so badly off the rails after she'd died. 'I wish I remembered her better.'

'You were very young when she died. She adored you.'

'Did she?'

His mouth widened into a huge smile that made her belly

flip. 'You would toddle after her while she worked, trying to "help". You had a toy vacuum cleaner and would drag it all over the villa, following her... She missed you when you started infant school.'

A flash of memory made Elsa's windpipe close. Her first day of school. Conchita enveloping her in the biggest hug and telling her to have fun.

She stared at Santi and an almost unbearable wave of sadness hit her. 'I'm sorry you lost her so young.'

'So am I.' His gaze penetrated through the shades they both wore, the intensity strong enough for her veins to turn to sludge. 'I would never have got through it without your parents.'

'What did they do?'

'Don't you remember?'

She shook her head.

'When my mother was ill, they were there for us every step of the way. They took her to all her appointments and treatments, kept her on her full wages even though she wasn't well enough to work, and they looked after me. They made sure I ate. Had clean clothes. Attended school. That kind of thing. When she died, they sat me down and gave me two options. I could live with my *mamá*'s family in Seville and they would pay her wages to support me until I finished my education, or I could stay in the housekeeper's cottage and live as a member of your family.'

'You chose us over your family?'

Santi shrugged. In his mother's year-long battle with cancer, not one member of his maternal family had made the effort to visit her. Not one hospital visit. All had cited the distance as their excuse, as if a six-and-a-half-hour drive on the country's excellent *autopistas* was a trek through the Himalayan Mountains. His grandmother, who'd had mobility problems, had been the only one to attend the funeral. He only looked out for her now because he knew that's what his mother would want.

He condensed his reasons to, 'They'd come to be strangers to me.'

She asked the obvious question. 'Why didn't you move into the villa with us? You were only fifteen.'

Because, for all their kindness and empathy, I was a rough, ill-mannered boy who didn't belong in the rarefied world your family inhabited.

Just thinking such thoughts made him feel like a traitor but he had no illusions about where he belonged. The Lopezes' world was one of riches and elegance. A whole world away from his.

Knowing his private thoughts would hurt her, he settled on, 'Because your parents foresaw that I would turn into the teenager from hell and wanted to protect you and Marisa from it.' His eyes found hers again and his lips twitched. 'They should have taken up fortune-telling. The rest you know.'

He waited for Elsa to say or ask something else, but she looked troubled.

'What's wrong, *chiquita*?'

She sighed and put her elbow on the table to rest her cheek on her palm.

'You must have thought I was the biggest brat in the world,' Elsa said heavily.

A crease formed in his brow.

'All that time I spent complaining about my parents and the general unfairness of adolescent life when I had *nothing* to complain about,' she explained. Santi had always humoured her whining. Given sensible advice when needed. Sympathised. Told her to pull her head out of her bottom when her whining got too much.

If she'd been a little less self-absorbed in those years

when he'd been her chauffeur, protector and friend, he might have opened up to her about his life.

To her relief, his eyes crinkled and he laughed. 'Your complaints were always entertaining.'

'But how did you put *up* with me?'

'Because you, *chiquita*, were *always* entertaining. Even when you were whining. And you know something else?'

She shook her head, fascinated at the change of expression on his face and the sensual tone that had entered his voice.

He stood up and leaned over the table. His breath was hot on her face as he growled, 'You're still entertaining but in a *very* different way. Now come here.'

CHAPTER TEN

SANTI PULLED OUT the cushions that transformed the area forward of the helm into a huge sunbathing area and lay down, then patted the space beside him. Elsa removed her sunhat with the shy smile he was becoming used to and curled into him. Beneath her caftan, she was naked.

For the longest time they did nothing but lie there curled together. Her knee slipped between his thighs. After carrying her to his cabin and making love to her again, he'd thought he was too sated to feel arousal again so soon but heat trickled into his loins, slowly, deliciously.

Desire. Pulled out of the shadows they'd both boxed it into and shining brightly like dancing fire.

Desire. Out in the open. No longer deniable. No longer denied.

He'd touched the fire and let it enflame him.

It would extinguish itself when they returned to Valencia.

'I need to ask you something,' he said before his arousal could take control of all his senses again. There were things he needed to know before their time together came to an end.

He heard her long intake of breath before she raised her face to look into his eyes. 'Go on.'

'That night. Was it the reason you moved to Vienna?'

It struck him then that he already knew the answer. He'd always known, just refused to acknowledge it. Within a fortnight of that haunting night, Elsa had gone.

Her stare held his. It seemed like a thousand emotions rang out at him.

Guilt pressed into his guts. 'I really hurt you, didn't I.'

It wasn't a question.

Hating the self-recrimination she could feel vibrating from him, Elsa traced the chain around his neck with her finger. 'Yes, but the blame never lay with you—it was all on me. I felt such *shame*.'

Until they'd given voice to the elephant in the room that had been there from their first clash of eyes in Vienna, Elsa had never thought about that night from Santi's perspective. Or how he'd asked her to leave numerous times and she'd blithely ignored him, going as far as to try to drag him onto the bed when *he*'d tried to leave the room.

All she'd remembered with any clarity had been his cruel words and the look of disgust on his face. The lancing sting of his rejection.

'Your rejection… That was the first real rejection of my life. I was so spoilt—'

'No,' he cut in. 'You weren't spoilt. You never looked down on people.'

'Thank you, but I *was* spoilt. I had the happiest childhood. Life was one big adventure and it felt that the world turned just for *me*. Your rejection was a sharp lesson in the reality of life and the first time there had been a real consequence to my actions, but I didn't have the emotional tools or maturity to handle it so, yes, I did move to Vienna to escape you. I didn't think I could bear to see you again.'

His hand tightened around hers. 'I'm sorry.'

'Don't be. It was for the best. I needed a fresh start. I

needed to grow up and learn to fend for myself. I needed to learn independence.'

'Then why didn't you learn to cook?' he teased.

'Stubbornness,' she said, glad of the lightening of tone.

He rested a hand on her hip and pulled her even tighter to him. 'I get why you needed a fresh start but why did that have to mean you turning into a loner?' Because Santi was convinced Elsa's Vienna years had been mostly spent alone. It hurt his heart to think of the vivacious young woman who'd thrived on company being by herself all that time.

'It wasn't intentional but my fresh start meant turning my back on the things that had got me into trouble, namely alcohol. How I behaved that night… I can't blame the alcohol, those were *my* actions, but all that rum…it made me lose my inhibitions completely and I was terrified of it happening again. I felt like I was a runaway train falling head first off the track and the only way to stop it was to slam my foot on the brakes. I didn't go to any of the parties I was invited to and eventually people stopped asking. If you can believe it, I was known as a goody-goody at university.'

He feigned shock. '*No!* Elsa Lopez a goody-goody?'

'They think I'm a goody-goody at work too.'

'Does that bother you?'

'Sometimes. When I overhear colleagues make plans for a night out I'm not invited to.'

He heard the wistfulness in her voice and fell silent for a moment. 'Has hiding away from life made you happy?'

'It's never felt like hiding away. More like self-preservation.'

'Okay, but has it made you happy?' he persisted.

Her silence gave the answer to that.

'Why didn't you come home?' he asked quietly.

'I don't know,' she whispered. 'I suppose…' Elsa sighed and rolled onto her back. A gull flew high over the yacht.

She wondered if it ever felt exhilaration when it swooped through the air. She hoped it did. Hoped it was capable of appreciating the freedom its wings gave it. Elsa used to wish for wings. She remembered being about four or five and climbing on the roof of the villa wearing her dressing-up fairy wings. She'd been convinced they would make her fly.

If Marisa hadn't followed her up and screamed for their *mamá* to stop her, she would have jumped. If her mama hadn't then thrown the fairy wings away, she would have tried again when no one was looking. Luckily, her faith in the magic of her fairy wings had stopped her trying without them until she'd jumped off that cliff thirteen years later.

She envied her younger self. She'd been free in her heart.

'When I'm in Vienna, I wear this persona,' she said quietly. 'People there accept me as this hard-working, strait-laced young woman and I can *be* that woman. There's no temptation. It's safe. *I'm* safe. And in control of myself and my life.'

'But not happy.'

'No,' she admitted reluctantly. 'I think I've forgotten how to be happy. Especially since Papá…'

Her throat hitched as her voice trailed off. The sound of her pain made Santi's heart cramp tightly and he had to suck in a breath to loosen it.

'You know what you need to do when all this is over, Elsa?' he said, breaking the sudden cloud of grief that had shrouded them, wanting, *needing*, to see her smile.

Her eyes held his starkly. 'What?'

'Let it go.'

It took a moment for the old joke he used to throw at her when she was in a particularly whiny mood to sink in. It was worth the wait. Her melancholy expression dissolved, her face creasing as she spluttered with laughter.

'If you start singing, I'm going to cook something and force-feed it to you,' she threatened.

'No singing, I promise,' he said quickly, making her snigger even more.

He propped himself on an elbow to gaze down at her beautiful face. 'But you do need to put it behind you. You can't let shame over an incident when you were only eighteen make you hide away from life for ever. You're a grown woman. If you want a rum and Coke, what's wrong with that? You're perfectly capable of stopping before you get close to losing your inhibitions. And if you don't want to drink, why let that stop you from partying? Do you really want to look at yourself when you're a little old lady and say, "I had some great times sitting at my office desk"?'

As he spoke, Santi had to acknowledge that the latter part of his advice could equally apply to him. When had he last taken time away from his business and simply lived for the moment?

The answer came to him immediately. Elsa's eighteenth birthday party.

It shocked him to know that really had been it. Five whole years without a break. He'd forgotten how good it felt to relax and do nothing, to simply enjoy being alive.

Right then, he felt more alive than he'd ever done. Every cell in his body was awake and zinging. Tomorrow they would be back in Valencia and this brief flare of passion between them would be over.

Covering her with his body, he kissed her. 'You're beautiful, Elsa Lopez.' He ran a hand over the contours of her incredible body. 'And sexy. *Very* sexy.' He cupped a breast and grazed his teeth over her neck, then took her hand to guide it to his arousal. Her gasp followed by a soft moan only made him harder. 'Feel what you do to me,' he breathed. 'This is all you.'

And then he showed her exactly what she did to him.

Elsa wrinkled her nose at the array of vegetables laid out on the kitchen counter. 'What are we making?'

After anchoring at sea for the night, Santi had announced it was time for her first cooking lesson. She'd agreed only because she couldn't think of a good reason not to.

'*Pisto*.'

Her mouth watered at the thought. She loved the Spanish take on ratatouille.

He picked a kitchen knife up and held it out to her, handle first. 'Your first job is to slice the onions.'

She took hold of the knife gingerly and stared at the onion, wondering if she was supposed to take the outer brown layer off first.

'Shall I show you how to do it?' he asked.

As there was no point pretending she had a clue what she was doing, she happily stepped aside.

Her mouth dropped open to witness Santi tackle the onion. For a man whose hands could easily be classified as bear paws without the hairiness, he had a deftness of touch and in less than a minute the onion was peeled and professionally sliced.

Done, he raised an eyebrow. 'Do you need me to show you how to dice a pepper too?'

Thinking of the way she'd massacred the pepper she'd chopped for their paninis, she laughed. 'Probably a good idea.'

He stretched an arm in front of her and grabbed a red one. The movement set off a wave of his cologne and in an instant Elsa's senses were filled with the scent of Santi. She leaned in closer.

'Here. Hold it like this and… *Chiquita*, what are you doing?'

'Sniffing you.' She slipped an arm around his waist, only to be deterred by his hand.

'No,' he said sternly. 'You are not going to seduce me into stopping your cooking lesson. I'm teaching you a valuable life lesson.'

'Can't you teach me another time?'

He lightly tapped the tip of her nose. 'Watch and learn.'

'I can learn when I get back to Vienna.'

'Schnitzel?' He laughed.

'It's actually nice. You should try it one day.' She almost added, 'with me', but quickly stopped herself. What was happening to them was nothing but lust. If it turned into something more then…

No, she would not think like that. She would not go there. She would not allow her mind to conjure delusions and spoil the happiness of today.

Music was playing and a song she liked came over the system. She tapped her foot along to the beat. If not for the gnawing fear of what tomorrow could bring, she thought this might be the happiest she'd felt in a long, long time.

She shoved aside the nagging voice that her fears for tomorrow were not only to do with her family's safety.

Her heart was safely enclosed and if she felt it straining for freedom, she simply tightened the lock around it. That was a valuable life lesson she'd taught herself…hadn't she…?

Shaking all the unwanted thoughts away, she peered at the chopping board now piled high with an array of vegetables. 'When did you last cook before this trip?' she asked.

He shrugged. 'Years ago.'

'You enjoy it?'

'Very much. It's therapeutic.'

'Then why employ a chef?'

He thought about this too as he continued to dice. 'I don't have time to cook. I work twelve-hour days minimum and travel a great deal.'

She watched him pull a pan out of a cupboard and felt the strangest welling of pride for him. 'You're incredible, do you know that?'

She only realised she'd spoken aloud when he raised a disbelieving brow and she hurriedly clarified, 'The success you've made of yourself. Our family business took decades to become as profitable as it is today but you achieved ten times as much in a fraction of the time.'

'I couldn't have done it without your father.'

'He helped, I'm sure, but it was your hard work that did it, so stop being modest. It doesn't suit you,' she added with a cackle.

Santi laughed at the delight on Elsa's face. How wonderful it was to see the joyful girl he'd known seeping out of the adult woman, as if she'd been hiding inside and just waiting to come back to life.

He'd laughed more these last few days than he'd laughed in years too.

When had he become so serious? He supposed the more pertinent question would be *why*.

He'd never set out to earn himself a fortune. He'd simply wanted to make something of himself and make the family who'd given him so much proud. His business model had been a hit and he'd quickly gained a reputation for honesty and reliability. Word of mouth had done more to boost his business than any advertising. Businesses trusted him to transport their goods across the world in a timely fashion and without damage to their stock.

More wants more, his mother had often said. He supposed there was something in that. The more his business grew, the greater his ambitions. The more he'd earned, the more he'd wanted to earn. As his wealth had grown so too had the trappings he'd purchased to go with it, none of which he'd actually taken the time to enjoy.

He poured a little olive oil in the pan. 'Now the vegetables are ready, we can start cooking. We start by sautéing the onion.'

'Sautéing?'

'Frying.'

'Why didn't you just say that?'

'Do you want to learn or not?'

Her face was completely deadpan. 'Not.'

He shook his head, amusement building back up again. 'You're lucky we're living in modern times where you're not chained to the kitchen.'

'I'd chew my way through the chains to escape.'

'I can well believe it. How have you not starved these last five years?'

'Restaurants, cafés and takeaways.' Then she added brightly, 'Marisa's gone all maternal and taught herself to cook baby food for Nikos.'

'Good for her.'

She laughed. 'She made sure Raul knows she won't cook for him.'

'I'm sure he was devastated.'

'Not devastated enough to end the engagement.'

'You really don't like him, do you?'

'Neither do you,' she reminded him. 'You know, when Marisa first said she wanted to get married, I thought she'd ask you.'

He turned his face to her. 'You thought Marisa would ask *me* to marry her?'

'It makes sense.' Elsa said airily. See, she told herself triumphantly, her heart was *fine*. Those months spent fighting cold sweats and living with the tightest cramping feeling in her stomach as she'd waited for the day her sister's thoughts aligned with her own had been nothing but echoes of her old obsession with him. Santi marrying Marisa had been an excellent idea because it meant her sister and nephew would have had someone with their best interests at heart.

If she'd almost fainted with relief when Marisa had announced she would marry Raul… Well, that was just another echo too.

'She's after a business partner for herself and a father for her son,' she said. 'You're practically family. You know every aspect of our business inside out. To be honest, I'm surprised you didn't suggest it to her.'

'The thought never crossed my mind.' Not for a second. Santi liked Marisa, was as protective of her as he was the rest of the Lopezes but they'd never bonded the way he and Elsa had.

His heart made a sudden lurch to imagine Elsa in Marisa's situation. The father of her child dead. Her father murdered. Expected to take over a multi-national corporation. A dangerous cartel doing everything in its power to drag the business into its nefarious dealings.

He couldn't escape the sinking feeling that had it been Elsa in Marisa's shoes, he would have been by her side in an instant with the biggest gun he could get his hands on and never let her out of his sight for a moment. He would have insisted she marry him and to hell with the consequences.

'I don't think your *mamá* would be happy for me to marry her daughter,' he commented through a throat that felt as if it had broken glass in it.

'What makes you say that?'

He tried to keep his tone light. '*Chiquita*, Lopez blood is blue. Rodriguez blood is red.'

'All blood is red.'

'I was speaking figuratively.'

'And I was speaking factually. Mamá loves and trusts you.'

Not enough to have allowed him to move into the main villa after his own mother had died, he thought, but kept that to himself. He felt bad enough thinking it, let alone vocalising it.

But he knew that for all Rosaria loved and trusted him, she would never consider him a good life match for one of her precious daughters. Marco wouldn't have either. Santi was like a stray fighting dog they'd taken in, fed, sheltered, taught to obey and protect its owner but with the owner always having a healthy respect for the dog's inherent nature. The dog had been one wrong move away from being metaphorically put down.

Rosaria, like her late husband, knew everything about Santi. She'd seen him at his worst. She'd supported him and treated him like he was of her blood… But he was still that stray dog.

He had made it to the very top. He'd reached an unimaginable level of success and wealth. He was good enough for anyone, and anyone who disagreed could kiss his backside. But in his heart he knew he wasn't good enough for the Lopez girls. The world he'd come to inhabit was their natural home. They belonged to it. He was the interloper tolerated only because of his wealth.

When this situation was over and he and Elsa returned to their normal lives, he would have to face the guilt of knowing he'd abused the trust Rosaria had put in him. He would have to visit Marco's grave knowing he'd be turning in it at the thought of Santi touching his precious daughter.

CHAPTER ELEVEN

ELSA KEPT HAVING to remind herself to breathe. She couldn't stop her fingers drumming on the dining table or stop her legs from shaking. She'd been a wreck from the moment her eyes had snapped open at the unholy hour of five a.m.

The cartel was being taken down. It was happening right now.

Until she'd woken that morning, being on the yacht with Santi had dulled her panic. His confidence and assurance that there would be no danger to her family had rubbed off on her and she'd spent their time sailing the Mediterranean falling under his spell rather than flaying her skin with worry.

If she hadn't had his calm presence with her now, she would likely have torn out every hair on her head.

As time ticked slowly on, she couldn't stop her mind veering wildly to imagine it all going wrong. She'd lost her father to this murderous group and now she couldn't stop thinking of her mother, sister and nephew all in the firing line, even though she knew that was ridiculous and the action would be taking place far from the Lopez estate.

But what if the cartel had a contingency in place to swarm the villa and take her family hostage?

The what-ifs were never-ending.

Her wild ruminations were interrupted when Santi

placed a plate full of pastries on the table and ruffled her hair with a gentle, 'Eat.'

'I'm not hungry,' she whispered. Her stomach and throat were so constricted she'd struggled to swallow the endless cups of coffee he kept making for her.

He stood behind her and laid his strong hands on her shoulders 'You need to keep your strength up,' he murmured, massaging her tense muscles. 'We might not hear anything for hours.'

She closed her eyes as a little of the tension racking her lessened. Only because he'd gone to the effort of preparing them for her did she eventually rip off a piece of pastry and pop it in her mouth. She might as well be eating cardboard. Did stress affect the tastebuds?

Elsa was about to swallow the last bit of pastry when Santi's phone rang.

Every part of her froze.

The hands still kneading her neck and shoulders froze too, but only for a moment.

Calmly, he picked the phone up from the table, swiped to accept the call, and put it to his ear. 'Felipe,' he said by way of greeting.

Elsa watched his reactions intently, searching for a sign, a tell, anything.

His eyes met hers. He nodded, lips curving into a smile.

She slumped in her seat and pressed a hand to her racing chest, and finally managed to exhale her pent-up breath.

Thank you, God. Thank you. Thank you.

Her own phone rang, pulling her out of her overwhelmed daze.

'Mamá?'

'It's over, darling. We're safe.'

Elsa pinched the bridge of her nose to stifle the threatening tears. 'You're really safe?'

'I swear.' Her voice lowered. 'I know how hard this must have been for you but it's over, and when I see you tomorrow I will—'

'Tomorrow? I thought there was an extraction plan to bring me home immediately?'

'There is, darling, but we were moved to a safe house in Geneva yesterday—'

'*What*?' Her gaze flew back to Santi, who was still discussing things with Felipe.

'It was a last-minute precaution taken by Felipe. Poor Nikos is teething and the flight hurt his ears so he had a terrible night and your sister hasn't slept. We can't put him through another flight, so we're going to drive back and stay in a hotel for the night. We'll be home in the morning.'

Until that moment, Elsa hadn't realised how desperate she was to be with her family and the guilt she felt at not being with them throughout the whole ordeal.

'I'm sorry I wasn't there with you,' she said quietly, sniffing back more tears.

'We'll be together again in the morning,' her mother promised, then her voice lowered. 'How have things been with Santi?'

Feeling her cheeks redden at the mention of his name, Elsa twisted to face the window so he couldn't see. 'Fine. Fine.'

'It made such a difference to Marisa and I, knowing you were in his care. It meant we could stop worrying about you. I do hope you two have resolved the…' she paused. '…differences between you.'

Elsa was very glad she'd turned her back to him for her mouth dropped open.

Her mother knew? Surely her father hadn't betrayed her confidence?

'I remember how your eyes always lit up when he walked into a room,' her mother said wistfully. 'I always hoped…'

'Hoped what?' she croaked when her mother's words hung in the air.

'That you would find your way back to him.'

A loud swoosh flew through her ears, like a wave crashing onto rocks. She pressed her burning forehead to the cool window and tried to think of something to say but her head was a jumble.

'I have to go,' her mother said. 'Have a safe journey home and I'll see you in the morning. I love you.'

Elsa's hands were shaking so hard she struggled to disconnect the call.

'Was that Marisa?' Santi asked. He'd been watching Elsa for the last minute, had seen her shudder and press her face against the window as if she'd been given bad news.

She shook her head. 'Mamá. They're safe.'

Then she burst into tears.

Sliding into the seat beside her, Santi hauled her into his arms and let her sob her relief, stroking her hair and kissing the top of her head until the tears ran dry.

'I can't believe it's finally over,' she mumbled into his chest, then tilted her face up at him. 'It *is* over, isn't it?'

'Yes, *chiquita*.' He bent his head and kissed her. 'It's over. All the leading members of the cartel have been arrested and their operations shut down. A handful of the lesser ranks in Naples escaped but they're powerless.' At least, he hoped they were. In the scheme of things, these four men and one woman were nothing but Santi suspected he wouldn't sleep properly until they were caught too. An international manhunt had already been launched to find them.

She nestled her face back against his chest and whispered, 'Thank you. For everything.'

He tightened his hold around her and pressed his mouth tightly to the top of her head.

Beats of dread ticked loudly in him. The time when he had to say goodbye to her, to let Elsa go, had accelerated with one phone call.

'Felipe's team will be here in around an hour. We should get our stuff together.' But he made no effort to disentangle his arms. This might be the last time he got to hold her like this.

She gave a long sigh then straightened and hooked her arms around his neck while wriggling onto his lap. Her nails grazed the bristles of hair on the nape of his neck. 'Felipe had Mamá and Marisa taken to Switzerland.'

'It was a last-minute judgement call.' He gathered her beautiful hair into his fist. 'I would have told you if I'd known.'

'They're safe. That's all that matters.' Her smile had a touch of melancholy to it but then her mesmerising eyes glittered with a hint of mischief. 'They won't be home until the morning...' Her hand drifted from his neck to palm his cheek. 'If we're extracted now we'll only be returning to an empty house...'

He stared into the green-brown depths, his heart inflating as her meaning became clear. 'You want me to call off the extraction?'

'Do you?'

Another day and night with Elsa? The thought alone was enough to put him into a state of instant arousal so hot it burned through any voice of caution. 'I think I could be persuaded.'

She kissed him with a hard, ferocious passion that stole his breath, pressing every inch of herself that should could into him as if she were trying to burrow into his skin.

When they finally came up for air, arms still locked

around his neck, she gave the most contented smile. 'Did that persuade you?'

He pretended to ponder.

Her teeth grazed his neck then, before he could guess what she intended, she slithered off his lap and dropped to her knees so her face was level with his crotch. Grinning wickedly, she put her fingers to the top button of his shorts. 'Let's see if this persuades you.'

No longer having to keep an inner ear and eye alert to danger meant that for the first time since he'd embarked on this remarkable journey, Santi was able to fully relax.

After Elsa had used her very recently gained talents to persuade him to spend one last day on the yacht with her, he'd called the extraction off and arranged for his private jet to collect them on the island of Mallorca in the morning. And then he'd carried her to his cabin and made love to her with nothing more than his tongue. His loins twitched every time he remembered her throaty moans of pleasure. They'd then moved to the sundeck and carried on in much the same fashion.

With the sun's descent telling him better than his watch that evening was fast approaching, his loins twitched again to see her now, as naked as the day she was born, face in profile, lying on her stomach, dozing. The successful takedown of the cartel had taken the worry off her shoulders. She'd had a spring in her step ever since, a carefree joy that was utterly infectious. How could anyone not to be in such vibrant company? This was the Elsa he'd always imagined she would mature into, but with a mountain of sexiness.

'How would you like to go out tonight?' he asked, tracing a finger down her spine, loving the way she shivered at his touch. 'Celebrate. Make the most of our last night together like this. Go for a meal and see where the night takes us.'

She lifted her head. The light in her eyes dazzled him before she gave a beaming smile that could have knocked him out with its power. 'I would love that.'

'We should think about putting some clothes on.' He cupped her smooth butt cheek. 'I would hate for a passing captain to train his binoculars on us and fall overboard with lust when he spied your perfect bottom.'

Her eyes pulsed. The lock of their gazes only broke when Elsa turned away and sat up with her back to him while she slipped her dress over her head. It pained him that despite everything they'd been through, she was still shy about her body around him. They'd spent hours naked yet she still pressed her thighs together and leaned forward and covered her breasts with an arm when doing something as simple as taking a drink of water.

Time and patience would, he was certain, see her lose the last of her inhibitions. But he wouldn't be the man to witness the final act of her blossoming. Come the morning and they would be over. The knife had barely penetrated his heart at this thought when she scrambled over to him and straddled his lap. The hem of her sundress bunched around her hips.

'Am I decent now?' she asked, fluttering her eyelashes.

He clasped her delectable bottom and mock-growled, 'Too decent.' His arousal thickened as she teased the folds of her sex over it. 'I much prefer you indecent.'

'Oh, do you?' She smiled innocently and sank down on him.

He groaned loudly at the all-engulfing pleasure and tightened his grip.

She pressed her cheek against his, raised herself then sank back down again. 'Is this indecent enough?'

He tried to capture her mouth in a kiss but was foiled when she suddenly sprang to her feet and took three quick steps away. Looking back over her shoulder, she said in the airiest of tones, 'I'm going to take a shower. Let me know if you need my help at the marina.'

Stunned, he pointed at the missile sprouting between his legs. 'You're going to leave me like this?'

She winked. 'I would hate to be responsible for a spike in boat accidents.'

Then she strode away, wriggling her bottom, leaving Santi with no choice but to laugh at her sheer provocativeness.

Elsa looked at her appearance and pulled a critical face. This was her first official date with Santi and she was dressed appropriately for a convent. She knew Santi wouldn't care what she wore but…

She froze on the spot.

Santi wouldn't care what she wore.

She could almost hear him. '*Chiquita*, you're beautiful whatever you wear.'

He thought she was beautiful. And it wasn't just words. It was in the way he touched her. The way he kissed her. The way he looked at her…

Her heart vibrated in a sigh.

With barely conscious thought, Elsa tugged the zip at the side of the dress down and then pulled it over her head and threw it onto the floor.

Eyes glued to the mirror, she removed her underwear and gazed at her naked reflection properly for the first time in five years.

The compulsion to weep hit her so suddenly that her whole body contracted from the force of holding it back.

She would not let anything ruin this evening. This was

an evening for celebration. The nightmare was over, her family were safe and she and Santi were embarking on something that might—and she was scared to jinx it by vocalising it even to herself—just might be the start of *something*.

But, still, she stared at her naked body and fought the tears as she finally accepted what her eyes were telling her, that she wasn't ugly, that her body was…just a body. No uglier or prettier than the average female body but beautiful in Santi's eyes.

Her chest feeling pierced with lightness, she opened the cupboard she'd stored her suitcase in and laid it on the bed. Inside it, having been stubbornly ignored since she'd first seen them at Santi's lodge…oh, but that felt like a lifetime ago…were the dresses Marisa had loaned her.

Santi was right. It was time to let the past go.

From as far back as he could remember, Santi had thought childhood cartoons where the rabbit or cat or dog or whatever's eyes popped out were ludicrous. That was until Elsa emerged from the cabin. His eyes might not be able to physically pop out but his jaw could certainly drop, and it did.

She held her hands out to the sides as she gave a quick twirl. 'Well? Will I do?'

Closing his mouth with a snap, he had to swallow a number of times to get some moisture going. '*Chiquita*, I'm going to be the envy of every red-blooded man in Mallorca tonight. You look…'

Like fire.

She wore a silk dusky rose, overlaid with gold lace wrap-around dress that was like no other wraparound dress he'd ever seen. This one was held with spaghetti straps that criss-crossed her otherwise bare back. At the front, the shimmering silk plunged in a V to meet at her midriff where bands of the spaghetti straps wrapped around her. When she'd twirled he'd glimpsed the loop low at the base of her spine where the straps tied together, and his blood thickened to imagine untying that knot and spinning her round to unwrap her.

His gaze swept down, following the dress's shimmering path to her feet, which were pretty in a pair of three-inch-heeled gold Roman-style sandals, then raked back up, over the bands around her waist, up the plunging V, where hints of breast were exposed, and finally back to the heavenly face and the thick sweep of fiery hair loose around her shoulders.

'Incredible,' he breathed.

Elsa felt herself glow at the thrill of his reaction to her appearance even as she absorbed every inch of *him*. There was nothing extraordinary about his outfit—not extraordinary for Santi anyway: black Egyptian cotton shirt, tailored black trousers, tailored charcoal waistcoat and handmade brogues. On his wrist was the watch he'd been wearing five years ago, around his neck the chain that had lived there for as long as she could remember him. Which was for ever.

She'd seen him in many different variations of the outfit but it felt like she was seeing him for the first time tonight. All the parts that made the total of him. The black beard and curly black hair. The creases around his eyes. The sparkle *in* his eyes. The muscles straining against his shirt. The rise and fall of his chest.

Her heart was fluttering madly, as if joy and excitement had been let loose together.

He held his elbow out. 'Shall we?'

She stepped forward as gracefully as she could considering her feet were straining to spring themselves at him, and slipped her hand into the crook, and happily let him lead her into the warm Mallorca night.

* * *

Elsa peered through the windows of the luxury car that had collected them from the marina. They'd driven through the beautiful village of Cala Deia with its honey-coloured homes, and affluent holidaymakers and residents alike enjoying the evening warmth in local restaurants and bars, and then taken a remote road, ascending through thick woodland until reaching a high iron gate that blocked further travel. An armed security guard approached from the sentry box to the right of the gate. Santi lowered his window and plucked a business card from his wallet, which he showed to the unsmiling guard who studied it before tapping something into a phone.

The iron gates slowly opened to reveal immaculately maintained grounds surrounding a sprawling sand-coloured villa.

'What is this place?' she asked as the car crawled to the villa's entrance, thinking it must be a luxury hotel.

'Club Giroud,' Santi said.

'Really?' Elsa hadn't thought her mood could feel any perkier considering she already felt that she was floating on air, but it did. She'd tried to sneak into the über-exclusive members-only club's Madrid venue once with a school friend who'd stolen her mother's membership card but both girls had been refused entry. Her surname had been no match for the stern doormen.

Santi picked up on her excitement and laughed. 'Really.'

'How long have you been a member?'

'A few years. It's good for networking.'

No sooner had they stopped than the two men standing guard at the bottom of the steps of the entrance opened their doors.

They climbed the steps with their hands clasped together.

'I hope you're not planning to network tonight,' she murmured.

'With you on my arm?' he said, feigning horror. 'I'd be too worried about someone whisking you away from me.'

'You should definitely keep me close to your side. To stop that happening,' she added.

'Don't worry.' They swept through the huge double doors that parted for them like the Red Sea. 'I'm not letting you out of my sight.'

Not for a second.

A hostess greeted them like old friends in the vast reception room and then they were led up two flights of cantilevered stairs. They continued down a long corridor where music and laughter could be heard coming from the myriad rooms they passed, then up another flight of stairs until they were on the roof terrace. Elsa couldn't help but sigh her pleasure at the sight that greeted her.

She hadn't realised how high up the villa was located and from this spot and this vantage point it seemed the whole of the western Mallorca coastline was spread out before her. The yachts in the distant anchorage bay seemed like toy boats bobbing amongst the waves. With the stars out in force on this moonless night, the whole setting was enough to make the heart sing.

Santi heard Elsa's dreamy sigh and smiled. Of all the Clubs Giroud scattered around the world, this, the most recently developed of them, was a significant departure from its usual gothic-inspired luxury. Possibly the setting had inspired the change to something more romantic.

Mallorca was a holiday destination. Club Giroud members who came here to dine would likely have partners and families in tow. The terrace was proof of this theory, as couples and families alike dined in the open air. He spotted Luis Casillas, a fellow club member he'd got to know in recent years and whose company he enjoyed, dining with his beautiful wife Chloe and their small daughter, and waved a hand in greeting as they passed.

They were shown to a table by the sandstone balustrade.

'Can I get you drinks?' their hostess asked when they were seated.

Elsa hesitated for only a moment before saying, 'A white wine spritzer for me.'

Santi raised a brow but held off saying anything until the hostess had gone.

A dress that showed three times as much flesh as anything else he'd seen her in and now this? 'Alcohol, *chiquita*?'

She gave a smile of such contentment that it pierced straight through his heart. 'It's time, don't you think?'

'What I think is irrelevant.'

'Not to me,' she contradicted softly. 'But what you said, about me needing to let the past go…it resonated. I *like* wine, and I'm old enough to know when to stop.' Then her mouth made the swirling motion and she added with a cackle, 'I don't think I can ever look a measure of rum in the eye again, though.'

Laughing, he took her hand and tugged it to his mouth so he could graze the knuckles with kisses.

Soon they were eating their way through courses of divinely cooked food and stealing forkfuls of each other's dishes and exchanging stories of the five years they'd missed from each other's lives. It was incredible to think that this beautiful woman, laughing throatily as she taught him how to swear fluently in German, was the same closed-off, frightened woman he'd met up with in Vienna a few days ago.

He'd just finished his lobster when Luis Casillas, carrying his sleepy daughter, waved goodbye and made a 'call me' sign.

Santi stuck his hand in the air in acknowledgement, and found his gaze following the Casillas family as they left the terrace with the strangest pang rippling in his chest at the closeness they so obviously shared.

He drained his wine. He wasn't there to mourn what could have been. He was there to enjoy his final night with the most beautiful woman to inhabit the earth.

He indicated Elsa's empty plate. 'Dessert?'

'Try and stop me.'

He grinned. 'What would you like to do after?'

'What are the options?'

'Off the top of my head, the club has a casino, a night-club, a jazz room—don't pull faces, *chiquita*, some people like jazz—and a—'

'The nightclub,' she interrupted decisively.

'You want to dance?'

Her eyes flashed. 'I want to dance with *you*.'

CHAPTER TWELVE

THE NIGHTCLUB WAS busier than Elsa had anticipated and had a far more glamorously seductive vibe than she'd expected too. So wrapped up in her Santi cloud had she been that it was a shock to bump into her old schoolfriend Lola. The porcelain heiress couldn't wait to show Elsa the ridiculously ostentatious diamond engagement ring flashing on her finger before introducing her to the man who'd bought it, an Italian aristocrat who liked to be accorded his defunct title of Conte.

When Lola took a breath from gushing about her wedding plans and clocked Santi, chatting to her fiancé and club members he was acquainted with, her eyes widened and she snatched Elsa's hand to drag her to the ladies.

'You and Santi?' she squealed. 'I can't believe you've finally pulled him. How long's it been going on? Tell me everything! I'm so jealous!'

'What are you jealous for?' Elsa asked drily, neatly sidestepping the other rapid-fire questions. 'You've got yourself a *conte*.'

Lola's eyes sparkled as much as her engagement ring. 'I know. But you have to admit… Santi…' She fanned her face with her hand. 'He's so *masculine*! Remember when we all fancied him? What's he like in bed? I bet he's *amazing*…'

'Have you set a date for the wedding?'·Elsa interrupted

with a smile. Five years ago she would probably have thrilled in sharing every little detail with her friend, but now... What she shared with Santi was private. Special. Wonderful.

Lola took the bait and happily blathered on about her extravagant plans while they made their way back to their partners.

Santi had moved to a round table on the edge of a dance floor and was clearly keeping watch for her as his eyes locked onto hers as soon as she re-entered the room. The crowd around him had grown in her short absence and he was chatting to a tall man she recognised. She smiled a greeting, sure he was the brother of another old school-friend, but before she could say hello she found herself pulled into an embrace by another face from the past.

Santi watched Elsa laugh as she disentangled herself from yet another pair of arms. Was there anyone she didn't know? All these faces, men and women of the kind he'd carefully cultivated working relationships with, these were Elsa's peers. Spain's elite. If he took her to any Club Giroud in Europe, she was bound to bump into someone she knew.

A crowd gathered around her, wanting to hear about her life in Vienna. Where it had taken Santi a good few years and a few extra billion in the bank to feel accepted in places like this, Elsa simply sidled in and was embraced by everyone. This was her world. She'd stepped out of it for five years but was welcomed back as if no time had passed.

Santi was accepted but he didn't belong, not in the way Elsa did. He was the interloper, the mimic octopus able to change colour and pass itself off as different sea creatures. He was a bad-mannered kid from the poorest part of Seville. All the trappings he'd accumulated over the past decade didn't change that. He didn't belong.

His beautiful Elsa did, and one day she would marry a

man worthy of her, maybe one of the men making subtle eyes at her now. A man born and raised in her world.

But she was still his for one more night and with a determination to make every minute count, he extracted himself from his conversation and weaved over to her.

Her smile as their eyes met dazzled him.

By the time they left the club, Elsa was no longer floating on air but soaring giddily over the clouds.

Who needed alcohol to feel drunk when dancing with Santi induced that same intoxicated feeling? Just being with him did.

She snuggled up to him in the back of the car, head on his chest, and closed her eyes to remember it all. The darkly illuminated, sensual nightclub. The pulsing dance music that had vibrated through her feet. The jostling of other dancers around them forcing her to attach herself like a barnacle to Santi…or so she'd told him, she remembered with a stifled giggle. Her surprise when Santi had thrown some moves that had had her clapping with delight. The time she'd used the ladies and had found him waiting outside for her and then pressing her against the wall for a kiss so deep and passionate that she'd been throbbing all over when he'd pulled away with a seductive grin.

It had been the best night of her life.

'Drink?' Santi offered when, hands clasped, they stepped back onto the yacht.

Her mesmerising eyes sparkled. 'Anything but rum.'

He rummaged in the small bar and found an unopened bottle of bourbon. He dropped ice in Elsa's glass then poured them both a measure before passing hers.

She accepted it with a sensual smile and raised the glass for him to chink.

Eyes fixed on her face, he took a slow sip. She copied him, barely flinching when the alcohol hit her throat, then, deliberately, poked her pink tongue out and ran it over her top lip.

The arousal that had risen and ebbed but had always been there throughout the night stirred.

What a night it had been. Relief that the nightmare of the cartel was over mingled with the lust and delight they'd found in each other had made it a fitting finale to an incredible week.

And it wasn't over. Not quite yet.

He took a step towards her.

Eyes gleaming, she took a step back.

He took another step forward.

She took another step back…then beckoned with her finger and turned to bound down the steps to her cabin.

Like a disciple tailing his leader, he followed in her wake.

The blinds of the cabin had already been drawn. Illumination from the marina filtered through them and blended with the light streaming in through the open door to cast the cabin in shades of grey.

She stood at the far end of the bed. Their eyes locked. She swallowed the last of her drink and placed her empty glass on the small dining table. She stepped over to him. And then she turned her back.

He gently fingered the knot of her straps at the base of her spine before doing what he'd fantasied about doing all those hours ago. He tugged at the knot. It loosened a little. He tugged again. It came undone. And then the dress fell apart.

He sucked in a breath.

He'd spent the evening lusting over this woman, having not the faintest idea that beneath the beautiful dress she was naked.

His throat closed, stifling the groan about to escape. His loins were on fire. *He* was on fire.

One quick shrug and the dress fell to her feet like a sheet. Still wearing her heels, she stepped over it and placed a hand to his chest. 'Your turn,' she whispered.

First she unbuttoned his waistcoat. Then she unbuttoned his shirt. Once that was removed and added to the growing pile on the floor, her hands went to his trousers.

Eyes still holding his, she fumbled for a moment before she managed to undo the belt. There was no fumbling with the button or zipper.

She stripped him naked without laying a finger on an inch of his burning flesh.

Done, she took a step back and appraised him like a lion about to strike its prey.

Santi had never been more turned on in his life.

'On the bed,' she ordered huskily.

He could hardly move his legs to obey. They felt as drugged as the rest of him.

Elsa watched this beautiful man whom she loved more than anything in the world lay himself in the middle of the bed. Her heart was so full she could barely breathe.

Her love for him had sneaked up on her during their wonderful evening together. It had started when she'd felt so protective about what they'd found together under Lola's deluge of questions, and had crystallised when a flare of panic had ripped her chest after losing sight of him for twenty seconds.

Her heart had given itself back to him. To fight it or deny it any longer was to live in more delusion.

Santi was her anchor. The one person she could always depend on. When she'd woken that morning, terrified of what the day would bring, her chest feeling like it had been injected with liquid nitrogen, she'd automatically rolled into his arms for warmth and comfort. For safety.

She was emotionally ready for him now, which she hadn't been before. Her years in Vienna had taught her independence and resilience—even if she hadn't learned how to cook, she thought with a giggle that cut through her stupor—and given her the tools to hold her own with him.

Her teenage love had been more of an obsession. An infatuation.

This felt solid. Deep. Abiding.

She'd fantasised all night about doing this. About making love to *him*.

No shame. No shyness. No self-loathing. Just this. Just them.

He'd done this to her. Santi had helped her to fix herself. He'd chased the shadows away. He'd helped her become the woman she'd always wanted to be.

Moving steadily to him, she kicked her sandals off then parted his legs and crawled onto the bed between them. Hands at his ankles, she dragged them slowly up over his muscular calves and even more muscular thighs. The only sound from Santi was the raggedness of his breathing.

His eyes stayed wide open, fixed on her. The thrill she felt to see the look in them had her closing her own and breathing deeply to keep control of herself. She ached to have him inside her, for their bodies to be crushed together, but there was something she needed to do first.

She straddled him as she'd done earlier on the sundeck, when she'd had to be clothed to do it. She'd teased him. Tormented him. Revelled in the power she had over him in this wonderful way.

Her old demons no longer had power over her.

She stretched forward. The tips of her breasts brushed

against his chest. She extended an arm and found the bedside light switch, and turned it on.

Santi lay there, fire burning through his veins, and was suddenly certain he'd died and gone to heaven. Elsa had turned the light on and then had sat back up, her sex gently rubbing against the tip of his erection.

For once, the relief he would have found thrusting straight into her was not the first thing on his mind. He was too entranced at seeing her display her beautiful body for him without an ounce of shyness. He wouldn't have been able to stop his greedy eyes from devouring every inch of her perfection if he had wanted to.

She traced her fingers over his hand then lifted it and placed it over a perfectly plump, high breast and exhaled a sigh. Her erect nipple rubbed against his palm.

He ran his fingers over the other breast. Felt her shiver.

Resting her hands lightly on his chest, she slowly sank down on him. He dragged a hand from her perfect breast to grip her hip, holding her steady.

And then he waited, too intoxicated with what was happening to draw air in.

Eyes fixed on his, she moved slowly, rising up to the tip and then sinking back down.

It was the most erotic thrill of Santi's life.

She rode him slowly, then gradually increased the tempo. He couldn't tear his eyes from her face, soaking in the way desire heightened the colour of her cheeks, the way her lips parted and soft moans fell, the way her eyes fluttered closed, the way her head swayed...

Elsa fought to hold on and savour this heady moment just a little longer but it was a fight she couldn't win, not with the glorious sensations building so deeply inside her, and when she felt her orgasm swell and break free, she threw her head back and cried his name as she rode the peak. The waves of pleasure ravaging her deepened when he suddenly sat up and covered her breast with his mouth before kissing her lips and wrapping his arms around her. Still riding the waves, Elsa threw her arms around him, holding tightly as he bucked furiously into her, his own release coming with a roar that echoed right through to her bones and into her frantically beating heart.

Santi turned the light off and enveloped Elsa in his arms. She wriggled a thigh between his legs and kissed his chest. His body craved sleep but his brain was still wired, reliving every minute of what they had just shared. Sensation still buzzed through him.

For a man who'd always rolled over and fallen unconscious straight after sex, the nights spent holding Elsa were like nothing he'd ever experienced. He would miss the closeness and affection as much as he missed her.

He ran his fingers gently up and down her spine. She made a noise much like a purring cat.

Slowly, the buzz in his veins settled, his thoughts dispersed and sleep pulled him into its clutches.

'Do you think it'll feel different between us when we get back home?'

His eyes snapped open.

Elsa's chin was on his chest. He could feel her staring at him.

He blinked vigorously, trying to clear his mind from the fog of sleep.

Her fingers tiptoed up his throat and rubbed against the bristles of his beard. 'This whole trip has been like a rollercoaster,' she said dreamily. 'It's strange as it's been one of the worst times of my life but it's been one of the best too. *The* best. I can't wait to see my family but I'm going to really miss this. Can we get away again soon, just the two of us? Take to the road or seas and just follow our noses?'

Elsa babbled on with a slowly tightening chest.

Why wasn't he responding? She knew by his breathing that he was awake.

'I keep imagining us going about our normal lives without all this drama and adrenaline, and—'

His hand suddenly gripped hold of hers. 'Elsa, stop.'

An icy prickle of dread pierced her heart. She lifted her head. 'What's wrong?'

His chest rose sharply before he released her hand and pulled away from her, straightening as he swung his legs off the bed.

His abrupt withdrawal left her chilled inside and out, and she fumbled for the bedside light, needing to look at his face and search it for what could be wrong.

When the dim light saturated the room, he hunched over and kneaded the back of his head.

She put a tentative hand to his shoulder. The muscles tensed at her touch. The prickle of dread was fast threatening to run into panic. 'What's wrong?' she repeated.

His words when they came were hoarse. 'When we get home, there is no us. I thought you knew that.'

A punch in the throat would have shocked her less, and had exactly the same effect. For the longest time she couldn't move it to speak. After numerous futile attempts, all she managed was, 'Santi?'

He twisted round to face her and covered the nape of her neck with his hand, gently holding her still while he stared into her eyes. 'This thing between us…' A grimace of pain flittered over his face. 'It can't go anywhere.'

Her bewilderment was stark and cut Santi to the quick. 'I don't understand,' she said in a strangely childlike voice.

He pressed his forehead to hers. 'It can never work between us.'

'But…but… Why? How can you know that?'

'I've always known it. I thought you did too.' Hadn't he made it clear? Hadn't it been as obvious to her as it had been to him?

Now cradling her head, he stared intently into her bewildered eyes. 'We've shared a unique experience. You said it yourself; a rollercoaster. We've been running on adrenaline and heightened emotions. Whatever attraction it set off…if it hadn't been for the circumstances, none of it would have taken root. When we're home things will feel very different, and you know it too—you just said it yourself. Sure, we could try and carry it on but it wouldn't last because it wouldn't be the same. It wouldn't feel the same.'

'You don't know that.'

'I do.'

A tear rolled down her cheek. 'You're not even prepared to try?'

He was going to hurt her. He *was* hurting her.

God forgive him. This was the last thing he'd wanted to do.

He'd eat glass for this woman. He'd take a dozen bullets for her and then come back for more.

He forced his voice to be steady so she wouldn't hear the lie, and hardened his heart. 'No. I'm not.'

This wasn't a mere punch in the throat. This landed like a full-on body-blow, and Elsa only managed to stop herself doubling over by summoning every ounce of pride she possessed.

He must have read something of her feelings for he took her trembling hand and pressed a kiss to it but the blunt justifications for breaking her heart continued. 'I have had the *best* time with you but we've been in a bubble. As soon as we land in Valencia, the bubble will burst. *Chiquita*, you're going to make some lucky man very happy but that someone can't be me. You deserve better.'

She snatched her hand away and shuffled back, trying desperately to retain some kind of dignity as she wrapped the sheets tightly around herself. A piercing of agony shot through her to know she'd opened herself to him, heart, body and soul. She'd given him the last of herself only that night because she'd believed...

'These days...' She cleared her throat. Nausea churned in her stomach, growing in intensity as the implications of what Santi was saying became clearer. All the hopes and dreams she'd allowed back into daylight...

One giant delusion when the lesson she'd learned at Santi's hands five years ago was not to indulge in delusion.

'These days we've spent as lovers,' she managed to continue, fighting with all her might not to let her anguish seep into her voice. 'You knew all along that once we left this yacht then that would be it for us?'

His face tightened into a grimace. 'At no point did we discuss a future together. Not once. You spoke of returning to Vienna only yesterday.'

'Yes, but...'

But that was before I realised I was in love with you, when I was still in denial, and even then I never thought we would be over the minute we disembarked. I never realised you saw me as only a quick fling.

'I said only a few hours ago that we needed to make the most of our last night together,' he said in the same clipped tone. 'How could you misinterpret that?'

'I thought you meant our last night together *here*. Like this. Before real life reclaimed us.'

'I'm sorry you misunderstood.'

'I'm good at that, aren't I?' An acrid taste filled her

mouth. 'But what did *you* think, Santi? That we'd skip off this yacht together and exchange one last tender kiss before, by telepathic mutual agreement, going our separate ways?'

His jaw clenched so tightly the bones threatened to poke out. His silence confirmed her fears. And roused her anger.

'Did you seriously think I would be happy with that?' She couldn't keep the bitterness from vibrating in her voice or her rising pitch. 'Did you see me in the future, gazing out of a window with a dreamy smile on my face as I remembered those wonderful days, just you and me, making love under the sun? Because let me put you right—all I'm going to remember is *this*.'

The moment he broke the heart she'd fought with all her might from giving back to him after he'd shattered it the first time.

No longer looking at her, he got to his feet. 'I'm sorry.'

His muscular legs disappeared into his trousers before he bent over to gather the rest of the clothes she'd stripped from him just a short time ago when she'd so briefly believed they had the foundations of something wonderful. It hurt to look. It hurt to breathe. It hurt to even speak.

But something nagged at her, tapping at her shell-shocked brain.

He closed the adjoining door behind him. For a long time she did nothing but stare at it.

How could Santi make love to her the way he had if all he'd thought of her as was some kind of short holiday fling? The way he'd looked at her. The way he'd touched her...

The nagging voice suddenly became clear.

She scrambled off the bed, grabbed an oversized T-shirt from a drawer and quickly shrugged her arms into it before barging her way into Santi's cabin.

CHAPTER THIRTEEN

'WHAT DID YOU mean about me deserving better?' she demanded.

Santi, who was sitting on the edge of the bed, lifted his head with a sinking heart. He'd known it couldn't end so easily.

'It was a figure of speech,' he lied with a heavy sigh. Everything felt heavy in him right down to the chain he wore around his neck, the last gift from his mother before her death.

Her eyes narrowed. 'Does this have something to do with my parents and what you think you owe them?'

'I don't think, I *know*.'

'You said something the other day about never betraying them. Is that what you see us as? A betrayal?'

He gritted his teeth. He could feel anger stirring in the combustible mix of emotions he was doing his damned best to keep a lid on. Where the anger was coming from he didn't know, but it was in him.

She folded her arms tightly across her chest. Bitterness ravaged her beautiful face. 'That's it, isn't it? It's nothing to do with us being in a bubble.' She stormed over to his unresponsive form and leaned forward to eyeball him with green-brown eyes wild with hurt and anger. 'Deny that you think you and I being together is a betrayal of them.'

Santi concentrated on breathing in and out through his nose, not prepared to open his mouth even for air, fearing that the rancid anger burning through him with all the other tumultuous emotions would burst free.

'Deny it!' she shouted, stabbing a finger into his chest. 'Look me in the eye and deny that you're throwing me away out of stupid, misplaced loyalty.'

He grabbed hold of her wrist before he even knew his hand had moved. '*Misplaced*?' he snarled in her face. 'Your *mamá* trusted me to bring you home to her. She trusted you would be safe with me, just as she and your *papá* trusted me all those years ago to keep you safe and out of the hands of men like me.'

'Men like *you*?'

'I put my teacher in hospital!' he roared. 'I battered him beyond recognition. I should have gone to prison for what I did to that man, so don't you dare accuse me of misplaced loyalty when *you*…' He drew the word out and let it hang.

At that moment he hated her, everything about her, but especially the way she could push his buttons and provoke him to anger and all the other emotions she elicited in him that no one else could.

'You have been pampered and cosseted and spoilt rotten your entire life, and what do you do the first time something doesn't go your way? You run. You ran away like a coward to Vienna because mean old Santi kicked you out of his bed. Where was your loyalty to your family then? To the business you'd promised to join? Your sister lost her partner when she was pregnant but even that wasn't enough to get selfish little Elsa back home where she belonged, not even after your father was killed, so don't you dare speak as if loyalty is something to be scorned when you don't know the meaning of the word.

'The only reason I wasn't locked up is because of your

father. Do you think for a minute he or your *mamá* would have done any of the things they did for me if they thought I would take advantage of their precious little Elsa? I have told you countless times that everything I have, I owe to them. Without them, I'd still be that poor, ill-mannered thug. I *am* still him, and knowing I've abused their trust *kills* me. I don't belong in your world and I never have. You think your father isn't turning in his grave at what I've done?'

Her face had turned ashen. Her eyes were wide, staring at him as if he were a stranger. A monster.

But there was no time for guilt to find its way into him for Elsa suddenly yanked her wrist out of his hold and rubbed it as if trying to rid herself of poison.

'The only thing he'll be turning in his grave at is what you're doing to me now,' she said icily. *'He knew.'*

Elsa watched the confusion play out on Santi's expressive face without an ounce of pleasure. She was too busy trying to keep herself upright.

It was his expressive face, she suddenly realised, that had been the cause of the nagging in her brain. His mouth had been telling her they were over but his eyes had said something very different.

She no longer cared. Santi had just vented his real feelings to her in the clearest and crispest manner. She couldn't misinterpret anything here. Any translator would come to the same conclusion—Santi *did* think she was a spoilt bitch. Something told her his words were going to haunt her for a long time to come but she wouldn't dissect them now, not in front of him, not when her heart felt like it was bleeding into her chest and one wrong word or thought could push her over the edge into a black pit of despair.

But she wouldn't run away. She wouldn't be a coward again. She wouldn't give him the satisfaction.

'Papá sat me down for a private chat when I was sixteen,' she informed him, enunciating every syllable of every word very clearly. 'He told me I was too young for you and that I should try not to make my feelings so obvious in case it made you uncomfortable and that all I had to do was wait a few more years.'

The shock that pulsed in his black eyes would have been funny if hate hadn't settled in her heart. She welcomed the hate and laughed anyway. Even to her own ears it sounded like a witch's cackle but she didn't care. Anything had to be better than the excruciating pain that had come close to paralysing her.

'He knew I was in love with you. He also knew some of what happened that night.'

His jaw dropped. His head shook sluggishly, left to right, right to left.

'He found me crying in my bedroom the night before I left for Vienna. All I told him was that I'd declared my feelings for you and that you'd turned me down—I was far too ashamed to tell him the rest of it. He said I had to be brave, and that life was long and people's feelings change. He said you and I had such a unique bond that all I had to do was hold tight and wait a little longer for you to see me as a woman.' She laughed again. 'Of course, I ignored his advice. After all, he didn't know the disgrace I'd made of myself.'

She forced her eyes to stay locked on Santi's. She would not flinch away from painful truths and memories. Not any more.

She'd never known him be so still. The man who zinged with energy was sitting on the edge of the bed like a statue. Only his eyes, fixed on her, moved.

'The only thing you owed him was to make something good of your life, and you've done that. You've earned your place in this world. Papá loved you like a son. Nothing, and I mean *nothing*, would have made him happier than for you to marry into the family just so he could have the pleasure of calling you that.' A sudden burst of nausea rose up her throat but she swallowed it back and forced herself to continue. 'And now I'm glad—*glad*,' she repeated venomously, 'that I ignored his advice. You're not fit to be called his son.'

He flinched. Good.

'You've strung me along for days. All this time you knew we had no future together and it's nothing to do with not wanting to abuse my parents' trust, it's because you're a bastard. How you have the nerve to say I need to let go of the past when you wear your past like a shield is beyond me but, still, I'm glad you've told me what you really think of me. Saves me wasting any more tears over you.' She folded her arms over her chest again and forced the muscles on her cheeks to form a smile before she fired her parting shot. 'As far as I'm concerned, you can go to hell.'

And then she stalked out of the cabin, slamming the adjoining door behind her.

Santi gave a sharp rap on the locked adjoining door. 'We need to go.'

There was no answer. He didn't expect one.

Elsa appeared on the deck two minutes after him, suitcase in hand, standing proud and elegant in a pretty cream fitted summer dress, long red hair flowing beneath her wide-brimmed sunhat. Her eyes were hidden behind her shades but he had no sense of her looking at him.

He attempted to take the suitcase from her but she stepped sharply out of his way and pulled it over the gangplank herself. She didn't bother to wait for him, setting off with her head held high.

The silent treatment continued in the back of the car as

they were driven to the airport and through the private security clearance. The first words she uttered were a pleasant, 'Thank you,' to his cabin crew when they showed her to her seat on his plane.

When, just after they'd taken off, his next attempt at conversation was rebuffed, he gritted his teeth and opened his laptop. If that's the way she wanted to play it, then fine. He had nothing to say to her anyway. He was just being polite.

He'd barely given his business a thought in the past week. The last time he'd checked in had been at his lodge by the lake in Austria. He couldn't believe how long ago that now felt.

Maybe if he'd given more thought to work during their trip and less to pleasure, he wouldn't have got into this mess, he thought grimly. Sleeping with Elsa had been a mistake, the consequences a mess of his own making.

Part of him wanted to apologise for the cruel things he'd said to her. The other part thought she could damn well join him in the hell she'd told him to go to. The biggest part of him thought he shouldn't think of her at all. So he didn't.

Mercifully, the flight to Valencia was short and he made a little headway with his work, deleting the three hundred and twenty-four emails he'd received since last logging on, before they landed on his private airfield.

He noted, with a sour taste in his mouth, that she was perfectly happy to let one of the cabin crew carry her suitcase off the plane.

Elsa couldn't help being impressed with the set-up at the airfield. This was the European hub of Santi's business. All around her stood ridiculously high warehouses the size of football fields and stacks of cargo containers. As she walked towards the waiting limousine, she took in every detail she could, right down to the scores of workers bustling around them. Anything rather than pay the slightest bit of attention to the man walking silently behind her.

She couldn't even look at him. She didn't dare. But she knew exactly where he was, about three steps behind and slightly to her right. Close but the furthest he'd ever been from her. Or was she the furthest she'd ever been from him?

Last night, after she'd locked the adjoining door, she'd surprised herself by falling asleep almost the moment her head had hit the pillow. She'd surprised herself even more when she'd woken that morning and found that she felt fine. It helped that she had something to focus on, namely returning to her family, and she increased the length of her strides to the limousine. She would be with her *mamá*, her sister and her nephew very soon. As long as she didn't look at Santi or engage in conversation with him, she was certain she would continue to feel fine. Empty inside but fine. No pain.

The driver got out of the limousine and tipped his hat in greeting.

She slid into the back. The driver shut the door. So intent was Elsa in not allowing any part of Santi into her vision that she didn't register the driver getting behind the wheel or putting the car into gear, didn't register anything until the car rolled forward and she realised they were leaving without him.

The panic injected itself straight into her heart without the slightest hint of warning.

'What are you doing?' she yelped into the microphone. 'Santi's not here.'

'Mr Rodriguez has made alternative arrangements,' the driver informed her.

Frantic, she pressed her face against the window, searching desperately for him, but all she could see was the back of his curly hair as he chatted with three of his staff.

He didn't look back.

He didn't see her drive away.

He didn't see the tears fall down her face or hear her muffled howl as the pain she'd boxed in punched its way free and doubled her over.

It took only ten days of living with her mother for Elsa to know she needed to leave. The last time she'd lived under the same roof as her mother she'd been a teenager. She'd made plenty of visits home over the years, often for weeks at a time, but those had always had an end date.

This was different. Elsa had moved back home. She'd resigned from her boring office job—now she really thought about it, she couldn't believe she'd kidded herself that she'd enjoyed it; she'd been bored out of her mind—and had all her possessions couriered over. In ten short days, she and her *mamá* had driven each other crazy. But in a good way. In the comfortable, familiar way they'd driven each other crazy when Elsa had been a teenager but without the added hormonal angst. She needed to leave, but was in no hurry to actually facilitate it. The terror she'd felt on The Trip, as she'd come to call it in her mind, that she could lose her family, was still there in diluted form. She suspected it would be in her for a long time to come.

If she could implant trackers in her mother and sister, she would. And they'd do the same for her. One day soon she would get a place of her own but it would be within a kilometre of them.

She was sitting in the orangery, reading through a pile of paperwork Marisa had given her to read on the family business human resources division, which Elsa was going to take over the running of when the current director retired in three months, when her sister walked in, holding baby Nikos in one arm and a collection of bulging bags hanging off the crook of the other.

'How was it?' Elsa asked. 'Did you find what you wanted?'

Marisa had been shopping for a dress for her engagement party and, despite babysitting offers from Elsa and their *mamá*, had taken baby Nikos with her. Elsa was proud of her—it was the first time Marisa had taken her son anywhere outside the estate. She'd lost her lover and her father within six months of each other. Her baby had been born without a father or a grandfather. Only now, with the cartel's destruction, could she breathe easily enough to take her son out of the estate and into the big wide world.

Elsa struggled with horrendous guilt. Her sister had been through hell and what had she been doing? Hiding and pining. She'd been monstrously selfish, and it didn't matter that Marisa had virtually ordered her back to Vienna after their father's funeral and the birth of her son. Elsa should have stayed. She should have been there for her in person and not just at the end of a phone.

She would make up for it, she vowed. She would be there for her family always and at all times, whether they liked it or not.

Marisa pulled a face. 'I don't know. I couldn't decide which one I liked the most so I bought them all. Will you have a look?'

'Sure.'

In Marisa's bedroom, Elsa settled on the bed with baby Nikos on her lap and waited patiently while her sister put the outfits on and paraded herself for Elsa's opinion.

When she emerged from her dressing room wearing the fifth outfit, a garish creation that made her beautiful sister look like an aubergine, baby Nikos threw his dummy at her.

Marisa burst into laughter and scooped him from Elsa's arms and held him up in the air above her head.

'You clever boy! Your aim is amazing! Your daddy would be proud. And you're right—it's a *horrible* dress. Mamá will take this one back.' Then she looked at Elsa and grinned. 'On second thoughts, maybe I should wear it. Raul will hate it.'

Elsa tried not to wince. With all the drama of the cartel's takedown, Marisa had reluctantly agreed to a short postponement, the engagement party now occurring in two days. Her enthusiasm for her future husband—which had always been tepid at best—had become downright cool in recent days.

She shuffled back to rest against the headboard and patted the space on the bed beside her. 'Come and sit with me.'

Marisa did better than that. Still wearing the horrible dress, she curled onto the bed, put baby Nikos on his back in the curve of her stomach, and laid her head on Elsa's lap, giving Elsa free reign on her corkscrews. Where Elsa's red hair was straight, Marisa's was the opposite, a mass of tight red curls that Elsa had loved playing with since they were tiny.

'Are you sure you want to go ahead with this?' she asked gently.

To give Marisa credit, she didn't pretend not to understand. 'I don't know any more. You joining the business changes things a little but I still need help and Nikos still needs a father.'

'Does it have to be Raul?'

'If not him, then who? Anyone else would want too much from me.'

Elsa understood. Marisa had been deeply in love with

baby Nikos's father. She twirled one of the curls in her fingers. 'I don't trust him.'

'Raul?'

'Yes. What protection did he offer when all this with the cartel was going down? Where was he? And where's he been since?'

Nowhere was the answer. Marisa's slime-ball of a fiancé's concern had extended to him dropping over for a quick coffee three days after the cartel had been taken down and taking her out for a meal. This was the man she intended to entrust her life and her son's life to.

Although Elsa took great pains not to think about the man she'd gone on The Trip with, she couldn't help comparing his actions to the slime-ball's. Not forgetting all the stuff he'd done before and during The Trip for her family, he'd since spent a morning on the estate going through their current security arrangements with their security team—luckily, she'd had prior warning and had been able to make herself scarce—and had had three brand-new cars delivered for each of the three Lopez women that would rival tanks for safety.

'I don't know what to do for the best,' Marisa whispered. 'It all seemed so simple before.'

Elsa picked up another curl. 'Go ahead with the engagement party if you must but don't rush into marrying him. If it doesn't feel right then don't do it, and it's not like baby Nikos doesn't have a male influence.'

That influence being Santi. Since being back home, she'd learned he'd taken to dropping in frequently armed with gifts for him, including the humungous fort-like climbing frame in the garden with a slide and swings and monkey bars he'd built himself. With any luck, baby Nikos would be big enough to use it sometime in the next decade.

'Why didn't you ask Santi to marry you?' The question was out before Elsa could stop it.

Marisa twisted a little so her face looked up at Elsa's. She reached up to gently pat Elsa's cheek. 'Because he belongs to you.'

CHAPTER FOURTEEN

SANTI PARKED IN a shaded area to the left of the Lopez villa and slowly crunched his way to the door. When, he wondered, would he approach this villa without apprehension knotting his guts?

Rosaria opened the door with a scowl that looked so much like the scowl her younger daughter gave when she was displeased that his heart came to a shuddering halt. Hands on hips, she scolded, 'Since when do you knock?'

He held his hands up and grinned. 'I'm sorry. I wasn't thinking.' Too apprehensive about the possibility of seeing Elsa.

'Apology accepted but don't do it again. This is your home, now come here and give me a kiss.'

After profuse kisses to the cheeks and a tight embrace was exchanged, Santi followed her inside.

How many times had she told him this was his home? How many times had Marco?

What had stopped him seeing it as such? Was it because he'd never been formally invited to live in it? Or because the cottage he'd shared with his mother had felt…

The answer suddenly punched him in the face. The *cottage* had been home for him. It was the place he and his mother had been at their happiest. It was filled with the furniture they'd shared, all their memories framed on the walls and surfaces.

The Lopezes hadn't kept him in the cottage because he wasn't good enough or safe enough to live under the same roof as their daughters but because they'd thought he'd want to stay as close to his mother as he could. They'd been thinking of *him*.

Once they'd settled in the living room that overlooked the garden and coffee had been poured, Rosaria's lips made the same swirling movement her daughter's made. 'You look tired.'

'Thank you.' A night out with Luis Casillas in Madrid was to blame for that, although their evening had come to an abrupt end when Luis's wife had called to tell him the youngest of their growing brood had a temperature. Luis had left so quickly it was like he'd channelled his inner roadrunner. Santi had carried on without him, downing shot after shot, trying not to envy his friend's beautiful family and his obvious devotion to them.

He'd woken with a thumping head and a mouth and throat that felt like sandpaper. He'd probably be sleeping it off still if Felipe hadn't called him.

Rosaria laughed. 'So, what brings you here today? You look like there's something you want to tell me.'

How well she read him. As well as his own mother had, and he felt a huge rush of affection for this wonderful woman who'd supported her husband in making the delinquent Santiago Rodriguez feel loved and worth something.

He would not think about the love he'd felt in the arms of her daughter. He couldn't. To remember it and to remember how he'd killed any chance of a future between them was to face the abyss.

He'd thrown it all away.

'Are you okay?'

He blinked. His mind had gone drifting. It kept doing that.

He cleared his throat. 'Felipe called with an update. I told him I'd pass the details to you.'

Before he could go any further, Rosaria rose gracefully from her seat. 'Let me call the girls. They'll want to hear it.'

She strode to the door and bellowed, 'Marisa. Elsa. Santi has news for us.'

Elsa's blood had stopped flowing. Cold white noise whooshed through her ears.

Marisa gave a smile so sad another strip tore off Elsa's heart. 'I'm your sister. Do you think I didn't notice you fall in love with him all those years ago?'

And then their mother's voice called out to them and her heart came to a shuddering halt and her fingers froze in the curl she'd been in the process of pulling apart.

'Marisa. Elsa. Santi has news for us.'

It felt like time had stood still. She might have sat frozen for ever if her sister hadn't gently covered her hand and pulled it away from her hair so she could sit up. 'Take Nikos for me. I need to take this monstrosity of a dress off.'

She obeyed but it was an automatic response. Holding her plump little nephew, who was currently trying to fit his entire fist into his mouth, she tried to get air into her lungs.

Was this what was meant by serendipity?

For ten days she'd gone out of her way to avoid talking about Santi and done her best to block him from her mind. Other than a quick debrief about The Trip, his name hadn't been mentioned by her family in front of her. Not until a few minutes ago.

He belongs to you.

'Are you coming?'

She lifted her head. Marisa had changed back into her jeans and blouse and was staring at her apprehensively.

Elsa passed baby Nikos to her then bit her lip. 'I can't,' she whispered.

Her sister's shoulders lifted before she sat on the edge of the bed and took Elsa's hand in the one not holding the baby. 'Yes, you can. Now dry your eyes. Don't let him see you like this.'

She hadn't felt the tears fall. So many times these past ten days she'd touched her face and been shocked to find it wet. So many times she'd passed a mirror and frightened herself at the redness in her eyes.

So many times she'd seen her *mamá* and her sister exchange looks.

No wonder his name hadn't been mentioned. If this was how she behaved when trying to go about day-to-day life, how would she act if they forced her to talk about him? There probably weren't enough tissues in the whole of Spain to cope.

Her whole 'I'm doing fine' act had been just that. An act. Another delusion.

But she would get better. With her family swathing her in love, how could she fail to? One day, she would wake and find the crushing pain a little less. She looked forward to that day.

Santi gripped his coffee cup tightly and worked on keeping his expression…expressionless.

He sensed Rosaria watching him closely as they made idle chatter while waiting for her daughters to appear. He suspected she knew that he and Elsa had been lovers.

If Elsa hadn't told him that Marco had not only known about her feelings for him but had approved of them, *welcomed* them, he'd be searching for Rosaria's icy disapproval. It's what he'd have been expecting. Because he was a fool. Too hung up on the mistakes of his past and humble beginnings to accept that everything the Lopez family had done for him had been because they loved him and not out of charitable endeavour. Too hung up on the past to accept he wasn't that rude, delinquent boy any more. He *had* earned his place in this world. He owed the Lopezes nothing but his love.

Elsa had loved him. That was something he accepted completely. In those short, sweet days at sea, she'd given herself to him like no one had ever done before. And he'd given himself to her.

In those short, sweet days he'd fallen totally, madly, irrevocably in love with her. It was a love he'd carried for her for five long years, just waiting for the right moment to spring free into the light.

And he'd thrown it away. He'd taken her love and discarded it like unwanted ocean debris.

He heard footsteps and murmured feminine voices approach the room. God, his hands were trembling. His heart thumped loudly.

Elsa followed Marisa into the room with a pounding heart and on legs that felt injected with water.

Santi rose from his seat and strode to them, placing a smacker of a kiss on baby Nikos's forehead and more refined kisses to Marisa's cheeks. Only politeness, Elsa was sure, made him extend the same courtesy to her, and she squeezed her eyes shut and lifted her chin as she braced herself for impact.

This was always going to happen, she reminded herself. Whatever her personal feelings, Santi was still family. He would always be a part of her life. She had to learn to live with that, especially now she was home for good.

The kiss, when it came, was over before it began, a quick brush of his beard against her cheek, the fleeting warmth of his breath against her skin and then done. He was already walking back to his seat before she'd opened her eyes, leaving his earthy, musky scent to torment her.

Her hands had gone clammy, and she wiped them on her jeans before sitting on the sofa next to her sister, pressing herself as close to her as she could. Thankfully, baby Nikos threw himself from his *mamá*'s arms to his aunt's, so she was able to stand him on her lap and hide behind him while Santi relayed his news.

Santi cleared his throat and tried to get his brain to unscramble.

Elsa wouldn't even look at him. He didn't blame her.

'Felipe has updated me on recent developments,' he began, then had to clear his throat again. He'd lost all the moisture in his mouth. 'Firstly, the cartel members who escaped have been arrested.'

Rosaria and Marisa both slumped and closed their eyes with relief. Only Elsa, too busy making faces at her nephew, gave no reaction.

'Secondly, the cartel members who came before the judge in New York have been denied bail.' That meant all of them would remain behind bars until their trials began. 'And thirdly…' he laced his fingers tightly, knowing the effect the next piece of information would have '…one of their members has struck a plea bargain. He's confessed to being part of the plot to kill Marco and named the other perpetrators directly involved.'

Silence followed this.

He couldn't stop his eyes turning to Elsa…

She was staring straight at him now. Tears fell silently like a stream down her face.

He hadn't thought there was any part of his heart left to break.

The thought of justice for their beloved father and husband was not something any of the Lopez women could celebrate. Not yet. They were too shell-shocked. None of them had believed the day would come. There had been days when Santi had struggled to believe it too.

He answered their many questions—well, Rosaria's and Marisa's; Elsa remained mute—over another coffee and then got to his feet. 'I need to go now,' he said before kissing Rosaria and Marisa goodbye.

Then he kissed Nikos and fixed his gaze on the still seated Elsa. 'Can I have a private word, please? It won't take long.'

'I'll take Nikos,' Marisa said, pulling him off her sister's lap before Elsa could refuse. 'Come on, Mamá. Let's give them some privacy.'

Elsa was trapped with him before her stunned brain had time to know what was happening. She arranged her face into her best attempt at nonchalance, crossed her legs and lifted her head, striking the pose her *mamá* had used when she'd demanded to know why Elsa's school report was littered with comments like 'Could try harder'.

Santi was on his feet. He rammed his hands in his pockets as he paced the room. If she didn't know better, she would think he was nervous.

'I owe you an apology,' he said heavily, coming to a stop in front of her.

She gave no reaction. She couldn't. Suddenly, she felt paralysed.

An apology was the last thing she'd expected.

'What I said to you that night in Mallorca...' Santi swallowed. What he had to say should have been said ten days ago. Every day he'd woken to darkness. Every day his first thought had been of Elsa, and the last thought, and every waking thought in between. 'It was unforgivable. I make no excuses. I was wrong to call you selfish. Everything I said was wrong. I lashed out. I think…' He grimaced. 'I think I lashed out the way I did because I wanted you to hate me. The pain I could see I was putting you through—it cut through me. Do you understand?'

She didn't answer. There wasn't a flicker of expression on her face.

'I couldn't bear to see it. Your pain. When you bleed, I bleed. When you hurt, I hurt.'

Still no expression.

'I'd spent so many years telling myself I wasn't good enough for you that I didn't dare imagine a future with you. I thought I had to end things but inside I was fighting it—my *heart* was fighting it. I thought it was wrong to feel the way I do about you but the only thing that was wrong was me.'

Her eyes closed. A solitary tear trickled down her cheek.

A burning sensation he'd not felt since the death of his mother stung behind his eyes. He pinched the bridge of his nose and took some deep breaths in a futile attempt to counter it. 'I'm sorry I hurt you, *chiquita*. If I could take those cruel words back, I would. You are…' He broke away with a muttered curse and impatiently wiped away dampness around his eyes with his thumbs.

'You are the most important person in my life. You have been for a very long time. I didn't know it was possible to love someone as much as I love you or how deeply I would feel it. It's like you're a part of me. The biggest part of me. And I sure as hell didn't know it was possible to miss someone as much as I miss you. Every day without you hurts a little more. What you said about us taking to the road or seas and following our noses… I can't tell you how badly

I wish I'd reacted differently to that because, *chiquita*, I would follow you anywhere.'

The slow blink of her eyes told him he'd said too much. It was the only movement she'd made the whole time he'd been talking.

Ramming his hands back into his pockets, he attempted a smile and failed. 'I should go.'

She blinked again.

He left the room and strode to the front door, staring straight ahead so he didn't have to acknowledge the two women and small child hovering close by. Down the steps and across the gravel he pounded, not stopping until the door to his car was open and he was secure inside.

Only then did he put his face in his hands and weep for the first time since his mother had died.

'Elsa?'

She snapped her eyes open to the concerned faces of her *mamá* and her sister.

Marisa crouched in front of her. 'What did he say?'

She shook her head slowly. 'He… He… *Loves* me.'

It had finally penetrated her stupefied brain.

Santi loved her.

It hadn't been a delusion.

He loved her.

She jumped to her feet so quickly she banged into Marisa and sent her sprawling onto her bottom.

'Sorry,' she cried over her shoulder, already halfway out of the living room and racing towards the front door.

The sun shone so brightly that the first touch of it blinded her. Only her absolute determination to get to Santi stopped her from stumbling.

Her heart crashed to a stop. His car was reversing out from its spot beneath the cherry tree and then, with her next breath, was put into gear and accelerating down the driveway.

She screamed his name at the top of her lungs and then, even though she knew it was hopeless, began to run after him.

As she pushed herself faster than she'd ever run before, her mind flew over the unrelenting misery of the past ten days. She'd been like a wounded bird that had lost its song but still tried to sing.

She'd been surrounded by the love of her family but the nights had been the loneliest of her life.

His car had almost disappeared. At any moment he would reach the electric gates. She couldn't reach him in time. In desperation, she waved her arms in the air, screaming his name over and over.

Santi slowed for the electric gates. As they opened with the speed of a snail on Valium, he wiped his eyes again.

The gap in the gates was almost wide enough to get through, just a few more seconds…

What was that?

Something had caught his attention. He looked around him then suddenly saw it in his rear-view mirror. The figure in the middle of the drive waving their arms and…

Without a moment's thought, he stuck the car in reverse.

Elsa could hardly see through the tears. Santi's car was just a black blob in the distance. Her thighs were screaming at her, her voice was gone and there was a stitch forming in her belly. She didn't stop, still ploughing forward, still waving, still…

The shape of the car changed. It became less of a blur, like it was closing on her…

Seconds later, barely two metres in front of her, it screeched to a stop, the driver's door flew open and Santi got out.

She didn't hesitate. She threw herself at him. Literally. She jumped into his arms without any fear that he wouldn't catch her. Her legs wrapped around his waist, her arms around his neck, his arms wrapped around her and their mouths found each other for a kiss of such passionate ferocity that if she'd had any lingering doubt it would have dissolved.

But she had no doubts. None at all.

She pulled her mouth away so she could gaze into the black eyes shining with pure, heartfelt emotion. 'I love you, Santiago Rodriguez. I've always loved you. I would follow you anywhere.'

The look on his face at this was something Elsa would remember for the rest of her life.

It was the moment their stars finally aligned and they both knew they would spend the rest of their lives together.

EPILOGUE

SANTI LIT THE match and held it to the kindling, dropping it when the small flames began to lick. He added some larger kindling and only when he was satisfied it had a good hold did he add the logs. Then he stepped back, placed the high fireguard around it and considered it with satisfaction.

There was something wonderfully primal about making a fire, he decided, and when his wife joined him in the lodge's snug wearing only a white towelling robe, hair damp from her bath, he felt something even more primal take root. Three years of marriage and his desire for her hadn't abated by an inch.

Snow fell heavily outside. Knowing how much Elsa loved to watch it, he'd kept the curtains open. He imagined Marisa and Rosaria, both retired to their rooms upstairs, enjoying the same magical scene.

The mulled wine was keeping warm, and he poured them both a cup, then stretched out beside her on the sofa.

'I'm afraid you'll have to drink this for me,' Elsa said, handing her cup back to him with a small knowing smile.

For a moment he was disconcerted. His beautiful wife was hardly a heavy drinker but only the other week, when they'd reached the tail end of their third voyage around the Caribbean on their yacht, she'd been happily sharing exotic cocktails with him…providing they had no rum in them, of course.

And then the penny dropped.

After three years of selfish togetherness, they'd finally decided a month ago that they were ready to create a family.

He twisted to look more closely at her face. His beautiful wife was glowing.

'You're not?' he breathed. How could it be possible? He'd never imagined it would happen so quickly.

She beamed. 'I am. Merry Christmas.'

He shook his head. He was going to be a father…?

He was going to be a father!

He made love to his wife in front of the log fire thinking he'd never imagined such happiness could exist.

* * * * *

HER DEAL
WITH THE
GREEK DEVIL

CAITLIN CREWS

CHAPTER ONE

CONSTANTINE SKALAS HAD waited a long, long time for this day. What had started as a young man's rash promise had become a plot. Then a plan. Today that plan had finally borne its intended fruit.

He intended to savor it.

And as a man who had dedicated a large portion of his decidedly debaucherous adult life to relishing all the many pleasures life had in store, he knew precisely how best to go about it.

There were any number of places he could have met the object of all his many plans. He was a Skalas, one of two owners of the sprawling, multinational Skalas & Sons. His father had once been the richest man alive, but Constantine and his brother, Balthazar, had doubled his wealth within the first year of their ownership. He had properties literally everywhere, homes and rentals and hotels, and could have chosen any one of them for today's long-awaited meeting.

Naturally, he'd chosen the one calculated to stick the knife in, and he hoped, give it a little twist for good measure. It was an estate in the quiet part of Skiathos, an island off the coast of Thessaly, Greece. Skiathos, where far too many bright young things flocked for the energetic nightlife in Skiathos Town, though Constantine had not availed himself of the local amenities, or talent, in longer than he cared to recall. And Skiathos was also where, once upon a time, he had been force-fed his father's new and unacceptable second wife and worse, had been required to contend with an awkward stepsister he had never warmed to in the slightest.

Though that was perhaps understating the case.

He had despised his stepmother. He had felt only slightly less opposed to his stepsister, who might not have been at fault for her mother's ambitious marriage—but she hadn't done anything to oppose it, either. Those feelings had not dimmed over time. His father might have thought better of his second marriage and summarily ended it, as he had been wont to do with his customary brutality, but Constantine could hold a grudge until the end of time.

And did. Happily.

He settled back in the chair behind the desk where the late and wholly unlamented Demetrius Skalas, his father, had once conducted his business when he'd called this house his primary home. It had been but a few years of madness before Demetrius had rid himself of the appalling British housekeeper, Isabel, and her hopeless daughter that he'd acquired for reasons unclear. As far as Constantine could tell, Demetrius had only married Isabel in the first place to really hammer home the fact he was moving on from his elegant and fragile first wife. The wife he'd crushed, then discarded, then mocked as she'd cycled deep into despair.

The wife who happened to be Constantine's mother, that was.

But Constantine was not going to think about his mother today, or he would lose his cool. And his quarry did not deserve his temper. She did not deserve to see anything but his vengeance.

He studied his father's desk as he sat there. Like all the things Demetrius had used as props to bolster his inflated sense of himself, the desk was a monstrosity. Constantine had entirely too many memories of being forced to stand on the other side of this very desk during those years, his eyes on his father if he valued his hide, while he gave a twenty-year-old's surly accounting of what he'd done with his monthly allowance. A tedious undertaking when he already knew it would lead to more of his father's brand of consequences. And all the while the wall of windows down one side—all of which opened up as doors to the terrace no one was permitted to use without Demetrius's never-proffered permission—let in the pine-covered cliffs. Unusual for Greek islands, as the tourists liked to caterwaul, but pine trees they were and they rose above the private cove the house sat over like the king Demetrius had imagined he was. And more, the great Aegean beyond beckoned, all while Constantine had been required to stand still and pretend penitence.

It had been torture, in other words.

A torture he intended to visit upon dear stepsister,

Molly, who his staff down at the gate to the estate had informed him had just arrived.

The waiting was exquisite.

After all these years, after all his plotting, after creating the perfect disguise for his true intentions and living it in full view of the world, it was time.

If he was capable of such things, he might have considered himself positively gleeful.

Constantine leaned back in the huge leather chair, itself a monument to a certain kind of overt masculinity. His father's kind, all bluster and bark, but unlike some of his toxic ilk, with a deadly bite beneath.

His father had died a few years back, and unlike Constantine's older brother, Balthazar, who had always splayed himself wide open with an unnecessary sense of responsibility, Constantine did not miss him. Perish the thought. The world was a far better place without Demetrius Skalas. His sons, in particular, were incalculably better off without him.

Not to mention, the old man's absence meant Constantine had finally been able to put the plan closest to his blackened heart into action.

He waited, smiling to himself when he heard the click of very high heels along the hallway floors that led to this study. He had not known which version of his stepsister to expect. But the heels were like a premonition, and then, in the next moment, she appeared.

She stopped in the doorway and regarded him.

Constantine gazed right back, aware of a certain electrical charge that seemed to fill the space between them.

No longer awkward or embarrassing, or anything like gawky, little Molly Payne, the housekeeper's daughter had transformed herself. She stood before him, framed by the doorway, and stared at him as if she stood atop some kind of catwalk and he was at her feet. It was adorable, truly. And he had seen her blond hair in a number of different styles, but today she had gone for big and lustrous curls, like a cat puffing itself up to make itself seem bigger in the face of a predator.

Poor little kitty, he thought to himself, darkly. *Your tricks and claws will not help you here.*

Her eyes were a stunning, arctic blue, and today she'd expertly applied the kind of cosmetics that took hours to achieve a barely there look, so that she looked effortlessly sultry, the cold color of those eyes honed to a laser point. Her pout was enough to raze cities to the ground, and that wasn't getting to her magnificent figure that had been splashed across every magazine cover in existence, then back again.

For awkward little Molly Payne had not had the good manners to fade off into obscurity when her mother's reprehensible marriage to Constantine's father had ended. He had imagined she would lead a perfectly unobjectionable porridge sort of life, perhaps away in one of those sad, lesser British cities, where everything was forever gray and depressed. Like she had been.

But no such luck. For instead, his stepsister had gone ahead and had the temerity to become universally, stratospherically famous.

"If it isn't the eponymous *Magda*," Constantine drawled, eventually, using her laughable professional name.

"Hello, Constantine," she replied.

Like all beautiful women whose looks were widely held to be objective fact, not subject to individual opinion, every inch of her was weaponized. Including that voice. It struck him like his favorite spirit, METAXA, smooth and complex before rolling on into a deeper, hotter intensity.

He had expected to feel the attraction that hammered him then, but it was far worse now that she was in this room than it usually was when he was confronted with her picture. Everywhere.

"I thought you would enjoy this trip down memory lane with me," he said, lounging back in the chair. His father had been a rigid man, his only excesses brutal. Constantine, by contrast, had created for himself the most dissipated, dissolute alter ego possible. It had started when he was young. He had learned, as his brother never had, that there was no point in attempting to live up to a madman's expectations. For every time a certain level was achieved, their father made up seven more. No one could possibly scale those heights.

Constantine had stopped trying. Then and now, he took great pleasure in polluting his father's legacy with his own brand of what he liked to call his libertine approach to rakishness.

The tabloids used other words. He delighted in all of them.

"Is that what this is?" Molly asked. For he refused

to think of her as *Magda*. "Memory lane? Funny, that. This particular road to hell always seemed remarkably unpaved to me."

"How droll. You've become so spiky over the years."

She did not shift from where she stood, shown to perfection in the doorway to the study. And Constantine had taken on a deep, personal study of the rise of Magda, a modern supermodel in a time when supermodels were widely held to be a thing of the past. He knew she was fully aware that the sun streamed in from without, lighting her beautifully, and dancing all over the exquisitely skintight gown she wore in a deliberately overbright shade of gold. The sunlight made her glow like an angelic host. He knew that she was well aware of the position in which she stood, designed to call attention to the impeccable lines of her body that left fashion designers beside themselves as they draped their latest creations all over her frame. Here, in this study, she simply looked magnificent. And untouchable.

Too bad for her that he had other ideas.

"Everyone grows up, Constantine," she replied. She considered. "Or, I should say, almost everyone."

"Was that a dig?" He made a tsking sound. "That is no way to convince me to be merciful, Molly. You must know that."

"I would prefer it if you called me Magda."

He grinned, enjoying himself immensely. "I am certain that you would. But I think I will stick with Molly all the same. Just to remind ourselves who and what we are."

Fascinated, he watched as a storm moved through that cool blue gaze of hers before she shuttered her gaze.

And then he waited, letting the silence spill out between them. Until, to his very great pleasure, she stopped holding that commanding position in the doorway and took a step farther into the room.

Betraying herself, he thought.

"I know you know why I'm here," she said, sounding far more brisk, then. "I suppose we might as well get down to business."

"Refresh my memory," he invited her.

"I see that we're going to play games. Lovely."

He remembered the sixteen-year-old who had foolishly confided in him and saw no trace of her on this woman's face. But that was just as well. Constantine did not traffic in guilt or shame, so he would never use those words to describe how he felt when he thought of that time. And yet sometimes it haunted him, all the same.

"Is that really necessary?" she asked.

"You will know what is necessary and what is unnecessary," he assured her. "Because I will tell you." He inclined his head, then waved a lazy hand. "For now, by all means, tell me your sad tale of woe, Molly."

"I do not wish to bore you." Her cool eyes glittered, like shards of ice, and he suspected she was thinking of a great many things she would like to do to him, none of them boring. All of them violent. "I know you remember my mother."

"As it happens, I have known a great number of grasping, petulant, jumped-up whores in my life," Constantine drawled, each word deliberate. Each word its own sharp blade. "And yet, you are correct, your mother managed to distinguish herself."

A faint splash of color stained Molly's cheeks. Her eyes blazed with fury. And he had the sudden, near uncontrollable urge to rise from his chair, throw himself across the room, and get his hands and his mouth into all of that fire.

But too soon, she reined herself in, iced over, and regarded him coolly once again.

Interesting, he thought. He would have to make a note of how she protected herself with that aloofness. And set it ablaze.

"I am not here to debate my mother's faults with you, or anyone," she said crisply.

"And yet I feel certain that should I wish to discuss your mother's many faults and terrible decisions, I will. Entirely as I please. With or without your permission. Molly."

She took a long, visible breath, but did not object. Because she was not a stupid woman, Constantine knew. And she was not in the dark as to why she was here, any more than he was.

"My mother has always fancied herself a businesswoman of sorts," Molly said, her voice ever so slightly strained. She moved further into the study that he knew she hadn't seen since she was still a teenager. It was unchanged. He watched with interest as she took that in, her gaze moving with arctic precision from the ponderous choice of art on the walls to the crystal decanter on the sideboard, which was the last in a long line of similar decanters his father had shattered against the wall.

Such pleasant memories. "This is not a business in the sense of Skalas & Sons, of course. What is? But whenever she found herself with some money—"

"Such as her divorce settlement," Constantine interjected silkily. "Three million euros to silently go away when she should have done so on her own, had she the faintest shred of shame."

Molly ignored that. He hoped it was hard. "She did some investing, here and there. And she began to imagine herself something of a hotel mogul."

"Surely that would be better termed a delusion and used to secure medical attention." Constantine laughed when Molly's frigid gaze swept to him. "I have many hotels. In my personal portfolio, not underneath the Skalas & Sons umbrella. I hardly think a few poorly chosen boutique options scattered about the globe make a mogul. But to each her own."

"Funny you should mention those few boutique hotels," Molly said softly, her gaze on him. "Because, wouldn't you know it, she's completely overextended herself and faces total financial ruin, because someone leveraged them right out from under her."

"What a sad story this is," Constantine murmured. "How lucky she must be that she has an internationally famous daughter who she can lean upon for support in such troubled times. Troubled times she brought upon herself, but I digress."

"I hate to continually tell you things you already know," Molly said, her voice acidic. She picked up a photograph from one of the incidental tables. A seemingly happy family shot until one looked closer and saw the look of worry on young Balthazar's face, the mutiny on Constantine's, and their father's grim expression that promised retribution.

If he recalled correctly, that time, Demetrius had beaten them both.

Ah, the manifold joys of family, Constantine thought dryly.

"But I know so little," he said. "Ask anyone."

Molly turned back to him then, and her gaze was a little too clever for his liking. Only because clever women boded ill, always. It was his own personal curse that he preferred them.

Not that his usual choice of paramour would make that clear.

His typical selections bored him, but they were beautiful. And the more vacant the woman on his arm, the more it was assumed that he, too, must also be shallow to his very core no matter how good he was at making money. He encouraged it.

Better that no one should ever see him coming.

"Since she left England to marry your father, my mother has always had one scheme or another," Molly told him. "Before these hotels, it was her own fashion line. Before the fashion line, she fell for at least three different scams."

He affected a vaguely sympathetic expression. "Con men abound."

"I used to think that she just had spectacularly bad luck," she agreed. She even smiled, though it was a cold curve of her famous lips. "Recent events have made it clear to me that no, she has one, very powerful enemy. And has always had this enemy."

Molly glared at him. Constantine grinned.

"That sounds ghastly," he said. "What do you suppose she might have done to gain such an enemy, if one exists?"

"Since you asked," Molly said, folding her arms before her, "she had the terrible misfortune of believing a horrible man when he claimed to be in love with her. Only in the end, lo and behold, it turned out he was not. But she only discovered that after a disastrous marriage that came complete with two unpleasant stepsons who made her life a living hell."

"Surely her choice of husband was the living hell she chose because it came alongside so much money," Constantine replied, his tone as smooth as it was dark. "These bargains are always so tawdry, are they not? But tell me, what sort of woman blames her stepchildren for her venal little choices?"

"Oh, you mistake me." Molly sounded as dark as he did, though three times as cold. And her gaze should have frozen him solid. "She doesn't blame anyone. *She* doesn't look back. But I do."

Constantine wanted to share his thoughts on the dreadful Isabel, Molly's mother, who should never have been permitted to set foot on Skalas property. Much less take up residence here. When all she should ever have been to Demetrius was a night's amusement. Possibly two. Who *married* the housekeeper after a weekend at a business acquaintance's old pile in the English countryside? Who then paraded about with a housekeeper on his arm?

Only Demetrius.

"Blame is such a funny thing, is it not?" he asked. "Oddly enough, I, too, have those I blame for the misfortunes that have befallen both me and my family. For my part, I find that what goes well with blame is power. For one is whining. The other is winning. And, Molly, you should know by now that I always, always win."

"I'm tired of playing this game," she replied, her gaze like ice. "You know that my mother is near enough to ruined and I'm on the verge of bankruptcy. You know it because you did it."

"I have had no interaction with you whatsoever since you were a depressed teenager," Constantine said mildly. "I suspect you are well aware that we've been at the same parties, from time to time, yet we somehow managed never to speak. How could I possibly be responsible for your inability to handle your finances?"

"She's my mother, Constantine." That was the first crack. The first hint of her emotions, and it was all he'd hoped for, a flash of deep, dark blue and that catch in her throat. "What am I supposed to do? Throw her out into the streets?"

He shrugged. "It sounds like that would be a good start if, as you say, she has had such…terrible luck."

Molly looked down for a moment and he thought he saw the faintest hint of a fine tremor move through her. Though it was gone so quickly, he couldn't be sure. And he didn't want to believe she was reacting quite in that way. Constantine only wanted her to feel the things he wanted her to feel. Not fall beneath the weight of them all. Where would be the fun in that?

For him, that was.

"I assume that this is what you wanted," she said after a moment, no sign of cracks or temper visible on her perfect face. "You left just enough clues. When I put the pieces together, it all made a kind of sick, strange sense. This whole playboy act of yours is just that. An act. You spend a lot of time and energy pretending a flashy car can turn your head and that you're as vapid as the interchangeable women you squire about. When the truth is, you're exactly as much of a shark as your brother, you just hide it. I'm sure you have your own, twisted reasons, as ever. I suppose it was silly of me to imagine that after making sure my teenage years were as hideous as possible, you would keep right on going."

"I think you'll find that teenage years, as a rule, are hideous for all." He smiled. "Even me. Though I am interested that both you and your mother seem to have no shortage of people to blame for your misfortunes. Anyone and everyone except yourselves, is that it?"

Again, a splash of color on her porcelain cheeks, but that was all that betrayed the emotions inside her. He was more fascinated than was wise, he knew that. But knowing it didn't change it any.

Molly regarded him as if he was the devil. It pleased him. "You set a trap and my mother walked right into it, over and over. Congratulations. Now why don't you tell me what it is you really want?"

So many things in life did not live up to expectations, Constantine knew. Most things deemed decadent, for example. The so-called charms of the yachting set who cluttered up the Mediterranean coastlines and bored him silly. Too many Michelin-starred restaurants, forever attempting to outwit their diners instead of simply feeding them. The notion that because a woman was beautiful to look at, she would be any good in bed.

But this. This was the exception that proved the truth.

For this was even better than he had imagined it— and he had imagined it in a thousand different variations, year after year.

"Why, I thought what I wanted was obvious," Constantine said, milking the moment for all it was worth.

Because he had waited all this time. Because his mother lay senseless in a long-term care facility, dead in all but name thanks to what had been done to her. Balthazar had handled the architect of their mother's downfall, the man who had seduced her then discarded her, then laughed when their father had done the same. Constantine was glad his brother had taken care of that egregious loose end. But for his part, he had never forgiven the woman who had truly imagined she could walk in and take their mother's place.

"Spell it out for me," Molly urged him. "I know you can't want my money, because you have far too much of your own. And anyway, all of my money is gone. Because someone had to take care of my mother's debts when you ruined her again and again—but I think you already know that. So what is it?"

"I told you when you called me, did I not? I do hate to repeat myself."

"In the very brief, *very* obnoxious phone call it took

you three weeks to return, you told me that there was a possibility my mother could reclaim her properties and retain her good name, such as it was." Her blue eyes glinted. "Your words, obviously. I'm betting it will involve intense humiliation for all the world to see, that being your specialty. Just tell me the shape of it."

"Intensity and humiliation are all a question of degrees," Constantine mused. Philosophically. "And perspective, do you not think? It should be obvious what I want, Molly." He smiled. "It is the one thing I am truly known for."

And he had the great pleasure of watching her face go slack with shock. He saw, very clearly and distinctly, the difference between Molly and Magda, because she lost completely that harder shell he supposed she must have developed over the years. And in its place was the face of a girl he half remembered, wide blue eyes, a sulky mouth, and forever where she didn't belong.

"You can't mean…"

"But I do," he told her, his voice low and deliberate. Revenge served cold, and it made him hot, everywhere. "I want you, Molly. Beneath me. And above me. And in all other ways. Naked, begging, and most of all, completely mine to do with what I wish, for as long as I wish, until your mother's debt is paid. In full."

She actually gaped at him. His smile widened.

"Did I not tell you it was a simple thing?" he asked silkily. "You should know this above all else, Molly. I am nothing if not a man of my word."

CHAPTER TWO

MOLLY PAYNE WANTED to die.

A not unusual occurrence in this man's presence. Or in the presence of any member of the vile Skalas family, for that matter, though in the years since her mother's escape from their clutches she had tried to block out her reaction to actually *standing before* one of them.

She'd obviously grown soft over the past decade.

Because this was much, much worse than her memories.

As far as Molly was concerned, the Skalas family was a scourge upon the earth. A very rich, very powerful scourge. When she'd heard the news that cruel old Demetrius had died, though she did not make a habit of thinking ill of the dead under normal circumstances, Molly and her mother had gone out to a lovely meal in London to celebrate. That mean old bastard deserved a few toasts to speed him along to hell, where he belonged.

But Constantine was a special case.

He had always been the seemingly nice one. Where his father was cruel and his older brother, Balthazar, distant and disapproving, Constantine had been friendly.

He had encouraged Molly, ungainly and terribly shy, to open up to him about what it was like to be the daughter of a woman like her mother. And she had told him, to her eternal shame. She had spent sixteen years filled with that desperate, helpless love on the one hand, yet cringing all the time at each and every obvious indication that Isabel Payne would do almost anything if she thought it would serve her ambition.

And the friendlier he was to her, the more Molly had told him things she should have kept to herself. Sacred, secret things she had no business sharing with anyone or anything but her own diary.

Things Constantine had gone right ahead and shared with the tabloids, and yet she had been so overawed by him that it had taken the better part of those terrible two years to fully accept that, yes, she was the source of all those gossipy stories about her mother's ghastly relationship with Demetrius Skalas. *Isabel's True Face Revealed*, and so on.

That was bad enough. Hideous, in fact. But such was his bitter genius that it had taken her many more years to realize that what he'd done to *her* was far more insidious than merely telling her secrets to a tabloid. Molly had come away from her mother's unhappy, if profitable, marriage to Demetrius Skalas convinced that she was a plodding, embarrassing bit of blancmange, destined for a quiet life of secretarial work, meals from a greasy local chippie with too much wine from the off-license, and the spiraling claws of despair. Had she not been discovered by a modeling agent on the Tube, of all the absurd stories she would have said were fake if it hadn't happened to her, she imagined that was precisely the life she would be living right this moment. As if those two short years in the Greek sun were a beautiful nightmare she'd had once, long ago while she lived out an unremarkable existence somewhere far away from the concerns of the Skalas family.

She'd come to realize that he'd wanted that to be her fate.

Her curse was that she'd spent even longer than that trying to justify the things he'd said and the way he'd said them to relieve him of any responsibility. It was her fault, clearly. She should have made it more clear that the things she'd told him were private. She had misread him, or misheard him, or taken it all in wrong because—as everyone had reminded her all the time in those days—she was so *sensitive*.

But no. Over the last few years, as Molly had begun to understand that her mother, for all her faults, could not possibly be *quite this* unlucky, a different picture of Constantine Skalas had emerged.

Now she knew the truth. The nicest, most approachable Skalas brother was, in fact, the devil.

The tragedy was that, like Lucifer himself—not called Morning Star because he was deformed or horrible—Constantine was beautiful. Ridiculously, absurdly beautiful.

And he knew it.

Everything about him was dark and rich and seductive. Dark brown hair that glinted gold in the Greek sun and always looked as if fingers not his own had moments before raked through it. His eyes were heavy-

lidded and suggestive, as impossibly dark and yet inviting as the bitter coffee he preferred. And he used his
unfair cheekbones to their full effect, always. He had
a generous, sensual mouth that was forever curving
with a hint of wickedness. Or grinning widely without a care. Or more often still, laughing lazily at all
the women who flailed about at his feet, all the lovers who trailed behind him weeping and wailing and
clinging to his trouser cuff, and the whole of the great
and glorious world that loved him all the more when
he treated everything and everyone in it as his.

As one of the Skalas brothers and thus one of the
wealthiest men alive, the truth was that much of the
world really was.

And for a man who never seemed to do anything
but lounge about, languid and bedroom-eyed, Constantine was obnoxiously fit. He was unnecessarily tall and
rangy, with long, lean muscles that he was forever showing off. Glistening his way across exclusive seaside resorts, shedding his shirt to crash a game of footie in
the park, leaping in and out of the odd plane yet living,
propping up beautiful women on his black-tied arm,
and always infusing all of his nearly overwhelming
sexual energy with more than a hint of lurking danger.

That was just the grainy pictures in the magazines.
Constantine in person was…worse. He had been shockingly attractive when they were younger, something
Molly had tried to tell herself had been something she'd
made up because she'd been such a young and foolish
sixteen. But there had been nothing wrong with her
eyes back then. He had been feral and gorgeous, al-

ways. And now, all of those relatively softer edges and blurred angles had disappeared entirely.

Leaving him relentlessly, ruthlessly, inarguably masculine. Every last inch honed to brutal, sensual effect.

And that was not the only tragedy.

Molly's deep and abiding shame was that even now, after all she knew about Constantine Skalas and all he'd done—and had yet to do to her, personally—she still had only to think about him and she felt everything inside her…melt.

She was pathetic.

Especially because, despite everything, she had not been adequately prepared for the reality of seeing him in his considerably mouthwatering flesh today. What was *wrong* with her? Maybe he'd been right all along when he'd suggested to the impressionable girl she'd been that she was simply wired wrong.

"Struck dumb in the face of my generosity?" he asked, sounding lazy and amused, as always. "I do not blame you. Being my mistress is a privilege, I grant you. Even under these vulgar circumstances, it would, naturally, constitute quite an elevation for you."

"Your mistress," Molly repeated.

Her mind couldn't take that on, much less the other insults packed into his words. She couldn't actually let herself visualize what *being his mistress* entailed because it was too much. It was an explosion of golden limbs and heat and his mouth…

Stop it, she ordered herself. *Dear God.*

And though it hurt, physically, she pulled herself together. Or tried. "Right. You want a shag. If I was paid for every man who wanted the same, I wouldn't need to come crawling to you because I'd be far, far richer than you'll ever be. But by all means, Constantine. If you're that basic and boring, I'm perfectly happy to lie back and think of England on my mother's behalf."

She didn't know why she'd said that. Molly had no desire whatsoever to trade her body for anything, particularly not when she already used it as a product—and as such, was keenly aware of the kind of slippery slope divorcing her body from her emotions could be. She was fully aware that there was a cottage industry of those who claimed to have had passionate affairs with her, and she liked that. The more people gossiped about her, telling each other and everyone else lies about all the scandalous things she was up to in her spare time, the less likely anyone was to notice that she did very few scandalous things at all.

But she also knew, because she was a grown woman who lived in the real world, that few things irritated men more than being laughed at. Obliquely or otherwise.

So she was totally unprepared for Constantine to throw back his glorious head and laugh himself.

And laugh. And laugh some more.

"Did I say something amusing?" she asked when he finally stopped. A bit peevishly, she could admit.

And then watched, her mouth dry, as Constantine rose in all his considerable glory from behind that dreadful desk.

She had nothing but terrible memories of this place. Which was no doubt precisely why Constantine, who had more houses than he had race cars and he had a fleet or five of those, had chosen this one for their meeting. It was likely purely for her benefit, so she could truly connect with the unutterably stupid teenager she'd been when she'd lived here. How she'd crept in and out of these deceptively welcoming rooms, painted in bright Mediterranean colors that made the sea and sun seem the brighter, trembling like a fawn every time she drew notice from anyone. Staff and Skalas alike.

This particular room had been where Demetrius had liked to exercise the worst of his power—and he'd had entirely too much power. He had loved nothing more than calling Molly in to stand before him, her heart pounding in her throat and her stomach in knots, while he shared with her exactly how embarrassing she'd been at whatever dinner had occurred the night before. How gauche and dull, when he'd expected so much more of her.

Constantine unfurling his magnificence before her while he stood in the very same spot where his father had stood before him was like…cognitive dissonance. Everything that had happened here had been dark. Even though she knew it had been typical Greek weather during those years, she always remembered it as if it had been dark and dreary, because inside her, it had. And then there was Constantine, who somehow seemed to blaze with a golden light when he should not have. Especially not now. But it had always been the same. He had all that Greek sunshine bottled up within him and everywhere he went, it was as if he lit up the world with every step he took.

It was annoying enough even when a person didn't know the truth about his wretched, twisted soul.

And here, of all places, it left her…shuddery.

"I think perhaps you're willfully misunderstanding me, Molly."

He sounded casual and almost offhand. To disguise his true intentions, as always. Accordingly, he was dressed like a businessman, instead of the more casual things she'd seen him in over the years. Not that she was looking, ever, but they were often in the same tabloids. His version of a business suit was always…rumpled. That was Constantine. Always slightly in disarray, so it was impossible not to look at him and imagine what bed he had just rolled out of. Or if he'd troubled himself to find a bed at all.

Stop shuddering, she ordered herself, and had to fight not to press her hand to her belly. It would do nothing to quell her internal reaction to him, but it would certainly give her away.

As he rounded the desk, lazy and languid and seeming not to move at all even as he did, she assured herself that it was not that she was uniquely susceptible to him. It didn't matter that he had pretended to be her friend or not. Or that he clearly was unhinged to have plotted out an elaborate revenge against her poor mother. Those things were factors, but not in the way her body reacted to him.

She couldn't help it if she was a woman and he was not just a man, but *him*.

It was a perfectly natural physical, chemical response. Molly certainly didn't have to *act* on it.

"You and I are going to start a flaming, passionate affair," he told her, oh-so-casually, as if he had summoned her here to chat about the weather. "It is going to be very, very public. I regret to inform you that like most women who become entangled with me, you will likely lose yourself. Fall in love, find yourself shattered, etcetera. It happens all too often."

"I'm not Icarus and you're not the sun, Constantine," she snapped at him. "I'm aware that might come as a shock to you."

His eyes gleamed. "We shall see. In any case, when I tire of you and your infamous charms, such as they are, I will discard you. Rudely and unfeelingly, I have no doubt. Then it will be up to you what you do afterward. Will you crawl off into obscurity as you should have done a decade ago? Or will you return to take your place on the runway, though you will be forced to accept that everyone who looks at you will no longer see whatever fashions you might be hawking, but my castoffs? Only time will tell."

Her brain literally would not make sense of any of that, because it all hinged on an impossibility. "You mean this is some kind of act we're going to put on... Right? Because, in case you've forgotten, you hate me. Remember?"

"I can only speak for myself," he said, sounding lazy and faintly amazed that she was asking. "But I do not *act* when I make love. And I do not make love, Molly. I make war. In war, I regret to tell you, there can only be one victor."

She knew she should have laughed at that. At him. It

should have been hilarious. If any other man had said such a thing in her presence, she would like as not have broken a rib laughing too hard. She would have raced out of the room, contacted every friend she'd ever made, and invited them to laugh at him, too.

But nothing about Constantine Skalas was funny. Because she believed him. He'd been at war all along, she had simply been too foolish to see it. And deep inside, where she had always and only melted for him, she knew he meant everything he'd just said.

And then some.

"Why would I ever agree to such a plan?" she managed to ask.

He smiled then, devil that he was, and it was heartbreaking. For he looked positively angelic. His eyes looked almost warm, as if he cared deeply about her—or anything—when she knew that was patently false.

"I cannot think of a single reason that you would." He shook his head, almost sorrowfully. "I would not, if I were in your place. But then, I would have left your mother to rot long ago."

"The way you've left yours?" she shot back at him.

And knew instantly that she'd made a huge mistake.

Constantine didn't blow up the way his father would have. He didn't throw something breakable across the room. He only studied her as if she were an experiment on a slide beneath a microscope—one he intended to dissect—while everything about him went still.

"Do not mention my mother again," he said quietly. So quietly it was very nearly a whisper, and every hair on Molly's body seemed to stand on end. "You will find that there are few topics off-limits to me. I'm not a man with any boundaries, and I mean that in every sense. But my mother is off-limits to you."

"I haven't agreed to do any of the things you suggested," she pointed out with a great surge of bravado she only wished she felt. "If I want to talk about your mother and the simple facts about her that every single person on earth knows—"

"I can't stop you, of course." He cut her off in that same quiet manner that made her spine hurt because she was standing so straight, so tall, for fear that if she did not, he would see how she shook. "But know this. Every time you mention my mother, I will take it as an invitation to vent my displeasure on yours."

And as ever, Molly felt that same sick rush of love and shame, frustration and longing that characterized her entire relationship with Isabel. If she could only find a way not to love her mother, her life would be infinitely simpler. If she could only harden herself and stop caring what became of Isabel, she wouldn't be standing here right now. She could have carried on living a life completely apart from even the faintest hint of the Skalas family, as had been her preference for years now.

But it didn't matter how many times her mother called her from the middle of what she liked to call her *little scrapes*. Or how many times Molly swore she would be done, once and for all, cleaning up all of Isabel's messes.

Oh, Moll, her mother would say in that rueful, smoky voice of hers, *I've really done it this time*.

And despite the number of times she'd received that

call, or had grudgingly agreed to let Isabel stay with her until she *sorted it*, which she never did, Molly still loved her. Molly couldn't help but love her. That was the whole of the trouble right there.

"Right," she said now, in Skiathos and in grave danger as well she knew. She kept her tone brisk. "No talk of mothers and I get to be your mistress, not merely a one-off shag. Brilliant. But how does that work, exactly?"

"How do you think it works?" Constantine's head tilted slightly to one side. Molly had the distinct and unsettling notion that he was less a man in that moment, and instead, some kind of overly large predator more usually found in the nature documentaries she watched when she couldn't sleep on whatever airplane she was on, jetting off to another job. "Have you not spent many, many years as a mistress to this or that man of appropriate means? What few there are in that tax bracket, of course. I am told it is very difficult to afford you."

That was possibly meant to be a joke, as there was nothing on earth or in the heavens above that a Skalas couldn't buy. Twice.

Molly opened her mouth to disabuse him of any notion he might have been harboring that she'd flitted about adorning the arms of the unworthy and unappealing men who thought they deserved her, no matter what the gossips liked to claim. But she caught herself.

Because if this was really going to happen—a possibility she couldn't quite allow herself to contemplate too closely, because it was too much, and too dangerous on a personal level after all she'd done to climb out of the abyss of her teenage years here—it would suit her far better that he thought of her as her alter ego. Magda.

Magda had been a creation of necessity. Molly Payne, awkward and shy, could not possibly have done the things she had if left to her own blancmange devices. But Magda could do anything. Magda had no fear. She was bright and strong, and when Molly was pretending to be her, the world around her was limitless. And usually hers for the taking besides.

Constantine insisted on calling her Molly, no doubt to remind them both of the power he'd held over her way back when. But clearly, he also believed everything he had heard about Magda. That could only work to her benefit.

Because Magda would think absolutely nothing about launching herself headfirst into a passionate love affair with the devil himself. In point of fact, Magda would find the whole thing unutterably delicious. She would laugh uproariously at the idea that she would ever be diminished by such a liaison. Not Magda. All Magda ever did was glow.

Molly regarded him for moment, collecting herself. Or collecting Magda, as the case might be, because that had always been much easier.

"Every man has a different set of requirements for the trophies he collects," she said nonchalantly. "And naturally, when the trophy is me, there are different considerations at play. My career is demanding and it will not stop being demanding to please the man in my life. Or even to accommodate him. And, of course, there is no possibility that I will ever waft about, waiting on a man hand and foot as some men long for. I require neither money nor the euphemistic *help* that such situations are generally made for, suiting all parties. So you see, it is indeed difficult to afford me, but not in the way you mean."

Well done, she congratulated herself. *Maybe next you can open up a brothel and make yourself the madam, since you're such a believable whore. That will be a terrific use of your talents. For lying.*

"That may have been your experience in the past," Constantine told her, a certain gleam in his coffee-dark gaze that made goose bumps rise all over her skin. "But this will be different. Because again, Molly, you are not the trophy here. You are working off a debt. Meaning, you will be the one doing the work. Because mark my words, you will pay. Again and again, until I am satisfied."

She believed him.

But she also knew him. And the Constantine she'd known, even if she'd deeply misjudged his vengefulness, had always been a glutton for attention. Good or bad, whatever worked. Molly had spent years trying to understand why, when now that she thought about it in the context of Demetrius's old office, it made sense. His father only doled out positive reinforcement every once in a blue moon, and usually to Balthazar. It had never seemed to bother Constantine much, for he was perfectly content to receive his father's negative attention. Just as long as he received it. And certainly all the behavior she'd seen in a thousand tabloid magazines over the years told her the same story. She didn't need a degree in psychology to work that one out—especially when she'd had a taste of the same hard school that had made Constantine who he was.

The hold Constantine Skalas had over her was insurmountable. Because like it or not, Molly could not bear to see her mother suffer. She could beat herself up about that all she wished, but she doubted it would change.

She knew it wouldn't change, or it already would have, at some point or another over the past ten years. Molly had watched her mother fritter away the fortune that had been her divorce settlement. Then she had drained the fortune Molly had built, too.

Molly did not care to imagine how many times Constantine had indulged his vengeful streak on her in that time when she'd been so blissfully unaware that he was the puppeteer controlling the strings, but it hardly mattered now. Because Molly knew that she was the only stepsister he'd had. That meant she knew a whole lot more about him than the average silly starlet who got mixed up with the famously beautiful and sexually voracious Constantine Skalas, imagining he'd be some kind of a lark.

When what he was, in fact, was lethal. Emotionally lethal.

But she felt that she could ignore all the goose bumps and that sense of foreboding that kept shaking its way through her, because she had her own weapons. Knowing him was the key.

He had rounded the desk and was now looming about within reach, which made her feel far too edgy. She drifted over to one of the chairs that sat about for decorative purposes, as far she knew, for never in her memory had she ever dared sit when summoned into this room. But sit she did now, draping herself across the nearest chair, the very picture of boneless ennui.

"Very well," she murmured. She draped one long leg over the opposite knee, letting her wickedly high shoe dangle sullenly, and waved a languid hand.

"Very well?" echoed Constantine, and he sounded... incredulous.

He moved to stand before her in all his rumpled male beauty that she knew she should have found malevolent. But her body refused to get that message. No matter how bored she tried to look, inside, she found it hard not to shiver. And melt. And shiver some more. Her breasts felt tight and high, her belly was tied in a knot that pulsed, and between her legs she was slick. Hot.

Desperate and aching.

You are a betrayer, she told herself sternly.

But what she did was *almost* shrug, then *almost* wave her hand, looking as deeply bored as it was possible to look without falling asleep where she sat.

"Very well then," she said, a little more slowly, as if he was dim. And watched that incredulity make his gaze narrow. She only sighed in response. "Let me know how you want me to do all this debt repayment. Let me guess. You'll want a sad, tawdry blow job here and now, because nothing says a man has power more than waving his little head around and making beautiful women genuflect before it. Or I know, maybe you want to toss me over some of the furniture for that shag, so it can be as dehumanizing as possible. I hear that's how the garden-variety seducer prefers to pave his way into deeper and deeper levels of sociopathy. You tell me. I doubt I'll notice the difference between this and the average photo shoot, if I'm honest."

And Molly had almost convinced herself that she was that jaded. That it wasn't even the usual Magda act. That she dripped scorn like a fountain and in doing so, had made herself untouchable, like stone.

Constantine laughed. A dark sound that sunk deep into her bones, making her feel as if they might shiver out of her skin, all on their own. As if the black magic sound of it might render her…someone else entirely than who she'd thought she was when she'd come here today.

Someone she was not at all sure she wanted to meet.

"Oh no, my little *hetaira*," he murmured, his voice another dangerous spell, and the gleam in his gaze a weapon. "That is not how this is going to go."

And then, standing above her like a judge on high, he reached down and hauled Molly to her feet.

Then slammed his mouth to hers.

CHAPTER THREE

MOLLY BURST INTO FLAMES, then exploded, and that was only a hint of the kind of heat that Constantine's mouth on hers generated.

It was only the start.

Her hands came up of their own accord, fluttering near his shoulders when she had never *fluttered* a day in her life. He was so big all around her when she was used to towering over most men. His mouth was so *hot*. And he angled his jaw as his tongue swept hers, making her shiver out as well as in.

His kiss was slick, wicked and insidious, and almost unbearably good.

He kissed the way he did everything. Lazy, reckless, and underneath it all, a dark edge of that same danger she really should have heeded.

She could taste him. Smell him. His tongue was a temptation, his sensual mouth a seduction, and she could hardly make sense of all the sensations that stormed in her.

Molly was lost.

All the dreams she'd had of him when she was a girl.

All the stories she'd told herself about what it might be like if ever he actually noticed her. All her wildest fantasies—this was better than any of that.

This was so good she wanted to cry. Strip off all her clothes here and now. Throw herself at him—

Which, she thought with something far too close to horror when he wrenched his mouth from hers, was going to make her plan for surviving this a little tricky.

She hated him in that moment.

Molly hated that satisfied, entirely too male expression on his beautiful face as he gazed down at her, his huge and unfairly hard hands wrapped around her upper arms to hold her in place. How a great boneless cat of a man like Constantine Skalas could somehow, magically, be as fit as if he worked his days away in the proverbial fields was an outrage. It was *unjust*, was what it was.

And meanwhile, she was absolutely certain that he knew full well the effect he had on her.

Her lips felt swollen. She could taste him on her tongue, something rich and heady that she was half-convinced had already gotten her drunk. He looked entirely too pleased with himself, so she was sure he not only knew all of that, but more, knew that her nipples had pinched tight with need while the core of her had gone molten.

Damn him.

"Kissing?" She called on all the acting she'd learned how to do to have the career she had, and to do it well. Every single time she'd had to contend with a horrible photographer, a grueling schedule, the usual condescending way women in her profession were treated, had been practice for this. And the faintly surprised but mostly bored tone she employed now. "Since when is there *kissing* when you're paying for it?"

Constantine's smile was a flash of white teeth, just this side of fangs. Or so she assumed when it hit her like a blow and made her feel tottery in her heels when she'd mastered stilettos back at age eighteen.

"I'm not interested in your ice queen act, Molly," he said, still smiling.

"What makes you think it's an act?" She tilted her head to one side and stood there woodenly, as if she had men's hands on her and their faces scant inches from hers every hour of the day. Which was not too far from the truth, though usually, at work, there was none of this spiky, brooding tension in the air. "I had a rough adolescence. My mother married a truly awful man and the blended family thing was hell on earth. But luckily enough, it cured me of feeling much of anything too deeply."

His smile took on that feral edge she remembered too well, though back then, she'd been foolish enough to mistake it for something else. Like empathy on his part. "I'm sure that's the story you like to tell, stepsister, but we both know it is not the truth."

"All right," she said, patronizing him. And making sure that he was fully aware that was what she was doing. "You know me better than I do. Got it."

Constantine…did something then, though she couldn't have said what it was. His hands were on her arms still, making her wish she'd worn some kind of sleeve to ward him off. Or to save herself, more like. That smile of his had settled into something worryingly *knowing* that she didn't like at all. And the gleam in his gaze was intense enough that it should have pierced her straight through. But then all of that changed, though she couldn't see how. It was as if he focused in on her, even more intently, and she lost her breath.

And he knew that, too.

"I think you'll find that there is no one on this earth who knows you better than I do, Molly. For your sins."

He released her arms and stepped back. And she was buffeted with contradictory sensations then. Relief. Loss.

And the heat in her rose all the while.

It did not wane, at all. Not even when it was clear that he was standing there, sizing her up the way they always did at work, as if she was a horse at market. Molly felt lucky that she was used to it. And more, that despite the reaction she was having, there was something soothing about being treated like a mannequin that took direction. It was her life's work, after all.

"The only things you know about me," she said, fighting to keep her voice even, "are the things I never should have told you when I was a silly teenage girl who believed that Constantine Skalas was actually my friend. But guess what? That girl is gone. You got rid of her yourself."

"You learned a valuable lesson," he replied, thrusting his hands into his pockets and giving her a long, thorough, deceptively sleepy once-over that made everything inside her prickle into high alert. "It is an act of supreme foolishness to trust anyone. Some don't learn this until it's too late. You learned it while you were but a girl. You should thank me."

"Thank you." Her voice was acidic. "And how proud you must have been to take it upon yourself to teach such a harsh lesson to a lonely girl. Such a humanitarian you are. I'm shocked you haven't collected awards for your services to mankind."

His smile was an exercise in seductive menace. "But we are not speaking of a hapless, awkward teenage girl, the daughter of a grifter of a housekeeper who fancied herself a replacement mother. As well as an actual mistress of the Skalas estates, rather than my father's tawdry affair that he dressed up in legalities for reasons that died with him."

There wasn't much anyone could say about Isabel that Molly hadn't thought herself. But that didn't mean she liked hearing it. "Yes, my mother woke up one day and just *imagined herself* your stepmother. Nobody pursued her. Or married her. Or told her to do as she pleased with the estates and the stepsons and everything else because, Lord knows, *he* certainly didn't care either way."

"My father is dead and cannot account for his decisions." Constantine shrugged, a masterpiece of Mediterranean nonchalance. "And would not have anyway, even had he lived."

"Right. You expect me to believe that while he was alive you changed the habits of a lifetime and took him to task for his behavior?" Molly laughed, and then laughed a little harder when she saw how little he liked it. "I'd like to have seen *that*. You know full well that the only thing he cared less about than what my mother did with his money was you. He likely would have cut you out of his will for suggesting otherwise."

She thought she saw the hint of a clenched jaw, which she told herself was a win. But was it really? Because the way he was looking at her...

"I'm interested that you seem to think insulting my father—and me—is a good way to begin a debt repayment program."

"Is it an insult to speak the truth about a man we both knew?" Molly shrugged, aware that when she did it, it was less a study of carelessness and more a sharp little gesture of disdain. She'd practiced it for years. "I wouldn't even say that's any kind of insider take on the late, great Demetrius Skalas. He was a complete mystery to me while my mother was married to him. Anything else I might have gleaned about him is public information." She counted off on her fingers. "He was a terrible person. His sons are terrible people. That's not my opinion, that's just a couple of incontrovertible facts."

Constantine smiled, and she regretted, deeply, that once again she couldn't seem to control her mouth in his presence. *Damn* him.

"Here are some other facts," Constantine murmured, all dark undertone and that glinting thing in his bittersweet gaze. "You have a martyr complex, for I assume you must get some sort of pleasure out of sacrificing yourself for your mother at every turn. Or why would you do it, again and again? She is a grown woman, capable of handling her own life—except she need not trouble herself with such things, because you do it for her."

Molly assumed he wanted a response from her, so she only gazed back at him, mutely defiant.

He continued. "For all that you travel about the world, command top dollar for pouting at the camera, and have entertained more rumored lovers than photographers, you're a very, very lonely woman."

She would die if he saw any kind of reaction on her face. *Die.* And still it took everything she had to simply continue to stare back at him as if he hadn't done that thing he'd always done. Smile and then skewer her.

"I know this because I watched you, Molly," he said, his voice getting quieter. But she watched his eyes. And the way they gleamed, that dangerous gold. "Every year you get thinner. Your eyes go darker. You become more and more brittle. Do not mistake me, your beauty, certainly a surprise to any who saw you as a gawky sixteen-year-old, only grows. But you're not happy, are you?"

She continued to stare back at him, but once the silence stretched between them, she gave an over-the-top sort of start. "Oh, my bad, is this the part where I actually respond to the man who's *blackmailing* me? I thought this was all rhetorical."

"I know what you eat, how long you sleep, even what documentaries you like to watch," he told her quietly, his dark gaze all gold, telling her clearly that he was showing her his weapons even if she hadn't heard him. "I know what you do when you're without one of your command appearance parties to attend in whatever city you find yourself."

"Why, Constantine. I'm flattered."

"You walk," he said, with a certain soft menace. And that time, she doubted very much that she managed to conceal her reaction. And then knew she hadn't when his gaze lit with victory. "Around and around and around whatever city or town you happen to be in, and you're not taking in the sights, are you? You prefer to go at night, almost as if there are demons you're trying to put behind you. Your mother, perhaps?"

"Wrong again," she replied, holding his gaze as if none of this scared her. When it did. When *he* did in more ways than she ever planned to admit. "I've only ever known one demon, Constantine. And he is standing right in front of me."

"I know you," he said again, clearly relishing this moment. Clearly enjoying this. "And when I have you, and I will, I will have all of you. And if there's nothing left after I glut myself on all you have, all you are, maybe you can see how it feels to put yourself back together." His dark eyes blazed. "The way my mother tried to do after yours took her place."

Molly was back home in London by evening, feeling as jittery as if she'd existed on nothing but caffeine and cigarettes for three weeks—a lifestyle she'd given up in her first year of modeling, because that led nowhere good. And was unsustainable besides.

It was a rainy, cold, and foggy May evening, and the shift in the weather from Skiathos to England's best plunged her instantly into a mood that was far too reminiscent of sixteen-year-old Molly. First plucked out of gray, miserable England and swept off to the dazzling coast of a Greek island, out of her depth in every possible way.

The sun had burned her skin a bright, feverishly painful red within an hour of her landing at the Skiathos airport. She should have known, even then, that it was only the first of many ways Greece would sear straight through her.

And when Isabel had finally left Demetrius and his power games, creeping back to England to lick her wounds and to hire a set of sharks to handle the divorce, Molly had felt the loss of all that terrible light and heat too keenly. It had felt like dying.

She felt the hint of that feeling again now, as her car bumped along the cobbled mews not far from Hyde Park and dropped her off at the Mews house she'd bought when her career first took off. A stone's throw from the Marble Arch, Hyde Park, and Oxford Street, her little house was a quiet retreat from the bustling, busy city all around her. It was also *hers*. All hers. She'd bought it with cash, filled with the naive hope that the one thing that was finally hers and only hers would stand as a symbol toward a bright future. The one she'd been determined to have, because she was sure she could make it different from the childhood she'd lived, the mistakes she and her mother had made in turn, and everything else she wanted to turn her back on.

Everything tainted by the Skalas family, in fact. And it had worked.

Her Mews house was a home, not an investment piece. It gave her four walls, three floors, and two lovely terraces' worth of peace. It was the only place on the planet where she could happily be herself. There were no pictures of Magda gracing the walls inside. There were no magazines. Inside, there were only the things she loved wholeheartedly. Books and art and other things she'd picked up in all the places she'd traveled. Bright colors and deep, soothing chairs and sofas, because every square inch of the place was meant for relaxation and recharging.

Out on the charming cobbled street as the car pulled away, Molly took a deep breath and let it go into the damp night. But the place still did its magic. Her shoulders lowered. That pounding in her chest settled. The knots in her belly eased…a little.

She let herself in the heavy door and heard the sound of music from the second level in what her real estate agent had loftily called her *reception room*. It was the heart of the little house. Kitchen on one end, a great hearth, French windows and a terrace over the cobblestones, and all the oversize, cozy things Molly had managed to make fit.

And since the last great implosion of her latest scheme, courtesy of Constantine Skalas, her mother, too.

Molly shrugged off the wrap she'd worn on the plane, hanging it near the door in her downstairs foyer. She kicked off her heels, flexing her toes against the polished wood floor as she padded up the stairs, absently reaching up to gather her hair, twist it back, then secure it in a thick ball on the top of her head. She walked up into the great room that had enough windows to make it bright and sunny on the days the weather wasn't foul, and she liked to sit out on her terrace and soak it in. And the clear nights, too. But tonight it was wet and cold, and anyway, even this magical little house of hers wasn't quite the oasis of calm when Isabel was around.

Her mother looked up as Molly walked into the room, looking flustered and determined all at once. "Darling. You're home at last. I've spent all day making the most *divine* pasta from scratch. As an offering."

"I can see that," Molly replied. The kitchen was a disaster. Pots and pans she didn't even know she owned were not only out, but half-filled with this or that, every single one of them noticeably dirty.

"Don't tell me you're not eating carbohydrates tonight," Isabel continued airily. "Pasta is the least you can do for yourself after the day you must have had."

And though Molly opened her mouth to say that no, obviously she couldn't eat bowls of pasta, she stopped herself. Because, actually, pasta sounded absolutely perfect for the mood she was in. She didn't want anything to do with all the feelings swirling around inside her. Might as well eat them instead.

Still in the slinky dress she'd worn to Magda up the situation with Constantine, she didn't comment on the state of her kitchen. She simply set herself to the inevitable task that would fall to her anyway, of washing the dishes as her mother fluttered about putting the final touches to her homemade masterpiece.

By the time they sat down at the table near the side

windows, Molly felt a bit better for having had the opportunity to lose herself a bit in the sheer drudgery of scrubbing and rinsing and drying, all better than thinking or feeling anything. It reminded her of long, long ago, when her mother had been a housekeeper in a grand house and she and Molly had lived in a small rented cottage in the village. On Isabel's days away she and Molly would cook up fanciful meals and then dress up to please themselves.

She'd spent so long trying to repress those years in Greece, she too often forgot that she and Isabel had, in fact, had a whole life before the Skalas family had crashed into them and crushed them flat.

"I'm quite impressed, Mum," she said after her first, marvelous bite. "I know you can cook when you have a mind to, but I would have thought pasta from scratch was a bridge too far."

Isabel was still the beautiful woman she'd been when she'd caught Demetrius's eye in the stately old home where her family had been in service, in one form or another, since around about the Norman conquest. Beautiful and young, since she'd had Molly when she'd been seventeen—and had never named the father. *He knows where we are if he can be faffed*, she'd said dismissively. *No sense in chasing after a man if he doesn't want to be caught. There are always more.* That attitude hadn't made much sense to Molly back then, when she'd been the object of scorn and derision in the village herself, little though Isabel ever took notice. Now she understood Isabel's lack of concern. She was very, very pretty.

Too pretty to be a housekeeper, the tabloids had

screamed when Demetrius had married her, then paraded her in front of the world.

He hadn't taken that from her, Molly thought with a rush of that same old love that got her into trouble. Nothing ever dimmed Isabel's spirits for long, and unlike many in her position, all of her looks were natural. No work.

At the moment, she looked rueful. "I'm not a total disaster, then," Isabel said with that self-awareness that always took Molly by surprise. "That's something."

"Of course you're not a disaster," she replied.

Isabel sat back in her chair, her bowl filled with pasta and aged parmesan steaming before her. "Go on then. Tell me what the damage is."

And Molly had intended to do exactly that. She had practiced fiery speeches on the plane ride home, each more bracing than the last. Hard truths were needed, she'd assured herself. It was high time she and Isabel *came to terms*.

It was always easier to fight with the people she loved in the abstract. Or the person she loved, to be more precise. Because it was only this one. Only and ever her beautiful, reckless mother, who for all her faults, loved Molly completely. Unconditionally. Even if that might not look the way Molly wished it would—like those long-ago fancy dress evenings, kitted out in costume jewels and pretending they were in Italy—it was real.

Molly knew that she could say anything to her mother. Isabel's guilt was a real thing. She had no qualm whatsoever about admitting fault, and apologizing, and taking it if Molly needed to shout at her.

But somehow, tonight, Molly felt that shouting at Isabel would be giving horrible Constantine Skalas exactly what he wanted.

I will need time to consider your charming proposal, she had told him with a regal disdain in that office.

Think of it less as a proposal and more as a lifeboat you do not deserve, he had replied, looking maddeningly handsome and inexcusably sure of himself. As if he already knew, as she did, that there was almost no way to get out of it and like it or not, she would be slinking back to him to do precisely as he commanded.

Still, she needed a bit of space, first. She needed to recalibrate. Because she'd expected that her temper would be involved, and she'd known deep down that what he would ask of her would feel unbearable, but what she hadn't expected was her response to him. That wildfire that raged in her still, and led to an insidious little voice inside wondering if really, it wouldn't be *too* bad, would it?

She'd wanted to rail at Isabel. It wasn't enough that Isabel had dragged her into the Skalases' harsh and cruel, glittering diamond-edge of a world back then, but now she was forced to return to it. To hand herself over to the architect of her first and greatest despair.

You are entirely too full of yourself, Constantine, she had told him. *No wonder you're so easily dismissed when you don't have a blackmail scheme in your back pocket.*

You are welcome to dismiss me, if you like, he had said in return. He'd even sounded encouraging. *My understanding is that you love that little house of yours in*

London. What a shame it would be if you were forced to sell it, to keep both you and your mother afloat in these uncertain times. He had smiled when she glared at him. *Alternatively, you can return in two days' time, ready and willing to begin our torrid affair.*

She was still having trouble with that. An affair with Constantine when she'd barely survived a kiss? A *torrid* affair?

What would become of her?

"You're awfully quiet," Isabel said softly. She blew out a breath. "Is it that terrible?"

And Molly couldn't do it. She couldn't tear out another chunk of her mother's heart. Because that was the trouble with Isabel. Yes, she was impetuous and ambitious and had always had ideas far above her station. It was tempting to think of it as thoughtlessness, but it wasn't. It was that heart of hers. Big and foolish, and entirely too willing to think the best of terrible people.

Molly knew. She had the same one in her chest.

"No, Mum," she said, and summoned up a smile. "It's really not bad at all. Who could have guessed that in all these years since last we saw him, Constantine Skalas stumbled over conscience?"

"No one will believe that," her mother replied dryly. "Least of all me."

"Well, he has," Molly lied. "You can rest easy. He needs me to play a role, that's all."

Isabel frowned. "If the man needs an actress, he has the whole of the West End at his disposal, to say nothing of his liking for all of those bland little Hollywood types. Why would he need you?"

"He's far too well-known to go out and hire someone. This little spot of blackmail helps him save face, that's all."

Molly almost believed herself, she sounded so matter-of-fact. She smiled, then kept smiling, even though her mother's gaze was entirely too knowing.

Maybe, if she just kept smiling, she would convince herself, too.

"And who knows?" she asked merrily. "It might even be fun."

CHAPTER FOUR

IT WAS NOT until Molly reappeared at the house in Skiathos two days later that Constantine admitted to himself that he hadn't actually known if she was coming back at all.

And he was not suited to uncertainty. Nor used to it.

Not since Demetrius had died, at any rate, taking with him his cruel reversals, endless judgments, and what Constantine had always thought was a truly sadistic delight in the art of the sucker punch, both literal and figurative.

He had not missed any of that since he and Balthazar had buried the old man with all the pomp and circumstance of a monarch, according to his typically narcissistic instructions. Constantine had stood in the famed Metropolitan Cathedral in Athens that surely should have crumbled around him at his entrance, to say nothing of his father's many offenses against God and man, and had tried to look suitably grim and somber.

When all he'd been thinking was, *good riddance, old man*.

He did not appreciate the return to unpredictability. He resented any and all memories of his father as it was.

It was one more charge to lay at Molly's feet.

Constantine had been forced to sit about in that odd old house he'd never cared for, waiting. He had felt so worldly at twenty that he'd thought having to leave his admittedly nonchalant studies in London at all was a personal attack. He had especially disliked having to spend that first year's holidays marooned on this island with a new family he'd despised, as his father had demanded. This time around, as then, he passed the time by outlining all the ways he would take out his retribution on Molly and her mother. It was an exercise that had once filled him with what he'd assumed was joy. By a process of elimination.

Surely it should have done so again, especially given the fact that *this time*, he had a great deal more leverage. Yet as the two days he'd given Molly dragged by, he found himself far more invested in her return to Skiathos than he should have been.

Because it was only one of the options he had before him, as well he knew. He should have been equally invested in all of them. Forcing her to sell that charming little Mews house of hers would deliver a serious blow, for example. He knew that. He should have been moving on that angle while he waited.

The problem was that now, having seen her in person again, Constantine was far more interested in the angles that involved the flesh. Her flesh and his. He had always viewed sex as akin to the hotel buffets he'd observed in the properties he owned—readily available and very,

very rarely worth the trouble. He had certainly never had to *convince* a woman to sleep with him.

In point of fact, he was far more often engaged in scraping lovers off, not obtaining them.

Yet Molly was different.

He told himself it was because of their history. Because of her déclassé mother and the fact they'd all been forced to share space—this space. That was what made her an obsession. That was why he sometimes felt haunted by her. And had for years.

But he had the taste of her in his mouth now and he couldn't seem to get past it.

And he had expected that Molly, in person, would prove the rule that photography was a very specific kind of magic. He'd expected her to look sallow. To have terrible skin, lank hair, or both. To make it clear, up close, that she had good bones but that all those pictures of her were simply make-believe.

Instead, he'd been astonished—and furious, frankly—to discover that if anything, the camera was unkind to Molly Payne.

Because she was far more beautiful in person than she'd ever been on film.

Constantine had been tempted to throw away all his plotting, keep on kissing her, and to hell with their past.

Really, that alone should have had him calling off this whole thing and moving against Isabel a different way. Because clearly, he was unprepared for the reality of his former stepsister, and the fact that he didn't wish to accept that didn't make it any less true.

That he'd woken in the night, his body hard and aching for her, his head filled with intense images of the two of them together, had not helped.

He'd stood out on his balcony in the dark, too aware that he need not suffer through his own desire if he did not wish it. He could go down into Skiathos Town and have his choice of women to slake his lust. If he listened, he could almost hear the sound of the island's nightlife on the breeze. And it had been a very long time since he'd had to control his own desires, if ever. He was not certain he had ever waited for a specific woman in his life. There was never a need for specificity when the world was filled with so many options.

Go, he had ordered himself. *Get a woman and get a handle on this madness now.*

But he hadn't taken his own advice.

And he did not wish to acknowledge the sense of something far too close to relief he felt when his staff announced Molly's arrival. Precisely two minutes before her two days were up.

It wasn't *relief*, he told himself now. It was merely a well-earned pleasure that his plan was continuing as it should, particularly now she'd returned.

He did not have her shown into his father's wretched study this time. He had spent his morning dealing with any number of tedious business concerns and was now sitting out on one of the many terraces, taking in the sparkling blue of the cove below him. Still, he knew the moment she rounded the corner, taking the outside stair from the front of the house, draped in bougainvillea all the way. And this time, there was no click of high heels against the stones.

Constantine smiled, for he could only assume that meant the battle was on.

Sure enough, when Molly finally presented herself before him—clearly in no rush—she wore a black dress that had to be at least three sizes too large for her elegantly slender frame. Her long blond hair was pin straight and tucked behind her ears. She even wore trainers. She looked like what she was, a model dressing down, but if she was trying to make some kind of point about how unglamorous she was in the everyday, it was ruined by the simple fact that there was no disguising the simple perfection of her features.

A truth he had spent very little time acknowledging was that her features had always been perfect. She had been a distracting, arresting teenager, something he at twenty had noticed and then studiously ignored. Her mother's beauty had been softer, more accessible. *More common*, he would have said. And had.

All of Molly's features, taken separately, had seemed too bold or too full-on. Like that mouth of hers or her commanding height. Even back then, the way they'd all come together had always and only led to being found stunning, not pretty. For she was nothing so simple as *pretty*. She was nothing accessible or easy. Hers was a haunting beauty, and a shapeless black dress could do nothing at all to disguise it.

"I see you dressed up for this auspicious occasion," he drawled, lounging in his chair as if he had spent the morning here, lazing the day away. He imagined she probably thought he had, and as ever, it amused him to let people think the worst of him.

"I thought you would appreciate the mourning attire," she said, smiling. "It seemed appropriate."

"You have no idea how much." He was wearing his unofficial uniform when in the Greek islands, or forced aboard a yacht. Linen trousers that breathed in the heat and one of his favorite T-shirts, and he was aware that when he had not bothered to shave, as today, it made him look disreputable. All the better. "Have you come to mount more arguments? To see if you can somehow change my mind? You won't, but it might be entertaining to hear you out."

"What would I do?" she asked, widening her eyes a little, though he did not believe the innocent act for a moment. "Appeal to your better nature? Does such an animal exist?"

Constantine found himself grinning at that, which was not precisely how he had planned to conduct his great revenge. But what did it matter if they ended up in the same place? They would. He would see to it they did.

"Then dare I trust that you are here for the long haul?" he asked her, idly, as if whether or not she stayed was of little personal interest to him.

Because it should not have mattered.

"You already told me I have a martyr complex, Constantine." She held her arms out at her side, as if she anticipated a crucifixion. "Here I am, ready and willing to be burned all nice and crispy on the pyre of your choosing."

"I'm delighted to hear it."

He stared at her for a long moment, taking in the mulish set of her chin and the way her clavicle presented itself from the wide neck of the dress she wore, begging for his mouth.

Oh yes, this was happening.

Finally.

"I'll be honest with you, Constantine," she was saying, her voice bright enough that she might have been at a cocktail party instead of her own doom. "You don't look delighted. I would say rather that you look a little…dark."

"You have no idea, *hetaira*. But enough small talk." He settled back in his chair and let his smile go lazy. "Take off all your clothes."

And she was not so mulish suddenly. She did not precisely jolt in surprise, but he thought he saw the hint of it, quickly repressed. Her eyes, that arresting, arctic blue, deepened into something that almost matched the Aegean Sea stretched out behind her.

Almost.

"You don't waste any time, do you?" she asked, still staring back at him.

"I like to start as I aim to go on," he replied. "And, Molly. You are stalling."

He saw her gather herself, and he wondered if she would balk now. It wouldn't surprise him. After all, she was clearly a proud creature, or she could never speak to him the way that she did. Constantine, too, knew something of pride, and could not imagine any scenario in which he would subject himself to another's will in this way.

But even as that notion bloomed in him, he brushed

it aside. They were nothing alike. He had no idea why he'd thought such a thing in the first place.

"And what happens if I can't go through with this?" Molly asked quietly.

"No one is forcing you," Constantine reminded her. He made a small show out of a shrug. "There is no gun to your head. You are not imprisoned here. The doors are open, the gate is unlocked, and you may leave whenever you wish."

"How generous." Her eyes glittered. "Yet if I do leave, you will ruin my mother. Possibly permanently. And who knows if you'll stop there. You might also take my house. Then make it difficult for me to work, I'm assuming. And probably, in the end, ruin me, too. Is that right? That has to be the goal or why bother?"

Constantine sighed as if pained. "It is a pity. But in life, there are consequences."

"This is how you sleep at night?"

He laughed. "Oh, *hetaira*, I have never had a night of troubled sleep in my life."

"Why would you? That requires a conscience."

"Now you're boring me." He shook his head. "Make your choice. Stay or go, as it please you. But if you stay, you heard my instruction. I would suggest you follow it."

"What a lovely invitation," Molly said, through her teeth. "How can I possibly refuse?"

Neither one of them pointed out that, of course, she couldn't.

Then, with a notable surliness he almost applauded, because she made so little attempt to hide it, she toed off her trainers. One, then the next. Then, with the level of sensuality Constantine would expect to see in a doctor's surgery, she pulled off the dress, tossing it onto one of the chairs nearby. Then she stood there before him in nothing but a pair of thong panties.

God help him.

And he could see that she had shifted into her work mode, as he liked to call it. She'd become the other version of herself. Magda. Her gaze became haughtier, sharper. The way she stood changed—to encourage, not touching, but looking. A fierce stance that commanded attention. She was suddenly imperious as she stared at him, almost as if she was challenging him. Did he dare to come before her without a camera to begin worshipping her with its lens, as most did when they beheld her?

And why not? Molly was a masterpiece.

She was all long, elegant lines and surprising curves. Two perfect breasts sat high on her chest, the nipples tightening as he looked at them. If Molly noticed, and Constantine was sure she did, she gave no sign.

Instead, Molly continued to hold his stare in that challenging manner of hers as she bent, stripped off her thong, and tossed it to the side as well.

Then she stood again, looking utterly at her ease. Her hands by her sides, her weight shifted to put her at her best advantage, and how could he not appreciate the view? He more than appreciated it.

"Well?" she asked, and not in the tone of one who had any doubts about what she was presenting.

"You have a very strange take on the idea of servitude," Constantine pointed out. "I find this amazing, given your mother's initial profession."

"Yes, cleaning a house is like brown eyes," Molly agreed, her tone like a lash. "Passed down generation after generation, by genetics. I was personally born with a broom in one hand."

"Here are the rules," Constantine said, ignoring that. "As you are well aware, this is the house where my father always insisted we live without a full staff. I assume because it gave him pleasure to make your mother do the housekeeping. I will not do the same."

"Whyever not? I was sweeping up before I could walk. A family trait."

"My assistant stays in the guesthouse and is rarely here in the main house. And never without advance warning. There are guards at the gate, as I'm sure you saw, but they do not venture within. I tell you this to forestall the inevitable argument you're going to attempt to have with me when I tell you that while we are here, unless I specifically tell you otherwise, you will be naked."

"Naked," Molly repeated. "I'll just be wandering about, draping myself on the furniture, naked. That doesn't sound hygienic."

"Do you have a medical issue that should be taken up with a doctor?" he asked, silk and menace and entirely too much delight. "Do I need to bring in a medical team?"

"I'm sadly all too healthy and not about to die from a stroke, which is a tragedy." She glared at him. "But in case you've forgotten, I sunburn very easily."

"That will not suit me at all," Constantine assured her. "But no need to fear." He nodded toward the table beside the chair where she'd tossed her clothes. "I brought you some sunscreen. Bring it to me, please. I'll apply it."

Then he watched, fascinated, as she looked from the tube of sunscreen to him, then back again, clearly fighting with herself.

He sat back and enjoyed the show.

And, if he was honest with himself, enjoyed the moment or two to pull himself together, because he had not quite anticipated the effect this would have on him.

Constantine had seen more beautiful women naked than he could begin to count, but this was different. She was different.

He was so hard that he ached. He *ached*. He wanted to throw all his years of careful planning aside and simply take her, as he knew he could. He had not imagined the way she'd responded to that kiss. He had not liked the way he had, come to that. He had meant it as a show, more than anything else. But somehow, what had started as an object lesson had turned into something else.

He was Constantine Skalas and he had spent the last two days reliving a bloody kiss, of all things. As if he was the gawky, awkward sixteen-year-old this time around. As if she had bewitched him, and that easily.

He would not allow it. He refused to allow the daughter of the unacceptable tart Isabel Payne, of all creatures, to affect him in this way. Or at all.

It was a physical reaction, that was all. She had made

an entire career out of her beauty. She knew very well how to elicit the reactions she wanted. He should not be so surprised that he was susceptible to it. What man would not be?

Because naked, Molly was even more beautiful than she was draped in all the dramatic clothing she wore on this or that runway. Once again, he was struck by the stark, glorious lines of her body. A work of exquisite art, angles and curves together, creating a woman no one could deny was exquisite.

And now, for as long as he wanted her, she was his.

Molly came to her decision. He could see it on her face in the split second before she swiped up the tube of sunscreen with one hand, then closed the distance between them. With a challenging look on her face as she stood there, naked, as commanded.

"Come closer," he told her, the terrible wolf to the not-quite-a-lamb, and when she did, he grinned. He held out his hand for the sunscreen, then waited.

And watched his favorite enemy as she fought, then surrendered, right there before him.

The way Constantine intended to see she did over and over and over again, until there was little left of Molly Payne but shattered pieces, and all of them in his hand.

CHAPTER FIVE

MOLLY HAD NEVER been more grateful for her chosen profession.

Because if it weren't for all her years as a model, could she have handled this? Could she have presented herself, so matter-of-factly, wholly naked in front of a man?

Not just any man. But Constantine Skalas, who had long been a shadow over her life whether she admitted it or not.

She tried to tell herself that there was nothing particularly worthy of her notice here. It was another gig, that was all. And luckily enough, she was more than used to finding herself in states of undress with very little privacy. If she'd been at all prudish about her body, she wouldn't have lasted a month in the fashion industry. Much less a decade.

Constantine took the tube of sunscreen from her, and Molly told herself to pay no mind to the fact that she was now standing between his outstretched legs. He took a long, lazy survey of her body, and she supposed she ought to have been grateful that he'd chosen to seat himself at the fanciful table she'd been enamored of when she'd been here the first time. This particular table was basically a shelf that ran around the trunk of a large shade tree, making it possible to sit out on this particular terrace in the high heat of a Greek summer day and enjoy the cool breeze from the sea without broiling.

It made her wonder exactly how calculating Constantine really was. But even as she thought that, she had her answer, didn't she? For here he sat in the shade, demanding her nudity, a convenient tube of sunscreen at the ready.

Molly really ought to have been ashamed that even now, when she had returned to Greece to trade her body for money—dress it up or down as she pleased, that was what was happening, and not, for a change, in the name of high fashion—even in the midst of yet another terrible thing he was doing to her, she wanted to excuse him. To give him some other reason for doing what he did.

When she should know better. The man was pure evil. More, he was proud of it.

He finally raised his gaze to hers again, sensual and heavy-lidded and, as ever, richly intense. She did her best not to react and her reward was the hint of a knowing smile in one corner of his mouth. He lifted an idle hand, then circled one finger in the air before him, telling her without words to turn around.

Molly complied, executing a sharp, crisp turn that would have made art directors sigh with pleasure in at least five languages. She presented him with her back and then she stood still—another skill that the average person assumed anyone could do. When, in fact, real stillness for more than a moment was significantly more difficult than most lay people imagined.

Constantine was also still, and she resented that about him. That he could simply do things it took others a lifetime to learn. Much less execute on a whim.

After a while she had the sense of some kind of movement somewhere behind her and braced herself, but she heard nothing that sounded like Constantine about to strike. There was the sound of the sea in the distance and the waters of the cove against the shore. She could hear the breeze through the trees. She was aware of bees buzzing, birds conducting their officious business, and wind chimes, somewhere near.

All of it seemed entirely too bucolic and sweet when she'd woken up in a gray and wet London morning. Especially when Lucifer himself was here with her. She should have been able to smell the sulfur.

She waited, but nothing happened. Time stretched out. She held her breath, but still, nothing.

The Greek sun she would have sworn she hated filtered down through the branches of the tree above her, yet because it provided her with a canopy, it felt like nothing so much as a kiss. And slowly, against her will, she began to feel the inherent sensuality of what she was doing. Standing there, letting the breeze caress her while the sunshine licked all over her, soft and sweet. There was salt in the air, and the scent of something sweet that she assumed must be flowers, and she was sorely tempted to close her eyes and drift off…

But it was as if he knew. As if he could tell. Because

the very moment she contemplated surrendering to this unusual moment she found herself in, he touched her.

It was torture in an instant. An exquisite, glorious torture.

And Molly had no idea why he'd turned her around so he couldn't monitor her expressions, because she was sure he would have seen far too much if he had. She felt her mouth drop open. Her eyes went wide. It took everything she had to keep her hands at her side, instead of letting them rise to cover her mouth. Her face. To do *something*.

Because Constantine was doing something so prosaic it should hardly have registered.

And yet.

His hands were big, faintly calloused from she knew not what, and slick with sunscreen lotion.

And it turned out that the most debauched and pointless man in the history of Greece was very, very detail oriented when it suited him.

He started at her hips, smoothing his hands to the small of her back, then all over her bottom, making sure to cover each curve. Then he slicked his way, ever so carefully, over her exposed inner thighs, down the backs of her legs, all the way along her calves to her feet, then up again.

Constantine said nothing while he did this. When he needed more sunscreen, his hands disappeared but always returned. The lotion was cool against her skin, but his hands were hot. Or she was hot. It was all *too hot*.

At some point he stood, and it took everything Molly had to keep from collapsing into a too-warm, coconut-scented puddle at his feet. Or even to keep her eyes open, because they drooped to half-mast as he rubbed lotion up the length of her spine. Then over each of her shoulder blades, then down the sides of her body, grazing her breasts at each side. But only grazing them, and then, as if he didn't notice, paying close attention to the backs of her arms.

"Lift up your hair," he murmured, though she did not mistake it for anything less than another command.

And in any case, she would have done anything he asked. Anything at all to keep his hands moving all over her like this, spreading heat and warmth inside and out and making her rethink her historic dislike of sunlight.

That was what it felt like. As if Constantine was sunshine and more, he was rubbing it straight into her bones.

"Turn around," he ordered her after a time, his voice gruff, and she didn't even think about it. There was no bracing herself now. No desperately trying to lock herself away somewhere inside her own head.

Perish the thought. All she could think about was more of that sunshine.

She turned again, and then everything seemed to ratchet up to such a high intensity that on some level, she was sure she had to be dreaming this.

Though she had never known a dream to be so tactile.

Constantine sat back down on the chair before her, picking up one of her feet and resting it on his broad, hard thigh. She had the strange notion that in this position, despite her nudity and all that was splayed before him, she should have felt regal, superior. Because she was not missish about being looked at, by any stretch of the imagination. He was below her, and surely she should have reveled in that.

But the truth was, she felt as if she might as well have been laid out before him on the ground, shuddering and boneless. She felt like a sacrifice. Yet for the first time in her life, she found herself questioning what that word really meant.

She had always used it in a passive-aggressive sort of way, particularly when it involved her mother and her *scrapes*. The sorts of angry sacrifices that a person made out of obligation, for example, meaning annoyances. Some larger than others but still, only annoyances.

But this man, this devil there before her, was running his hands up her slender calf, his attention seemingly so fixed on what he was doing that it made her feel hollowed out with a kind of shivering within.

And Molly found herself contemplating the notion of *sacrifice* in a new light. Everyone had seen those movies of girls dragged screaming to terrible deaths in the clutches of horrible monsters that heroes would then ride in to vanquish. *But what about the other girls?* she asked herself then, almost dreamily.

The ones who woke in the night, hot and desperate to wear a crown of flowers and a white dress. The ones who felt their very cores run hot at the notion of walking, of their own volition, away from the lights of the village, into the dark. The ones who shivered in delight at the idea of surrendering themselves wholeheartedly to the monster who waited there.

Why didn't they get any songs or myths? Why did no one tell their stories?

But she already knew the answer. No one mourned the girls who flirted with their own disasters. Mourning was for the good girls, the ones who behaved properly on the way to their deaths. All this time, Molly had been certain she was good.

But Constantine's hands taught her otherwise.

He did not look up at her, almost as if her reaction to what he was doing was incidental to him. And for some reason that made everything...tighter and hotter and wilder, until she felt molten straight through.

He is preparing your body for his pleasure, a voice inside her that sounded far too much like her own whispered then.

Molly should have been horrified. And yet she... was not.

She would not describe the breath she couldn't catch, or the way her nipples stood proud, or even that slickness between her legs that she was half-terrified and half-hopeful he would see as...horrified.

If he noticed her obvious arousal, he ignored it, moving with a certain briskness up the outside of her thighs. Then over her mound, ignoring the way she jolted as he made sure to rub lotion to cover all she kept bare, save for a tiny strip. Surely now he would shift everything over into a sexual place. Surely now he would make some kind of claim.

But instead, he sat forward. And took another age

to move his slick palms over her belly, below and then above her navel. Eventually he made his way to her rib cage, where he climbed the length of her torso as if he could do so all day, and only stopped when he reached the under slope of her breasts.

Now her breath was coming in shallow little pants, and Molly should have been ashamed. Deeply ashamed. She should have held her breath until she passed out rather than show him how he affected her.

But it was as if her body was going to do as it wished. Or maybe he was simply that talented, even when it was something as small and seemingly nonsexual as the application of sunscreen.

It had never crossed Molly's mind that the man might actually have earned his reputation.

Constantine took his time putting more lotion on his hands, and then he moved again, standing once more so he could slick his hard palms over her breasts.

And then…he played with her.

Either that, or he was under the impression it took a remarkable level of detailed touching and caressing to protect her breasts from the sun. Not that Molly could really remember the sun or her usual aversion to it at this point or the world they both lived in.

There was only Constantine. There was only his touch.

He massaged her breasts with his palms, teasing her nipples into even stiffer points. Until she could do nothing but arch her back, let her head fall as it would, and press herself into his hands.

She'd never felt anything so delicious her life.

And somehow, without any idea how it happened, Molly found herself closer to Constantine. Had he pulled her there? Or had she simply drifted there of her own accord until she might as well have been in his arms.

Then his thigh was between hers and she found herself pressing the place she ached the most against his brutally hard, deliciously tough thigh. Then rocking herself there, lost in the rhythm of his hands on her breasts and her own movement on his thigh.

And then everything was slick heat and astonishment, and that coiling, shuddering, shimmering tension inside of her.

In the distance, or at her ear, she heard his gruff, dark voice muttering something she didn't understand. Greek, maybe. Or another incantation. It was too hard to tell.

And then she came apart.

Molly was a thousand shards of glass and still she came apart. Still the shattering went on and on.

She was dimly aware that she was still riding his thigh, that his palms were still working a rough magic against her nipples. And the connection between those two things was so intense, such a bright and impossible shine, that she felt as if all that light and wild heat was inside her. Then shattering outwards like all of that glass.

And then, for a time, she knew nothing at all.

It was only when she felt his hands on her shoulders, turning her and then guiding her down into the chair he vacated, that what she'd let happen here impressed itself upon her.

What she'd let happen and worse, what she'd done.

It took one breath, and then the shock of that realization hit her. Hard.

And right behind it came a wallop of shame. Liberally infused with the kind of self-recrimination she had last felt quite this keenly right here in Skiathos. And back then, she had never been naked in this man's presence, much less flung herself into his hands with so much heedless abandon.

Had she really been thinking about happy maidens scampering up mountainsides to fling themselves, breasts first, at the nearest scary thing they found?

It cost her more than she wanted to consider to lift her gaze again, then to do her best to regard him coolly. Because it was all she could do.

And he was waiting.

"You come so prettily," Constantine told her, standing there before her with a little half smile on his perfect mouth and the glittering roar of heat in his gaze. "I hope you enjoyed a little taste of what awaits us on this little journey of ours. And the next time, Molly, you will have to beg me for your release."

"I think I can promise you that will never happen," she said, scraping up a truly miraculous tone of voice considering what was happening inside her, all scorn and haughty amusement.

But it was lost on him. All he did was let that half smile grow a bit deeper.

"Don't make promises you cannot keep, *hetaira*,"

he advised her in a low voice. "You will not like how I correct a broken promise, I assure you."

She could see that he was aroused himself. Yet he seemed to disregard it. To not even notice it, somehow, when she had always been under the impression that Constantine Skalas, above all men, was ruled entirely by that impressive length she could see pressed against his trousers.

Yet all he did was indicate the tube of sunscreen, still with that smile.

"Don't forget your face and neck," he said. "You're already quite red. Though I do not think it is sunburn. Yet."

And then, to her astonishment—and what she would not have admitted was something far more complex than that, and a whole lot closer to disappointment— he simply turned and left her there.

She sat there, in the shade of that tree, for a long, long time.

And then longer still, as there was no getting past what had happened. What she had not only allowed, but had obviously reveled in.

Eventually, she took his advice and put sunscreen on her face and neck. Then sat there, certain that he must have been watching her, or waiting for her to…do something. It would no doubt indicate what was next on the naked blackmail menu for the day.

The shadows changed, yet Constantine did not reappear.

So even though she would have happily put it off longer if she could, Molly had no choice but to stand up, face the house behind her that she still hadn't gone inside this time, and then actually walk in of her own volition.

The house already made her feel vulnerable, and she shivered as she stepped inside, and not because of the temperature. She could see ghosts of her younger self everywhere she looked, and having to walk through these rooms literally naked, stripped down and vulnerable, did not help. She padded through the various living areas, trying not to see her memories play out before her, but there was no sign of Constantine.

Gritting her teeth, she moved on, making her way back to that dreadful study once more. But he wasn't there, either.

Eventually, she found him in the grand master suite that was its own wing of the house. She had not, obviously, spent much time here, as it was Demetrius's domain. And woe betide anyone who went somewhere he did not wish them to go. She had only vague memories of the way the suite was set out, with a sitting room here, a media center there. She told herself it was pleasant, by contrast, to walk through rooms with no ghosts at all.

But there was Constantine, and he was something far worse than a ghost. He was stood out on yet another balcony, his gaze on the sea beyond, speaking in impatient Greek into his mobile.

And yet somehow, Molly knew that he was perfectly aware of the very second she stepped out behind him. If not before.

He gave no indication that he cared either way if she was there, but she knew that he did. She just knew.

Constantine finished his conversation, and not particularly quickly, then turned, shoving his mobile in his pocket as he faced her. And she was struck—again—by his wholly unfair beauty. He was too masculine, too sexual, and yet somehow fitted perfectly here, where centuries back he should have been a god.

First monsters, now gods. She was losing it.

"You are lucky you did not attempt to defy me and dress," he said, though he sounded sorrowful. "I was so certain you would."

"Maybe you don't know me as well as you think," she replied loftily, and would keep to herself that new stab of self-recrimination. Because it hadn't even occurred to her to put her clothes on. What did that say about her?

Nothing good, she replied to herself. Nothing that wasn't more monsters and gods and willing sacrifices.

"I have a number of calls I must take today," Constantine told her, his dark gaze moving over her and making her feel as if he was still touching her. "I trust you can amuse yourself without supervision?"

"Am I allowed to amuse myself?"

His gaze gleamed at her dry tone. "In any way you like, save one. I already told you that your pleasure is at my command. And only when you beg me, Molly. I meant it."

She wanted to shake apart again, into a thousand new pieces because of that. And she was sure that he could see how close she came to doing it.

Instead, Molly pressed her bare feet into the smooth stone below, ordering herself to breathe. To remain calm. To use all the lessons she'd learned over time here.

Among them, to stand about wearing or not wearing all manner of strange things while others stared at her.

Pretend this is a job, she told herself. *Because it is.*

"I don't think you need to worry about me running off to pleasure myself at the slightest provocation," she managed to say, just this side of withering. "I realize this may come as a surprise, but some of us are not quite so obsessed with endless sexual exploits as others."

"You could have fooled me."

That voice of his was dark like silk, and it curled in her like a threat.

She thought she should refute that. Fight him. Stand up for herself, for God's sake.

But Constantine only smiled. "You will stay in your old bedroom, naturally."

"Naturally," she repeated. Because that would be more torture, wouldn't it? "How appropriate."

His eyes brightened. "I saw that you brought only one small bag. I brought it in, but you will not need even that. If I wish you to dress, I will provide whatever it is I think you ought to wear. Nightly, we will have dinner and you will wear whatever is left on your bed. And nothing else. Do you understand me?"

"With perfect clarity," she said. After all, her entire adult life had been about being *someone's* life-size dress-up doll. Why not his?

"Wonderful." The way he looked at her was predatory, though he did not move from the rail behind him. As if he was letting her know he could have. As if he was making sure she knew that everything that happened—

or didn't happen—was entirely of his choosing. "Off you go then, Molly."

But she didn't move. She found herself scowling at him instead. "I have to say, I really thought the naked sex object thing would be a lot more about the shagging and a whole lot less about the endless mind games."

Constantine laughed, throwing his beautiful head back and making the Greek sky dim a bit behind him. "What would be the fun in that?"

"I rather thought the forced shag was the point. And the fun, from some perspectives."

"Oh, Molly. You've read this situation entirely wrong." Constantine leaned back against the balcony railing, regarding her with more of that deep male satisfaction that made her feel as if the ground beneath her feet was not stable at all. "I have no intention of forcing you to do anything."

"Except making me come here, then forcing me to prance around naked for your entertainment, you mean."

That smile of his was…confronting. "I don't recall kidnapping you to get you here. Or tearing off your clothes. Or, for that matter, forcing you to orgasm while engaged in so prosaic a task as simple sun protection."

She felt herself flush, and there was no stopping that. "No, of course not. But persuasion is just a pretty word for force, isn't it?"

"It's a completely different word," Constantine said dryly. "And besides, I think the word that is the most germane to our situation is *consequences*. You don't like the consequences of some of your choices, that is all."

"I don't like the consequences of any of my choices," she retorted. And thought, *Or my mother's.*

"Such is life, *hetaira.* And someday, I have no doubt, you will dine out on all the stories of my wickedness. What a monster I am, how terrible, and so on. But between you and me, here and now, let us be clear. I have always given you choices. You always will have choices. And where there is choice, I think you'll find, there is no force."

She laughed at that. In disbelief. "Says the man with a sword hanging over my head."

"But therein lies the truth you're so desperate not to face," he replied, with quiet intensity. "That is not my sword. It is yours. By any estimation, you should never have had any money troubles again. And yet here you find yourself, naked before me, because of the choices you made long before you had the faintest idea what was waiting for you here. Blame me all you like. I'm used to it." He shrugged, the very picture of unconcern. "But when you're alone, Molly, and can look at yourself honestly, if you dare—remember. Blame yourself first."

And then he turned his back to her, leaving her to stew in his words for far too long. Before she slunk off inside…to do just about anything but look at herself in a mirror, honestly or not.

Because Molly already knew she would not like what she saw.

CHAPTER SIX

"I BEG YOUR PARDON." His brother Balthazar's voice was bright with amusement, and Constantine could practically see the look on his face, even though he was holed up far away on a private island down where the Aegean flirted with the bigger Mediterranean. He and the woman who was the daughter of the man who had destroyed their mother who Balthazar had married and impregnated, though not in that order. "Did you say Molly Payne? Our Molly Payne?"

"Perhaps you know her better as Magda," Constantine murmured. "Ridiculous as the name might be, and much as it pains me to admit it, she is universally known."

Balthazar laughed, which was a strange, new thing he did since his wedding. When, by rights, his marriage should have been as cold as the revenge he had always intended to wreak on his bride's family. Constantine could not get used to a lighter side of his grim older brother. It was…disconcerting.

"I don't know her at all, brother," Balthazar said. "No matter what name she uses. Because she was our stepsister for approximately five minutes and then I promptly forgot her."

"I did not."

The inadequacy of that statement clung to Constantine as the silence dragged out between Balthazar and him. Inadequacy and the fact that while he'd expected his fascination with Molly to wane after ten days in her constant company here in Skiathos, it had not.

And that, too, was putting it mildly.

His brother didn't have to know that. Just as Balthazar didn't need to know that Molly was currently dozing in a sun lounger that she'd pulled up beneath one of the umbrellas near the pool that was cut into the cliff below from the house, making its own level in the steep hill. Or that Molly came to him in the mornings, always naked and defiant, and he made sure to put the sunscreen all over her skin—though there was, sadly, no repeat of her ecstatic first reaction to his touch.

Was she fighting the simmering, greedy thing between them as hard as he was?

And did she understand that what he was doing was getting her not only used to his touch, but dependent on it—so that when she begged him for her release, as he knew she would, she would mean it?

Because sometimes that was all he thought about. Another thing he did not intend to share with his brother.

From his vantage point on the balcony off the master bedroom, he could see her where she lay. He could see how she glowed. She was stretched out on the lounger with a book in one hand and not a stitch on, which she had taken to as if it had been her idea in the first place.

She wafted about the estate in the same manner, often frowning at him as if it was bizarre that he was actually wearing clothes.

He hadn't expected that his nudity decree would humble her—she was a woman who was not in the least ashamed of her body, and he liked that. It made her all the more beautiful. But he had expected some pushback, and there was none.

Her own way of fighting back, he supposed.

Constantine wanted her. Badly.

But the waiting only made the wanting better. And it would make her inevitable destruction better, too. Or so he kept telling himself.

"I wouldn't have mentioned Molly Payne at all," Constantine said into his mobile. "But she and I are undergoing a small negotiation that is taking more time than expected. I didn't want you to worry unduly if you heard mention that I wasn't in the office."

He ran the Skalas & Sons operation from their London base, but he traveled so much under usual circumstances that it was not as difficult as it might have been to handle his office from afar. And besides, there were so few members of his staff who understood that he was in no way the character he played for the world. He liked it that way.

But his brother was a different story.

"I did not realize that I was your keeper," Balthazar said, sounding amused when he was usually anything but. "Or your boss."

Constantine knew that most of the world was convinced the Skalas brothers hated each other. They had split the company after Demetrius's death—in the sense of their responsibilities, though too many people seemed convinced it had been a civil war. Balthazar spent most of his time in New York, Constantine in London. And because each one of them had chosen his own city and headquarters, and saw no reason to live in each other's pockets, this was seen as evidence of their undying loathing for each other.

Neither one of them had ever bothered to set the record straight.

The truth was far less interesting. They had grown up under the foot of a cruel man who'd pitted them against each other. They had not learned how to be close. Neither one of them, therefore, had ever craved it.

And yet, when Balthazar had chosen to marry his enemy's daughter, a move Constantine grudgingly admired as truly leaning into the long game when it came to revenge, Constantine had stood as witness. He had taken his place at his brother's side in the traditional role of *koumbaro* at the wedding and had been fascinated to discover that his always cold, always business-minded brother was far more emotionally involved with his pregnant new wife than Constantine had expected.

More than he'd thought was even possible for a Skalas, for that matter.

And he had found that while he had not known how to be close to Balthazar growing up, or if such a thing was wise with a father who sought always to crush them both—using whatever weapons came to hand— it seemed less a mystery now that they were grown men. He could simply be a brother. Just as Balthazar could in return.

Though it was easier to think such things and far more difficult to know what to do when opportunities arose to actually *be* brotherly in the way others, as far as he was aware, simply knew how to do since birth.

He found himself scowling down at Molly's beautiful form, laid out for his pleasure. And was too aware that Balthazar was perhaps the one man alive who would fully understand what he was about here. But that didn't mean Constantine knew how to go about telling him.

Money was easier. It was either made or lost. The numbers never lied.

They also never had *opinions*.

"I ran into Isabel at a charity thing some years back," Balthazar said, sounding nonchalant and conversational. Two things he had never been before his wedding. Constantine did not know whether to applaud or ask if Balthazar was feeling well. "She seemed far less of a gorgon than I recalled, it must be said."

"You are mistaken," Constantine bit off, staring at the gorgon's daughter. "She remains every bit the horror show she was then. Did you forget what she did?"

"I'll never forget what she *represented*," Balthazar said, with a not particularly subtle inflection on that last word. "But what did she *do*, really, except marry a man neither one of us liked much either?"

Constantine took that as an opportunity to steer the conversation away from the thorny topic of Isabel Payne, but he was still brooding about it when he and his brother ended the call.

And he continued to brood about it until dinner that night with Molly.

Because he liked her to dress in the evenings, he also allowed his staff in then. He had his cook prepare them the kind of meals he always preferred when he was by the sea. Light and fresh, assembling local ingredients and letting the dishes they ate look as colorful as the table they ate them on.

Tonight he waited for her on the low terrace, the one set even further down the cliffside than the pool. It was accessible only by a winding path, meandering this way and that, with nothing but the sea there below. At night it was lit by lanterns, all of them making little halos against the hill when he looked back up toward the house.

How had he failed to notice how beautiful it was here when he was younger?

But then, he knew. Every moment in this house had been a trial, and when he'd stormed off to Skiathos Town in the evenings, his focus had been on oblivion, not taking in the sights. And he didn't like to think about what his brother had said. He didn't want to ask himself what Isabel or her daughter had actually *done*.

They had been here. That was enough.

As always, he heard her coming a few moments later. And was perhaps too grateful to turn from his thoughts to watch Molly as she moved in and out of the halos strewn across her path. Then stepped onto the terrace that had lanterns everywhere, casting her in a golden glow that seemed to beat back the night sky.

For glow she did. Still. Perhaps always.

Her blond hair swirled all around her and the dress he had chosen for the evening was a splash of a deep blue that made her look almost otherworldly.

"Your dress-up doll is reporting for duty," Molly said. Then executed a sharp pirouette, swirling around before him in a manner he knew she meant to be mocking.

But he did not feel in the least bit mocked. Because the way this particular dress clung to her was a revelation. The fabric clung and swung, both calling attention to and yet concealing everything at the same time.

Constantine had discovered that the more she was dressed or undressed according to his whim, the more possessive he became. And he enjoyed knowing that she wore nothing but the dress, as he had requested.

As if he might, at any moment, have his hands all over her. He liked her to spend a lot of time, every day, thinking about that possibility.

He knew he did.

"I apologize that my sartorial selections do not live up to those of a woman renowned the world over for her style," he said dryly. "Which, as far as I can tell, involves wearing extraordinarily ugly things as a measure of defiance."

"You're not wrong," Molly agreed. She drifted closer to him and accepted the glass of wine he handed her. "But fashion is a self-conscious art by its very nature. Style is innate."

"Now you sound like one of those dreadful magazines. I thought you were more often seen draped across their covers."

Molly took a sip of her wine and, not for the first time, he was struck by her total lack of self-consciousness. She was disarming, this stunning woman who should have been prostrate in her room, weeping at the cruelty being visited upon her here. Instead, she seemed effortlessly charming—as she had been each and every one of the past ten days.

As a strategy, he was forced to admire it. Because she chose to engage with Constantine as if he was her host. Not her jailer.

When she was naked, it was easy to remember their actual roles here. But these dinners blurred the lines. They made him almost forget why they were really here—and he knew he couldn't allow that. He should put a stop to any part of this that did not serve his vengeance.

But though he told himself the same thing every night, he kept on with these dinners anyway.

He chose not to ask himself why.

Molly was studying him, her gaze cool but not unpleasant. It was clearly a part of her charm offensive—and he assured himself he was merely learning how she operated. Her weaknesses and fragile spots. Her surprisingly effective weapons.

"When you wake up of a morning," she said, "I doubt very much that you preen about in front of your mirror until you have achieved exactly the right level of casual chic. Mixed liberally with contempt at the very notion of casual chic, obviously. I think you likely… just get dressed."

"I pay other people to worry about my wardrobe," he

replied. And smiled. "I already know I will look good in it, after all."

She lifted her glass in a mocking toast. "There you have it. Innate style. If you were fashion conscious, there would be more preening."

"You can't possibly be suggesting that you pay absolutely no mind to what you wear," he objected, mildly enough. "When you might happen to find yourself on a red carpet at any moment."

Her blue eyes looked something like merry. "No, of course not. What I'm saying is if I chose to wear a garbage bag to a red carpet, I would do it with such élan that garbage bags might very well become the rage afterward. That's style."

Constantine looked down at her and couldn't shift the same brooding mood he'd been in since his conversation with Balthazar.

"You're not the girl who lived here all those years ago," he said, in an abrupt growl. "Sometimes it's hard to imagine you could possibly be one and the same."

Her expression changed. And he had a quick, uncomfortable bolt of recognition at the sight, because it was instantly clear to him that she was acting a part. The charming, artless version of her was a role. Perhaps it really was a part of her, too, but it was a part she used for her own devices. Why did Constantine find it so difficult to remember that she could not possibly have scaled the heights she had were she not capable of working a room? Just as he was.

That did not sit well. At all.

"Did you expect me to be sixteen, then?" she asked

quietly. She gazed at him with those sharp eyes of hers, and Constantine suddenly felt exposed. The lantern light washing all over him didn't help. Her mouth curved. "Oh. You did. Let me guess how you thought *that* would look. You expected that there would be weeping. Maybe even a tantrum or two, since I was always accused of throwing those, though I never did. You expected me to turn bright red every time you deigned to look at me directly. And best of all, pick up where we left off, with me whispering my secrets into your faithless ear so you could use them against me."

That was as good a description of what had happened between them as any, Constantine knew. So why did he dislike it so intensely?

"If I'd wished for you to be sixteen again, I would hardly insist on your nudity," he pointed out. "It would muddy the retroactive teenage waters, don't you think?"

"Constantine." And Molly shook her head at him as if she'd expected better. "How could you possibly imagine that the same approach would work on me twice?"

"I am only pointing out that I thought there were only the three versions of you. That sixteen-year-old girl, you, and the role you play as Magda. I had no idea how many *other* versions of you there were."

"Maybe there's only one version," she replied, her cool blue gaze somehow filling him with fire. "Maybe you're the one who splintered into a hundred pieces, so long ago you think everyone else did the same."

"I am not the one with an alter ego, *Magda*," he said, with a laugh.

But she only smiled.

And then the food arrived, thankfully, before he could chase down whatever he saw in that gaze of hers that left him feeling… Edgy.

They ate in the lantern light. Perfectly grilled fish, local delicacies, and a few of Constantine's favorite forms of comfort food. Spanakopita. Saganaki. Honey-drenched sweets and strong coffee to finish. Far below, the sea threw itself at the cliffs and up above, the Greek summer sky put on a show as the stars beamed down.

And it had been ten days, yet Constantine—who had long regarded himself as wholly irresistible to women, because he had yet to meet one who had not said so her-self—was no closer to demolishing *this* woman than he had been before she'd arrived on the island.

That was the trouble, he told himself. That was why he did not feel quite himself. She was proving to be far harder to crack than he'd anticipated.

"How did you get into modeling in the first place?" he asked.

Her gaze flicked to him, looking something like amused. "Small talk? Really? I was wandering around your house today, naked from head to toe, and you think *small talk* is the appropriate response?"

"Is it that you cannot answer the question or that you do not wish to?" was his cool response.

She shrugged, managing to make even that a kind of pointed blade. "A modeling agent approached me on the Tube. I was eighteen and foolish enough to go around to the address on the card he gave me. That's it. That's the story. It was all fairly cut and dried, I'm afraid."

"But you must connect the dots for me." Constantine

toyed with the stem of his wineglass. "Because the girl who left Skiathos would never have imagined that anyone could consider her modeling material."

He did not know what he liked about the arctic blast he got from her then. Only that he did.

"You saw to that, didn't you?"

"I saw to it?" He sat back in his chair, taking his wine with him. "I'm guilty of a great many things, Molly, but I do not recall putting together a campaign against your... What is it you accuse me of? Your self-confidence?"

"But of course you did," she replied, with a certain simplicity that seemed to slice into him. "It was your only goal, I assume. That and extracting private sentiments from me that you could sell to the tabloids."

"I never sold anything to the tabloids," he replied.

It was true. He'd given away those stories for free.

"I'm actually delighted to have the opportunity to discuss this with you," she said, with a strange light in her eyes, propping her elbows on the table between them. "I used to dream about doing this, though when I did, it was less *discussing* and more...beating at the side of your head with a stick of some kind. But, you know. Bygones."

"I'm afraid I'm not following you." He eyed her, and that light in her gaze. "Surely you are not complaining that I was *mean* to you? I know you were a sensitive girl back then, Molly. But really. There is a vast difference between *meanness* and a person simply not catering to you in the way you would like."

"Sensitive," she repeated, as if tasting the word and

not finding she liked it overmuch. "Isn't it funny how that word is used as an insult? Think about what it means. Yes, I was very *sensitive* to your manipulations. And your father's. And—"

"Are you comparing me to my father?" His tone was light, but he doubted his gaze matched. "Do you dare?"

If he expected Molly to back down, he was in for a disappointment. She only gazed back at him, her expression neutral enough, save the arch of her brows.

"My mistake," she said in a cool tone designed, he knew, to rub him the wrong way. It worked. He hated that it worked. "There are no similarities. Your father isolated a woman here, constantly veering back and forth between treating her as a lover or treating her like the help. Either way, she was an object entirely at his whim. There is, naturally, no overlap whatsoever between the two scenarios."

"Is this an example of the sensitivity you claimed not to have?" he asked darkly.

"Am I the sensitive one, Constantine? It seems you're the one having a reaction."

He was having any number of reactions, and he doubted very much that she would like it if he shared them with her. He did not care how long it took him to get himself back under control, so long as he managed it. He did not like how close he'd come to losing control altogether. He did not care, at all, for how this woman affected him.

But he didn't walk away from her or this situation he'd created, either.

"I believe you were going to tell me how it was that I

hurt your precious teenage feelings, making me somehow responsible for your lack of self-confidence at the time." His shrug, it turned out, was no less a weapon than hers. "Though I think you will find that many a teenage girl is in the same predicament. It is the *teenage girl* that does it, not me."

"How many teenage girls do you know who had their confidences funneled directly to the gossip rags?"

He eyed her. "Do you imagine that I will apologize for this?"

Her lips curved, but there was only frigid cold in her gaze. "A Skalas? Apologize? The very earth would tremble."

"If you resent finding yourself in these crosshairs, Molly, I would suggest that you address yourself to your mother. As she is the one who put you there."

Molly scowled at him. "I get it, Constantine. You didn't want a stepmother. Boo-hoo. It may shock you to discover that I didn't particularly want a stepfather, either. Particularly not one like your father, who was, at best, sadistic. And that's about the nicest thing I can think to say about him."

He made a scoffing sound, but she didn't subside. Instead, she leaned over the table, still aiming that scowl right at him. "It amazes me that you seem to think my mother, a housekeeper with no formal education whatsoever, managed the astonishing feat of *trapping* Demetrius Skalas, who was at that time the richest man on earth. *Trapping him.* What a joke. If she had that kind of power, why would she have stopped with a simple trap? Why wouldn't she have used her power to either make him a better husband, or, failing that, kill him off so she could live out her days as a very wealthy Skalas widow?"

Constantine couldn't say he liked either one of those questions very much. "You are naive in the extreme if you don't know precisely how your mother ensnared my father."

"Because… What? Demetrius Skalas, once again the richest man in the world—and also well renowned for the parade of women on his arm all throughout his marriage—suddenly tripped over one particular woman and could no longer function? My mother worked some kind of spell, is that it? And he was susceptible for only as long as it took to race off and marry her. Then, in another bit of magic, he became completely impervious to her in every way." She rolled her eyes. "Come on, Constantine. You can't really believe any of that."

He found his ribs were too tight, suddenly. He was too aware of his pulse, and the way it racketed around inside him. He glared at her, wishing the lantern light didn't make her look even more beautiful than she already was. Because the beauty was distracting, and somehow made the charges she was levying against his father—and against him—seem that much starker.

And something he almost wanted to call painful.

"Nothing you can possibly say to me is going to make me change my opinion of your mother, Molly," he said.

When he could speak with the voice that was only dark with warning, not bright with his temper.

"Of course not," she said quietly, her arctic blue gaze

pinning him where he sat. "Because if you did that, you would have so many other unfortunate questions to ask yourself, wouldn't you? If you're wrong about my mother, then all the years you spent sandbagging her every move would seem…vicious, wouldn't they? If you're wrong about my mother, this price you intend to extract from me by naked days and romantic nights really does make you a monster, doesn't it? And that's not even getting into what you did to a lost teenage girl who could have used a friend. The less said about that the better, I think you'll agree."

"I think that's enough," he managed to growl.

"I'm sure it is," Molly said with a rueful little laugh that set his teeth on edge. "It gets scary straying that close to the truth, doesn't it?"

He was on his feet, though he didn't recall when he'd decided to move. Constantine stood over the table, staring down at her, and for all her talk of what was and was not a spell, he felt cursed.

She had haunted him for years. And over the past ten days, that haunting had only grown worse. Because everything had gone according to plan here, except his reaction.

He had wanted her to be lulled into a false sense of security. He had wanted her to stop worrying he might pounce on her at any turn and to embrace both the insistence upon nakedness as well as the sunscreen he ritualistically applied to her body every morning.

But while she seemed to have acclimated with ease, all Constantine seemed to do was lose sleep.

"You seem to have forgotten your place," he managed to get out.

But Molly rose, too, like a shimmering blue flame. She was a gloriously tall woman, no doubt used to looking men in the eye. Or looking down at them. Yet she had to tilt her chin to manage it with him, and Constantine found he liked that he did not loom over her as he normally did over women.

Because it put her mouth that much closer to his.

"You'd better teach me my place then," she shot back at him. "Don't you know? We Payne women have a terrible habit of casting spells on unwary men like witches of yore, then making them do our bidding. Behold my success, for it has made me...your plaything."

"Shut up," he growled at her.

And then he took her mouth in a fury.

It had been too long since that last kiss. It had been *too long*.

He found his hands on the sides of her jaw, holding her mouth right where he needed it. He kissed her and he kissed her, a wild taking. A claiming, possessive and dark.

He kissed her until he realized that if he didn't stop, he would take her right there, out on the terrace beneath the stars.

And that was not the plan.

Just as the fire that coursed through him was not the plan, because it threatened to undo everything. It got in his head, it made him far too hard, it made his hands move over her as if all he'd been put on this earth to do was worship the glory she wore so easily.

He kissed her until he thought it might break him, and then he thrust her away from him.

And took some solace in the fact that however wrecked he might feel, she looked worse. Her blue eyes had gone dark, needy.

The sound she made was of loss.

"Tonight is our last night here," he told her. "We have a series of extremely high-profile events to attend, Molly. Remember. This affair will be very, very public."

"Is it an affair? Or an impromptu bit of theater you've set up for your entertainment?"

But she didn't ask that quite as sharply as she might have. And he could hear the tremor in her voice. He could see the flush on her face and against the fabric of that dress of hers, the telltale press of her hard nipples, giving her away.

"Don't you worry about when our affair will begin in truth," Constantine said, dark and hot. "You'll know. You'll find yourself on your knees, begging as beautifully as you do anything else."

And then he left her there, still obviously trying to hide the fact that she was shaken before she could tell that he was, too.

CHAPTER SEVEN

MOLLY SHOULD HAVE EXPECTED, Constantine being Constantine, that the publicity tour he had apparently put together in his spare time—all while seeming to do nothing but drive her to the brink of distraction with his daily sunscreen ritual, then taunt her every evening—was comprehensive. And would catapult them to the forefront of every gossip's mind, not to mention every tabloid's main page, with a vengeance.

Because vengeance was his goal, and she needed to remember that. She had almost started to think that his goal was to keep her completely off balance, because he was succeeding at that, and brilliantly.

Though she thought she would rather fling herself from one of the Skiathos cliffs, like the Gothic heroine she told herself she was, than admit it.

That next morning he drove them both in a simmering silence to the Skiathos airport. His jet waited for them there, prepared to whisk them off across the world to Los Angeles, stop one on their world tour. It might look like a romantic interlude to some. It was meant to look like a happy accident of press appearances while engaged in some of that high-profile celebrity charity that famous and infamous people alike used the way teenagers used the hallways in their schools, all see and be seen.

But Molly knew the point of it was neither romance nor charity. It was her eventual humiliation. He'd said so.

"If we are attending some kind of gala event," Molly remarked as they started their descent into a surprisingly clear day over the Los Angeles basin, "does that mean that you have also selected my wardrobe? Or is this more naked time. That *will* cause a stir."

Across from her, Constantine barely looked up from the laptop that had consumed his attention for the whole of their flight. Too busy checking for mention of himself in several languages, she could only assume. Because it was too strange to think of Constantine Skalas actually *working*. Surely that was what Balthazar was for.

She couldn't have said what Constantine was for, save her own, personal destruction.

"Your role is simple," he said now. "Keep your mouth closed and act adoring. Easy enough, no?"

"Easy, yes," she agreed. "But unusual, certainly. I'm not exactly known as the shy and retiring type."

Constantine slapped his laptop closed as the jet's wheels touched the ground. His gaze seemed to touch hers with a similar impact. "But you are besotted, *hetaira*. You hardly know yourself. Your body betrays you with the things it wants and you tell yourself you ought to be horrified, when in truth, all you are is wildly, madly in love. So much so that it is astoundingly visible to all and sundry and possibly even from space." Then his mouth curved in that mocking way that always seemed to pierce straight through her. She assumed he must know that. "Or is that too much of a stretch?"

"Don't you worry," Molly said, as if trying to soothe him. She smiled. "I'm very, very good at my job."

But she was just as happy when his attention was redirected to his mobile, because that had all been…a little too close to the truth for her liking.

Because she had the terrible fear that despite all her tough talk, she was more in danger when it came to Constantine Skalas than she ever had been, even back when they'd lived together in Skiathos the first time.

Because the teen girl she'd been then had never imagined he would look twice at her. Not really. Whereas the grown-up version of Molly was a little too aware that at any moment, there was the possibility he might kiss her again.

Or more.

Why hadn't he done more?

She had spent ten days wandering around naked all over his estate in Skiathos, pretending she didn't feel half-feverish at the thought, waiting for him to put his hands on her at any moment. To her dismay, it was nearly all she thought about, unable to understand why it was that he simply kept her…wanting.

Maybe the wanting was why.

If so, it worked. It drove her mad. She had lounged about near the pool every day, near the sun if not quite in it, imagining that every stray breeze was his touch. And even though ten days of forced idleness should have driven her crazy, she had never felt particularly idle. Too busy was she…imagining.

Because the things that had happened inside of her the first time he'd put that sunscreen on haunted her. Not to mention the things she'd done. God, the things she'd *done*… She still daydreamed about it. Those hands of his, all over her breasts. That hard thigh thrust between her legs. Her absolutely shameless display as she'd rocked herself against him… How she'd moved her hips, making no secret of the fact that she was pressing the molten, aching core of her femininity against his hard-packed muscles.

Deliberately. Desperately.

Molly wasn't sure why she hadn't died from embarrassment. Instead, she had lived. And now relived those moments, over and over and over again, and if she was honest with herself, not because she was attempting to browbeat herself with guilt and shame. Not at all.

She had managed to keep herself contained every other time he ran those hands, slicked with lotion, all over her skin. She had simply packed those sensations away as she did every time she stepped in front of a photographer. She felt as she was told to feel. She moved as she was told to move. She was a canvas who existed for others to paint their vision all over her.

It was harder than it sounded, but during the day, it worked well enough. Even at their typically fraught dinners, she did her best to funnel her feelings away while she dressed in what he'd left for her. And because she was dressed for his pleasure, she took the evening meal as an opportunity to vent her spleen.

The truth was, she'd gotten used to it. She had gotten used to Skiathos, and while the fact she had no choice but to be there again could never make her love it, she found herself becoming something like affectionate for the place, after all.

But it was when she went to bed in that bedroom that had been hers once before that everything she kept at bay all day long swamped her.

At first she thought it was just as well. He might excite her to a fever pitch, but there was nothing to say she couldn't handle her own pleasure as she pleased once she was alone.

Except she didn't.

Because Constantine had told her not to. It was as simple as that. And her own obedience to this man who made no secret of the fact that his aim was to destroy her appalled her. It made her wonder, not what spells her mother might have worked back in the day, but why she, personally, was cursed with an inability to treat Constantine as he deserved in turn. Or even think of him as she ought to.

But however appalled she might have been, she didn't disobey him.

And as they rode in the back of a limo through Los Angeles, a city she knew well, she had to assume that all of this was part of his game. Her uncertainty. Her feeling of being forever off balance. Even his rules about sunscreen and the clothes he insisted she wear, so that at all times, whatever touched her body was his. It was a game, all right.

What Molly didn't understand was why she kept playing right into it.

The house he took her to sat propped up high in the Santa Monica Mountains that ran through the center of California's largest, most sprawling city. They took one of the canyon roads up from the valley floor, a winding, slow affair. Slowly they climbed into the foothills, one tight curve after the next, passing houses that defied gravity and nature as they clung to the sides of cliffs. A grand, if vertical, mansion next to what looked like an old cottage, all tucked away in that southern California lushness that always surprised her. Think of Los Angeles and what came to mind was traffic, but the city was much more than that. The mysterious hills, where coyotes roamed and some nights, it could seem as if civilization was far, far away. The famous beaches and beyond them, surprising pockets of charming little places that still felt small and close-knit. Old flower-children's retreats in far-off canyons, beautiful architecture, and the smell of citrus and salt on a sweet spring breeze. As she looked out her window now she saw hummingbirds darting between one blossom and the next, all of them bright and plush, and around them, great swathes of green and fruit-bearing trees. Outside, the air was scented with a hint of smoke, rosemary and sage, and the sweetness of too many flowers to name.

They made it to the top of the hill and stopped at its crest. The house they'd arrived at looked wholly unremarkable from the winding street outside. It was overgrown with exuberant vines of bougainvillea that reminded her of Greece, thick curtains of jasmine she knew would bloom at night, and an invitingly green arched trellis that led to the unassuming front door of what appeared to be a very modest bungalow.

Molly knew it wasn't. Even before she exited the limo she knew that despite appearances, there would be nothing modest about any place Constantine Skalas frequented.

And sure enough, the house cascaded down the side of the cliff, a jumble of sleek modern levels flowing in and out of each other, creating a poetry of indoor and outdoor space. Rooms that were enclosed had as few opaque walls as possible and the rest was all glass, looking out over the enduring tangle of the City of Angels, stretched out as far as the eye could see. And because the day was clear, she could actually see the thick blue ribbon of the sea in the distance.

It was stunning. Because it was his. How could it be anything else?

"We leave for the red carpet in two hours," Constantine informed her. And shook his head as she began to speak. "I don't want to hear excuses about how much time you need to make your appearance. You claimed you could appear in a garbage bag, did you not?"

"I was being facetious."

He smiled, nothing but challenge in his gaze. "I want to see magic."

"Garbage bag magic?" She kept her voice light. "Who knew such a thing existed?"

But the intensity of Constantine's stare did not waver. "Magic, Molly."

"Then magic it will be," she assured him. What else could she say?

"My staff will assist you." He nodded toward a woman who waited there at the edge of the glass room, her gaze lowered.

Molly smiled at him. "You are too good, Constantine. Really."

And her reward was a searing, almost painful blast from those coffee-dark eyes.

A warning she really should heed, she knew. But she couldn't seem to do that.

Molly followed the woman down a series of exposed staircases, moving in and out of the glass enclosures. Then she led the way into a room that had been transformed into the kind of salon Molly knew best. Racks of clothing stood ready, and more, she saw a fleet of men and women she instantly recognized as stylists and beauty estheticians, armed with the tools of their trade.

Very well then. This was a test he wanted her to pass, and Molly did not *pass* tests. She aced them.

"What is this red carpet for, exactly?" she asked the woman beside her as she scanned the clothes provided. She recognized most of the designers from the cut of their garments, as clear to her as if they'd been labeled.

"It's a gala event," the woman told her, and then outlined exactly what charity the gala supported and more importantly, the expected celebrity content of its guest list as well as the kind of press expected.

"We do have some suggestions," the woman began.

Molly smiled at her. "I think I've got it. But thank you."

She remembered being interviewed by a journalist once who had spent the better part of the interview making snide, not particularly *passive* aggressive remarks about how low-maintenance and carefree she, the journalist, was. *She* couldn't imagine spending *twenty whole minutes* on her appearance, much less the hours and hours that Molly did. And she certainly didn't waste so much brainpower *worrying* about *clothes*.

Though, of course, she'd been speaking to Magda.

That is why, Magda had told her imperiously, *it is the words you type with your unmanicured fingers that go into magazines. While it is my face that graces the cover.*

There were a lot of things Molly found herself uncertain about lately, but fashion, style, and how best to use both as her best weapons were not among them.

She changed swiftly into the smock waiting for her, and then handed herself over into the clutches of the beauticians, making her preferences known when it came to nail polish, toenail polish, brow shape, and the cosmetics themselves. She and a makeup artist had a robust discussion about lip shade and a smoky or unsmoky eye. And when she told the hairstylist her concept for hair, he agreed, his eyes lighting up.

And then all of them got to work.

One hour and fifty minutes later, she stood before the mirror with her hastily assembled team around her. She took a look at herself from each side, critically. Then she lifted her gaze so she could see everybody standing behind her. And beamed.

"You are all absolute stars," she said, and meant it. "This is complete perfection."

Then she walked upstairs to present herself for Constantine's inspection, two hours to the second after she'd left his side.

And had the distinct pleasure of watching him do a double take.

He had been waiting for her with a drink in one hand, looking out one of the enormous windows over the city that lay before him as if displayed on a platter. He glanced at her, then looked back outside—only to whip that gaze back to her again.

She strode toward him, letting him take in the look she'd selected. "Does this garbage bag meet with your approval?"

For his part, Constantine was dressed in what should have been sober black tie, unremarkable in any way. But it was Constantine wearing it, so he looked not only faintly rumpled but as if the effort of standing upright was almost too much for him, so profoundly was he a creature who ought to have been horizontal. Stretched out lazily in the nearest bed, and not alone.

"I expected something ornate," he said, but she didn't think it was criticism.

Molly turned in a full, slow circle for him before he asked—or twirled that finger of his—so he could see the full effect. "You asked for starry-eyed adoration. And I think we can agree that I've delivered it."

She already knew how the pictures would look. She

had picked the simplest gown on offer, in a deep, luxurious blue. It looked like nothing much on a hanger, but she knew the designer well and had known at a glance that it would hug her perfectly and more, make her skin look luminous. She had the makeup artist make her look fresh and dewy, with a little bit of glamour around the eyes, on the off chance she couldn't quite pull off full-on adoration at all times. And to top it off, the hairstylist had created a breathtaking bit of ponytail art that made her look like the girl next door.

Molly looked like innocence personified, and next to Constantine, she might as well have taken out a billboard announcing that she was Little Red Riding Hood, and he the Big Bad Wolf.

She could see by the way he grinned, slow and sure, that he agreed.

"The only question," he said as he drew close, then took her arm in a possessive grip that made her whole body tighten, then melt, "is whether or not anyone will believe that a woman such as Magda could ever be innocent."

"Love makes innocents of us all," Molly said quietly, wishing those words sounded as arch as they had in her head. "Isn't that the story you're selling here? Magda, a known whore who is also the daughter of whores, is rendered into a Disney heroine at one touch of your wicked hand. What tabloid could resist such a lovely tale?"

He was still holding her arm, that hard palm of his wrapped around her bicep, which meant he was much too close. She knew his scent, now. She knew his heat.

And the danger of his heavy-lidded gaze that only seemed to grow worse with time.

Or perhaps it was that she grew more susceptible with each day that passed.

"Why would anyone resist?" he asked, his voice rough.

And for a moment, while he gazed at her, she forgot where she was. She forgot who she was. The California sun streamed all over them both, but all she saw was the rich dark of his gaze. Her heart thudded. Her blood seemed to sing in her own veins, loud and clear.

When he turned away, steering her toward the door, she realized she had been holding her breath. And more, that she'd wanted absolutely nothing in that moment but to feel his mouth on hers again.

But Constantine did not kiss her that night. He waited.

First there was the red carpet in Los Angeles. Then it was a jaunt across the Pacific to Singapore, then on to Dubai, and then, in quick succession, Rome, Madrid, and then finally to Paris.

They had made exactly the splash Constantine had wanted. The world was obsessed with them. No one had ever seen Magda look so sweet, so smitten. No one had ever seen Constantine look even remotely possessive— of anything.

The public was hooked.

What worried Molly was her dawning realization that she was, too.

She was careful to remind herself—she tried to remind herself—that if he expected her to put on an act, he was likely doing the same. No matter how it felt sometimes.

In all, the trip took two weeks. It was a jumble of time zones, flashbulbs, and the flights in between, tucked up in that jet of his. Kept stocked, after the first week, with tabloids from too many countries to count. All featuring their faces.

"It makes a difference to actually *try* to make it on the cover of the tabloids, I suppose," Molly had said somewhere in the beginning of their second week. "A bit inside out, if you ask me."

"I want to be certain that for the rest of your career, no matter what happens, you will be asked about me," Constantine had told her, with that smile of his that let her know this was a part of his revenge he loved the most. He liked to study her over the edge of his laptop, where he did who knew what. "Of course, a girl can only model for so long. As you might imagine."

Molly had not shared with him that no one knew the expiration date on a model's career more intimately than the model in question.

"Handy, isn't it, that you can go right on being a bastard forever," she replied instead, smiling wide.

And had pretended not to notice it when she'd gotten a real laugh out of him for her trouble.

Because all the while, the tension between them grew. A tension she tried to tell herself had to do with his great revenge and only that revenge…but she knew it didn't. It was rooted in the way he touched her. Every time skin met skin, an electricity that only seemed to rage brighter and longer between them flared. And never dimmed. It was every event where they were stood next to each other, always touching, always gazing adoringly at each other.

Always acting, she told herself.

Only acting, surely—though more and more, she feared that wasn't what she was doing at all.

They landed in Paris in the early afternoon and because it was Paris, Molly took extra time preparing herself for the evening ahead. That night, she went for more drama overall, but compensated for that with an understated face and a flat shoe that would be seen as edgy. Particularly amongst the fashionistas of France.

It was a typical evening. Too many pictures taken. Too many faces, all of them avid and insinuating, not much more than a big blur before her. Another formal dinner where she ate heartily no matter if she liked what she was served or not. Because Molly distinctly disliked the fact that as a model—a woman whose job it was to maintain a certain body shape—she was constantly observed when food was around. It tired her.

We must take our rebellions where we can, she told herself as she smiled at a sharp-eyed society doyenne seated near her, then ate a huge forkful of creamy pasta just to watch the other woman recoil.

Like many of these events on their little tour, there was also dancing. And no matter how many times she told herself that she was used to it, she wasn't. No matter how many times Constantine gathered her into his arms and looked down at her as if nothing else existed save the two of them, she wasn't ready.

You will never be ready, a voice inside her pronounced.

And in another sense, she'd been ready since she was sixteen.

Maybe that was why, when they made it back to a Parisian penthouse apartment that, like all of the Skalas properties she'd sampled on this trip, commanded astonishing views, Molly…lost it.

If this night went the way all the other nights went, she and Constantine would sit about drawing blood and scoring points over drinks. Then he would take himself off and she would find herself lying wide awake in another strange bed, her hands between her legs yet unable to give herself the relief she craved.

Tonight, she thought that going through this same routine of hers might kill her.

"I was promised a very specific kind of torture," she said, standing in the great living area with the City of Light shining in all around. Molly could hear that her own voice sounded…distinctly unhinged. "You made it perfectly clear this was supposed to be a real affair, or else how could you possibly destroy me at the end of it?"

Constantine, pouring the usual drinks at the bar across the room, turned. "I beg your pardon?"

"To be honest, Constantine, it seems to me that after all this jetting about the planet, not to mention starting off the whole thing with a one-way nudist colony, I deserve some kind of compensation."

"Why would you think that?" he asked mildly, though his gaze had gone glittery in that way that made everything inside her cartwheel about. She should have been used to it by now. And yet was not. At all. "Surely I cannot have given you any reason to assume that your feelings matter here? I did try to avoid it."

"Perish the thought," she said grandly. "I'm only looking out for your interests. If, after all, this is nothing but a little act we're putting on for the press, well. That's a different scenario than the initial bold threats that were issued. With, I suppose, a dose of compulsory nakedness from time to time, just to keep everyone honest?"

Constantine swirled the liquid he held in a heavy tumbler in one hand. His eyelids, already so seemingly sleepy, seemed to droop even lower. It made his gaze seem all the brighter.

"Why, Molly. I am shocked. Are you asking me for sex?"

Was she? But she knew she was. "And if I am?"

She didn't know what she was doing. Or maybe that was a cop-out. Maybe she knew exactly what she was doing. Maybe what she'd said to him was true, after a fashion. She was putting out all this effort. She was already linked with him in the press and everywhere else. The whole world thought she was engaged in a torrid affair with *the* Constantine Skalas, which did not horrify her the way it should have. Oh no.

Molly knew, keenly, that the sixteen-year-old idiot girl who'd been so enamored of him would have loved to find herself in this situation. Had, in fact, wished and dreamed and hoped for precisely something like this to have come along back then.

What she couldn't seem to handle—because the

longing for him had become a pulsing thing between her legs, on the insides of her wrists, at her temples, in her throat, *everywhere*—was not getting the opportunity to actually have that affair.

Because she'd spent her whole life not having affairs.

Not only with Constantine Skalas, but with anyone. The world kept turning and people were out there having life-altering sex, apparently. All while Molly just writhed about in photo shoots, selling sex to the camera yet having none herself.

If he was going to blow up her life anyway, she might as well enjoy the fire while she burned. Why not?

And since she had the distinct impression that they were going to end up in bed together anyway, once he finished playing his little revenge games, Molly could admit that she took a certain pleasure in moving things along her own schedule.

Because she had the feeling it might very well be the only thing she would control when it came Constantine. Ever.

"I thought I made it clear," he said, still regarding her in that way that made her want very much to squirm. If she was a person who squirmed. Until tonight, she never had been. "If you want me, you must beg. I do not mean pretty words, though I fear I do require them. I will have you on your knees, naked, begging for the privilege."

"You really do like a pageant, don't you?"

He gave a very Greek sort of shrug, more his chin than his shoulder. "The only people who do not care for a pageant, *hetaira*, are those who know one will never be thrown in their honor."

"Fair enough," she murmured.

And it was one thing to want sex at last. Right now. But another to do what he was asking. To debase herself—

But who was she kidding? She had already debased herself to the moon and back for this man, and more, had loved it more than she'd hated it. What was a little more where that came from?

Letting out a long sort of breath—a soft sound of surrender—Molly reached around to the side, where the zipper of the current dress she was wearing was cunningly concealed, and zipped it down. She let the gown fall, then pool around her feet, then she kicked it aside.

She let him look at her for a moment, stood there in nothing but heels and a push-up bra, and then she kicked her shoes aside and pulled off the bra at the same time. It was so easy to undress, she thought a little wildly, even though it took hours to get her looks put together so she could look effortless in public.

That is because fashion is always about sex, a beauty editor had once told her grandly.

Tonight Molly agreed.

Naked, she glided across the room until she stood before Constantine. And the longer she looked at him, the more her heart thundered inside her chest.

And the slicker, and hotter, she felt between her legs.

"Beg," he ordered her, though his voice sounded slightly hoarse. Rough like his hands would be against her skin. "And make it good, Molly. I've been waiting for it for a long, long time."

Molly took a deep breath. She wanted to smile but found she couldn't.

Instead, she did the only thing she could.

The thing she'd been wanting to do for longer than she cared to admit.

She sank down onto her knees before the devil himself, tipped her head back so he could see her face, and begged.

CHAPTER EIGHT

AT LAST.

Constantine had waited so long. All the plotting. All the planning. The angry seed of vengeance that had been planted so long ago when his father had brought home a new bride. The small, wiry green shoot of fury that had developed when dreamy Molly, unaccountably, had shot to prominence as Magda.

Those years when he'd seen her face everywhere. Like a taunt.

And the exquisite, almost unbearable weight of what had dragged on between them now for nearly a month.

All for this.

This.

He would not say that he was used to her nakedness by now, for who could ever grow used to the sight of such perfection? He would sooner be dead than *used to* her.

But it was a different thing altogether to see her on her knees before him, graceful and gorgeous, and her head tipped up to him. Showing him, in case he'd had the slightest shred of doubt, that she hungered for him as he had always dreamed.

As he had been so sure she would.

Those arctic blue eyes were filled with heat, and Constantine could feel the weight of her hunger, its sharp claws, deep in his sex.

He could not wait to get inside her at last.

But all he did was swirl his drink in his glass and regard her idly. As if he was on the verge of boredom, but was trying to be polite, and he had the pleasure of watching her expression change as he looked at her.

He wanted her off balance, even on her knees. Maybe especially on her knees.

"That is a very pretty picture you are presenting to me, Molly," he murmured. "But that is your stock in trade, is it not? Pretty pictures. Pretty images. None of them you. You don't even use your own name."

"Did I misunderstand the stage directions?" she asked, and for some reason, the warm undertone in her voice, that thread of laughter when surely she should have been more mindful of her own surrender, was nearly his undoing.

Why was it that he could not seem to remember that what was happening here was serious? It was revenge. It was not the place for laughter. He should not have *liked* her.

"This is the trouble with beautiful women," he told her, and it was harder to sound as disaffected and jaded as he usually did.

But then, that was nothing new. He had been acting

unlike himself when it came to Molly for far longer than he cared to recall.

Once again he was struck by how at ease she was in her skin. It was powerful. It made her seem something like mystical, adding to the glory of all her elegance. She settled back on her heels now, her breasts jutting out and her blue eyes gleaming with more than simply that hunger, now.

God, the ways he wanted her.

Especially when she smiled at him, that clever little curve of her lips that made him feel almost…silly. "I can't wait to hear the thoughts of an inveterate bedpost-notcher when it comes to women," she said. "Such things are always so incisive and hard-hitting, aren't they? And not at all patriarchal. I'm surprised you haven't already written a book on the subject, given how many women's names you've likely forgotten in your time. In the last week, even."

"Here is the thing about beautiful women," Constantine said again, refusing to rise to her bait. And then, as he considered it, astounded that he had to caution himself against such a thing in the first place. "A beautiful woman assumes that the *fact* of her is sufficient. That she need not think or do or say anything further. She exists, therefore that is all that need be expected of her. Her mere appearance on any scene should do all the thinking, doing, or speaking necessary, and she therefore assumes it will."

Molly's head canted slightly to one side, and he could no longer see any of that humor in her gaze. He should have been thrilled.

He told himself he was *thrilled*.

"Beautiful women are born with a face that they did not choose," Molly said quietly. After a moment that stretched on too long for Constantine's comfort, and he was the one who was in control. He was not the one on his knees. "And they are taught, over time, that people will react to that face. That strangers and loved ones alike will treat that face in ways that have absolutely nothing to do with the person behind it. You learn quickly that it is far better to simply present yourself and see what the reaction will be first. It's safer."

Something seemed to crackle between them, a new and more dangerous heat.

"Molly." Constantine said her name as if he had never tasted it in his mouth before. As if he'd never tasted her, when the reality was, he had never been the same since he had. "Nothing here is safe. Not for you."

He expected her to quail at that. To shrink down, there where she knelt before him, or shrivel a bit. To show some hint that she was torn into a thousand pieces as he could feel he was. As he would rather rip off his own head before showing her he was.

But instead, this confounding woman—his once-upon-a-time stepsister and his current obsession—smiled.

A big, wide sort of smile that made him want to shout out his frustration loud enough to topple the Arc de Triomphe. And yet, at the same time, it made him want to taste that smile himself. And then the rest of her.

Now.

Why could he not compartmentalize this woman as he had every other thing in his life?

"No one expects an intricately plotted revenge plot to be *safe*, Constantine," she said in mock quelling tones, and he could hear too well the laughter in her voice again. It was its own heat. "That would completely defeat the purpose of all that plotting. All the demands for naked sunscreen application. And our current grand tour of the romance that wasn't."

"If this is still a joke to you," Constantine said, and it hurt him to say it so lazily, but he managed it, "you might as well get dressed and take yourself off to bed. I told you the only circumstances under which we will have sex, Molly. Mockery is not among them."

She sighed a little. "I didn't realize we had to be as solemn and serious as death. I have to tell you, every story I've ever heard about the irresistible charm of Europe's finest playboy—and I think you know there are a great many stories—was a lie."

"Not a lie," he found himself retorting, when he did not need to respond to her provocations. Surely that she wanted him to respond was reason enough to refrain. "But not for you."

"I do enjoy being special," Molly murmured, her eyes too bright on his. "It's because of an experience I had when I was but a girl, you see. I'll tell you the story. Once upon a time, I had an evil stepbrother straight out of central casting who tied himself in knots to make certain I knew that while *he* was marvelous in all ways, I was destined for nothing at all but a life of sodden beige porridge."

"You must be speaking about Balthazar," Constantine replied, sounding significantly less lazy than before. "As I have never trafficked much in either the color beige, nor, happily, porridge. Sodden or otherwise. I would rather eat paste."

"Constantine." She knelt up again, raising her hands before her in what looked like supplication, even though he could see that all that heat and all that humor in her gaze was still right there. "You may have to lead me through this, as I'm a little rusty. I believe I picked up your deeply subtle attempt to let me know that merely kneeling before you as a woman you consider beautiful is not enough. But I'm afraid my begging skills aren't my strong suit."

"You can start by taking this seriously," he growled down at her.

And again, found himself something like confounded when all she did was smile wider, her eyes sparkling as if he just recited a love poem.

"I take this very seriously, actually," she said. She paused, almost as if she was debating something, but then blew out a breath. "I've never done this before."

"Beg for it?" He should not have felt that as a particular triumph, and yet he did. "I would not know myself, but I'm told it can add a certain…intensity. If not for you, then for me."

"Not so much the begging part," she said softly. "*It*, Constantine. The deed itself. This will be my first time and I want to thank you, in advance, for making it so soft, special, and beautifully caring."

Despite himself, Constantine laughed.

Hard.

Because the very idea of Magda, whose many lovers pranced about the planet giving interviews about exactly what it was like to sample one of the most beautiful women in the world—interviews that had long driven him mad—claiming to be *untouched*?

It was preposterous. Hilarious.

And somehow, it reset something in him. It settled him. If she needed to play games to get through this thing between them, then who was he to deny her that opportunity?

Constantine had always liked a game or two. It only made things more fun.

"Yes, of course," he drawled, trying—if not too hard—to sound more serious then. "I should have known at a glance that you were a virgin. I'm honored indeed that you have chosen to hand over such a glorious prize to your enemy."

Her smile grew practically beatific. "Constantine. You're not my enemy. I'm afraid that's always been a one-way street. Left to my own devices—those being, you know, when no one is mounting a coordinated campaign to crush my mother, taking both her money and mine—I don't think about you at all."

He shook his head, as if in disappointment. "Liar."

Then, finally, at that single growled word, her smile faded.

And he watched, transfixed, as the heat took over.

It was possibly one of the most beautiful things he had ever beheld.

He could see it all then on that beautiful face of hers.
Heat, growing by the moment. Need and longing, a
match for his own. And that same wild, incoherent desire that stormed through him.

"That is a lie," she admitted. And when he only held
her gaze, she swallowed. "And I'm not kneeling here,
naked yet again, to lie."

"I would hope not."

Molly's blue eyes were nothing like cold any longer.
No hint of ice.

He felt the heat there like a punch to the gut. And
lower still.

"Please," she said then, in a very different voice. This
time she sounded husky. Greedy, at last. "Please, Constantine. I want to stop playing games. I want... I..."
She faltered, and it seemed so real to him that he almost believed... But no. She was nothing if not an ace
game player. She wasn't famous by accident. "I want
you inside me."

And Constantine had played this out inside his head
a thousand times. More. He had intended this begging
scene to go on forever. He had wanted abject pleading.
Perhaps proof of overwhelming arousal while she was
at it, but certainly Molly on her hands and knees. A bit
of time prostrate at his feet, even.

But in all his planning for this moment, it had never
occurred to him that he might want her this badly.

He had wanted her, clearly. But he'd spent years telling himself that his attraction to her was all a part of his
revenge and why it would work so beautifully. Not...a
wanting in its own right.

And Constantine had made himself wait so long. He'd made himself hold back, though such a thing was not in his nature. He had waited and waited—

The waiting ended then. With a crack so loud inside him he was shocked it didn't tear down this building they stood in, then topple Paris to the ground.

He was shocked he still stood.

But in the end, it was that simple.

One moment he was worried about his plan, the next he was done.

Constantine reached down, unable to control himself a moment longer, and hauled her to her feet. He got his hands in the thick mass of her blond hair, shaking it free of its pins, then slammed his mouth to hers.

And the taste of her burned in him as it always did, so intense and so hot he could not believe he was not scalded.

But it wasn't enough. Not tonight.

He gathered her against him, plundering her mouth, and he wanted more. More of her taste. More of that sleek, glorious body of hers pressed against him. He could feel the points of her nipples, a sweet agony against his chest.

It was too much.

Everything about her was too much.

Because with every taste of her, every little way she melted against him, it was as if she was somehow blazing straight through all those boundaries he had always kept strong and secure. As if she was the one melting him, from the inside out.

Constantine needed to get inside her. He needed to

vanquish her, once and for all, and no other way had
worked yet. Surely that would.

It was the waiting, he assured himself. He had never
waited for another woman, not in any sense. It had created an unreasonable hunger—but it would be assuaged
soon enough.

Now, in fact.

Once again, all the plans Constantine had toyed with
over the years seemed to disappear, in so much ash and
smoke.

He lifted her up into his arms, then carried her over
to the nearest long, deep sofa, where he laid her out like
an offering. To his deepest, wildest greed.

The longings he dared not admit, not even to himself.

Molly might be a martyr, but she was his. *His.* And
he intended to lick up every last drop of this sacrifice
laid out so temptingly before him.

He tore out of his own clothes, tossing them aside in
his haste to finally get as naked as she'd been in front
of him all this time. And he only slowed when he saw
her eyes grow wide. He watched as she flushed, a rolling splash of color that moved from her cheeks to her
neck, and then all over those sweet breasts.

Sure enough, her eyes were dilated. Her lips were
slightly parted, as if she found him just as overwhelm-
ingly tempting as he found her.

Good, something in him intoned, like a vow.

And say what she might about enemies, he knew full
well that she hated him. He wanted her to hate him. But
that meant he knew that if she was looking at him like
this, she meant it.

That gave him a little sliver of space to breathe in.

Better yet, to remember who the hell he was.

To slow it down and take control, before he exploded like an untried boy.

It almost felt like a blessing when he stretched himself out over her, there on that long couch. They both fit, if closely, and he could prop himself up on one elbow. Then look down at the work of art before him.

He took his time looking.

"Constantine…" she began, and there was a little break as she said his name.

He was already hard enough to hurt. But that catch in her voice really took him over the edge.

"Quiet, *hetaira*," he ordered her, dark and low. "This is not a time for talking."

Then he leaned down and set his mouth to her breast. He toyed with her hard nipple with his tongue while his hand busied itself with its twin.

Molly arched up against him and cried out, and so he kept going. Back and forth between each of her lovely, perfect breasts as she writhed and bucked and then, to his delight, shuddered into her first release since long, long ago in Skiathos.

She was so responsive it made his chest feel tight.

She was so responsive he *ached* to thrust himself deep within her, now.

But he didn't. Not *right now*, anyway.

He took her mouth again and settled himself over her, aware on some level that he was rushing things. That he had wanted, badly, to lay her out like a feast and take his time with each and every course.

But he couldn't seem to do it. He couldn't seem to wait another moment.

He fished around for his trousers, pulling out protection and sheathing himself with one hand. Molly's arms moved around his back to hold him, and Constantine had never been aware before of how good it felt to have a woman grip him like that. While her eyes were so wide, her face was still flushed, and she was already looking at him as if he performed miracles.

Just wait, he thought with dark pleasure.

But the waiting, at last, was over.

He settled the broad head of his sex at her entrance, reveling in her softness. Her sweet molten heat.

Below him, Molly pulled her lip between her teeth and nearly undid him with that alone, then gazed at him as if she was close to overwhelmed already.

When they hadn't even started.

"Hold on," Constantine advised her.

And then, finally, he began to thrust deep inside her—

Except he didn't.

Because he felt what could only be the innocence he had thought was a fine joke she'd made. A game she wanted to play.

But it was no joke.

Molly Payne—*Magda*, for all that was holy—lay beneath him, wincing slightly. Her nails were digging into his back, she was holding herself taut, and she was a virgin.

A virgin.

Constantine knew that this could not be. It could not.

Because if she was a virgin, that meant that he did not know her at all. And more, that every single thing he had thought about her as he'd plotted out his revenge was wrong. That he'd been completely and utterly off course.

And if he was wrong about something he had long since accepted as an incontrovertible fact, what else was he wrong about?

Something in him pitched, then rolled.

"Molly…" he gritted out, in genuine pain.

But she scowled at him, this impossible woman. This *virgin* in the body of a *hetaira*, the ancient Greek term for a courtesan.

How could he have been so wrong about her?

"Don't you dare, Constantine," she gritted out at him, her scowl deepening. "Don't you dare stop now."

And then, to his astonishment, she thumped him one in the ribs.

Hard.

CHAPTER NINE

IT HURT, BUT MOLLY had expected it would.

She'd been told a thousand stories of terrible, horrible pain the first time, but people didn't seem to let that stop them from having sex. She didn't intend to let it stop her.

Because there was something right on the other side of the pain. Something almost seductive, like a new kind of fire. Molly knew that no matter what, she wanted to taste it.

For his part, Constantine looked poleaxed. He stared down at her, an expression she couldn't begin to interpret on that beautiful face of his.

And to her impatient fury, he didn't move.

So she did.

Molly might not have done this before, but she understood the mechanics. Or she understood them well enough, anyway, to lift her hips and try to press herself into that bright, sharp pain. Especially when it made him tight all around her, that astonishing body of his nearly vibrating as he held himself still.

"Molly—"

But she ignored him, rocking herself against that insistent press of his need until it hurt too much to bear. Then she pulled in a ragged breath and impaled herself.

And then lay there beneath him, panting.

Impaled and panting.

"That was very foolish," Constantine gritted out, in dampening tones.

"Only if it's bad." Molly laughed a bit at that, aware that it was shaky at best, but that didn't make her stop. "Is it going to be bad?"

And he still didn't look…quite like him. Something of that internal storm that so marked him was gone. Or not gone, exactly, but not the same. His dark gaze seemed flooded with gold.

Meaning she did, too.

He shifted over her so he could brush moisture she hadn't known was beneath her eyes away with his thumbs, as he held her head in place. Not in a way that made her feel held down, but in a way that made her feel precious.

She melted a little at that, inside and out.

"No," he said gruffly, his gaze intense. "I can promise you, it will not be bad."

And then he kissed her.

Molly found it was different from the kisses that had come before. She would have said it was sweeter, but this was Constantine—and he was *inside her*. What sweetness could there possibly be?

And yet she thought of the honeyed sweetness she'd eaten in Skiathos, the richness on her tongue.

Constantine was better.

He kissed her and he kissed her, as if he wasn't buried deep inside her body. As if there was no hurry whatsoever. His chest brushed against her breasts as he held her face, and she hadn't thought that she was tense at all until she felt herself relax beneath him. Until she was melting into that kiss, pouring herself into the dance of his tongue and hers.

And slowly, surely, everything changed.

Until she felt as if both of them were liquid sunshine, tangled all around each other. The newness, the shock of his penetration began to change, too, rolling into a kind of molten thing. Bright. Warm, then hot.

Then hotter still, laced through with all that shine.

And only when she sighed a little against his mouth, running her own hands up and down the glorious planes and muscles of his back, did he lift his head and smile down at her.

She thought he was about to say something, likely something cutting and indisputably *him*.

But instead, he began to move.

And it was unlike anything she had ever experienced before in her life.

The heat of it. That unbearable, unimaginable slide, each one hotter than the last. Each one sending intensity and sensation searing through her. Into her limbs, lighting her up, making her dig her heels into the sofa they lay on so she could lift herself up to meet each impossibly beautiful thrust.

She'd spent her whole life posing for pictures and pretending, but this was real.

This was him, and her, and a slick joining that changed her every time he plunged deep inside. Changed her, then taught her.

Then it made her new.

Until she not only couldn't tell the difference between the two of them, she lost track of all those differences she'd maintained within herself, too.

This was too real for separations. This was too powerful.

Molly felt a different kind of quaking come over her and almost protested, because it was too soon. She wanted this to go on forever. And she couldn't tell if she cried because she knew it couldn't or because of the sudden surge of wildfire ecstasy that ripped through her, making her arch up against him and cry out.

She thought she might even have said his name.

But he didn't stop. He kept going, and that explosion shifted as his thrusts grew harder, more demanding.

All that golden light turned to fire. And her whole body seemed to light up, burning red and hot from the inside out.

And he knew. She could tell he knew, because he gathered her beneath him, his hands gripping her hips, as he pounded into her.

Molly met him, reveled in him, and to her surprise, shattered once more.

And that time, heard her name on his mouth as he followed.

She could feel a kind of oblivion beckoning, but she fought it off, because she didn't want to miss a moment of this. Of Constantine, his face next to hers and that remarkably powerful body of his laid out over her as if wanting her that much had made him weak.

How had she missed out on this for so long?

But on the heels of that thought came another one, and she almost made a sound in response. What if she had given in to one of the many invitations she'd received over the years and done that with anyone but Constantine?

She shuddered at the thought.

And nothing had been settled between them, but she didn't care. Because Molly might have been lost as a sixteen-year-old girl, but she'd been perfectly clear about one thing. That it was him. That it had always been and would always be him.

And she'd been right.

"Come," he said in a low voice.

Molly didn't have time to think about how or why his voice was different, only that it was. Because he was lifting her up, hoisting her into his arms as if she was one of those dainty, tiny girls who men were always toting about as easily as they heaved pints to and fro.

She felt a delicious sort of softness everywhere. She liked it. And so she did nothing at all but tuck her head beneath his chin, the better to contemplate the gorgeous strength of his collarbone, his neck, the underside of his jaw as he moved.

He carried her into the bedroom he'd claimed in this penthouse when they'd arrived, then brought her to a large, ornate bed that looked like the sort of thing whole French revolutions had been fought to protest.

Fitting, really, for Constantine Skalas.

He placed her down on the grandiose bed, then straightened, looking at her with a dark, unreadable look on his face that probably should have made Molly feel self-conscious.

But it didn't. Nothing could. Not when she felt like this, loose and beautiful and made entirely new.

His jaw tightened, and he turned, walking off into what she assumed was the en suite bathroom.

Sure enough, she heard the sound of water, and for once, was perfectly happy to simply stay where she was and wait to see what might happen.

Constantine was there at her side again in a moment, with a warm, damp cloth he pressed between her legs, and that was what made her suddenly feel…vulnerable.

"I had no idea that you were serious." His voice was almost too low to hear, a thread of darkness between them. Almost. "It never occurred to me that you could possibly be an innocent."

"Not anymore," she said brightly, and she didn't know what to do with that look in his eyes. She didn't know what to do, so she got back onto her knees, and ran her hands over his chest where he stood beside the bed. She reveled in the feel of her palms against his skin, his muscles, *him*.

"Molly."

Her name was a command, but she had no intention of heeding it. She let her hands wander where they would until one made its way down that fascinating arrow of hair to find his sex. Almost accidentally.

He was so hard, though not as hard as he had felt inside her. She wrapped her fingers around the width of him and he thickened, and Molly smiled. Because that, too, felt like a power she wished she'd known she'd had all this time.

"Molly," he said again, now sounding very nearly stern. "I do not think—"

"Can we do that again?" she asked, smiling up at him. She tipped herself forward so she could rub her aching nipples against his chest and taste all the parts of him she'd admired on the walk here. His corded neck, his bold jaw. "Please? I'm begging."

He made a low sound, but then his mouth was on hers again. And he was picking her up and turning her, rolling with her down onto that wide bed, until they were tangled up with each other again.

Constantine rolled to his back and let her explore him, but when she went to take his hardness in her mouth, he gripped her beneath her arms and hauled her up the length of his body.

"I want to," she said.

"We do not always get what we want, Molly," he told her, then kissed her until she melted against him once more.

He taught her how to sit astride him, then take him deep inside her from that different angle.

She rocked her hips against his, staring down at him in a kind of wonder. He looked up at her, his expression so fierce, his hands moving almost restlessly from her breasts to that place where they were joined.

He pressed a thumb down hard at her center and she dissolved, almost sobbing out at the sharp pleasure of it.

Then he flipped her over onto her belly and came

into her from behind. He slid one arm beneath her hips to lift them at an angle so that he could pound his way into her, once again taking her from the middle of one explosion and throwing her like a catapult straight on into another. And another still.

And when the last one hit, she heard him roar behind her.

Then she knew no more.

Molly didn't know what woke her, or how she knew that it was later. Much later, by her guess, and she knew instantly that Constantine wasn't in the bed with her. She'd slept but she'd been always aware of him beside her, wrapped around her, hot to the touch.

She sat up, her heart pounding at her as if in fright, but then she saw him.

He stood by the window, and for once, she got to gaze upon his glorious nakedness instead of the reverse. The lights of Paris flowed all over his perfect form, making him seem unreal. Like one of the statues in the Musée Rodin, where she had spent many a stolen afternoon while at loose ends in the city.

He put them all to shame.

"Constantine?" She hardly sounded like herself, but that didn't shock her. She didn't feel like herself either, not any longer.

She felt like his.

He didn't turn toward her, and yet she knew, somehow, that he had heard her all the same. A small, shivery thing teased the nape of her neck.

"I hated your mother long before I met her," Constantine said, his voice gravelly, his gaze on the city be-

fore him. "I hated the idea of her, probably before my
father ever met her. But then, there she was. And she
had a name and a face, and told me to call her Isabel,
as if we were friends already."

Molly had spent her life wanting to have this conversation, and now that it was happening, she wanted
no part of it. She wanted to fly across the room and
throw her body against his, hoping that could distract
him from whatever he was about to say. But just as he
seemed to stand there, frozen solid at the window with
Paris at his feet, she couldn't seem to move, either.

She could only watch the light move over his dark
form. And wait.

He seemed to grow even more frozen as she watched.
"But as luck would have it, my new friend Isabel gave
me more than enough reason to hate her, personally."
Constantine let out a laugh, though there was no humor
in it. It sounded like a weapon, and this time, it wasn't
one aimed at her. Why did that make her ache? "She
tried, you see. She tried so hard. Not just to make my
father happy, a doomed endeavor if ever there was one.
But she went out of her way to try to love me, too."

He turned then, and Molly caught her breath. Because his face was a mask of anguish. Sheer torment.
His eyes blazed with it, and she hated that, too.

"Constantine. I don't understand—"

"And how dare she love me so easily?" Constantine
gritted out, as if she hadn't spoken. "When my mother's life was a spiral of despair. When my own mother
had never been any good at loving anyone or anything
because she was so focused on my father—anything to

get his attention, good or bad. How dare a stepmother come along and try to do what she had never managed?"

That hit Molly like a blow. Hard into her belly.

She whispered his name. And he laughed again, that awful sound.

"Your mother was *kind*, Molly. Understanding. *Warm*. And oh, how I loathed her for it." He moved toward her then, and it felt like fate. Like doom. Then he stopped at the end of the bed and it felt a whole lot more like heartache. "But then you came."

"You don't have to do this," she managed to get out.

Maybe she meant, *Please don't do this*.

"But I do." He raked a hand through his hair as if he would rather have put it on her. She wished he would. And her heart was beating so hard against her ribs that she was surprised she wasn't rattling with the impact of each hit. "You were so soft. So astoundingly innocent."

"I think you mean stupid."

Constantine shook his head. "It was obvious to anyone who laid eyes on you that you could be easily chewed up and spit out and more, would never have the slightest idea what had happened to you."

It was a searing sort of pain, she found, to imagine her former self like that. Particularly as she knew it was true. And more, could see too well the gap between the girl she'd been then and the woman she'd become.

"Again, I think the word you're looking for is *stupid*," she managed to say. "All I knew of the world was the village I came from. Our neighbors might not have liked my mum much. They might have watched me a little too closely, forever on the hunt for evidence that I was either like Isabel or looked a bit too much like one of their sons, since Isabel never named my father. But at least I knew my place there."

"You had no business turning up in our world, Molly. You weren't made for it. You made the terrible mistake of imagining that people, at heart, were basically good. No doubt another gift from your mother."

"Yes," she said quietly. "You treated me like a friend and I believed you meant it. I've had a long time to beat myself up for that, Constantine. A lot of years to regret it, but do you know what? I don't. I would rather see the world as more good than bad. Or what would be the point of living in it?"

"How can you possibly continue to be this naive?" he asked, his voice filled with sadness and something like wonder at once. "The fashion industry should have succeeded where I failed and beaten this out of you years ago."

Her smile was rueful then. "Oh, it did. So did you, Constantine. But cynicism is a choice. And I decided I would not choose it, despite all provocation."

It hadn't always been easy, because there was a certain ragged pride to be taken in weathering the storms of a volatile industry. Not to mention fame, fortune, and the joys and horrors inherent in both.

But she had decided, with great deliberation, that she would rather be happy.

Wasn't that why she'd sought Constantine out? Oh, she'd told herself it was to face down the architect of her mother's financial ruin. She'd assured herself it had less to do with her own demons and far more to do with protecting Isabel.

Yet she knew better. Deep down, she had known that she was never going to be happy until she either exorcised the devil…or embraced him.

He was staring at her as if she'd sprouted new heads. "The Skalas family has ever been a pit of snakes. I would rather have gone off to war than sit down to a family dinner when I was a child. You were woefully unprepared. Outgunned and outmaneuvered before your plane landed on Skiathos. I had every intention of snapping you like a twig. I wouldn't have thought about it twice. If anything, your total destruction would have amused me."

She cleared her throat. "My recollection is that you did precisely that. And happily."

Constantine let out a small, harsh sound. She could not call it a laugh.

"No, Molly. Not quite. Because you lit up when you talked about your mother."

Molly's voice hardly seemed to work any longer. "Is that a bad thing?"

His smile was merciless. "You knew her flaws, but you loved her. It was obvious. It made your whole face change even as you shared your frustrations with me. And the stories you told me, your little village secrets, did something I thought was impossible." That smile carved a deeper groove on his beautiful face and she understood, then, that his lack of mercy was aimed at himself for once. Not her. "You made me feel sympathy for Isabel, Molly. And I couldn't forgive it."

"Constantine…" she whispered.

"I never sold your stories to the tabloids, Molly. I was so determined to punish you for the things you made me feel that I gave them all away. For free."

Molly sucked in a breath at that. Her head was spinning. She had so many questions she wanted to ask him, but he was still glaring down at her in that stern, uncompromising way that should have made her faint.

Or something better than fainting, maybe. Something to address the way she prickled all over with that heat she now knew all too well.

"I don't require these confessions from you," she told him then. "I don't even want them."

She wanted to tell him she forgave him, but she didn't quite dare. Even if, as she let that notion take root in her, she knew it was true. Or she would never have taken off her clothes for him. She would certainly never have writhed about in his hands on that first day, all abandonment.

But there had been something about all those sun-drenched days on the island. Something about baring her skin and letting the breeze and the light find her wherever she was. Something about opening herself wide to Constantine's gaze and never wavering, never hiding, never falling apart.

Molly had forgiven him, yes. But she'd forgiven herself, too.

"I do not care if you want this confession," Constantine said tightly, as if this was a fight they were having. He certainly looked as if he was prepared to wade into battle, so tautly did he hold himself. "And despite all that, I'm sure I would have forgotten you in time. Isabel's relationship with my father didn't last, because nothing my father touched ever lasted, except the fortunes he hoarded. You were no threat. I could have gone quite happily about my life and never thought of you again, Molly. That was the goal all along."

She found herself staring back at him at that, mutely, not certain how to respond to that, much less the ferocity she could see stamped all over him.

"But instead, you became Magda. And you were everywhere. It began to feel not only as if you were hunting me, but as if you had played me from the start." His laugh then was dark. "There I was, the jaded and worldly Skalas son, stamping out an innocent for my amusement the same way my father had always trodden on anything that dared attract his notice. But no. That whole time I thought I was crushing you into the dirt, you had one of the most famous women in the world right there inside of you. Ready to come out the moment you left Skiathos and escaped my family. You became my obsession."

"I can't imagine why you would care what happened to me."

"Can you not?" His voice was a bitter lash. "Because I felt guilty, Molly. *Guilty.* You are the only thing I have ever felt guilty about in my life. Because for all I have always reveled in sin, for all I have sought out the darkness and the lowest of places, you did not deserve what I did to you. *And I knew it.*"

Now there was no stopping the way her heart catapulted against her chest. Now there was no hope of doing anything but sitting there, waiting to see what he would lob at her next. What mad grenade. What bomb she wouldn't see coming.

"Now it turns out that once again, you have shamed me," he said quietly. Ferociously. "Your innocence is my guilt made new. It proves that all along, I was never who I thought I was. And you… You have been even more pure, from the start, than I imagined anyone could be."

Molly felt turned inside out. Or maybe she only wished she had been, when all she could see was the rich darkness of his gaze turned bleak.

"This is a lot of talk of guilt and shame," she said. She found she could move then, so she did, crawling down the length of the bed until once more she could sit there before him, her knees beneath her. "And it seems to me that if we're going to spend the night castigating ourselves for the despoiling of innocence, there should be more despoiling. Don't you think?"

"You are not hearing me," Constantine thundered at her then. "You are the only thing on this earth I have ever felt for, Molly. First it was guilt. Then it was fury. And now—"

"Constantine," she said, desperate and greedy, her heart a great clatter. Needy and sure, at last. Absolutely sure what this was—what this had always been. "Shut up."

Then she launched herself at him.

And he caught her.

Molly might not have known what she was doing, but she knew it felt good.

And this time was different all over again. This time

was slow. Constantine put his mouth on every inch of her body, as if committing her to memory, one lick of heat at a time.

He settled between her thighs and drank deep from the heat of her core, until all she could do was sob out his name like a prayer.

It felt that sacred.

Then he set her before him on her hands and knees and took her that way, a slow, delirious rhythm that made every part of her body seem to come alive. Then burn bright.

Only when she was sobbing again—but this time in the grip of that fiery need—did Constantine flip her over, gather her beneath him, and drive them both home.

When she woke again, it was morning.

Daylight poured in through the windows, bright and sweet. Molly felt deliciously battered from head to toe, and as she stretched she laughed as she found so many interesting tugs in new places.

She did not see the note until she sat up and looked around for Constantine. He was nowhere to be found in the vast bedchamber, but the note had been clipped to the pillow beside her.

She picked it up, trying to make sense of the words written across the heavy card stock in a slashing, dark hand.

It was a simple message, direct and to the point.

Molly felt it like a stab wound through her heart.

YOUR DEBT IS PAID IN FULL.

CHAPTER TEN

CONSTANTINE FLEW BACK to his antiseptic penthouse in London, a modern masterpiece of low-slung furniture and strange objects that he found neither artistic nor functional. He hadn't chosen any of it himself. It was the work of the sort of interior design firm who catered to wealthy clients like the Skalas brothers, as it meant their work was always aspirational. The flat had been the subject of at least six different fawning articles about Constantine's *keen eye* and *flair for esthetics*.

It looked like a bloody surgery, he thought now.

But then, that was why he'd chosen it and let the firm run wild. He didn't want his home to be anything like the house in Skiathos. Memories lurking behind every door, rooms filled with art and nostalgia and ghosts. *Feelings* oozing from the walls. He had wanted his primary residence to stand as a visual representation of what he was.

Not the playboy, but the sharp-edged angel of vengeance he had made himself into.

He looked around the clean lines and soulless expanse of the penthouse and told himself he was fine. *Terrific*, even.

Constantine experimented with that theory upon his return to the Skalas & Sons London headquarters, dedicating himself to his work in a way he never had before. Meaning, visibly. He showed up at the office, did not send his usual proxy to board meetings, and generally turned the place on its ear by destroying the long-held fiction that he was the useless Skalas brother who did nothing at all, as a vocation.

And it was only after his trusted assistant suggested, very carefully, that he rethink his approach to the people who believed the hype about him—that he was lazy, sybaritic, more often to be found facedown in a sea of women than in the boardroom, and if he wished to change this that he do so at a more sedate pace—that Constantine accepted the fact that he was not, in fact, fine.

In any way.

If he was brutally honest with himself, he wasn't sure that he would ever be anything like fine again.

Because he had excavated entirely too many of his own deep, personal motivations, and the feeling that left in him was unbearable.

Constantine preferred the clarity of revenge. The force and thrust of a life committed to nothing but vengeance. Every temper, every dark *feeling*, every wild and stormy thing within him—it had all been excused by his focus on getting even with Molly.

And through her, at last, Isabel.

Now all he could think about was Molly. That wasn't new. But the way he thought of her had changed. Instead of brooding over what he would do to her and the many ways he would crush her and her mother to dust, he woke in the night in a fever of need. Instead of finding ingenious new ways to put pressure on Isabel, he found himself lapsing into daydreams about sunny afternoons in Skiathos and the sheer glory that was Molly on her knees before him, smiling up at him as if she wanted him.

As desperately and comprehensively as he wanted her.

Constantine suspected he had changed. That Molly had changed him, somehow, with her frankness and her laughter and that spirit of hers that had seemed to bloom brighter the more she was tested. The more he had tested her, the stronger she had seemed.

His revenge had backfired spectacularly, loath as he was to admit it, even as one week turned into another, then another still, and he was as unsettled as he'd been when he'd left Molly in Paris.

Because everything was different. *He* was different, and he disliked it intensely.

It was possible he disliked *himself* intensely.

Because he'd seen himself too clearly. He could not seem to claw his way back from that.

"You do not sound well, brother," Balthazar commented when Constantine finally gave in and called him. He told himself it was only because his brother, too, knew the lure of revenge. And the particular way a woman could twist it all around—for how else was there to explain Balthazar's shockingly uncontentious marriage? "And how can that be? For I have never seen you look as happy as you did while engaged in your little experiment with flashbulbs and infamy."

"You're the last person in the world who should believe a press release," Constantine said tersely, glaring out at London as if his brother's face hovered there above the Shard.

"I would never believe a press release," Balthazar returned with a laugh. A *laugh*. Constantine still couldn't believe his older brother *laughed* these days, as if it was an ordinary, everyday thing instead of wholly out of character for the man he'd been until now. "But I'm referring to the expressions I saw on your face. Please remember, I actually know you. And more, am all too aware that you would make an absolutely dreadful actor."

"You're confirming my aptitude, then. For I assure you, it was all an act."

"If you say so." Balthazar was quiet for a moment, and Constantine could hear the sound of the sea in the background. It made him wish, with a deep passion he would have sworn could not possibly exist within him, to return to Skiathos.

To go back in time, and stay there for far longer than ten days, with nothing to do but appreciate Molly's sun-kissed limbs. And this time, not to *wait*.

His fist was clenched so tightly his bones ached. He forced his palm open, scowling as he did it.

"But why do you use the past tense?" Balthazar asked at last. "Do I dare even ask this question?"

"Molly has paid her debt to me in full," Constantine said. His voice sounded gritty. Rougher than it should have, and he was afraid he gave far too much away.

Surely this is why you rang your brother in the first place, a voice in him said testily.

Constantine rubbed his aching hand over his face, wishing he knew how to do more than *want*.

On his end, Balthazar made a considering sort of sound Constantine opted not to interpret. "Has she indeed. That is enterprising of her."

And Constantine had half a mind to throw his mobile across the cavernous great room he had heard described as *containing a loftlike vibe*. Surely a little bit of destruction would liven the place up. Chip one of the sharp edges of his furniture that was decidedly not made for human habitation. This was a flat to admire from afar, or peer at in the pages of architectural magazines, not *live* in. Because Constantine did not *live* anywhere. He traveled between places and personas, always with the same goal in mind—revenge.

But now he had no goal and all his years of plotting vengeance sat heavily in him. He wanted to take the strange overly modern pieces in this flat and hurl them out one of his vast windows. Because it did not escape his attention that he had taken Molly on a tour of only his most beautiful properties. As if he had needed to make sure that a creature as beautiful as she was could only ever be surrounded by similar beauty.

As if he had imagined that he could bask in both. He had.

Now he stood in the reality of his life, such as it was, without her. Without the idea of her that had sustained him for years. And without the live, flesh-and-blood woman who had turned him inside out.

And it was cold. Impersonal. Incomprehensible in places.

He was all of those things.

And here he was on the phone to an older brother who had only ever been another soldier in the same dreadful foxhole. It had never occurred to Constantine that a brother could be—or should be—anything else.

But he wanted…

The mawkishness almost drove him to his knees, but he knew. What he wanted was a friend. Constantine certainly had none of those. If he wanted one, he would have to take his chances here.

And so, feeling very much as if he was flinging himself off his own balcony in lieu of his terrible, uncomfortable furniture, he told Balthazar…everything.

Everything he'd told Molly. And more besides.

When he was done, he felt sick. And something like hollow. And his head pounded so hard and erratically that he wasn't entirely sure he would hear Balthazar as he spoke.

Or maybe he only wished he wouldn't.

"A wise woman once told me that the best revenge of all is living well," Balthazar said. "And I must tell you, I've taken it to heart."

Constantine let out a dark laugh, not at all surprised to find that he was rubbing at his chest. As if he could press his heart back into place. "I live well enough as it is."

"The key is happiness, brother. If money could buy it, we would have had a far better childhood than we did."

"Happiness," Constantine said, pronouncing the word as if he wasn't sure how the syllables came together. Or if it might sting him while he worked it out.

"We could talk all day about the many sins of Demetrius Skalas," Balthazar continued. "And in fact, I would enjoy it. There's nothing about that man I admire and I take it as a personal challenge to make certain that I never hand on any part of him to my children."

"I will also take this challenge," said Constantine, who until that moment had never so much as considered the possibility that he would bring a child into this world.

And yet the moment he considered it, he could only think of one woman who could possibly be the mother to those children. His children.

Their children.

The thought of Molly, ripe with a child they'd made, made him hiss out a small breath as if he'd been punched deep in the gut.

"But we must also talk about our mother," Balthazar was saying, unaware that yet another sea change was sweeping his brother away as he spoke. "Both you and I went to such lengths to avenge her, though our approaches were different. I was furious about what had been done to her. You were furious at what was done to her memory."

"I fail to see the difference," he managed to say.

"You want her to be a saint, Constantine." Balthazar's voice was quiet, but direct. "When, like the rest of us, she was only a person."

"She is still a person," Constantine gritted out.

"You and I both know that isn't entirely true." His brother's voice stayed quiet. And powerful. "One of these days, when she has stopped clinging to what little life she has left in her, you and I will do what we must to honor her. But in the meantime, do you imagine that if she were not in that bed she would applaud what you were doing?"

"I like to think she would."

"Constantine. The only reason she stopped the downward spiral she was on was because she hit the bottom too hard to get up again. You know this. Our mother was a woman of grand obsessions. First with our father. Then it was her lover." And his voice was harsh then. For he had taken that lover down. "Then came many other lovers, and worse by far, the chemical inducements they provided her. But the one thing our mother was never obsessed with was her children. I choose to take that as a compliment. She couldn't take care of us. We could take care of ourselves, and we did."

Constantine stared out the window, but he didn't see London. All he saw was Molly. And then, almost superimposed over that face of hers that seemed to be lodged inside him, what dim memories he had of his mother before he'd lost her.

Because Balthazar was right. His mother had always been obsessed. Frantic and fragile. And while it was true that their father had been cruel to her—the way he was cruel to all who crossed his path—it was also true that she had never done much in the way of fighting back.

Not like Molly, who had found a way to stand tall in the worst possible circumstances. Even on her knees she had towered over him. Because that was the difference, wasn't it? A person either had that flame inside, or they didn't.

They either stood up or lay down.

He didn't think it was positive or negative, necessarily, but it did make him wonder why it was he was so determined to avenge a woman who would never, ever have avenged herself if given the opportunity.

And she would never have applauded you, that voice inside him told him harshly. *She barely noticed you as it was.*

He raked a hand through his hair. "When did you become a font of wisdom?" he asked his brother. Grumpily.

Balthazar laughed. Again. As if laughter was now a staple of his daily life. It was hard to imagine. Impossible, in fact, and yet he kept doing it.

"Right about the time you decided to call me for advice," he said then. "I suppose we can call this a brand-new day, Constantine."

When their call ended, Constantine did not fling his mobile across the room. He stayed where he was, staring out his windows until he saw London again. No superimposed faces. No ghosts. No regrets.

And when he did, he took a deep breath, then stalked out of his surgical flat and headed for one of his cars in the attached garage.

He drove out of the city, following a route he knew all too well. He took it as often as he could. At least once a month when he was in London, and he tried never to stay away for more than six weeks at a time.

Knowing full well that if their situations were reversed, his mother would not have maintained the same visitation schedule. In fact, it was likely she would never visit at all. It wasn't as if Constantine didn't know this. Of course he did.

But he couldn't say he'd truly *felt it* before now.

When he arrived at the long-term care facility where his mother waited, he took the steps two at a time, presenting himself to the duty nurse who knew him by sight.

"She's doing well," the cheerful woman told him as she ushered him down the same familiar hallway he'd walked for years, always lit up with that same, enduring thirst for vengeance that had animated his every action since he was twenty. "I do think it's that Good Samaritan of hers."

Constantine blinked at that. "I beg your pardon? A Good Samaritan?"

"Oh yes," the nurse said as they reached the door of his mother's room. She looked at Constantine with a slight frown between her brows. "She comes in most every week? I know I've mentioned her before. It's been years now?"

"Yes, of course," Constantine murmured, though he had no memory of any Good Samaritan. But then, would he have listened to anything that didn't serve that cold knife edge inside him? That intense focus on revenge? "How lovely."

Constantine supposed it was nice that someone else was visiting his mother. And yet when he walked inside and seated himself in the chair beside her bed, he knew it didn't matter. People made all sorts of claims about patients in the same state as his mother, and maybe they were right. But not about his mother. As he took her hand and looked down at her, at her still dark hair and soft face, he knew the truth. She was not trapped in there. On the contrary.

She was at peace.

A peace he knew she had never found while she was alive.

His conversation with his brother kicked at him. He looked into his mother's faintly lined face, looking far more at ease now in her endless sleep than she ever had when she'd been awake. She had forever been falling apart when they were children. As terribly as Demetrius had bullied his sons, he had bullied his wife even more. And when she did not cower or cry enough for his liking, he'd made sure to hurt her in other ways. Appearing with his mistresses in public. Making certain she always knew his unfaithfulness was epic and constant.

Constantine was not convinced he had ever seen her smile. Not a real smile. Not one that required anything more from her than good manners.

And he had loved his mother, truly he had, but looking back he could not say with any conviction that she had felt the same. They had been raised as much by nannies as by her, which had suited everyone.

Particularly when she had started taking lovers of her own.

And then, when Demetrius had thrown her out, it was not as if she had worked tirelessly to make sure she maintained contact with her children. She had always been far too busy recapturing what had been taken from her—or at least, that was his memory of the excuses she'd made at the time.

His father had delighted in calling her selfish, which had been laughable coming from him.

The truth was, Constantine thought now, she had earned that selfishness. She had earned any life she wanted after surviving Demetrius.

Why don't you deserve the same? something asked inside him.

But he put that aside, because he knew better. He was a Skalas male, not the victim of one. It was different.

"I'm so sorry, *mitéra*," he found himself saying, there alone in the room with only the quiet beeping machines that kept her alive for company. "I put you on a pedestal. And how was that so different from what my father did, if in reverse? Who knows how things could have been if I had only let you be who you were. Not what I wanted you to be instead."

He understood that the opportunity to know his mother had been taken from them both. And it was possible that had he come to know her, he might not have liked what he found. He understood that his mother was weak in many ways, but so, too, had his father exploited that weakness for his own amusement. Most of all, Constantine understood that he had been young when his parents had made the decisions that would mark them all.

Too young, and time had not been on his side.

Still…wasn't that what he did? He decided that there was a certain truth, and then he charged directly at that truth, forever. He would accept no complications, no complexities, no mitigating circumstances. Only what he accepted as truth existed, nothing else.

How else could he have missed the fact that Molly had been an innocent?

He thought that might haunt him forever.

Constantine kissed his mother on her soft cheek, whispered a goodbye he knew she couldn't hear, then rose.

And when he turned, there was a woman standing at the door.

For a moment he didn't recognize her. Perhaps he didn't want to recognize her.

He took in the pretty face, the quietly elegant way she held herself. And how startled her cool blue eyes looked as she beheld him.

Isabel.

The first thing he'd done after leaving Molly in Paris, when he'd returned to his offices in a fury, was to restore everything he had taken from Isabel over the years. And from Molly.

With interest.

He'd considered it wiping the slate clean.

And he couldn't tell if he was pleased to see Isabel now, or if it only added to how hollow he felt. How dark and empty, all the way through.

Constantine held himself tightly, as if standing at attention would make this confrontation easier. A confrontation he knew, if left to his own devices, he would have avoided forever.

"If you came here to thank me for not ruining you, or indeed to take me to task for coming so close in the first place, I'll save you the trouble." He inclined his head. It was not Molly's majestic act of kneeling, but then, he doubted he possessed her strength. "It is I who owe

you an apology, Isabel. For too many things to count."
The words he needed to say clogged his throat. They
actually *hurt*, but he made himself say them anyway.
"I am sorry, Isabel."

It occurred to him that it was possible she'd come
here to gloat. To taunt him. To take a piece out of him
for what he'd tried to do to her daughter as well as to her.
And he would take it, because he'd earned it, and he—

"Oh, Constantine." Isabel let out a laugh that reminded him entirely too much of her daughter. It was
warm and husky, filled with life even as it sounded a bit
rueful. "You have always been so touchy, haven't you?"

If he stood any straighter he would break in half.
"...touchy?"

The older woman sighed. She gestured toward the
bed. "I come to see your mother all the time."

Constantine stared at her, because her words didn't
make sense. On any level. Isabel Payne came to visit
his mother? Whatever for? Dimly, the nurse's chatter
about a Good Samaritan came back to him. Could it be?

He shook his head, baffled.

And found himself wholly unable to speak.

"She and I have a lot in common, for our sins," Isabel said, sounding far too wise for Constantine's taste.
"I like to think we could have been friends, if things
had been different."

"I'm not entirely certain my mother was capable of
having friends," Constantine forced himself to say, as
a kind of olive branch, though tearing the words out
of him felt more like ripping trees apart than extend-
ing branches.

"Everyone is capable of having friends," Isabel replied. Her eyes were too blue. Too much like Molly's. Too capable of seeing straight through him. "But like most things, not just anyone will do. It has to be the right friends."

Isabel moved further into the room, holding herself like a person who had every expectation of being welcome wherever she went. Something, he could see now, she had handed down to her daughter, along with those blue, blue eyes. Because Constantine was the one who suddenly felt out of place. Who stepped back as if this was a hospital room Isabel belonged in, not him.

Which was currently also how his life felt around him. Misshapen, because Molly had been in the middle of it.

But then every muscle in him tensed up when Isabel reached out and laid her hand on his arm.

Her gaze on his was far too warm. Far too knowing.

"You should hate me," he gritted out. "Why don't you?"

"I have spent too much time being hated myself," she replied. "I would never inflict it on another. Or myself. What a waste. Might as well chain yourself to whatever you're hating and leap into the sea. That's the kind of power you give it."

Constantine thought of the stories Molly had told him about her childhood, more when she'd been sixteen than now. Back then he'd been far more interested in piecing those stories together to make them scandalous. *SAD SINGLE MUM TO SKALAS BRIDE! PREGNANT AT SIXTEEN!*

Only now did it occur to him that Molly had not been as naive as he'd imagined her back then. She had already faced all manner of close-minded ignorance. All he'd done was show her that such mean-spiritedness wasn't the unique province of small country villages.

He kept thinking it was impossible to hate himself more. And in that, too, he was wrong.

Isabel squeezed his arm and he stared down at her hand, still astounded that she had simply…reached out and touched him. As if he was a regular man instead of this monster he'd become.

A monster far too like his father.

"And I want to apologize to you, Constantine," she said softly. "I should have tried harder to get through to you, but not in my usual clumsy way. I know I only made things worse."

Constantine couldn't breathe. He couldn't cope with this. It was as if this woman was a tsunami, ripping into him years ago and now again, and in all this time he still hadn't figured out how to survive her.

Maybe he never would. Maybe all these years of plotting and planning and honing himself into what he'd thought was the perfect weapon for his revenge had all been leading here, to a quiet care facility and a soft hand on his arm.

Maybe he had always been meant to go out with a whimper, after all.

"Some people aren't worth these efforts, Isabel," he managed to say, though everything inside him seemed to rock wildly back and forth. "There's no getting through to them. No matter what you do, or what you try, it will always be futile. There's nothing clumsy or elegant that could ever be done to reach them where they've gone, and good riddance."

Isabel squeezed his arm again, as if that was a normal thing that people just…did. And worse, smiled at him. As if she couldn't see what a monster he was, when she should know better. When she'd been married to his father, the worst monster of all.

"I suppose vengeance can be elegant," she said as if this was nothing but happy cocktail chatter. "It requires surgical precision, doesn't it? I think you'll find that in contrast, love is often clumsy, Constantine. Or it wouldn't hurt so much, would it?"

And it was not until that moment, with Isabel Payne's hand on his arm, his own mother there in the same room, and his heart flayed wide open, that Constantine understood at last.

He was in love.

All this time, all these years, all his grand plans… and he was *in love*.

And the moment that was clear to him, at long last, there was only one place for him to go.

CHAPTER ELEVEN

MOLLY WAS ENJOYING a quiet evening in—or more accurately, brooding with wine yet again, because that appeared to be all she did when left to her own devices since she'd returned from Paris—when a terrific pounding started up on her front door downstairs.

She had long since removed any buzzer from her property, because the paparazzi had regularly abused it. Anyone who wished to contact her should have her mobile number, and if they didn't, they shouldn't contact her. Packages and other such deliverables she had delivered to her agent's offices instead. Where they could be picked up at her leisure or delivered by messengers she recognized.

There was no reason anyone should be pounding on her door.

She set her wine aside and stalked across to the windows that opened up onto the balcony that sat up above the street. She stepped out, breathing in the warm air. It was full summer in England. Light held on until late and even though it was just as likely that it would take a cold turn by morning, it was impossible not to feel a bit giddy.

But when Molly peered over the side of her balcony to see who was abusing her front door, she found she did not feel giddy at all.

Because Constantine stood there. Staring up at her as if *she* had left *him*, naked in a bed in a different country.

"I thought my debt was paid in full," she said, her voice going a bit echoey against the cobblestones.

Or maybe she was feeling a bit wobbly herself. She was clinging to the rail, though she told herself it was because it was his neck she would like to wring, not because her knees felt much weaker than they ought to have.

Because Constantine was here. Here, at her door. And he looked even more darkly beautiful than she remembered.

And all she seemed to do was remember him.

She had spent a lot of time imagining him in different places, and different poses—and a thousand different *positions* because her body longed for him in ways that made her shiver—but she hadn't imagined him here. All of that simmering Greek glory, out on the cobblestones with London brooding about in the background. Rumpled and hot-eyed and almost too recklessly masculine to look at directly.

It was almost too much to take.

"This isn't about *debts*," he retorted.

A bit loudly, to her surprise.

Almost as if he…felt something.

But this was Constantine Skalas. There was more likely to be a sudden stampede of unicorns along her cobbled street than there was for him to catch a terrible case of *feelings*, like a bad flu. And it was even less likely that if he did, he would come here to share them with her.

After all, their relationship had been a lie when she was sixteen and more recently nothing but debts and dares. A *hetaira* indeed.

Because she'd looked that word up once she'd come home, thinking he'd used an endearment. She should have known better.

"Then there's no reason for you to be here, is there?" she asked coolly, glaring down at him. "After all, ours was a transactional relationship at best."

"I'm not here to talk about transactions!" he thundered at her.

Even more loudly.

She responded by going arctic. "My mistake. Are you here to *talk*? Do you do *talking*, Constantine? Is that part of your revenge fantasy?"

His eyes blazed. And she had the strangest notion he was about to explode. Right out in the open.

Molly wanted to see that more than she wanted her next breath. And equally wanted to protect him from it. She despaired of herself and her endlessly stupid heart.

"Do you truly wish to shout at each other?" he asked her, biting off each word as his gaze incinerated the world around him. "In public?"

And she had to think about it.

Because she was certain no good could come of letting that man into her house. No good could come of letting herself get close to him again. Physically, that was.

Does anyone get close to Constantine Skalas? the bitter voice inside her asked.

Still, the last thing she needed was to have someone make a video of this confrontation and splash it over the internet, which she knew they would. Because who needed the paparazzi when everyone had a mobile in their hand? She scanned the windows opposite her and didn't see any telltale twitching curtains, but that didn't mean anything.

Eyes were everywhere. That had been the first lesson Constantine had taught her.

She turned on her heel and slammed her way back into her house, running down the stairs to the front door and then waiting there a moment, desperately trying to get her breath under control.

But she gave it up as futile and tossed the door open.

Constantine brushed his way inside, then stood there, glowering at her in her own hallway as she slammed the front door shut, locking them in.

Together. And alone.

Not that it mattered if they were alone or with ten thousand people, surely. Not anymore.

Her heart, predictably, beat too hard anyway.

"There's no reason for you to be here," she told him, her voice hot and potentially unhinged, but she couldn't worry about that. "The note you left me in Paris did all the talking you could ever need to do. My debt was paid. Is that how a *hetaira*'s term was usually ended? I'm not conversant on the finer points of relinquishing a courtesan."

"A *hetaira* is not any old run-of-the-mill courtesan, Molly," he began, frowning at her.

"Did you really come here to debate the finer points of an ancient Greek insult you were using as an endearment?" She actually laughed, and not in a way that indicated she found anything funny. "Because I would rethink that approach, if I were you."

"You don't understand." He moved closer, but stopped, clearly reading the scowl on her face. Was she happy about that or disappointed? "Molly, you must know I didn't leave you because you were some kind of courtesan and I was finished. I left you for your own good."

It had to be said that she had not seen that one coming.

But she didn't like it any better for being unexpected.

"How noble." Her voice was scathing. "Next time, leave a tip."

His face darkened, and she hated the part of her that couldn't simply hate him the way she should. That wanted to make him feel better, even now.

"Everything I told you that night was the truth," he said, his voice as intense as it was rough. "And it is mine to regret that it took me so long to understand that in all this time, what I thought was vengeance was never that at all. Never. It would have been far easier for me if it was. My curse all along was that I never hated you or your mother the way I thought I should have."

That mapped a little too closely to what she'd been thinking, and she didn't trust the way her heart kicked at the idea of a connection between them.

She scowled to cover it. "You have a very funny way of showing it, then. And yes, I'm aware you made some restitution, but that's just money, Constantine. God knows you have far too much of that."

It occurred to her then, as he glared down at her with too much of that ferocious intensity that shouldn't have stirred her at all, that she was trapped with her back to her own front door. She couldn't have that.

Molly pushed her way past him and didn't look back as she marched back up her stairs. Then into her great room, where she swept up her wine along with the bottle. And then stood there, glaring balefully, as Constantine followed.

Because it just wasn't fair. He had neglected to shave today and his jaw looked deliciously rough. His hair was its usual mess. He was wearing nothing interesting at all, a T-shirt and jeans, except it was instantly clear that neither item was the sort of thing a regular person could buy in a store. Just like he was no regular person.

He still looked like a statue that begged to be cast in marble. And now, despite everything, all she could think about was that she knew how he tasted. Every part of him. Looking at him again now, all she could think about was how he had moved inside her, changing everything.

Changing *her*.

And then he'd left her all the same. The way he'd warned her he would at the start.

He'd even warned her that she would fall for him.

And fool that she was, she had.

"I thought that you did it all rather beautifully, really," she said as he stood there in the middle of the quiet, soothing retreat that she would now always remember with him in it. Damn him. She would have to move. "It all went according to plan. I knew better than to let my feelings get involved, and yet they did. And you left me, as you promised you would. Did you come here to pick apart the corpse?"

"Molly." Constantine's voice was urgent. His bitter coffee eyes wild. "I love you."

Something inside her detonated. She could feel it. But Molly didn't move, even as she felt everything inside her...liquefy. She clutched her wineglass in one hand, the bottle in the other, and thought very seriously about throwing the bottle directly at his head.

But she didn't.

She didn't know how she didn't.

"That's very flattering," she said, making her voice absolutely frigid. "But you don't."

"I do," he said, frowning at her with a certain level of arrogant outrage, no doubt because she hadn't flung herself prostrate on the floor before him in abject gratitude. "You must know that you're the only reason I have feelings in the first place. It took me a long time to realize what they were, that's all." He raked a hand through his hair. "I had to let go of my mother. I had to see her for who she was, not who I wished her to be. I had to take a good, hard look at why I wanted her on a pedestal in the first place. But I did that, Molly. I did it and I even accepted how I felt about your mother, and why. When I tell you that I love you—"

Deep inside, she could feel a kind of tremor, but she fought it back.

And she had to shut him up before that tremor took her down. "Constantine. You're just talking about yourself. You can hear that, can't you? That's not love, I think you'll find. Though it might be some abnormal psychology that you should probably look into when you leave. Which I can only hope will be shortly."

He stared at her as if she was the one acting erratically.

"You are mistaken," he bit out. "I love you, Molly. I wonder if I always have."

He *wondered*.

Molly felt everything inside of her…blow up.

She thought of that girl, lost and lonely, torn away from everything she'd ever known and shunted off to that blinding island, with the Greek sun that blazed on her only one of the things that shined too brightly to look at directly. She thought of the horror she felt when she'd realized what Constantine was truly about, when she'd read those stories he'd placed. And all the contortions she had gone through to convince herself that it had all been her fault, not his.

Then there were all the years in between, where she had made herself into the very thing that girl could never have imagined she'd become. Anti-beige. Anti-porridge. And all along knowing, somewhere deep inside of her, that she was doing it because of him.

At him.

He had made her feel small, so she became giant.

Epic.

She remembered when it had begun to occur to her how strange it was that her mother kept having so many runs of notably bad luck when, whatever else Isabel was, she had never been stupid. And how Molly had felt when she'd traced it all back to Constantine himself.

When he'd made certain she could trace it back to him.

And she could remember with perfect clarity leaving this very house that morning, so long ago now, to fly down to Skiathos and face him at last.

Molly had known the truth then, hadn't she? She called it nerves. Anxiety. A history she wanted nothing to do with, she'd assured herself, but she'd known better.

She'd been excited.

Thrilled that she would see him again, at last, no matter the circumstances.

That was the long and the short of it. She had gone to Skiathos to confront him about the things he'd done to her mother and her, the campaign he'd deliberately waged against her family *for years*, and she'd been *excited*.

There had been those ten days spent naked in the sunlight, then dressed for his pleasure when the stars came out.

There had been their press tour, all those hours spent together flying from place to place, and the performance they both put on so well for the cameras. The *dancing*. The *gazing*.

All to be left on the very night she'd given him her innocence, called her a whore, and had abandoned her. Not in that order.

"The fact of the matter," she hurled at him, slamming the wine bottle down on the nearest table and slightly surprised it didn't shatter with the force she expended, "is that you should thank your mother. Because you've been using her as an excuse for your entire life."

"Molly—"

But she was just getting started.

"You focus with all your might on blame and retribution, because that's much better than asking yourself why it is you've been hiding behind that poor woman since you were a kid. Isn't it, Constantine? You built a whole alternate persona based on sex and promiscuity, perceived indolence and carelessness. All the while hiding the truth of you, deep inside."

"That feels a bit pot and kettle, wouldn't you say?" he bit out. *"Magda?"*

"Magda is a stage name," she snapped out. "It's the difference between putting on a costume and taking one off, that's all. I'm not hiding anything, Constantine. I'm not two people. I'm not hiding in Magda—she's a part of me." And she knew as she said it that it was true. Maybe it hadn't always been true, but it was now. She leaned in. "She's always been a part of me. It's what I call the part of myself that can handle the bright lights, the applause, the strange and glorious things that come when your face is your currency. But that's not what you're doing."

"Oh no? Then what is it I'm doing, if you are suddenly the expert on healthy and unhealthy divisions of personalities."

"You'll do anything to avoid feeling an emotion," she said. Like she was handing down judgment. "Anything and everything. Everybody knows men who sleep around like that don't *feel*, so no one expects you might, do they? Boys will be boys and so on." She shook her head. "And left to your own devices, you think… You really, truly believe that a lifetime spent in a sick pursuit of vengeance against a stepmother who never did anything to you except try to take care of you is *love*."

He looked like he might explode. Or as if he had. As if this was the explosion. Maybe it had claimed them both already.

Molly realized she might not be able to tell.

"I just told you I loved you," Constantine thundered at her. "Do you think that's easy to say? Do you imagine that I've ever said it to another living human being? Because I haven't. It's only you, Molly. Don't you understand that yet? Whatever you call it, however twisted it's been, it's only ever been you. I love you, whether you believe that or not."

She didn't know where her wineglass had gone. Molly surged toward him, stopping herself just before she made a critical error and threw herself at him.

Because she knew, somehow, that would not end the way she wanted it to. She would not pummel him the way she wanted. She would end up kissing him and if she did, she would lose this moment forever.

Molly knew she couldn't allow that to happen.

"You need to feel all the parts of love, Constantine," she threw at him. "And you don't. You can't. It's not just sex. It's not just connection to another person. As wonderful as those things are, they're only one half of the whole. You have to feel its opposite." When he gazed back at her without comprehension, she made a small sound of frustration. "You have to feel the bad as well as the good to get the whole. Like loss."

He jolted as if she'd slapped him, with a wall or two in her hand. "I have no idea what you're talking about."

She moved closer to him, and she knew somehow, deep inside, that it was because she didn't know how to stay away.

But that was future Molly's problem.

"You loved your mother and you lost her," she said, very intently. "And I'm not pretending that's an easy thing. Or that I would know what to do if I lost my mother, because I know I wouldn't."

"My mother..." He shook his head. "I visited her just today. She—"

"You lost her," Molly said again. Firmly. "As far as I can tell, you lost her again and again. And so you blamed my mother. Then you blamed me. And you arranged your entire life around revenge—on me, because I made you feel something when you thought only she could."

"Not something," he gritted out at her. "*Love*, Molly."

"Have you ever stopped to take that in, Constantine?" she asked him then. "Have you ever allowed yourself a moment, just a single moment, to grieve?"

And she watched as that rocked over him. As he stood there before her, Constantine Skalas, rendered... not a devil. Not a scourge. Not the playboy or the reckoning.

He was no more and no less than a man.

At last.

My man, a voice in her said, with a kind of certainty that seemed to ring deep inside her, like a bell.

And she stayed where she was, holding her breath, as he visibly fought to accept what she'd said to him. While between them, all the fury and explosiveness seemed to ease, until it almost felt as if they were back in Greece. Where there was nothing but a breeze from the sea, faintly calling wind chimes, and the sunlight all over the both of them like a blessing.

He stood there like that for some time. And when he found her gaze again, she could have sworn there was a different man there behind those dark, rich eyes.

He reached over and ran a finger down one cheek, and her foolish heart lurched.

"Do you love me, Molly?" he asked her, his voice a rough scrape. "*Can* you love me?"

She might have fought on, had he thundered at her some more. Had there been more of that exploding, that heat.

Had he not touched her like that, as if checking to see if she was real.

Had he not…simply asked.

"I should hate you," she whispered. "I want to hate you."

He nodded at that, a sharp movement. As if he had already accepted how this was going to go. Not in his favor.

"You have every reason to hate me. I can't blame you." He blew out a breath. "In fact, I think I ought to encourage you to hate me as much as possible. It's only what I deserve."

Molly searched his face, his dark gaze. Did she want to be strong—or did she want to be happy?

She knew the answer even as she asked it.

Carefully, deliberately, she reached across that space between them to take one of his hard, magical hands in hers.

"I've been really, really bad at hating you, Constantine. For as long as I've known you. I'm afraid it just doesn't stick." She looked down at his hand, because there was too much emotion behind her eyes and thick in her throat. "If you want the truth, I've been in love with you since I was sixteen years old. And all these things you've done to me, I forgave a long time ago. I suppose that makes me as naive and stupid as I've ever been, but that doesn't make it any less true. Even if it is naivete, well, I prefer it to the sad and jaded alternative."

It seemed to her like an eternity, though likely no more than a second before his fingers were on her chin, tipping it up so that he could look at her directly. So he could look *into* her, she thought, as her breath caught.

"I love you, Molly," he said, as if he was taking a solemn vow. "I've never loved anyone else. I've never known how. And I'm nothing if not single-minded. If you let me, I will dedicate my life to learning how to love you so well, so deeply, and so perfectly, that you never question for a moment that you are anything but adored. Never stupid. Never naive. Simply mine, from the start."

She blew out a breath, feeling that tremor inside of her loom again, but Molly knew what it was now. She wasn't afraid of it.

There was heat, and her endless need for him. And beyond that, or mixed in with it, that *something else* that had always been there. That had pushed her along this path until she'd found him again. That had made her *excited* to face him in Skiathos when she should have been anything but.

And she'd named it now, hadn't she? Or he had.

It was love. It had always been love.

Just waiting there all this time for the two of them to see it.

"You silly man," she said softly, and smiled when his arrogant brow rose. Because he was still Constantine Skalas, after all. And would she love him if he wasn't? "You're here. You came after me and thundered in the street. You look tortured, as you should. And I'm tempted to say I already feel sufficiently adored."

"That's just the beginning, Molly," he promised her hoarsely.

"But," she interrupted him. She pulled her chin out of his grasp and smiled at him in the cool way she knew he would take as a challenge. And sure enough, saw his gaze grow brighter. "I'm afraid there are consequences for outrageous revenge plots."

"Consequences?" he repeated.

"In life, there are always consequences, Constantine," she said breezily, echoing something he'd said to her what seemed like a lifetime ago. "You might not like them, but there are consequences all the same."

He considered her for a long moment, and then, slowly and wonderfully, he grinned.

"Never let it be said that Constantine Skalas cannot

face the necessary consequences of his choices," he drawled. "I live for them, in fact."

"I'm glad to hear it." She gave him her most imperious, most Magda look. "Why don't we start with a little abject groveling?"

"I wouldn't know where to begin," he said, though his eyes gleamed.

"I think you do know," she said. She waved a languid hand. "You can start naked, obviously. And we'll move along from there."

Constantine's grin widened. She thought he might balk, but instead, he merely stripped off his T-shirt and tossed it at her. Molly found herself laughing as she batted it away from her face, and then she stood there, feeling buoyant and joyful and fizzy with it, as he toed off his shoes, rid himself of his jeans, and then presented himself before her, beautifully naked.

And undeniably hers.

"This is a very good start indeed," she told him.

"You have no idea."

And then Constantine showed her his version of a grovel.

He knelt there before her, drawing one leg over his shoulder so he could lick her straight over the edge.

Into her first hint of forever.

And true to his word, that was only the beginning.

CHAPTER TWELVE

TEN YEARS LATER, Constantine sat on the lowest terrace down the cliff from his Skiathos house, waiting for his wife.

These days, he savored the waiting period.

First Molly had taught him to love. Then she taught him to grieve, and he had. It had taken time. It had been a journey, as he'd learned grief often was. Nor did it ever go away. Not really.

But only once he'd allowed himself to truly face what he had lost had he found hope. Laughter. And the wholeness of love. The good and the bad all mixed in together to make a life.

There, in the arms of this woman he did not deserve, who had forgiven him and loved him and given herself to him like pearls before the swine he was, Constantine Skalas learned at last how to be himself.

Just him.

For her.

The path had not always been easy. But then, what worth having in this life was ever easy?

They'd fought. They had gone through dark times

both of their making and imposed upon them from without, but they'd come through it stronger. Closer.

All of it possible because of Molly, Constantine knew.

He became a brother to Balthazar, and in time, a friend. He and Molly had married on the same island where Balthazar had taken his own bride, and all four of them found a new future. And built a new kind of Skalas family, drenched deep in the love they'd worked so hard to find.

When their mother finally slipped away, some five years ago, Balthazar and Constantine had stood together, shoulder to shoulder, and allowed themselves to mourn.

Constantine and Molly had spent this far brighter decade building themselves the marriage they wanted. Then adding to it with the children Constantine had only ever wanted with her. Molly had retired Magda when she felt the time was best, and was considering the many offers she'd received, looking for what moved her. In the meantime, she was as stunning as he'd imagined she'd be, big with his daughters. Three in rapid succession, and then a squalling little thunderstorm of a son to cap off their collection.

And with Isabel as their magical, marvelous grandmother, Constantine knew that his son and his daughters would live the kind of life he could admit, now, he wished he'd had all along. His children were loved, and they knew it. His children were happy, and he worked hard to make sure they would always remain as close to that state as possible.

His children saw, every day, that he loved and honored and respected their mother. And that she loved him back. That their parents laughed and danced, fought and made up, and always, always, put each other and the family first.

He couldn't wait to see who they became, these four bright souls he would let nothing crush.

But Skiathos was for him and Molly alone.

He heard her on the path, as he always did. And when he turned to enjoy her approach by the light of all those same gently glowing lanterns, he smiled.

For she had worn the filmy, see-through gown he'd left out on their bed, so he could see her beautiful figure. Her curves were rounder now, after the four children she'd borne him, and her smile was brighter. Because here, and always, she was his.

And he was hers, entirely.

Love kept getting better all the time.

"You almost kept me waiting, *hetaira*," he murmured as she came to him, here in the place where they came to lie naked beneath the sun and remind themselves of all the ways they'd untwisted each other over the years.

"Never fear," she said as she approached. "I will always be your courtesan, my love. Especially here. Ready and willing to accept whatever consequences you render for the unpardonable sin of *almost* making you wait, the horror."

"And I will always be your husband, Molly," he replied, a vow he could never make enough. "A role I hope I will one day deserve."

She settled herself in his lap and gazed down at him

with those arctic blue eyes that warmed for him. Always for him. He saw their past, their future. This beautiful present in these days they liked to steal for themselves, just the two of them, so they would always remember.

Not that he would ever forget.

And then the love of his life, the mother of his children, his perfect *hetaira*, kissed him as if she was breaking a spell. Or casting a new one.

The way she did every day.

And Constantine kissed her back with a hunger that only grew, year by year.

While all around them the lanterns glowed, the sea whispered far below, and forever was right here, tangled up between them and stretching out into eternity.

No revenge necessary.

Only love.

* * * * *

MILLS & BOON

Coming next month

HIS BILLION-DOLLAR TAKEOVER TEMPTATION
Emmy Grayson

"Mr. Cabrera?"

The husky feminine voice slid over his senses and sent a flash of heat over his skin. He took another deliberate sip of his wine before turning his attention to the second woman who had invaded his space this evening.

Her.

The blonde woman he'd locked eyes with before Alejandro's arrival now stood before him. The neckline of her dark blue gown plunged down in a V to the silver ribbon wrapped around her slender waist. From there the dress flowed into a long, billowing skirt that reminded Adrian of the waters of the Mediterranean before a storm.

His eyes drifted back up to her face in a slow, deliberate perusal. Lush silver-blonde curls enhanced her delicate features. Violet eyes stared back at him, and her caramel-colored lips were set in a firm line.

"Yes," he finally responded, his voice cool, showing that, despite the unusually intense effect she was having on him, he was still in control.

She stepped forward and held out her hand, bare except for a simple silver band on her wrist. Adrian grasped her fingers, pleasantly surprised by her firm grip.

"My name is Everleigh Bradford. Congratulations on your Merlot. It's exquisite."

"Thank you." He arched a brow. "While your compliments are appreciated, was it necessary for you to ignore the 'Balcony Closed' sign and invade my privacy?"

Everleigh's chin came up and her eyes flashed with stubborn fire. "Yes."

Intriguing… There were plenty of men who would have cringed at the slightest hint of his disapproval. But not this woman. She stood her ground, shoulders thrown back, lips now set in a determined line.

"You're a busy man, Mr. Cabrera. I need to speak with you on an urgent matter. I'm sorry for breaking the rules, but it was necessary for me to have a moment alone with you."

Her honesty was refreshing. A night with someone as bold and beautiful as Everleigh would more than make up for his past few months of celibacy.

He infused his smile with sensuality as he raked his gaze up and down her slim form once more, this time letting his appreciation for her body show. "I would greatly enjoy a moment alone with you."

Everleigh's cheeks flushed pink. The blush caught Adrian unawares. Was she an innocent or just playing a role? Much as it would disappoint him, she wouldn't be the first to go to such lengths to catch his attention.

"This has nothing to do with sex, Mr. Cabrera."

"Adrian."

Her lips parted. "I... Excuse me?"

"Please call me Adrian."

Those beautifully shaded violet eyes narrowed. "This is a business discussion, Mr. Cabrera. First names are for friends and family."

"We could become friends, Everleigh."

What was wrong with him? He never teased a woman like this. He complimented, touched, seduced... But with this woman he just couldn't help himself.

Perhaps it was the blush. Yes, that had to be it. The delicate coloring that even now crept down her throat toward the rising slopes of her breasts...

"We will never be friends, Mr. Cabrera," Everleigh snapped. "I'm here to discuss your proposed purchase of Fox Vineyards."

"Then let's talk."

Continue reading
HIS BILLION-DOLLAR TAKEOVER TEMPTATION
Emmy Grayson

Available next month
www.millsandboon.co.uk

COMING SOON!

We really hope you enjoyed reading this book.
If you're looking for more romance, be sure to
head to the shops when new books are
available on

Thursday 13th May

MILLS & BOON

LET'S TALK

Romance

For exclusive extracts, competitions and special offers, find us online:

 facebook.com/millsandboon

@MillsandBoon

@MillsandBoonUK

Get in touch on 01413 063232

For all the latest titles coming soon, visit
millsandboon.co.uk/nextmonth

MILLS & BOON

THE HEART OF ROMANCE

A ROMANCE FOR EVERY READER

MODERN

Prepare to be swept off your feet by sophisticated, sexy and seductive heroes, in some of the world's most glamourous and romantic locations, where power and passion collide.

HISTORICAL

Escape with historical heroes from time gone by. Whether your passion is for wicked Regency Rakes, muscled Vikings or rugged Highlanders, awaken the romance of the past.

MEDICAL

Set your pulse racing with dedicated, delectable doctors in the high-pressure world of medicine, where emotions run high and passion, comfort and love are the best medicine.

True Love

Celebrate true love with tender stories of heartfelt romance, from the rush of falling in love to the joy a new baby can bring, and a focus on the emotional heart of a relationship.

Desire

Indulge in secrets and scandal, intense drama and plenty of sizzling hot action with powerful and passionate heroes who have it all: wealth, status, good looks…everything but the right woman.

HEROES

Experience all the excitement of a gripping thriller, with an intense romance at its heart. Resourceful, true-to-life women and strong, fearless men face danger and desire - a killer combination!

To see which titles are coming soon, please visit

millsandboon.co.uk/nextmonth

JOIN US ON SOCIAL MEDIA!

Stay up to date with our latest releases, author news and gossip, special offers and discounts, and all the behind-the-scenes action
from Mills & Boon...

 millsandboon

 millsandboonuk

 millsandboon

It might just be true love...